Going Barefoot

A Lost Key Mystery

Jeff Hutcheson

Pneumanaut LLC
Gainesville, GA

ISBN: 978-1-7365683-0-9 (Paperback)
ISBN: 978-1-7365683-1-6 (eBook)

Cover Art: Corazon Guzman-Thornton, Artist
Cover Design: Lieve Maas, Bright Light Graphics

Publisher's Cataloging-In-Publication Data
(Prepared by The Donohue Group, Inc.)

Names: Hutcheson, Jeff, author.
Title: Going barefoot / Jeff Hutcheson.
Description: Gainesville, GA : Pneumanaut LLC, [2021] | Series: A Lost Key mystery ; [1]
Identifiers: ISBN 9781736568309 (paperback) | ISBN 9781736568316 (ebook)
Subjects: LCSH: Young women—Gulf Coast (U.S.)—Fiction. | Beachgoers—Gulf Coast (U.S.)—Fiction. | Oil spills—Florida—Fiction. | Real estate developers—Florida—Fiction. | Intuition—Fiction. | LCGFT: Detective and mystery fiction.
Classification: LCC PS3608.U8587 G65 2021 (print) | LCC PS3608.U8587 (ebook) | DDC 813/.6—dc23

Chapter 1

Dedication

To Sherri, my wife, my soulmate, my muse.

Table of Contents

Bailey

The sunshine-yellow Jeep bounced along a worn-out beach road as the legendary music of Lynyrd Skynyrd boomed, a spirited woman in her early thirties behind the wheel. Singing loudly and off-key, she tilted her face toward the southern sun, breathing in the salty air.

"Ooouuu… Oouuu… ooouu—Oh! Crab balls!"

Reluctantly, she pressed the brakes and downshifted. The Jeep came to a halt behind a line of cars, stalled by a construction zone ahead. Slapping the steering wheel, she peered over the windshield, and blew the horn in protest. The driver just ahead shot her an annoying look. Noticing his Indiana license plate, she slid back down into her seat, sighed, and turned down the music. A parked Jeep and rock and roll just didn't quite go together.

"I don't know why they bother to fix this road," she mumbled. "It's just gonna wash out again. This should be a Jeep-only road."

The elderly Indiana driver poked his head out the window studying the road work.

Hooking her arm over her door, Bailey leaned out and said, "What's the holdup? Are they on break or something?"

The tourist turned back to her. "Looks like they're stuck."

Bailey sighed again, leaning back in her seat. She glanced to the white envelope peeking out of a handbag on the passenger floorboard. *Pretty soon, I might not have to worry about construction along the beach.* But that didn't help her out of this jam.

She stood up again and yelled over her windshield, "This should be a Jeep-only road!"

For a long time, Old Gulf Beach Road had been just Gulf Beach Road. It had gotten 'old' after the new State Highway 90 came in only a few years before, and the DOT paid less and less attention to maintaining it. Still, on weekends and holidays, the tourist traffic found its way to this majestic route that snaked right alongside the sugary white sands and the blue-green emerald gulf waters of Florida's Panhandle.

She blew her horn again.

"Hey, lady! I'm stuck, same as you!" yelled the snowbird.

Yes, but this is my beach. And now it was under construction, clogged up and making her late. Still, remembering her mother's reprimanding voice, and suddenly mindful of her southern roots, she sweetly called to the Indiana visitors.

"Sorry, I'm not honkin' at you. I'm honkin' at those workers up front." Noticing several energetic heads bobbing in his car's back seat, she asked, "Y'all here on vacation?"

"Yes. The wife and I brought our three grandkids. It's been a long drive. Is there another way around?" the Hoosier asked.

Six more cars had already lined up behind her. Turning around was not an option. Circling back would take way too long to get where she was going, where she went every morning.

"No, I'm afraid you're stuck." *But I'm not!*

With a smile born from a playful idea, she plopped down back into the driver's seat, cranked up the volume on her stereo, and turned her Jeep toward the water. This section was shallow enough to drive through the waves. Flooring the gas, she sped along the ocean side of the stopped cars, spraying the construction crew with saltwater and sand.

"Aww, geez, Bailey!" she heard above the curses and objections.

Laughter, mixed with the tune of "Sweet Home Alabama," trailed behind as the yellow Jeep zipped away.

Chapter 2

The Tropical Palm

Unimpeded by any more roadblocks, a few minutes later, Bailey pulled up to a diner with a neon palm tree and a large sign, not quite clean, that read, "Tropical Palm." The place had needed a paint job about five years prior, but Bailey loved it with no makeover. She parked and went inside. The low rumbling sound of conversations, the smell of bacon, and the clinking of dishes greeted her like an old friend. The waitress behind the counter smiled. "What's up, Bailey!"

"Hey, y'all. Another beautiful day!" Bailey replied, and almost giggled.

A sizeable man wearing an apron and a cook's hat looked through the opening from the kitchen. The wrinkles on his aged, weather-worn face and the tattoo of anchors on his arm were signs that he was no stranger to hard work or hard times. The bright stare of his hazel eyes conveyed that nothing got by him, not in his diner. Stories of the places he'd traveled in the Navy, the people he had encountered, always fascinated Bailey. Now and again, while telling his tales, he would pause and stare off into space, as if remembering something he couldn't forget but couldn't find the words to speak out loud.

When he saw Bailey, his face softened and melted into a smile as if he'd seen something good in the world.

"Hey, sunshine!" he said, flipping an egg on the grill. "Found your Prince Charming yet?"

"You found your treasure yet, Max?" Bailey teased, glancing up at the picture just above the kitchen window of an old treasure map neatly matted and framed. Next to it, in another frame, hung the first dollar they ever earned from the Tropical Palm.

He leaned through the window. "I'm telling you, that map is real. That ain't no pawnshop knock-off. I found that thing when we moved into this place."

Bailey glided up to the counter, sat on a stool, and swiveled back and forth playfully. "In other words, no, you haven't."

"One day." He winked. "You wait an' see."

A waitress ambled over, carrying a pot of coffee. She looked about the same age as Max. "Well, that ain't today. Today we got mouths to feed. You can look for lost gold tomorrow."

Bailey smiled. "You caught yourself a real treasure hunter here, Mary."

Mary poured her a cup of hot black java. "Oh, he's been goin' on about that for twenty years. Besides, he's my treasure, hon."

Bailey sipped the hot coffee.

"You're a little late today," Mary said, glancing at the clock.

"Got stuck behind some traffic on Gulf Beach Road."

Mary chuckled. "You didn't set up a toll booth and charge the tourists again?"

"Ha!" Bailey laughed. "One of my teenage ideas. But it was a good one. Tourists should pay."

"So, what will it be today?" Mary asked.

Bailey gave her a look that said 'seriously?'

Mary hollered back. "The usual for Bailey gal here."

"Surprise, surprise," Max's voice echoed from the grill. "You know one day you might want to try somethin' else on the menu. There are other things I can cook, you know."

"Max," Bailey said, and then they all joined in, "shrimp and grits."

Bailey's smile shined like a light glowing from deep inside.

The daily paper, *The Mullet Wrapper*, had been left on the counter by a previous patron. The front page blared "*Abandoned Oil Rig Still Leaking!*" with a close-up picture of a bird covered in black slime and an offshore oil rig in the distant background. Bailey noted today's date, Wednesday, February 5, 1992, then scooted the newspaper aside without even glancing at the headline. She swiveled her seat back and forth again and smiled at Mary.

"You've got a little extra sunshine today. What's going on?" Mary asked.

Bailey pulled the letter from her handbag, held it up next to her wide grin, and gave it to Mary.

"I got invited to apply to be an agent at Thomason Brothers Realty in Mobile!" Bailey beamed, bouncing side to side.

"Well, congratulations, hon. I'm not the least bit surprised."

Bailey pulled a folder from her bag and held up a glossy piece of paper with bold print.

"I thought I'd create an ad to show them what I would do if they hire me! What you think?"

Mary read the flyer and took on a proud maternal look. "Bailey, I'm impressed. This promo is so professional looking."

Then Bailey finished with her tagline. "Your Home is Waiting for You!"

Mary's face took on a sad, compassionate expression—the look one might give a wounded puppy.

"What?" Bailey said, surprised.

"It's a lovely idea, hon." Mary smiled at the young agent. Then she picked up the discarded *Mullet Wrapper*, opened to the real estate section, and laid it in front of Bailey.

"What are you gonna do about these?" Mary asked, tapping Bailey's ad in the newspaper. "These are your condo listings, not in Mobile, but here in Lost Key."

"I'll finish selling those or refer the listings out. It depends on how it goes with my tryout. I really like finding these," Bailey said, pointing to the residences portrayed on her new proofs. "Houses are so beautiful, and when the people walk in, I know right away. I can feel it. It's all about the feeling. Condos, well, there's good money, except anybody can sell them. But finding a home for someone, some family, that's like… indescribable!"

"We have homes here, too. You've sold quite a bit of them," Mary said with a note of caution in her voice.

"You know, Mary, it's a big deal to get invited to apply for a position there. I have to follow up on this." Bailey's eyes became alert with a please-don't-challenge-me expression.

Mary got the message. "I know, and you'll do fine. I just wish Thomason Brothers were over here. Lost Key is your home."

Katie, another waitress, walked by, balancing a stack of dirty dishes on a tray and glanced at her old cap, hanging on the rack in the corner.

"Home is where you hang your hat, I always say," she joked, laying the stack of dishes in the reception window.

Katie had arrived at Lost Key two years before, without two dimes to rub together. Bailey remembered how Max and Mary had met her when she was standing at a four-way stop holding a sign that read, "will work for food." Instead of giving her a dollar, they took Katie to lunch, which led to a conversation, followed by a job at the Tropical Palm. Katie had been a faithful employee and member of the family ever since. She now had plenty enough money to buy new clothes, but she kept that tattered hat like a child keeps an old blanket. It reminded her of the days before the Tropical Palm when her home was actually where she hung her hat.

Max's burly tattooed arms set a steamy plate of food in the receiving area. "Home is where your treasure is," he said, winking at Mary.

"You mean, where your heart is, dear." She walked over, retrieving the freshly cooked dish.

He smiled. "Of course, dear."

Bailey was enjoying this banter among friends until she felt a tightness in her stomach. She stared down at her lap with a somber expression. "Home is for other people," she whispered.

Out of the corner of her eye, Bailey caught Max and Mary stealing glances at her, but they said nothing.

Mary brought the plate over to Bailey but held onto it for a moment till Bailey looked at her. "You know, hon, sometimes we're already home and don't even know it."

An almost imperceptible watery film shimmered in Bailey's eyes. Mary smiled and gently brushed one of Bailey's bangs away with her free hand. Then she set the plate of food in front of her.

Mary said, "Well, you can do anything you set your mind to, young lady. Remember that. You got the looks, sweetheart, and brains, and that," she searched for the right words, "fire inside. If Mobile is what you want, then go get 'em, dear. Though I can't quite see you liking it over there." She looked lovingly at Bailey. "You just be careful. There's a meanness in this world."

Bailey sniffed and looked down at her food. "Yum, smells good."

Bailey's breakfast consisted of shrimp and grits, with a side of crispy bacon. Max had even added 'Bailey's Breakfast' to the menu. It was a popular item, too. "Here's your toast and orange marmalade."

Bailey's smile returned. "This is just great," she said, shrugging her shoulders. A warm shiver ran up her spine, and the knot in her belly eased.

Mary leaned on the counter. "So, honey, about that Jeep of yours. Any passengers yet?"

"Sure. Me and Keri went for a great ride yesterday to the Pensacola mall and—"

"You know what I mean. Any passengers of the male gender?"

"Well, yeah, Kevin. He and I went to the garden show last week."

Mary just looked at her.

"He's a guy," Bailey said.

Mary peered over her glasses and said, "Kevin is a wonderful man, but he's never gonna date you, or any other girl for that matter. Hon, a pretty thing like you can have your pick."

"Nope, don't need any boyfriends!" Bailey shouted playfully. "No romance in my Jeep!"

Mary looked disapprovingly.

"Come on, Mary, I'm eating here. You are ruining my breakfast."

"Let her be, Mary," Max said. Then he looked at Bailey. "I think one day, honey, you're going to meet your Prince Charming, just you wait."

"Prince Charming exists only in fairy tales. I prefer real life."

Max nodded somberly, as though he'd seen a lot of real life.

Mary wasn't ready to let it go yet. "What about Benji? He came looking for you, you know."

"Oh please, he reminds me of that cartoon dog. Rufus or doofus or something like that. You just want to say to him, 'Hold still.' Then punch him in the nose. He'd probably smile that goofy smile, too."

Katie chuckled as she walked by to refill the coffee pot. "You go, Bailey. All men suck. Don't let them catch you."

Bailey blew her a kiss.

Mary looked disapproving again. "Not *all* men," she said before looking back at Bailey. "Not everyone is like… him, dear. What he did to you was just awful. Horrible."

"Mary," Max said, as he peered around the corner at his wife and shook his head.

"Just makes me sick is all. First, that so-called husband cheats on you, then cuts you out of the family like that. Lord knows what lies he told the kids. You may not have been their biological mother, but you were their real mother."

Bailey stiffened and looked away. Mary meant well, she knew, but even the thought of those events made her nauseous. She stopped eating and focused her gaze toward her friend.

"Men leave if they ever bother to show up in the first place. I'm not going to give them a ride to whatever fantasy they're chasing."

Mary started to reply but heard the stern voice of her husband.

"Mary! Let her be."

Mary held her comment, looked at her husband, then patted Bailey on the forearm. "I'm sorry, hon. I don't mean to upset you. You just got to find the right one, dear." Then she smiled at Max. "I did."

His stern look softened into a smile. "I'm the lucky one," he said, and resumed cooking.

A pinkish tint in her cheeks matched Mary's smile. "I knew the minute he walked in that door. I was waiting on that table over there," she said, pointing to the one near the front door, "and in comes this dashing sailor. I knew it right away. Even spilled coffee in a customer's lap. You'll know, hon."

Bailey kept eating. The only thing she wanted to know was how good the bacon tasted. Then she spotted the clock on the wall. "Oh, it's 8:27! I've got to go!" She finished her meal, reached for her wallet, and realized she had forgotten it.

Mary waved her hand. "Don't worry about it, dear. Pay me tomorrow. I know I'll see you at 7:57."

"You got it." Bailey sailed out of the café, her white boat-shoes almost skipping across the floor.

"Hey, wait!" Mary ran after her. "You forgot your ads!"

"How could I forget those?"

Bailey hugged Mary and bounded outside.

"You go get 'em, Bailey! They'll be lucky to have you!" Mary shouted after her.

Bailey stopped short of her Jeep, eyes wide. She gasped and blinked in disbelief. Slowly, she circled her Wrangler, scarcely able to take in what she saw. Hundreds of dark spots and black streaks stained her shiny jewel. *Is that mud?* She could only hope. She touched a blotch, smearing the thick glop between her fingers. It was sticky.

"That looks like oil," said Mary, who had walked out upon noticing her distress.

"What?" Bailey managed to say.

"Don't worry. It won't damage your Jeep. You can wash it off. You may have to wax it, though, to get rid of the streaks."

"But where did it come from? They're not paving the roads anywhere. All I did was drive through a little water to get around the construction..." She looked at Mary. "Is there oil in the water?"

"Afraid so, hon. It's likely from one of those damn oil rigs out there. They say some leakage is normal. I bet it's from that new company, Trident Oil. They just went belly up, had to abandon operations. They're suing the government now, claiming unfair regulations cost them profits."

"Well, if they aren't operating, shouldn't the leak stop?"

"Oh, hon, the leak is why they shut down. Frankly, I wonder if the company ever really repaired it. Ah, hell, who knows how many of them rust bucket rigs are leaking out there. I think it's getting worse."

"I'll say! Look at this!" Bailey said, pointing to her Jeep. "This is a lot of oil! Not just a little leakage."

"I swear we are ruining our planet. Pollution will be the end of all of us," Mary added. "Lost Key will be swallowed up, one giant gooey pit." She hugged Bailey. "Go on, girl. You're gonna be late for your appointment. There is nothing you can do about this anyway. Things happen for a reason. Lord only knows what this one is."

Chapter 3

Bailey drove toward her appointment, no music
this time. Her eyes darted back and forth, scanning the faces of any pedestrians she passed or oncoming drivers in the next lane. She just knew everyone was
staring.

*How embarrassing. People must be thinking, 'what kind of
person would just let her Jeep stay trashed like that. If you're not
going to care for it, then, why have it?... Amateur, swamp trash,
weekend real estate agent.'*

Fortunately, just ahead, was the good ol' Sea-n-
Suds car wash right across the street from the Emerald Green, where her appointment would be waiting.
She checked her watch. Ten minutes to nine, ten minutes to meet the Joneses. *I've got time.* She ignored the
fact that she had never washed her car in less than
half an hour. She was too particular. One clean spot
demanded cleaning the other dirty ones as well. The
tires screeched as she pulled into the car wash just a bit
too fast. She parked in the first empty stall, made quick
work of getting the top fastened, then rolled up the
windows. The Sea-n-Suds offered your basic car wash,
several brick stalls with a mounted spray hose overhead
that you could maneuver around your vehicle. They
had other custom options too, but Bailey only had time

for a quick wash, not a complete detail. She opened the door and sprang out.

The attendant waved from inside the small office then yelled through the open window, "Hey, Bailey."

She waved quickly. "Don't have but a few minutes today, Cricket. Got an appointment and I don't want to be late."

"Only a few minutes? To wash your Jeep?" He chuckled. "That'll be a first. I've never seen you take less 'n half an hour."

"Well, not today." She grabbed some loose change from her cup holder, and hastily put the coins into the machine. The compressor kicked on, and the water began to spray.

Cricket came out of the office. That wasn't his real name, of course. He'd garnered the reputation as the best fisherman in all the panhandle. He used mostly crickets and some lures. Today, as with most days, he sported an old stained fishing vest and equally "broke-in" camouflage ball cap with 'I'd rather be fishing' stitched across the front. Since he always wore the cap backward, unless he was actually fishing, you could only read it if he had his back toward you. The *Mullet Wrapper* he had been reading was squeezed under his arm. Judging from the empty stalls, it was a slow day at the car wash. Besides, Bailey knew he liked talking to her, his most frequent customer. She thought he might just like her anyway.

He looked over the black spots speckled alongside the car, scratched his beard, and said, "What did ya run into there, Bailey?"

"Oil," she said flatly.

"Oil? But where—"

"In the water. I was trying to get around that construction traffic on Old Gulf Beach Road."

"That explains it then."

"Who knew the water was dirty?"

"Um… everyone?" He held up a copy of the *Mullet Wrapper* displaying the front-page news story about the oil rig leaking.

"Oh," Bailey remarked but kept washing.

"I'm sorry, Bailey." And he was. "If that's oil, it'll leave some nasty streaks, maybe even take off some of yer paint."

He's right. I'll never get this clean. That stuff is going to strip the color right off the side.

She clenched her teeth.

"Yeah, so I've been told."

Despite her fears, as Bailey sprayed the side of the Jeep, the black spots vanished! No streaks, no stains, no residue. She paused, then washed faster. The sprayer felt like a magic wand in her hand, and every wave blasted away the dirty grime and left a pristine, sunshine yellow. She laughed.

"Would ya look at that?" Cricket said. "You sure ya ran into raw crude?"

"I thought so. But who cares as long it comes off my Jeep?"

Bailey quickly waved the wand back and forth, spraying the rest of her beloved vehicle. The black sludge washed entirely away. Her treasure shined again.

"Now that's what I'm talking about," she exclaimed. "That's the cleanliness of a pro!"

She put the sprayer back so fast she almost missed its holder. The water still gushed, spraying her and Cricket and all the surrounding vicinity.

"Hey, watch it!" Cricket shouted as he brushed the drops off his fishing vest.

"So sorry," Bailey giggled, but she wasn't because his fishing vest was waterproof anyway. "I got to go!"

She climbed back into the driver's seat and tilted the mirror toward her for one last-minute check. Except for a few lingering soap suds, she looked as though she'd been caught in an afternoon shower. Only it was a sunny day, and it never rains soapy water. *Well, so much for looking professional.*

Cricket knocked on the window. She rolled it down, and he handed her a towel.

She smiled. "Thanks, Cricket."

The towel helped, but not quite enough. Bailey dialed the heater in the dashboard to its hottest setting and highest fan speed and aimed the vents directly toward her.

"There, that should do the trick."

"You're only goin' across the street. Oh yeah, that's plenty of time to dry," he teased.

Bailey laughed and threw the towel at him. "Oh, shut up."

She drove off and shouted, "Bye."

Her clothes were damp, she was late, but her Jeep was clean.

Chapter 4

Selling Airspace

Bailey leaned against the railing and looked over the balcony. From fourteen floors high, she had a clear view of the coastline stretching from Orange Beach, AL, to the right, and Panama City, FL, to the left. Giant dark schools of fish swam erratically just offshore in the blue-green gulf waters. The gentle waves crashed and foamed. Sounds of children laughing floated to the balcony along with the seagulls' squawking. Two porpoises surfaced in the distance, arching their backs and fins as if inviting her for a swim. Blue and white parasols shaded pairs of lounge chairs and dotted the seashore, looking like tiny umbrellas in God's giant ocean margarita. She closed her eyes and turned toward the bright sun. The warm gulf breeze caressed her face. She breathed in the sweet smell of the saltwater like a sacred incense and smiled.

She glanced at her watch, 9:30 a.m. Fortunately, they were late, allowing Bailey's clothes to dry, mostly. Her anticipation grew. Maria and John seemed like nice people, at least on the phone. *I just know we are going to be great friends.* Bailey could hardly wait to meet them and their two kids. *What were their names? Oh yes, Jonathan and Samantha.* She always heard them in the background laughing and playing, or sometimes fighting as brothers and sisters do. They would be there any minute to see Condo 1401. The two-bedroom corner unit offered lots of light, an open kitchen, and living room areas. *I can't wait till they walk through the door. They're going to love it! I just know it!* She had fun adding a few extra touches, like a beach blanket, sand buckets, and festive drink glasses with tiny cocktail umbrellas. Still, it was hard to match a family with a condo when she had never met the family.

"You try too hard," Margaret Jane, her broker, always said. "You don't need to match the family with the condo, just show them the space." But Bailey never just showed the unit. She wanted the Joneses to have an experience of home.

Hearing a knock on the door, Bailey hurried to open it.

"Hey!" She smiled, "You must be John."

"Yes, I'm Mr. Jones. And you are Bailey."

"That's me." They shook hands. "Come on in." Bailey gestured like an usher to a grand palace. Mr. Jones tucked his newspaper under one arm and stepped inside. Bailey leaned out the front door and looked right and left along the balcony.

"Where's Maria and Samantha and Johnathan?" she asked.

"Ah, turns out, my wife and kids couldn't make the trip. We just have too much going on to take a vacation as we planned. So, it's just me."

Though disappointed, Bailey said, "Oh, well, glad you're here."

She led him inside and began giving a tour of his new home. Showing houses was the part of her job she loved. Mr. Jones walked and looked but said nothing.

Bailey kept trying to read his expression, careful to talk about things that he was interested in, while not saying too much. But oddly, she couldn't tell if he even liked the place.

"And here's the main bedroom, and bath, two sinks, and a stand-up shower with a separate tub." She paused. Still no comment, but at least he nodded. They walked to the balcony. "And this is your backyard." She took a step back, watching his expression.

He smiled. "Well, that is beautiful." He looked for a moment and then said, "Okay, let's talk about price."

Really? Whatever reaction Bailey expected, that one didn't even come close.

"Would you prefer to sit on the balcony? We could take in the sun and the breeze while we have our meeting."

"No, thanks. Inside will be fine."

They walked inside. Mr. Jones sat on the couch and Bailey in the chair next to the sofa.

Still getting little reaction from the buyer, Bailey continued. "So, it has been fully updated with the latest appliances."

He put up his hand to stop her. "Thanks, I'm sure all that is fine. It's the beach location I most want. This condo isn't our home after all, but a vacation spot and potentially rental income."

"Rental income?" As soon as she said the words, she wished she hadn't. They had never talked about renting it out.

Tossing one hand in an upward gesture, he said, "Problem?"

"No. No, of course not. It's just I had imagined this as your beach home."

"Our home? It's a little small to be our home." He looked around. "It's a little smaller than I expected. It seems pricey, too."

"It's the same price we've been talking about."

"Well, it turns out we are kind of strapped for cash right now. What I'm hoping is that we can cut some of the cost. Perhaps y'all can reduce some of your fees"

Are you really John Jones, the customer I have been talking with for the past couple of months? His tone was almost opposite what she had heard on the phone, more business-like, not friend-like.

"Well, you could make a request and see if my company will accept it, but these are in demand. This is one of the few finished units."

His brow wrinkled. "You're our agent? Right? Aren't you supposed to look out for us?"

Bailey blinked and tipped her head to one side. This meeting was going nothing like she imagined, nothing like she hoped. "Technically, I'm the listing agent," she said. "And yes, I do care about your family."

"I see. When we always got you on the phone, I just assumed you were out agent. You even acted like our friend. I guess agents are just agents, right? It's just about making money."

"No. It's about more than money. It's about helping people find a home." Bailey's jaw clenched, but she held her composure.

"Okay, we will make a full price offer. We saved a little so we can put twenty percent down."

Whew! Well, that sounds good, back on track now. The muscles in her jaw eased.

"That will be an attractive offer, Mr. Jones."

"We've already pre-qualified with a mortgage company back home. We are ready to go."

"Fantastic, I'll draw up the paperwork."

He hesitated. "One condition."

"Is there something else?" she asked, her senses going on alert again.

"Yes. I mean no offense, but I'd like to discuss your commission."

"My commission?"

"Yes. By my estimates, you and your company will get about seven percent?"

"That's correct." She felt her stomach tighten. Bailey had been around long enough to know this discussion wouldn't lead anywhere good. And that it was better to stay vague.

"Your take should be somewhere around $5,000 to $7,000, am I right?" he pressed.

"Sounds about right." Her shoulders slumped slightly.

"To be honest with you, Miss Evans, I just have trouble with all these commission fees. I mean, seriously, do you think you did $7,000 worth of work here? Or even five for that matter?"

Bailey wondered why every time someone said, 'let me be honest', it always turned out to be a prelude to deception. Her jaw clenched again.

"Mr. Jones, I don't control the fee structure, and yes, I do think I've done my work faithfully and diligently."

"Again, no offense intended, I'm sure you are a nice gal and all. But really what are we talking about, a few phone calls and a half-hour visit? You probably have a department at your office that prepares the paperwork."

Bailey stared, no longer able to hide her irritation or disappointment. All the calls, the listening, thinking through the options, then to come to this.

He continued. "I appreciate the way you called us and kept us informed."

"I did more than that." Her face turned slightly red. She knew it was never good if she had to justify her work, but the words spilled out anyway. "I pulled strings to get you an early viewing. This condo isn't even on the market yet, but it will be next week."

"And I, we, appreciate that, Bailey." Mr. Jones said with a calm, even tone. "You made us feel like your friend even though you are just doing your job. I mean, this has been the most pleasant exchange with a real estate agent we've ever had."

"Well, I'm not just doing my job, Mr. Jones." She caught herself talking a bit louder than before, so she lowered her voice. "I had hoped we could be friends. I've been looking forward to meeting Jonathan and Sam."

Speaking softer, he said, "Bailey, I don't mean to upset you. I just can't see clear to paying all these commission fees. We did stick with you as our agent because we felt like we were friends, and that you'd understand and help us out. You know, give us a break. A thousand dollars seems more than fair. I mean, come on," he said, looking around. "You're selling airspace, and it's over-priced airspace."

"Airspace?" Bailey's words sounded more like a challenge than a question. She crossed her arms and stared at the buyer. If the Emerald Coast was like God's great margarita, then this must be the worm in the tequila bottle. She had often wondered how that worm would taste. Maybe it smacked like the word 'airspace.'

Bailey had never thought of condos as airspace before. As much as she disliked the thought, he had a point—these things sold at exorbitant prices, even though they appraised at or above market value. But what bothered her more, she felt devalued. Just as bad, she felt manipulated.

"I'm not trying to cheat you out of a commission; just be realistic and meet us where we can afford."

Bailey glared at him in silence. *You don't want to rip me off. You just can't help yourself?*

He leaned forward. "Let's make a statement that this condo racket is overdone and overpriced. I'll even go up to fifteen hundred dollars. That will still be a good rate of return for the time you've had to put in. Don't you think?"

Bailey sat and said nothing. She looked away, out the window, fighting off a volcano of frustration about to erupt.

He sat next to her and put his arm around her shoulder. Instead of comfort, it felt condescending, as if her commission were some amateur demand.

"We'll even give you a key, " he said. "You can use the place as much as you want."

Seething anger boiled inside Bailey. Instead of exploding, she shrugged his arm off her shoulder and stood. "That wouldn't be appropriate."

"It's for friends."

Oh, now we're friends, huh? My friends would never treat me this way.

Bailey took a deep breath, summoning her best agent mode. Her eyes went colder, business-like. "My company won't budge on its commission policy."

"I think they should," he pressed.

He laid a copy of the local paper he had brought with him on the table. The headline screeched, *Abandoned Oil Rig Leaking.* "Why has no one told me about this?"

Surprise and curiosity took over as her mind flashed to Cricket, holding up his copy of the paper, and another one that she pushed aside at the diner earlier. This was the third time this morning she had seen this picture and heard about the spill. *Must be a sign. They come in threes, don't they? I should have known about this.*

"You think I knew about this?" she said, re-focusing on Mr. Jones. "You think my company knew about this?"

"I think your company should come down off its commissions," Mr. Jones repeated. "This property, this whole area is losing value, and you and your company need to take some responsibility."

"We didn't cause that!" she said, almost yelling.

"But you knew about it." He stood.

"I just found out today! On the way over here!"

He shook his head and pointed his index finger toward her. "The only reason I'm still in this deal is that I'm thinking long term. When the leak is stopped and the spill cleaned up, then the values will return. Hopefully."

"I can't make promises on behalf of my company," Bailey said.

"But you can control *your* commission. It's still a grand. Not bad for what, a day's work when you add it all up. I'm generous when you consider the oil in the water and on the beach. Besides, it would really help us out. If you can do that, I'll sign this paper right now and make an offer."

Bailey thrust her hands on her hips, her eyes blazing. *What an ass! You had this planned all along. That's why Maria and the kids aren't here.* She imagined how good it would feel to slap him hard across the face. She could almost see the red handprint she would make on his cheek. Instead, she sighed. Her more professional self prevailed over her angry instinct to lash out. *Take the deal in hand,* she told herself. *Nothing is moving right now, and the company needs the sales. And you need the money.* All indications pointed to the market trending worse. She thought of her new opportunity awaiting in Mobile. *You're on the getting-out end of this anyway.* She took a deep breath and found herself handing him the contract. "Okay, sign here," she said robotically.

She got the deal. She sold the condo. But she didn't get to meet the family, didn't get to watch the expression on the kids' faces. Her decorating didn't matter. Her umbrella drinks and sand toys didn't grab his attention. He didn't acknowledge her phone calls, her time thinking, and imagining what it would be like for them living there. What closed the sale was her willingness to cut her commission by almost eighty percent.

All the Jones's previous niceness seemed like a dream she had invented. Now even the promise of meeting Maria and the kids carried no excitement.

Disappointment gave way to anger. *How could I have been so wrong about this guy? What a condescending jerk! I just conceded that this is overpriced airspace and sold it at less than one-quarter of my commission. What's wrong with me?*

Mr. Jones finished signing and initialing all the documents. He wrote a check for the earnest money and handed it to Bailey. "You're upset."

Bailey gathered the documents and didn't answer. *Damn right, I'm upset.*

"Come on, Bailey, don't be that way. I'm just trying to be fair here. It's nothing personal."

Bailey stared coldly. *Really? You not only cheat me out of my commission, but now you want me to be okay with that?* She didn't say that. Again, she managed her most professional demeanor but with a sharper tone. "I've got to go, Mr. Jones. I'll get the paperwork in to the office. Enjoy your rental property."

They stood, and he extended his hand. Bailey gave him a cursory handshake. Mr. Jones got the real estate agent now, not a friend. She picked up the margarita glasses she'd planned to leave as a welcoming gift and packed them in her bag but left the sand buckets for the kids.

Holding open the door, she waited for Mr. Jones to exit first.

As he walked past, he said, "You've got some growing up to do, kiddo. Time to live in the real world."

He donned his sunglasses, smiled, and strolled out the door. Bailey's head hurt, and her stomach knotted. She jammed her key into the lock and twisted hard, securing the door behind her. Then she headed in the opposite direction from Mr. Jones.

"Screw you!" she yelled as she turned the corner.

Chapter 5

Dirty Water

Instead of going back to the office, Bailey drove down a winding road that ended at a small cove, in a marshy section of Lost Key. She knew Keri would be working there today. She needed to see her best friend. The foliage thickened, and the underbrush softly screeched against the sides of the Jeep. Slowly the road transformed into marshland. Tire-worn tracks succumbed to long thin blades of grass and thick scrub brush as life insisted on remaining wild and undefined by human-made machinery. This path earned the stature of a Jeep-only road. She turned left and parked at the edge of the boggy bayou. She met Keri here often. They claimed this place as their sacred playground. The soil squished as she stepped out of the Jeep. Bailey felt comforted knowing this was protected wetlands. The diversity of life evoked a child-like wonder. Strange, colorful insects buzzed, multicolored birds chirped, and frogs croaked. Several varieties of fish swam aimlessly, their darkish shapes visible beneath the shallow water. And of course, there were the sea turtles, darting left and right, heads bobbing just above the surface, blissfully floating along as if this were their private swimming pool.

Bailey loved coming here, especially when her best friend was working. Keri was an expert guide to the vivid marsh life, pointing out things that most people miss. Bailey spotted her just up ahead, wading in water-proof boots, shorts, and the official blue pullover shirt of the National Oceanic and Atmospheric Administration, where she worked. She topped off her uniform, wearing a navy ball cap with NOAA stitched across the top in bold white letters. Bailey smiled and waved. Keri looked up at her friend and returned the greeting. Though glad to see her, Keri's shoulders slumped slightly forward, her gestures slower as if moving underwater. *She's not having a good day.*

"I wouldn't come out here," Keri shouted. "The water is dirty." She slogged toward Bailey, who had stopped at the water's edge. Keri held up her gloved hand covered in slick, gray-black mushy stuff. Bailey then noticed that farther out in the marsh, the water had turned opaque black toward the ocean.

"That's oil!" Keri said. "If that damn rig out there keeps leaking, our marshland we fight to protect won't be here." She slung off the gooey substance and swore. "It will be just like Louisiana, probably worse."

"What do you mean worse?"

"Well, no one cares about this little cove, Bailey. It will be worse because this won't make the national media. Part of the problem is that the abandoned rig isn't leaking enough. It falls below the government's threshold to investigate." She kicked at the oil in the water. "This stuff will kill the roots of the plants, then kill the wildlife, the birds, and the fish that make a home here. It will be a sandbar... Dammit!" she exclaimed, slinging the sludge from her glove. Keri was close to tears. "And Snaps, if Snaps starts eating this stuff, it will make him sick or worse."

"Have you seen him yet?"

Keri shook her head.

"Won't all the oil dissipate? It is a pretty big gulf."

"Some… maybe in the open water. Not here, though. When it gets here, it has nowhere else to go. That's how we get this marsh. The currents carry the silt and the sand to this place."

She threw off the remaining muck from her free hand and swore again. Her voice broke. Bailey put her arm around her. Keri let out an anguished wail of frustration. Then, suddenly, her expression changed.

"Ohhh!" Keri splashed forward a few yards into the marsh again.

"What is it?" Bailey asked. But then she saw what had grabbed her friend's attention.

A little bird flapped about as if it had a clipped wing. Only it wasn't a clipped wing that kept it from flying. Instead, the same blackish-gray goop that crept ever inward had covered the fledgling like a heavy straight jacket, hiding its feathers, squelching its song. The oil had so consumed it that one couldn't even tell what kind of bird it was.

Gently, Keri picked up the struggling creature, cupping her hands, making a safe nest for rest. "This is what I'm talking about!"

She carried it over a few yards to cleaner water and began bathing the sticky mire off the distressed creature. Bailey stepped forward to help, not caring that her boat shoes and white cargo pants would get wet and stained. Cool water engulfed her feet as she sank slightly into the muddy bottom.

"See," Keri emphasized, holding the bird gingerly. "They come in for fish, food, or land and rest, and this is what happens. They get this sludge shit on them, and they can't get it off. Then they drown or starve because they can't fly or move very far."

As Keri gently bathed the feathered friend, the bird's wings became cleaner, and it began to flap and chirp.

"Would you look at that," Keri said. "The oil is washing right off. It's usually stickier."

One final splash of water on its back and she turned it loose.

The bird soared and sang as if to say thank you.

She took a deep breath and smiled. "Well, we saved one anyway."

"Maybe it won't get any worse," Bailey said, even though she wasn't convinced.

Keri stared defiantly out at the ocean horizon. "Thing I can't figure is why so much oil is collecting in this cove?"

"I thought you said the currents brought it here."

"They do, but there is an unusually large amount running for about a half-mile stretch along this coastline. I'd expect oil to settle here more than other places, but not in such quantities. It's odd. The rig is a good way offshore, yet a boatload of it collects right in this area."

"You think there's more oil spilling out than anyone realizes?"

"That's likely. Some oil companies low-ball their leakage reports. Hell, this stuff is probably not from just one platform anyway."

"You mean there is more than one leaking rig out there?"

"There are hundreds," Keri said. "I'm not exaggerating. Not only that, but many are simply abandoned. Who knows how many of these are polluting my Gulf!"

"Wow. I had no idea."

"Of course not. Those responsible don't want any-one to know. But still… why is all the oil accumulating like this? I go about a few hundred yards in either direc-tion and it clears up. I'd expect to see tar balls farther along the beach."

"So, what makes this such a popular destination?"

Keri shrugged. "The currents do strange things, I suppose. The oil is moving like a river."

They searched to make sure no other wildlife needed a bath. They saw splotches of dark oil in every direction, but no other birds in distress.

As they were sloshing their way back to drier land, Keri said, "So, what's on your mind, girlfriend?"

Bailey looked away. "Oh, nothing. At least nothing compared to the battle going on right here." She gave Keri a darting glance. "Just wanted to see my friend."

Keri studied her for a moment, tilted her head as if she could see something else at a different angle, then said, "I know that look. What did you do?"

Bailey shrugged and shook her head.

"You gave away your commission, didn't you?"

Bailey turned her head, hiding an embarrassed smile. "Well, not all of it."

"Dammit, girl!" Keri's voice rose, the vein in her neck bulging. "Don't let them talk you into that! You're worth every penny and more!"

"I know, I know." Bailey felt grateful to have a friend like Keri. Someone who cared enough to fight for her, to give her an earful if she needed it. Someone who saw her and could see through the facade. A friend who just 'gets you' is a true gift.

"Do you? Well, then believe it." Keri sighed and lowered her voice. "I'm sorry. I'm just extra upset over all this crap." She picked up a shell and threw it in the direction of the oil rig. It skipped three or four times before settling in the water.

"Nice toss," Bailey said. "Let's go for a walk." Looking around, emphasizing that they were standing in two feet of marshy water, she added, "Preferably on dry land."

"Yeah, that sounds good. I could use a break." As they walked over to her bag of supplies, Keri said, "You know I had a feeling they weren't the people you thought they were."

"Oh yeah? What's that supposed to mean?" Bailey said sharply. But she knew what it meant.

"You know." Keri lowered her voice and took a soothing tone. "Some people just want to buy a house. They're not…" she paused, then gently said, "family."

Bailey straightened in a jerking motion. She sighed, tilted her head back, closed her eyes, and said, "Yeah, I know." Then she looked downward. "I know."

"I'm just lookin' out for ya, my friend. You start adopting clients and giving away your commission in Mobile, and you won't last a month."

Bailey nodded.

"You look tired," Keri said.

"I am. I just need a nap, that's all."

"Take extra care of yourself. Last time you got too stressed-out you slept for a week."

"I'll be fine," Bailey said, and gave Keri a sideways hug.

They reached the bag of supplies. Keri pulled out a small vial, opened the lid, and walked back toward the oil-stained water. "Before we go for that walk, first let me gather a water sample for the lab."

"You analyze the water?" Bailey asked, grateful the topic had changed.

"Yeah, got to get a water quality sample, standard procedure for any environmental event like this that affects the wildlife and ecosystems. We send them for analysis at our offices in Pascagoula and Pensacola." She scooped some water/oil into the vile and held it toward the sky and frowned. "Hmmm."

"What's wrong?"

Keri studied the murky liquid carefully. "I'm not sure. This stuff seems thinner, less dense than a sample from a regular oil spill. Maybe that's why we could clean the bird so easily." She walked over and showed it to Bailey, tilting the vile one way then another. "See how it doesn't separate, but mixes?"

"Yeah, I do," Bailey said. "What do you make of that?"

"Not sure. But this doesn't look like any crude oil I've ever seen. Oh well, the lab can tell me exactly what weird crud we are dealing with." Keri's face brightened with an idea. "When are you headed to Mobile?"

"I'm going to an orientation day after tomorrow," Bailey said.

"Would you mind taking this to Dauphin Island Marine Center?" I know it's a bit out of your way, but my friend Jade is interning there. She can run a quick analysis for me with their equipment. I'll get results a lot faster than if I send it off to our NOAA lab."

"Sure thing."

"Thanks. That would be a big help. Plus, I think you'll enjoy meeting Jade. She is super cool."

"Great. I look forward to it."

Bailey took the vile of oily water. She held it up to the sky, studying it the way Keri did. Then a flash of light caught the corner of her eye, startling her. She saw a man wearing all black and dark sunglasses lowering a camera. *Did he just take our picture?* Her heartbeat quickened. She shaded her eyes with her free hand to get a better look.

"Who's that?" she exclaimed, pointing. But the mysterious photographer had stepped into the foliage and out of sight.

Keri looked. She didn't have to shade her eyes, because the brim of her ball cap already did. "Who? I don't see anyone."

"A man was just there, wearing black. He had a camera in his hands." *The sunlight must have reflected off the lens.*

"Maybe a tourist." Keri shrugged.

"What tourist wears black to the beach?" Bailey felt an uneasiness in her gut that she tried to dismiss, but it lingered. "Also, I think he just took a picture of us."

Keri looked again. "I don't see anyone now. You sure this wasn't one of your—"

"Yes, I'm sure," Bailey said sharply. "I saw him! He's real." She saw more, too. Her mind played vivid images of a large man with indistinct features getting into a black sedan. Bailey continued staring at the spot in the brush where the light flashed. Her breathing grew rapid and shallow. Her eyes peeled wide. She put her hand over her pounding heart.

Keri reached out to her friend. Bailey jumped at her touch.

"It's okay," Keri said. "It's okay. Just some tourist; don't make too much out of it. They are always coming here, taking pictures."

Bailey nodded and took slow, deep breaths. She felt her body relax.

Keri said, "This is the most beautiful spot in all of Lost Key, well, for now." Suddenly she looked to the right.

Bailey turned and immediately saw the ripples on the surface that caught her attention.

"Snaps!" Keri sprinted back to the edge of the marsh. "That you?"

A small greenish head peeked just above the water. Trailing behind was a grayish-green shell, only the topmost portion breaking the surface. Part of the shell was discolored, forming a natural heart shape. They had thought of painting the heart a bright pink color, but their better judgment stopped them. It would have been dangerous for their sea turtle friend. Sometimes his survival depended on his ability to blend into the natural environment. They both squatted down, beckoning Snaps to swim to them. He darted one way then the other, then paused. The turtle was carrying a semi-circle object in its mouth.

"What's he got there?" Bailey asked.

Keri shook her head. "It looks like an old pottery handle, maybe." She smiled. "He's always bringing me stuff. Snaps, where did you get that?"

The turtle continued his swim, carrying its treasure away.

Bailey exhaled with delight. "Glad he's okay."

They stood watching their turtle friend paddle gently into the reeds.

Bailey said, "Come on, let's take that walk and enjoy this natural beauty."

"Sounds good," her friend replied. "That way, you can put off having to face your boss-lady a little longer."

Bailey laughed. "Maybe we can walk all day."

Chapter 6

Hard Lessons

The old faded leather crinkled as Bailey leaned back on 'the couch.' *Boy, if this thing could talk.* She wondered about the clients and the agents who had sat in this very spot. Today it felt like an actual hot seat. Though the furniture couldn't talk, it did smell. Or was it something else? No one knew for sure. Lost Key Realty used to be the Cross Bones Bar. The sofa had endured as one of the items left over from the old tavern. Despite the deep cleaning, the fresh paint, and even a couple of new walls, a strange bar-smell lingered throughout the office. No one had yet pinpointed precisely where the smell originated. One day you would swear the couch stank. Another day the smell seemed to be inside the cinder block walls. The invisible odor appeared to move around the office like a drunken ghost that didn't realize the bar had closed.

Bailey clutched her arms across her chest, anticipating the sting of an emotional paddling. Several times now, Bailey had made this same choice. Several times they had had this conversation. She glanced up to her picture on the nearby wall celebrating her as this month's top agent. She always thought the posed glamour shot seemed artificial, her dark hair pouffed out, makeup just a bit thick. Now that vibrant professional seemed a stranger. Besides, she was the only full-time agent left in this waning company.

Yet the look on her boss/friend's face worried her even more than the impending reprimand. Margaret Jane's short blonde hair still shined, but her eyes were puffy and tired. Her brow wrinkled, her shoulders curled, and she leaned slightly forward as if pressed by a heavy invisible weight. MJ stared at Bailey and said nothing.

Don't just look at me like that, so disappointed. Yell at me! Say something! I deserve it; Bailey thought before breaking the silence, "I was stupid. I don't know why I keep giving away my commission. You're right, I know."

When she said it out loud, it opened the door to the critical voices inside her head. *Because you really shouldn't be a fancy real estate agent. If you paid as much attention to your business as you do cleaning that Jeep. If you'd just stayed married…*

Bailey felt a hand on her shoulder. MJ had walked over and now sat next to her.

Patting her leg, MJ said, "Bailey look at me."

Bailey brought her eyes to meet Margaret Jane's.

"You're not stupid. Don't talk about yourself that way."

Bailey shifted, feeling undeserving of this kindness.

"Let it be a lesson," MJ said in a calm voice. "Learn from it, but don't beat up on yourself."

"I don't get it. We had such great conversations on the phone. Maria and the kids didn't even show up."

"It happens to all of us. We start thinking of clients as friends, but it keeps happening to you," MJ said. "You can't help but feel what you feel, just don't give your commission away."

Bailey nodded then looked at her picture again. "What happened to that girl?"

"You mean the one who convinced a developer to work with her as the exclusive listing agent for an entire Condo complex? No one has ever done that in our company's history, nor any other agent in this whole area. And not just any condo either, but the Emerald Green, the newest, most luxurious development on the Gulf Coast."

Bailey sat a little straighter. "I guess I did do that, didn't I."

"Damn right, you did. And not only that, you shared your listings with other agents in the office. For some, that is the only reason they had any income this year. It certainly kept them from being laid off sooner. You have a golden heart, Bailey."

Bailey felt warmed by Margaret Jane's flattery and relaxed her arms.

Her boss continued, "Then you manage to give away your commission." She shook her head slightly. "You spend your well-earned money trying to help your clients; buying school supplies for their kids, paying their first month's mortgage, and even buying one a refrigerator. You can't stay in business operating this way."

"I know," Bailey muttered. "It always seems like the right thing to do at the time."

"It's not," MJ fired back. "It's not your job to fix their problems. Whatever those problems are. And…" she paused. "You can't use your clients to fix your problems, either."

"Now, what's that supposed——"

"Ever since your ex-husband cut you off from seeing his kids, you seem to be trying to adopt every family that wants to move here."

"I do not!" Bailey said just below a shout.

MJ raised her eyebrows and pursed her lips.

"Do I?" Bailey yielded.

"I can understand it," her boss replied compassionately.

"They were my kids!" Bailey said, her voice cracked, her words broken by surging emotions. "I know I wasn't their biological mom, but I raised them for six years. I was their mom. Then he runs off with some floozy and still gets everything. It's not fair."

"No, it's not, Bailey," MJ said softly. "But still, customers are not friends. Customers are not family."

"Customers are customers, I know," Bailey finished the thought.

MJ shook her head and smiled faintly. "Also, I didn't realize the oil leak was front-page *Mullet Wrapper* news. That's not good for business. It's already a tough market. Now it's only going to get worse."

Bailey thought of the number of For Sale signs she'd seen in the area, all marked with "reduced price" across them. Fortunately, the For Sale sign staked out front of Lost Key Realty had avoided that label so far. MJ had told everyone she planned to sell the building and work from home. Yet everyone knew that she wanted to sell the company altogether and retire. But few understood what a big decision it was for her.

Bailey glanced at the picture of Margaret Jane's father on the wall behind her desk. Next to it was a picture of her grandfather. Lost Key was not just another real estate company; it was Margaret Jane's family legacy. Even if she couldn't get a full fair price, she would never put a reduced sign out front.

Then MJ looked sternly toward Bailey. "This time, you violated your employment agreement. You do not negotiate commission fees without going through me."

"I know. I'm sorry," Bailey said.

Margaret Jane sighed and rubbed her neck. "Makes me almost glad I'm selling this place, that way I don't have to fire you."

The words landed hard. Bailey straightened as she felt her body tense. Her boss had never, ever, threatened to let her go.

"We are going to keep this between ourselves. But listen to me. You can't do this in Mobile! Understand?" She stared hard at Bailey as if to drive her point home.

"Yes, ma'am," Bailey quickly answered.

"Fortunately, it's not a total loss," MJ said. "We'll still make something out of the deal. Let's just get it closed."

Margaret Jane stood gingerly. Though she had the legs of a runner and the suntanned, toned body of a windsurfer, she moved as if she were much more aged. She grunted as she hoisted herself using the arm of the couch.

"Tough day today, MJ?" Bailey asked.

"Yep, today I feel like an old woman." She steadied herself and walked carefully back behind her desk.

"Docs still don't know what is causing this?"

"Nope. It comes and goes. Kind of like the smell in this office." She raised the window. "Stinks in this room today."

"Oh, Margaret Jane, I hate seeing you like this."

"Thanks, me too. I'll be back to my old self soon enough."

Bailey hadn't seen MJ's 'old self' in quite a while. She wondered how much longer her mentor could keep running a real estate company, even if it was a legacy.

MJ gazed at her protégé for a moment as if pondering a decision. She opened her top desk drawer and pulled out a legal-looking document. She pushed it across the desk toward Bailey.

"What's this?"

"Here's a way you can make it up to me." MJ's smile returned. "I've got a new buyer. They are willing to pay top-dollar for the Penthouse Suite at the Emerald Green." She smiled more fully and raised both her eyebrows. "There's more." She leaned forward. "They are developers, Bailey. They want to build a whole subdivision here."

Bailey could hardly contain her surprise and excitement. "What? Seriously?" She stood.

"This could save me and be good for the town, too."

Bailey turned over the possibilities in her mind. "Who are they? I know all the developers in the area, and none of them have any plans to build right now."

"The company is called Acheron Developers ."

"Never heard of them."

"Me neither. The organization seems to be brand new and well-funded. So, time to climb back on the horse, or in your case, the Jeep." She winked. "This is just what your broker ordered, a paying client with no time to get all romantic about it, just business. Just get him to sign here."

"This is only the signature page. Where is the rest of the contract?"

"I sent it over already. We negotiated by phone. It's out of the ordinary, but the CEO is also going to make an offer on our company."

"Wow! Congratulations, MJ. Sounds too good to be true."

"It ain't over till it's closed."

"Has he smelled the place?" Bailey teased.

MJ frowned. "Just get it signed for me, please."

Ever since Bailey had worked at Lost Key Realty, MJ always handled her paperwork, and never completed her contracts piecemeal.

"You must be feeling bad."

"Yeah, the episodes seem to be getting worse and longer. Docs say I've got to rest."

Bailey could see the fatigue weighing on her friend and mentor. "This can wait till you feel better."

"No, now is as good a time as any. We have a buyer interested. Sign him while he still is." She handed Bailey a note typed on company letterhead.

"What's this?" Bailey asked.

"It's a letter authorizing you to act on my behalf for this transaction. Technically, it's not necessary, but Martin is a stickler for proper documentation."

She felt the compliment of this gesture. MJ practically offered to hand over Lost Key Realty to Bailey on more than one occasion. But Bailey held no desire to run things. She wanted to sell clients their dream home.

Bailey warmed at her boss's trust. "All right then. Are you sure about this? I might give away the store this time."

They both chuckled.

Margaret Jane nodded as if Bailey's reaction was confirmation that she made the right decision. "Trust your judgment but bring me back a signed contract."

Bailey headed for the door. "You got it."

Company protocol dictated that Bailey let the receptionist know her schedule, and where to reach her. Eddie was filling that role since the layoffs.

"Eddie, I'll be…"

Eddie's eyes were closed, and his head had tilted back. A snore escaped from his open mouth with each breath. Shaking her head, she snickered and headed out the door.

Chapter 7

The 'Privateer'

The S-shaped structure of the Emerald Green rose nineteen floors tall, constructed to seem like it grew out of the dunes. The shell of the building was mostly complete, yet a good number of the condos around back still needed windows and drywall. Construction had halted as the market softened. The downturn in sales had been further impacted by the oil continually creeping inward. Bailey let out a deep breath, putting her hand over her heart. *So many unfinished units.* This could have been her greatest real estate accomplishment. Bailey had always imagined the Emerald Green as a magical community. She envisioned the grounds around it teeming with life—families having picnics, children laughing and playing, each unit a welcoming home. It seemed MJ was right. She projected her longing for a family even on this inanimate, incomplete structure, as if plastering the walls could fill the hole in her soul. *Why don't you click your heels three times? You might see a yellow-brick road, too.* She shook her head. That community dream now seemed about as likely as Oz. The castle of wizards and colorful characters, now a mostly empty building of concrete and stucco, with unfinished rooms and strips of plastic blowing in the wind.

"Maybe condos are a fancy name for airspace," she scoffed as she climbed out of her Jeep.

Resolved to get the papers signed and get on to Mobile, she stepped into the elevator and rode it to the top, the nineteenth floor. When the door opened, sunlight flooded the compartment. She smiled. She walked toward the corner unit. The nineteenth floor housed only three larger condos. This one faced east toward Panama City. To reach Unit 1901, Bailey stepped around a pile of drywall, and some loosely stacked boards. She discovered someone had left the door ajar. *The manager must've let them in. Darn.* She always liked being the first to introduce clients to the view, and from this unit, the view was more intoxicating than one of Keri's salt-rimmed margaritas. Light and color poured into the room from floor-to-ceiling windows, offering full, extended vistas of God's natural handiwork. From the balcony, it didn't matter if you turned your head left or right. Either way, one could see up and down the beach as far as visibility would allow. This unit also overlooked the last pristine area of Lost Key, the marshland Keri had been working, and the place where Bailey splashed the workers.

Two men stood on the balcony, talking intently. Bailey approached and felt the warm, humid air blowing through the open sliding-glass door. The ocean breeze brought the smells of coconut sunscreen and grilling hot dogs, and it also carried sounds. Sometimes if the wind blew just right, you could overhear a conversation on the beach from any balcony in the complex. Muffled yes, but one could still hear it. Today, mixed among the faint sounds of beach life, Bailey overheard the two men arguing on the balcony.

"Martin, I'm telling you we only have a short window for this to work."

"That's why I hired you, Stanley, to do my worrying for me."

"There's no way to control the outcome. Too many things can go wrong," he said, shaking his head. "If word of this gets out, this whole thing could blow up in our face."

"That's not going to happen."

"That's what you said in Antigua."

The taller man, the one called Martin, leaned in, his face now inches from the other. Martin stood only a mere three inches taller but seemed to tower over him.

"We were betrayed in Antigua," Martin said with such cold conviction that even if the other man disagreed with him, he didn't dare voice it.

Stanley, the man on the right, took a step back, threw his hands up, and shook his head.

"Don't you hear what I'm saying? It's dangerous! It's a matter of *when* not *if* this story is going to break!" He paused. "We don't need this one, boss."

The taller man straightened and placed both hands on his partner's shoulders. "Oh no, my friend. This deal is the culmination of what I, what we, have been working toward all these years."

Stanley held his gaze. "It's not going to bring them back."

Martin lowered his hands, his nostrils flared, and his jaw muscle bulged. Bailey wondered if Martin might haul off and hit his "friend."

He glanced off as if looking at a distant memory. Then his voice grew icy. "I'm going to get what's mine. They owe me. They owe my family."

Just then, both men saw Bailey standing in the doorway. An awkward silence felt weightier than the hot humidity. *Something does not feel right,* she thought. Martin stepped toward Bailey. He wore tight, tan, form-fitting pants, knee-high leather boots, cracked and faded over time and wear. His off-white shirt seemed not quite clean, unbuttoned at the top of a thin collar, exposing his tan chest and a gold necklace with a gold medallion that looked like an ancient coin hanging from the end. His face was also tan and rugged, with a strong chin. A small scar trailed down the right side of his cheek, a visible sign of past adventures and maybe a scuffle or two. His dark, inky black hair was pulled back into a ponytail, except for one braided strand dangling along the right side.

Seriously? Tell me you don't dress like this every day, that you're on your way to a costume party.

"Who are you?" he said, eyes narrowing. He spoke in a slight French accent now.

"Umm, I'm Bailey Evans from Lost Key Realty. I'm supposed to meet a buyer here for this condo." She extended her hand, but he didn't offer his.

"Where's Margaret Jane?"

Bailey lowered her hand. "She's not feeling well and sent me on her behalf." She handed him the letter MJ had written.

His expression softened, and with an almost forced politeness, he said, "Of course. Forgive me. I was not expecting you, and it's been a tiring day." He passed the note to Stanley.

"No problem."

"Let me try again. Hello. I'm Martin Delahaye, CEO and president of Acheron Developers ." He extended his hand this time, and she shook it. His firm grasp suggested confidence, a man accustomed to taking charge. His hand felt rough and rugged. A shiver ran down Bailey's spine, and she wasn't sure if this was excitement or apprehension. Instinctively she wanted to recoil, but she composed herself. A feeling of déjà vu surprised her. *Easy, Bailey girl. Don't weird out here; just get the deal signed.* Bailey smiled cordially and felt her face flush. His dark brown eyes disoriented her like tinted windows hiding the man inside.

"Pleased to meet you," she managed to say.

Martin motioned to the other man. "And this is my associate, Stanley."

Bailey returned his handshake as well. It felt unexpectedly cold. "Nice to meet you, Stanley."

His slick-backed hair shimmered, and not a strand moved in the breeze. A blue blazer draped over his left arm. He sported khaki pants and a short-sleeved pullover.

"I was just leaving," he said.

"No, why don't you stay," Martin commanded. "This signing won't take long."

"Certainly." He complied with no hesitation.

Martin's minion?

Bailey suddenly noticed she felt a dull throbbing headache. But she felt something else. Something both captivating and off about them. Martin looked like he had stepped out of an antique clothing store. She couldn't get a read on Stanley, and Bailey wondered where he'd rather be. The answer seemed clear: any-where else. *Well, Margaret Jane, you don't have to worry about me adopting these guys. Come on, Bailey, don't blow this. Just get the contract signed. Don't oversell. Answer the questions the client needs answering.*

"This is the finest unit available," Bailey began. "One of the best views, an excellent choice. Any questions I can answer?

"No, I think we are fine." Martin shook his head and smiled.

Are you flirting with me? Bailey stared into his eyes. She couldn't help it. His dark pupils compelled her with the irresistible force of a mystery. If she looked deep enough, she might uncover some guarded secret. No longer content to just get a signature, she wanted to know more about this man and his intentions.

"Margaret Jane told me you have plans to develop Lost Key," Bailey said.

Slowly, he took off his coat. Bailey's eyes tracked his movements as he slid his arms out of his jacket. The white, almost sheer, long-sleeved shirt clung to him, revealing the lean, cut muscles of his arms and shoul-ders. He handed his coat to Stanley.

"I have big dreams for this area." He extended his hand in a gentleman's gesture to escort the lady. "Come, let me show you."

When Bailey put her hand in his, a warmth radi-ated up her arm like a tingly electrical charge. Oddly, her head hurt worse as well. For an instant, in her mind's eye, images flashed, an unwanted slide show. Bailey saw strange, violent visions, a woman's face, ter-rified, then her head bloody, a scream, an old bar, a sinking boat, then a beautiful woman with red hair and a mischievous look on her face. She gasped and quickly withdrew her hand.

Martin held her in a penetrating gaze. "Are you all right?"

"Yes… yes." She took a deep breath and touched her temple. "I've just got a headache is all."

Martin squinted as if not convinced of the explanation. Bailey met his eyes again, surprised that the thought he might be dangerous somehow made him even more attractive, and at the same time, more repulsive. She gawked a bit longer. Though quite sure she'd never met him before today, he seemed familiar somehow.

"Have we met before?"

"No. I'd remember that." He responded pleasantly, but she could tell the question bothered him.

He motioned toward the far end of the balcony. As they walked to the railing, Bailey smiled as wide as the view. She could see everything about Lost Key—the real estate office, a multicolored spec amongst the few buildings that dotted the otherwise green brush and blue waters; the marshy inland bay waters, where Keri worked and Snaps lived and played. Wispy white beaches outlined the waterways like brushstrokes from a divine painter. She could barely make out the Tropical Palm on a distant point jutting out into the bay. She almost waved but remembered herself. She was on duty.

"My big dream is to give this…" Martin made a broad sweeping gesture, "scrub-brush town what it deserves."

He said 'deserves' through pursed lips, as if tasting a bittersweet, forbidden fruit.

"What it deserves?" Bailey asked.

His lips curved into a slight smile.

"Yes. This community deserves my development." He seemed both pleased with himself and confident in his ability to accomplish it. Bailey longed for a renewal of Lost Key, as did MJ and most of the locals. *Most of this "scrub brush" could use a face-lift. The marsh would look good with some beautiful homes around it.* However, he didn't seem like any developer she had ever encountered.

"Margaret Jane said you were a developer," Bailey stated, her face a question mark.

He nodded. "I think of myself as more of a privateer."

"A privateer? You mean like a pirate?" Bailey chuckled.

Martin responded in a deadpan tone. "An entrepreneur."

"I'm sorry, I meant no offense."

Martin didn't acknowledge her apology. He squinted, scanning her more closely.

"I believe you have a signature page for me?"

"Right here." She lifted her leather case slightly.

"Come, we can sign the documents inside. We'll be more comfortable." He motioned toward the living room. He put his other hand on Bailey's shoulder and began escorting her inside. Her arm tingled at his touch, and then she saw another image flash, this time of a tiny boat, an old fisherman hauling treasure, a flag with a skull and bloody sword, and a name.

"Morales," she said out loud, and to her surprise, with a slight Spanish accent.

Martin stopped abruptly. "What did you say?"

Stanley gaped at her, glancing back and forth between Bailey and Martin.

Martin shot him a subtle but stern look. Stanley quickly regained his composure.

Whoa, what's happening here. Bailey wanted to break contact with Martin, but not be blatant. She purposefully dropped her briefcase. "Whoops." It worked.

"Careful," Martin said.

But he never looked down at the case. Instead, his dark eyes remained fixed on Bailey.

Okay, you're starting to get creepy. Just get it signed. Just get it signed.

Motioning toward the couch, Martin said, "why don't you have a seat."

"Um… okay." Bailey went inside and sat down. She began to shuffle through the papers in her briefcase.

"Stanley, would you get Miss Evans a cup of water?"

"Thank you. That would be great. And some aspirin if you have any," Bailey added.

Stanley filled a glass from a pitcher of water at the staged welcome area in the foyer. Bailey wasn't sure where he got the aspirin—must have brought it with him.

"Thank you," she said as he dropped two pain killers in her hand. He nodded but said nothing. She sipped the cold water. *Mmm, that tastes good.*

"Just outside, you said a name, 'Morales'," Martin stated flatly.

"Oh… did I? I must have been thinking about my old friend John Morales. He just moved away. Sorry about that; my mind wanders sometimes."

Bailey never lied convincingly, and she could tell Martin wasn't buying this one.

He kept still; his eyes locked upon her.

Finally, she said, "Let's review the contract that Margaret Jane sent you."

Martin seemed impatient but motioned to Stanley, who then laid a small stack of papers on the table in front of Bailey. She flipped through them. They were Lost Key Realty documents, all familiar and all standard. Then Bailey gasped when she saw the sales price of the company.

"That's it? It's worth way more than that."

Martin glanced at Stanley.

His minion said, "No, Miss Evans, it's not. Your production is way down. The company has laid off everyone except yourself, and another part-time agent. Your broker has not taken a salary in six months."

"What?" Bailey exclaimed. "I didn't know that. I mean, I knew times were tough, but not this bad." *MJ, why didn't you tell me?*

"I'm afraid so," Martin said with an eerie calm. "But as you can see, we have added a few contingencies so that everyone benefits."

Bailey read further and said, "So, you will purchase this condo at full price, no money down, and you promise one percent of the profit on the overall development as part of the sales price for the real estate office?" Bailey raised an eyebrow and looked at Martin. "That could be quite an offer."

Martin nodded then said, "You know how these things go, Miss. Evans. It could be a lot of money. Maybe even several million."

Bailey thought of the uncompleted units in this development, the stacks of boards, loose nails and hanging plastic she'd stepped past to get on this floor.

"Yes, I do know how these things go. It could also be a lot less. Maybe nothing."

She gazed at the privateer, her stomach twisting in knots. More than just her strange intuitions about Martin, this deal fell way outside the norm. The offer only promised money to be paid down the road and in the future. Anything could happen between now and payday. It contained too many contingencies, messier than she liked. MJ would never tolerate this kind of complicated contract. But then this was a messy time, an oily mess. *MJ did negotiate this*, she reminded herself, *but she is also not feeling well*. Bailey felt protective for her friend and mentor, not from a sense of duty, but out of love and loyalty. If this deal worked, MJ could retire, take care of her mother, and finish putting her daughter through college. If it didn't work, or if it wasn't real, then her friend would be in a worse situation, totally broke *and* out of a company. If, if, if, the iffy-ness gave Bailey pause. The contract also referenced an addendum which Martin had not provided.

"May I see the rest of the documents please," Bailey asked.

Martin shifted in his seat then said, "I've already negotiated the details with your boss. I'm running late for another appointment."

"I understand," she said, and then waited.

The privateer motioned to Stanley, who then laid a half-inch stack of documents on the table.

"That is my revised offer with appropriate contingencies," Martin said.

Bailey raised one eyebrow and began flipping through the documents.

"This is quite an addendum."

"Oh, it's all standard stuff, legal mumbo jumbo, some guarantees, and it spells out my protection and assurances."

He waved over to his associate again. This time he laid a sizeable thick manila envelope next to the other docs. The package was sealed and stuffed so full it looked like it might burst at the seams.

"That's the other materials that your boss requested, more detailed building plans, timetables, etc."

You and MJ must have had quite the conversation.

He signed the contract and the addendum pages and pushed the stack back to Bailey.

"Give me a few minutes to look these over."

"Of course. Take the time you need, Miss Evans," he said calmly but seemed irritated to have to wait.

Bailey sat back, flipped through each page. Nothing unusual jumped out, pretty standard stuff. MJ had not initialed a couple of pages. *Maybe she missed these.* She saw something on the appraisal too.

"Environmental testing?" Bailey asked.

"Yes. I need to assess the impact of the spill before I purchase."

"But the office isn't near the water."

"This condo is."

"Oh, okay," Bailey said. Though not an unusual request from a buyer, she didn't trust his answer.

Martin nodded impatiently. "Let's move this along, please."

Despite feeling unsettled, she had no real reason not to proceed. Plus, MJ was counting on her. Bailey took pen in hand, ready to sign. Just before she made her first mark, she abruptly turned toward Stanley. "What did you say?"

He shrugged. "Nothing."

Yet, Bailey could have sworn she heard a clear, distinct voice, just above a whisper, saying "don't sign." She shrugged and re-focused on the contracts.

"Don't sign!" the voice spoke again.

She looked at Martin, then Stanley. Their lips never moved. *What is wrong with me today? I can't even get a document signed.*

Martin stared at Bailey and said, "Everything okay, Miss Evans?"

"Oh, I'm so sorry. Yes, yes, everything is okay. I just thought I heard something." *Breathe… keep it together.*

"You sure?" Martin asked, acting concerned.

"Yes, I'm fine." *And would you stop staring at me?*

Martin half-smiled as if he could hear her thoughts. As she moved pen across paper, suddenly, her signature, an activity she could do without thinking, became complicated. Her fingers felt uncoordinated and sluggish as if the air had thickened around her hand. She labored over each stroke, every letter like carving her name in wood, not putting ink on paper. *What the heck?* Finally, she completed her first signature on the first spot required. She shook her hand, trying to wake it from this strange, bewitching spell.

"I'm sorry, I seem to have a cramp."

Martin and Stanley glanced at one another but said nothing.

Slowly, she finished signing and initialing all the appropriate boxes and lines, shaking her hand each time, each signature more arduous than the one before.

Finally, she completed the task. *Whew! Now let's get out of here!* She stood.

Martin stood more slowly. He handed a check to Bailey. "Here's my deposit. Will that be enough to hold this unit?"

The check was made out to the escrow company.

"Um... yeah... yes. It will."

He pushed the large, sealed manila envelope closer to Bailey.

"And please give this to Margaret Jane. As I said, these are the papers we talked about."

It was more substantial than she expected. *There's an unusual amount of papers in here.*

"Have your office call me and set up a meeting. I want to get the testing going as soon as possible."

"Will do." *Good answer, agent Bailey.* She grabbed her papers, stuffing them and the thick envelope into her bag.

Once outside, she squinted under the bright sunlight and donned her glasses as she walked away.

Usually, Bailey would be excited having sealed a deal, especially since she hadn't given away hers or the company's commission. Instead, she felt conflicted, unsure if this transaction was a good thing or a horrible mistake.

If this deal goes through, I will have helped MJ land the biggest real estate deal to end her career. This way, she can go out with a bang. Maybe this will even save Lost Key. She felt a sharp pang of grief. *I just wish...*

A feeling of dread haunted her. Thoughts she couldn't explain kept lurking in her brain. What were those images she saw? They seemed so real.

She replayed the whole experience in her mind. She saw every detail as if she were watching a movie in her private theatre. *Why was Stanley so worried? What is going to blow up in their face?*

Hey, you got it done, Bailey. She tried to reassure herself. *You got the deal and a huge one at that.*

Yeah, if he delivers on all his promised payments. I've got a bad feeling about these people.

She could almost hear Margaret Jane's voice. *Business is business, and clients are not friends, they are clients.*

Still, maybe I should say something. But what? Hey, Margaret Jane, better call off the deal. These guys are creepy. He's not a developer. He's a pirate. Really? Geez, Bailey. Now I'm not romancing the client; I'm having nightmares about him.

A bell dinged, and she realized she was in the elevator but didn't recall stepping inside or pushing the button for the ground floor. She also became aware she'd been talking out loud. Quickly scanning the interior, she exhaled loudly, relieved to find no one else with her. The doors opened, and the silhouette of a large man blocked the entire exit.

He wore black sunglasses, slacks, and a short-sleeved shirt. His thick neck bulged with muscle, and he seemed a solid square piece of granite more than a real flesh and blood person. A tiny device attached to a cord descended from his right ear, adding to the inhuman effect. It reminded Bailey of the kind of communication device used by some evil villain in a spy movie.

"Miss Evans," he said, extending his hand, palm up. "I work for Mr. Delahaye. My instructions are to escort you to your car."

"Oh, thank you, but I don't need an escort. It's not far."

She started to walk out, but the man did not move. He made no threatening gesture; he just didn't move, and so she could not escape.

"Sorry, ma'am, but it's my job."

Bailey felt her body tense. She swallowed hard and said, "Very well, then."

I guess I don't have a choice.

He stepped aside.

"Thank you."

She walked toward her car, head lowered, clutching the satchel containing the freshly signed papers. She stopped.

"Oh, you know what, I didn't drive today. My friend is picking me up."

The granite man chuckled and then motioned gently with his tree trunk- sized arm.

"Your Jeep is right over there, Miss Evans. I made sure no one bothered it."

Bailey's heart skipped. *You know where my Jeep is? How long have you been watching me?*

"You know this is a safe place, and that's not necessary."

"Like I said, just doing my job, ma'am. Sometimes people act unfriendly to developers and those associated with them."

"I'm not affiliated with this company. I'm just getting some papers signed."

"Yes ma'am, of course."

She reached her vehicle and climbed inside. The Jeep embraced her like a warm cocoon.

"You have a nice day."

As she started the engine, she noticed the man speaking into a small microphone on his shirt lapel.

What the hell was that? Her mind swirled as she drove away. *That's supposed to make me feel safe? That's it. I'm gonna tell MJ what I think about this guy—got to get this off my chest. She'll know how to sort this out.*

She quickly arrived back at the office and scurried inside, startling Eddie awake.

"Hey, Bailey. What's up?"

"Napping again?" She walked past him toward Margaret Jane's office.

He started to deny it as usual, but Bailey interrupted. "MJ here?"

"No, she stepped out for a few."

Crab balls! she thought. *Oh well, maybe I'm making too much of it.* But her gut told her otherwise.

She went into her broker's office and laid the signed contract and thick envelope on her desk.

Done! I got it signed and delivered.

Glancing at the large sealed envelope, she started to reach for it, then withdrew.

Let MJ read it first. If there's something I need to know, she'll tell me.

On her way out, Bailey grabbed her new ads for Thomason Brothers, and Keri's vial of oil she had left in her desk drawer.

Now go home, pack a bag, and head to Dauphin Island Marine Center.

"Tell MJ the new listing is on her desk. I'm heading to Mobile for tomorrow's interview. Thanks, Eddie."

"Sure thing," he said. "Hey, congrats on the listing…" The rest of his sentence cut off as the door closed behind her.

Chapter 8

Jade

Dauphin Island Parkway was a lonely, almost deserted stretch of road. Bailey drove through sections that seemed cut out of the dense scrub brush and short trees. The closer she got to the water, the more the ground became sandy, beach-like. Now and then, the foliage opened, providing a quick glimpse of the blue-green water around, and each time it did, Bailey smiled. Finally, she came to the DI Parkway bridge. The thick underbrush receded, giving way to wide-open views of the Gulf on one side and the inland waterways on the other. She relished the panorama. She inhaled the gulf air like fresh oxygen. The smell of the ocean evoked feelings of familiarity that ran deep down to her bones. When she reached the other side, a short time later, she turned into the parking lot of the Dauphin Island Marine Center.

Several local universities had adopted DMC as an extension of their educational services. Many budding marine biologists from all over the country flocked here for training. DMC had also attracted many tourists over the years, providing a place where the public could learn about the unique ecosystems that make up the Gulf Coast. They could view and sometimes even touch the living attractions on display inside.

As she parked near the entrance, Bailey saw a group of children exiting, single file, from the Marine Center. They held hands and were led by an adult in front and another in the back of the line. They paraded toward a yellow school bus, with the words Mobile Elementary School on the side. Bailey's stomach cramped as she remembered another young boy and another such field trip. She recalled holding his hand and could almost hear him call her 'mom.' She let her gaze linger on the children passing by, talking and laughing. One commented about the cool porpoise, another about the big manatee. "I like the sea diver," another said. "He looked like GI Joe." Then she took a deep breath as the bus drove away.

Walking through the front door, a blast of cold air refreshed her. A cheerful receptionist immediately greeted her. The attendant wore khaki shorts and a navy blue polo shirt, with the company name and logo embroidered in white on the left front.

"Welcome to Dauphin Island Marine Center!" she said as if delighted to meet Bailey.

"Thank you. I'm looking for Jade." Bailey realized she didn't know Jade's last name.

"You must be Bailey?" The attendant smiled.

"Yes, I am," Bailey answered, surprised.

"Jade is expecting you. Follow me."

Wow! First-class service.

They walked past the displays and the aquariums. Bailey felt like a school kid, too.

I love exploring, she thought.

Each beautifully colored section created a world all its own. As Bailey passed the turtle display, a larger one looked up at her, as if to say, 'How's Snaps? '

Then the attendant turned right and opened a door marked "Staff Only." They entered a hallway of glass windows on either side, which provided a view of working labs. This was where the research happened. Men and women in light blue lab coats peered under microscopes and wrote on tablets; some gave presentations to small groups. The attendant opened the last door on the left. A young woman, early twenties with fiery red hair and a tattoo of a dolphin on her neck, greeted them. Bailey could see more tattoos on her arms, where the light blue lab coat stopped just below the elbows. Underneath, Jade wore a white T-shirt with a black leather vest, black skirt, and fishnet stockings with tall black leather boots.

What do you know, a *goth girl in the deep South*, Bailey thought, and grinned wide.

"Hi! I'm Jade," the redhead said, stretching out her hand with precise movements. Bailey shook it. Jade gripped her hand firmly and confidently, maintaining eye contact with Bailey the whole time.

"I'm Bailey, a pleasure to meet you."

"Keri called and said you might be coming by. I think she's a little upset with you, by the way. She seemed peeved that you didn't call her before you left to come over here."

"Yeah, I had a last-minute change of plans." *Why am I explaining myself to a girl I just met?* "Thanks for relaying the message."

"You have something for me?"

"Oh, yes." Bailey reached into her purse and took out the vial Keri had given her and handed it to Jade. "Keri took this sample from the spill, over in Lost Key."

Jade held the small glass cylinder up to the light and studied it. "Hmm. It doesn't behave like crude oil."

"That's what Keri said, too."

Jade looked back at Bailey.

"Okay, groovy. I'll be glad to run an analysis." She gestured with her hands as if trying to put parameters around a problem. "Anything for Keri. She's awesome."

"Yes, she is," Bailey agreed. *Keri said I would enjoy meeting you. She was right.*

Bailey surveyed the lab. "Cool workspace."

"Yep, works for me. We got great equipment and all the latest computers." She grabbed a flat rectangle object from her table. "And even the newest floppy disks."

Bailey examined the 'disk.' "That's neat, newer '90s technology."

Jade smiled. "Yeah, way awesome. They're smaller than the original and hold more data.

"Not very floppy, though."

Jade snickered. "No, the floppy disk is inside."

"Oh, of course," Bailey said, as if she understood. "What will they think of next."

"Tell Keri I'll give her a call as soon as I know something, maybe in two days." Jade looked up and to the right like she was calculating. She counted with her fingers as if punching an invisible keyboard in the air. "Maybe three."

"Okay, thanks. Nice to meet you."

"You too. We should hang out sometime."

Really? "That would be awesome."

"Groovy." With that, Jade made the motion of a check mark with her index finger in the air and turned to get back to whatever work she had been doing.

As she walked through the doorway, Bailey asked the attendant, "Know any good hotels around here?"

"Nope, sure don't," she replied, again seemingly delighted to answer.

Just then, Jade's voice called from behind them. "You need a room for tonight?"

Bailey turned around to see Jade leaning into the hallway.

"Yeah, I got a meeting tomorrow at Thomason Brothers Realty."

"My roommate is gone. I got extra space. You can stay at my place if you like. You said you wanted to hang out sometime. How about tonight?"

"We just met," Bailey said, raising her eyebrows.

Jade looked at the clock. "No, we didn't. We met five minutes ago," she said with a smile and holding up five fingers. "I got a good feeling about you, Bailey. I trust my feelings. They are never wrong. Besides, any friend of Keri is a friend of mine."

Touched by her kindness but not sure what to say, Bailey borrowed one of Jade's words. "Groovy. I'll meet you back here after work."

When they reached the entrance, the attendant smiled and said, "Have a great evening," before locking the door behind Bailey.

Bailey ambled to her Jeep—the parking lot empty now except for a black sedan in the far corner near the entrance.

Well, got that done. Two for two, Bailey. Got the contract signed, and the sample delivered. And I even made a new friend.

As she reached for the door handle, she noticed a flicker of light in the corner of her eye, like a reflection.

Instinctively she looked just in time to see the tinted window on the driver's side of the sedan rising. Before it closed completely, she saw the top of someone's bald head. The engine cranked, and the car drove away. She thought of the granite-man who escorted her to her car. His head was bald too.

What was that flash?

Her senses heightened, and a feeling of dread surged.

Nah, come on. You're imagining things.

Rationalize as she might, uneasiness lingered.

Chapter 9

Welcome to Thomason Brothers

ailey arrived at Thomason Brothers Realty at 8:47 the next morning, her ears still ringing from the punk bar Jade had taken her to last night. She'd stayed out a bit later than she intended, but only had a few sips of one margarita. Today, she needed all her senses clear and sharp.

The office looked newly constructed. Just off Airport Blvd, it occupied an acre all its own. Bordered by a full wraparound porch with several white rocking chairs, and shaded by lush oak trees, it felt cozy. Warm yellow paint with white trim on the shutters added to the welcome.

She parked, then scurried out of her Jeep, up the steps. She paused just outside the front door, took a breath, and straightened her favorite dress, one handed down from her grandmother. Though a bit dated, the garment retained a timeless elegance that Bailey thought would capture vintage Mobile. She smiled, pleased with her choice. *This ought to make a fun first impression.* As she stepped into the foyer, everyone stopped and looked.

Am I in the right place? A couple of dozen people filled the reception area, all milling about, waiting, dressed in their best. Several men sported three-piece suits, except one who wore a wrinkled brown suit and shoes not quite polished. *Probably the only suit he owns,* Bailey thought. Several women looked like they'd stepped right out of a fashion catalog. Bailey's eyes were drawn to a blonde-haired lady wearing a red business suit, a white silk blouse underneath the blazer. The form-fitting skirt accented her perfectly, stopping just above the knee. Very classy shoes, easily costing a few hundred dollars or more, completed the outfit. *Wow.* Bailey spotted another glossy-haired woman wrapped in a tight-fitting mid-thigh-length dress. The low-cut sleeveless top revealed her smooth tan shoulders. She carried a tiny matching purse because there was no place to put anything else. *She's beautiful, and she flaunts it.* Bailey noticed more than one man stealing a glance at both women.

How can men not know their 'stealth stares' are so obvious?

Bailey caught a glimpse of herself in the lobby's full-length mirror. Though she loved the elegant, well-made hand-me-down, the contrast embarrassed her. The black flats paled in the shadow of the designer shoes she'd spotted. Rather than vintage Mobile, her outfit conveyed thrift-shop next to the silk blouses and expensive clothes. She felt like an outsider even before she heard that critical inner voice.

I told you so; you don't belong here. You're out of your league. I tried to warn you.

She touched her temple as the critic in her head went on and on, louder and more persistent.

Come on. It's not too late. Let's get out of here while we still have a shred of dignity left.

"Shut up!"

Everyone stopped talking and stared. Horrified, Bailey realized that she had spoken her thoughts. More than two dozen pairs of eyes examined her like vultures circling.

"Where did she get that dress, a box in the attic?" one person whispered to her friend. Yet her comment echoed in the quiet.

Chuckles rippled through the group. Shame boiled in the pit of Bailey's stomach, its heat spreading to the top of her head.

"Look at her face. It's all red!" another said a little too loudly.

Really? You had to mention that, did you? Gawd, I hate that!

When she did something embarrassing, her face blushed. It perplexed Bailey why someone had to call attention to that natural response. When they did, she thought for a split second that somehow she could control her reaction and 'will' her embarrassment away. Often, that only made her face redder.

The brunette walked over. "You okay, honey?"

She looked sincere, but the way she said it, with a syrupy extra southern drawl, felt so condescending. Her look of concern seemed just as phony, like an artificial emotional implant.

Then the blonde, the one in the red business suit, sauntered over with an irritated look. Bailey wondered whether she had come alongside only because the brunette had grabbed the limelight.

"Don't worry, it's going to be all right," she said and glanced at the brunette who looked away.

Bailey felt her face flush again. She wanted to flee, but there was no place to go. Bailey focused on an empty spot on the wall and took a deep breath, gathering the resolve to look composed. Instead, she felt the urge to cry.

No, not now. Not here.

But she could feel the tears coming. *What was I thinking? Maybe this isn't the right place for me.*

Bailey turned to leave but paused as a woman with a clipboard in hand entered the lobby. Whoever she was, this lady commanded the room without saying a word. She wore a blue business suit, elegant and classy, her black hair neatly cut at a medium length, and half-glasses hung around her neck with a golden chain. As she approached, the two women stepped back from Bailey, who still had that fish-out-of-water look.

"What do you have in your hand?" the woman asked, donning her half-glasses to get a better look.

"It's my ad for when I sell homes in Mobile," Bailey said in a sheepish voice as she handed over the glossy paper.

One of the ladies snickered and let out a smile.

The woman looked up at the heckler over her glasses. She said nothing, just stared, holding her gaze until the room quieted.

Returning her attention to Bailey, she said, "Outstanding! You created this?"

"Yes, I did." Her shoulders relaxed.

"Are you Bailey Evans? From Lost Key Realty?"

The mention of her name surprised Bailey, and further silenced any hecklers and the invisible critics. Someone prominent from the company knew her name. A gentle calm came over her. Bailey stood straighter.

"That's me."

The woman extended her hand. "I'm Ann Swanson. I'm the broker here. Nice to meet you."

"Nice to meet you."

Bailey sensed that all eyes were on her again, but this time looking with envy.

Ann scanned the group. "Thank you for coming. You are all here because you received an invitation. We are looking for a few agents to bring into our family. Today is the beginning of a process to see if you have what it takes to become our newest member. Welcome to Thomason Brothers Realty."

Ann turned toward a perky, sandy-haired young lady sitting behind the reception desk.

"Meet Joy," Ann said.

Smiling, the young receptionist rose and waved. Her big glasses made her even more adorable.

Everyone clapped.

"Joy is your link back to the world, your communication hub," Ann continued. "Be nice to Joy. She can be your best ally."

That sounded like both a warning and an invitation. "Now, follow me to the conference room, and let's get started."

The blonde-haired woman sidled up next to Bailey.

"Nice recovery. I'm Mandy, pleased to meet you."

"Hey, I'm Bailey." She felt hopeful. "Thanks for before, for coming over."

"Sure thing. We've got to stick together."

I could use a friend about now, Bailey thought.

The tour continued into a plush conference room; luxurious blue carpet accented the deep shiny mahogany table. Six comfortable executive-type chairs completed the ensemble.

Ann said, "We have three such rooms; the other two are unavailable. We use them for writing contracts. That is what we love around here. Nothing makes our day more than contracts."

She gestured to several offices behind her. "This section is the heart of how Thomason Brothers supports your business. All contracts and listings go through here. Submit your paperwork, and our competent staff will take care of the rest. We'll review your documents, check any contingencies, and monitor the entire process to closing. We don't want you to worry about anything but selling."

Ann led them past the supply room containing several copy machines, prepared customer packets, marketing materials, and mailboxes for the agents—all the things you would expect in a well-run office. One item stood out.

"What's that?" someone asked, pointing to a tall cylindrical tank in the corner.

"That's helium for your open house balloons," Ann said.

The candidates murmured with delight.

"It's for balloons only!" Ann added sternly.

They kept walking till they reached a larger room full of central cubicles where agents were busy working, and all seemed to be having a good day. Some smiled. Some waved.

"All agents begin here, with your own cubicle space. Those offices around the room," pointing to the several outer offices around the far wall, "are for the top producers."

Mandy asked, "how much production does it take to get into one of those offices?"

"How many offices do you see?" Ann asked.

"Six," Mandy answered.

"Make it into the top six, and one of those offices is yours."

"That's what I want," Bailey exclaimed.

Ann winked. This time no one else snickered. They continued to a large classroom in the back. Two more attendants greeted them, offering a sparkling cider and a piece of fine chocolate.

"Please, everyone, sit down and relax," Ann directed.

The room was arranged theater-style, with several rows of chairs facing a big screen. Everyone found a seat and quickly quieted, listening for what was next. Ann walked to the front and addressed the candidates.

"I've been in real estate for thirty-five years. I've sat where you're sitting right now. I came up in this business selling homes just like you will do. I've sold real estate in New York, Atlanta, and San Francisco. So, how did I end up here in Mobile, Alabama? Of all the companies I've worked for, of all the bosses I've worked with, Thomason Brothers is, far and away, the most exceptional. They model integrity. They walk their talk. We're in the top ten real estate companies in the US, and that's just in terms of production. When it comes to class, we're number one."

Applause broke out in the room. The lights dimmed, and a projector flickered to life. A montage of pictures flashed on the screen, showing the covers of magazines that featured the company, candid shots of celebrities, politicians, and business tycoons shaking hands—or laughing with—one or both Thomason Brothers.

Ann continued her presentation. "Our company is consistently featured in *Real Trends* magazine. Real Estate tycoon Warrington Bouchée refers to Robert and Johnny as "the best of the best." A picture of Mr. Bouchée with the brothers on each side filled the screen. Bailey watched with wide-eyed wonderment.

"They are in negotiations now with Mr. Bouchée to expand this company. The *Business Street Journal* reported this as the best-run company in the last twenty years. This organization is the crème de la crème, ladies and gentlemen, the gelato of real estate companies. You won't find one better… anywhere!"

Again, applause erupted from the group.

She gave her last comment the reverent pause it deserved before continuing.

"Ladies and gentlemen, it is my great pleasure to introduce you to the owners of this magnificent company, Johnny and Robert Thomason."

Two men entered casually and smiling. Johnny had dark chestnut hair and wore the most beautiful black silk suit that Bailey had ever laid eyes on, period. A bright yellow tie with a blue diamond pattern complemented his attire perfectly.

That's awesome!

With shoulder-length blond hair and a slightly unshaven face, his brother, Robert, seemed just the opposite. He wore dressy slacks and a collared shirt, pink with no tie.

So, one formal and the other casual, how interesting.

Everyone stood and clapped.

"Please sit down," they said.

Johnny spoke first, "Welcome to the first day of your new career."

Bailey noticed that Mandy and her friend sat in the front row. They stared and winked like a couple of shills at the Robert and Johnny show.

Are you gonna drool, too?

Johnny continued, "If you are sitting here today, you've made it to an exceptional place, and it's no accident. We believe you're meant to be here right now, and some of you are destined to stay."

Robert spoke next. "Yes, we don't just hire employees. We help you find your path in real estate. You see, we want to find the people aligned by the universe to join our group. Think of your colleagues as more than coworkers; we strive to be friends, even family."

Bailey hung on every word as if she had found water in the desert.

A spiritual real estate broker? Aunt Lee would love this.

Robert continued. "We are a business, yes, but more. This company is a mission, our life's work, our calling. We want to work with those who understand this."

Johnny chimed in. "We'll teach you the latest business skills, the next cutting-edge techniques. We'll provide top-notch support and the most up-to-date technology. We are living in the nineties after all."

He held up a small device.

"For example, this is the latest car phone."

Audible gasps, then applause, filled the room.

"Wow, I can't believe how much smaller that is than the old car phone," Bailey exclaimed.

The front row ooohed and awed again, a bit too loudly.

Johnny continued. "No big old battery packs to lug around."

Then he held up another device.

"This is the latest pager. We can now send brief, typed messages directly to you."

Again, they gasped in amazement.

"The car phone is up to you, but the alpha-pager we supply. If you work here, you will not work alone. We've got your back. The organization exists to support you as you build your business. For now, enjoy the refreshments. Several of our agents have made some time for you. I suggest you get to know them, ask what they do. Have fun."

They lifted their glasses in a grand toast. Then, Johnny, Robert, and Ann left the group to mingle and talk.

Bailey stood and bounced up on the balls of her feet.

"This sounds amazing," she said to the man next to her in the crumpled suit. "Hi, I'm Bailey."

"I'm Remington, but my friends call me Remy; nice to meet you." He didn't bounce. "What did he mean by 'our calling'? Calling to work here? I mean, it sounded like some kind of church or something."

"I don't know. But it reminded me of my Aunt Lee, who says we all have a destiny, and you know it when you feel it."

Remy nodded, "I just need to make a living. I got a wife who's expecting."

Bailey smiled, "Congratulations!"

"Yeah, it's exciting, well," he chuckled, "really exciting!"

"Of course it is!" Bailey said.

Ann returned to the conference area and found the agents and the recruits mingling, laughing, and talking. She had a look of contentment as she watched the happy and productive workers. She walked over to Bailey. Conversations lagged as the newbies lost focus on their gabbing and tracked Ann's every move.

"Bailey, could you join me? The brothers would like to meet you. They want to speak with you about the ad you created."

Bailey's eyes grew big. She grinned wide and, again, bounced on her toes. "Yes! I'd love that."

She glanced at Remy as she walked away and mouthed the words, 'can you believe this?'

Chapter 10

A Sign

Ann led her past the jealous stares of many other candidates. Mandy dipped her head slightly as Bailey passed with a respectful nod—not the gesture of a new friend wishing her success, but that of an opponent competing for the prize.

When Bailey stepped into Johnny's office, she quietly gulped. *I'm not in Lost Key anymore.* A lush oriental rug blanketed the gleaming wood floor leading to a stunning mahogany desk that sat at the far end of the room. Floor-to-ceiling glass doors opened to a serene garden. This office looked and felt like 'success,' and Bailey loved it.

She noticed an easel off to one side, holding a square shape draped by a silky green cloth. *It must be a painting waiting for the unveiling. What art is worthy of this office?*

As they entered, both Robert and Johnny stood and greeted her with friendly smiles and firm handshakes. Johnny invited everyone to a sitting area next to the garden. They sat in four comfortable chairs encircling an artistic round glass coffee table.

"Would you like something to drink, Bailey? Coffee? Water?" Johnny asked.

"Yes, water would be fine. Thank you"

"I'll get it," Robert chimed.

Robert returned with the water and some ginger cookies on a silver tray. The name Thomason Bros marked each wafer.

Ha! These are so cool!

Johnny said, "Bailey, we are very impressed with your ad."

"Oh, thank you. I imagined myself as an agent here and what kind of ad I would create, and this is what I came up with."

"Visualization is a great skill," Robert commented. "The first step in manifesting."

Ha, I know someone else who talks like you... manifesting.

Johnny continued, "So where did you get the idea for the slogan?"

"Umm, it just came to me," Bailey began. "When I thought about it, isn't that the difference between selling a condo on the beach, and selling a house in this fine town of Mobile?"

Easy, Bailey, don't oversell.

"I mean, I sell condos all the time. It's easy, and the money is good, but, I don't know, it's not like the buyers are going to be there all the time. And there is no cute neighborhood, or quaint street, or pretty yard. I mean, really, you're just selling airspace once you get off the ground floor."

They chuckled.

"I hadn't thought of it like that," Johnny said, "but you know, you're right." Then looking at Robert, "A irspace, I love it."

I hadn't thought of it that way myself till the other day, Bailey mused.

Then Johnny's expression took on a solemn look. Bailey felt in trouble for some reason. She knew this wasn't a coffee meeting, but serious business, and their life's work.

Johnny followed up with a strange question. "Do you know any of the Guillroy people? Dave Epstein? Mark Flyer? Julie Roth?"

Bailey paused briefly after each name and gently shook her head no to each one. Finally, she concluded, "None of those names sound familiar."

"What about Creative Designers?" Robert asked. "Ever heard of that company or know anyone who works there?"

"No," Bailey answered. "I don't know that company. Are they out of Mobile?"

"Yes, they are," Ann said.

Then Bailey straightened quickly, "Wait... have I seen their name at the bottom of your brochures?"

"That's them," Johnny affirmed, leaning slightly forward. "So, you do know that company."

"Only by your promo materials. I've never actually been there."

The brothers exchanged glances, and then both seemed to relax.

"Thank you," Robert said. "The reason we're asking is that we have a new ad campaign we are about to unveil later today. We don't mean for this to sound like an interrogation, but let me show you, and it will become clearer why we are so curious and why we are asking you about strangers you've never met."

He walked to the easel and gently removed the silky green covering, revealing a 'worthy' piece of art all right, but not the kind of painting Bailey first thought. Instead, she saw a professional rendering of the company's new slogan. It was precisely her slogan. 'Your Home is Waiting for You!'

Her mouth fell open, and she sprang to her feet. "No way!"

"Way," Robert said. "Your idea is the same kind that we are about to unveil."

Bailey gazed in wonderment. The similarities between what she had created, and the company's new ad were so striking that this seemed more than just a coincidence. It felt like a moment of divine synchronicity. One of those times that you are in tune with the muses, or the planets line up, and you feel connected to something larger than yourself. It defies description really, and yet evokes wonder, at least for those attuned to the magic of the universe.

No one said anything, and their silence revered the moment.

Oh no! Bailey suddenly thought. *What if they think I stole this idea?*

She turned to face the brothers. "I really did come up with this idea on my own, " she said, knowing how defensive she must sound.

"Relax, Bailey," Johnny consoled. "We believe you. We didn't mean to sound accusatory. But we had to ask."

"I understand," Bailey replied, staring again at the ad.

Robert said, "I think this is one of the most extraordinary signs I've ever seen since we started the company. Bailey, you are aligned with who we are and who we want to become as an organization! I believe our meeting is more than coincidence."

Bailey returned to her seat with the expression of a little girl beholding a magic moment.

Robert leaned in, "I'm delighted you've come. I hope our company fits you as well."

Johnny nodded approvingly.

"I think you've got the makings of a terrific agent, Bailey," Ann concluded.

Bailey, so happy she couldn't speak, dipped her head in agreement.

Though seemingly pleased by Bailey's reaction, Ann still kept her tone professional. "Now, you'll have some work to do and some changes to make."

Bailey began to come out of her cloud and back to the room. Without thinking and completely excited, she said, "I'll do it. Working here is like a dream. I'll do whatever it takes."

Johnny stood, and then so did everyone, "Fantastic!"

Ann gestured for her to follow. "Come with me, kiddo, and I'll lay it out for you. Then if you still want to come on board, come on."

As they walked to the door, Bailey saw a large foam board leaning against the wall, a master rendering of a new neighborhood with the words 'LOST KEY' written in bold letters across the bottom.

Her heart skipped. "What's that? Are you starting a new development in Lost Key?"

"Well, we had hoped to build a nice beach subdivision in that area," Johnny replied. "But the market over there isn't good. Plus, we learned an oil spill is driving the values even further down. We just couldn't make the numbers work."

Robert added, " And now there's some new developer in town that seems to be trying to corner the market."

"You mean Martin?" Bailey asked.

"Yeah, that's the one," Robert said. "Do you know him?"

"No, I only just met him."

"We've never heard of him." Robert looked puzzled. "We couldn't find where he has ever developed anything. It's like he sailed in from out of the blue. I get a weird vibe about that whole situation."

"Me too," Bailey said. "I met him the other day. He bought one of the end units at Emerald Grand. Said he had big plans for the whole area. He did seem out of place. He even dressed like a… pirate."

They chuckled.

They laughed at my joke.

Bailey smiled, then studied the drawings again. She felt lighter and energized. She could envision the vibrant community, feel its life leaping right off the picture.

"This is beautiful," she said.

"Thank you," Johnny said. "We were quite excited about that."

"Just not meant to be," his brother added.

"He is even buying Lost Key Realty," Bailey said.

Johnny's face scrunched in a look of puzzlement. "Why would he bother purchasing a real estate office?"

Bailey shrugged. "It could be good if his project goes well. Everything is in deferred payments."

Johnny looked at his brother, who also seemed concerned. "He appears to be more of an opportunist than a real developer. He may be one of those types who takes advantage of a bad situation and breezes through for the quick buck.

"I hope for Margaret Jane's sake, he's legit," Bailey said.

"Well, we *do* have a good feeling about *you*, Bailey," Robert said, changing the subject.

"We all do," Ann added. Then she opened the door. "Would you excuse us for a moment, Bailey? Just wait for me with the other agents. I'll come to get you."

Bailey glided effortlessly back to the gathering as if floating on air. When she turned the corner to the conference room, she saw Remy across the way and couldn't help but blurt out "I've got the job! They want to hire me."

The agents clapped, as did Remy and a couple of the candidates. The brunette, the one Bailey met earlier, did not.

Mandy applauded and approached.

"Impressive." Again, a competitor's nod. "You're off to a great start. But I thought we all have the job. That's why we're here. If you got an invitation, it means you've already got a chance to work here. I could be wrong," she feigned. "The real question is, can you keep it?" Then she acted as if embarrassed, "Oh my gosh, I'm sorry. I don't mean to rain on your parade. That's extra special to be taken back to meet Johnny and Robert right away."

"Oh, umm, no problem." Bailey shuffled her feet, as if off-balance.

"Anyway, way to go," Mandy said, patting her on the shoulder. "What did y'all talk about? Any hints as to what I might face if I get called back?"

"No, not really. The brothers asked about the ads I created. My theme is almost identical to the new ad campaign they are unrolling soon."

"Really? What an amazing coincidence."

"Yeah, it's kind of surreal. I can hardly believe it myself."

"That is quite..." she paused. "What word am I looking for... well you said it best, unbelievable. I know I can hardly believe it either."

Bailey tilted her head and furrowed her brow, not sure what to make of that remark. "Well, it's true."

"Oh, of course it is. I didn't mean to imply that it's not; it's just, well, amazing! Such a super coincidence, and at such an opportune moment. But wow, good for you."

Mandy's eyes darted to Ann, who was just returning. Then she smiled and lifted her sparkling cider toast. Bailey returned the gesture.

As their glasses clinked, Mandy said, "Well played," just loud enough for Ann to hear. Sneering, she walked away.

Bailey looked to Ann, who did not react to the comment. A quiet unspoken question filled the space between them.

"Oh no, no," Bailey began. "It's not like that... I didn't play anything..."

Ann lifted her hand, and Bailey stopped.

"Okay, Bailey," Ann said and then motioned for her to take a seat.

Bailey saw Mandy smirking from across the room. Once again, Mandy lifted her glass. Bailey thought of a rotting piece of fruit that still looked good on the outside, but you didn't dare bite into it.

I bet you're the kind of girl who steals other women's husbands.

She glared until she looked up and caught a disapproving stare from Ann. Bailey's face turned a bright shade of red, but not from embarrassment this time, but hot anger was boiling to the surface. She scowled at Mandy. She wanted to scream, yell something, or throw her glass at her. She thought of various other obscenities. She started to walk over to Mandy but was interrupted as Ann began to speak.

"Folks, let's gather around and take your seats."

Bailey sighed and tugged on her dress as if to straighten a wrinkle.

"Everything okay, Bailey?" Ann asked.

Oh no, Bailey thought. *Did Ann see me angry like that?*

"Yes," she managed to answer and sat down.

Then Ann addressed the group.

"Congratulations, you all have an opportunity to become part of a great company. You're all hired!"

Ann raised her glass in a toast. Cheers and applause broke out. Bailey felt bewildered but managed to celebrate.

Mandy was right; we've already been hired. She thought she was one of the few. *Will everyone get that same special meeting with Johnny and Robert?*

Ann proceeded. "You're not permanent yet. First, you need to go through some training, and then some field time. I'll meet with each of you to go over the requirements and expectations. Thomason Brothers sets the standards in this town. We'll help you get oriented and provide support as you find your rhythm and pace. At the end of the trial period, just a few of you will earn your permanent spot. So, for now, enjoy the refreshments."

She looked at Bailey. "I'll start with you, Bailey. Come on back to my office."

Chapter 11

Expectations

Books neatly lined the shelves in Ann's office. Her desk remained clear. Any loose papers sat stacked in the appropriate trays on one corner, efficient and well organized. Bailey sat on a plush tan suede couch next to an end table adorned with a lamp emitting a soft glow. Ann's family pictures hung on the wall, along with awards of excellence and the magazine covers featuring her, including *Real Estate Inc.*, *Mobile Life*, and *Business Now*. Behind her desk, a window wall provided a view into the garden area. Though Johnny had the larger office, Ann's space still expressed professional, mixed with serene and elegant. Ann sat in a posh matching chair across from Bailey.

Bailey asked, "So, we're all hired?"

"Yes, everyone here has a shot at being an agent. But not everyone gets a meeting like you had, and never on their first day. I have rarely seen the brothers as excited about a potential agent as they are about you."

Bailey beamed and felt elated. "I'll work hard, I promise."

"I know you will. I'm not worried about that. Margaret Jane speaks highly of your work ethic." She paused… "Tell me what happened back there with Mandy."

"Mandy?" Bailey asked.

"Yes, the sandy-blonde in the red suit you were talking to when I walked in just a few minutes ago. You looked upset."

Bailey shifted a bit in her seat, uncomfortable yet impressed. Her new boss didn't miss a thing.

"I wouldn't... it was nothing, nothing to worry about."

"Good, because one of the values here is teamwork, collegiality, even with sandpaper-type people."

"No problem. I'm good."

Ann handed her a notebook, the orientation manual for new agents.

"This will cover a lot of details, how the office functions, where to find stuff, how to order your business cards, support materials, and paperwork. It's your business. You manage it, but it's Thomason Brothers' name under which you operate. That's a respected name in this town and indeed around the country. We set the standard, and others follow."

Bailey laid the notebook in her lap and sat straighter. "I understand."

Ann nodded as if she recognized the hungry look and the determined spirit.

"I'm your broker, and I manage the office and the agents. Come to me with questions and for help."

"Got it," Bailey said.

Then Ann said, "If you're going to work here, you will have to move here."

Bailey's expression changed from confidence to uncertainty. Ann's words unsettled her.

"Yes, I figured as much." She looked away, surprised by her sense of hesitation. Although she was grateful for this opportunity, and despite the allure of Mobile, she found herself more worried about the recent events in Lost Key. The oil leak continued creeping slowly inward; a mysterious developer from out of nowhere, that even this company didn't trust, buying up everything for next to nothing.

"Are you okay with that?" Ann asked.

"Um… yes. Yes, fine. Just a lot to take in."

"I understand," Ann said. "Our agents live in or near the neighborhoods they sell."

Bailey gave a quick nod. "Just curious, so when would I have to move to Mobile?"

"Right away. One big hindrance to success, especially for a new agent, is too long of a commute."

"But I can get here in an hour," Bailey protested.

"More like an hour and a half, and that's if the traffic is good," Ann stated matter-of-factly.

"I'm not that far. I like the drive."

"You have to move here to work here," Ann said.

Bailey sat quietly, then Ann's tone softened before she offered a concession to the hard rule.

"It's just for the first few years, and then you can live anywhere you want. You'll be a known and established agent, and it won't matter. Our experience has shown that it's best in a family town like Mobile to have local agents. Also, there is no way you can meet quota and spend three or more hours driving back and forth from here to Lost Key every day. You must be readily available to sell homes. Can you move here?"

Bailey had dreamed of moving to Mobile, talked about it with her friends. Now on the precipice of her dream, she thought of her beach she loved, the smell of the salty air, and the gentle sound of the breaking waves. Bailey thought of the Tropical Palm and the breakfast she ate every morning, Mary's encouragement to find a man, the warning from Katie not to, and the gentle giant Max who always made her feel like family. She thought of Keri, her friend, her lifeline to sanity. Her heart ached. *I'll be back a lot. I mean, after all, it's not that far.* She thought of Lost Key Realty, quaint, cozy, and haunted by smells of its former life as a bar. It had been her career home. Yet, it too was being sold. Its best days behind it. There was no foreseeable future there. She knew that her beloved community was changing, but she did not anticipate it would also be suffering and vulnerable. She both wanted to follow this new adventure and stay close to protect her home.

"Bailey? You still with me?"

"Oh, um, yes. Yes, I can move here."

Ann squinted her eyes as if assessing what Bailey just said. "Good. Now one more thing…" she peered over her glasses and continued, "you will need to wear business suits, business attire. Upscale casual is okay, but old fashioned is not. Okay?"

Bailey folded her arms and sat straighter. Again, she felt underdressed. Ann was politely saying that wearing your grandmother's dress wasn't going to cut it. Ann was not her friend but her boss; on her side, yes, but not a buddy. Bailey liked the clearly defined boundary.

"All I have are beach clothes." She looked down at her grandma-dress. "And… something borrowed." She met Ann's gaze. "I was going for a Mobile-vintage kind of look."

Ann raised an eyebrow and shook her head.

"But I can go shopping!" Bailey said, smiling at that idea.

Ann scribbled something on a small pad, then tore off the note and gave it to Bailey. "Try this place. I got a feeling you'll like it. Tell them I sent you."

"Wow, thanks!"

"Also," Ann said, "you'll have to drive another car."

"What!" Bailey abruptly stood and then quickly sat back down. "I can't drive my Jeep?" She spoke without thinking, so the words came out a bit louder than Bailey's usual tone.

"You can't sell high-end homes in a Jeep. What if you need to take customers around and show them houses? How will you wear a suit in your Jeep?"

"But I love my Jeep!"

"You can keep your Jeep. You just can't drive it around selling homes here. At least not until you get established. Sorry, kiddo."

Bailey frowned. Her head moved side to side as if her ears heard an irritating screeching sound like fingernails raking a chalkboard. Bailey huffed and felt a knot in her stomach. The sparkles of this opportunity had begun to fade.

"Bailey?" Ann snapped her fingers. "Hello…"

"Yes, okay, yes." She sighed. "If that's what it takes, I'll do it." But her words had a forced quality about them.

"Bailey, take some time and think about it. Take the weekend. We would love to have you on the team. But it also should be the right fit for you. We want happy agents here. I think you've got the gifts to make an outstanding real estate agent for this company. That's why we have this probationary period. Becoming our agent is a big decision and a big change. We try to provide people a space to ease into this." She stood, and Bailey followed suit. "Go treat yourself to something fun."

"Thank you," Bailey said, shook her hand and left.

Bailey walked out of Thomason Brothers as if in a trance. A few folks said bye, and Joy said, " See ya soon." Bailey painted on a smile and returned their salutations. She climbed into her Jeep and held the steering wheel tight as if she were holding the handrail of a roller coaster. She sat, trying to settle her feelings. These past few days felt like an emotional ride of ups and downs and twists and turns.

She took a deep breath and turned the ignition. Music blasted loud, but she turned it off, not in the mood. She drove through Mobile and headed back home. The city that had once intrigued her and left her full of wonder suddenly felt strange and mysterious. The ancient oak trees hanging over Government Street, once a shady caress, now seemed to be slowly squeezing the breath right out of her. She drove through the tunnel and out onto the causeway.

The closer to the beach she got, the better and lighter she felt. But something wasn't right back home either; an eerie feeling sent a chill throughout her body. Filled with an overwhelming desire to get back to Lost Key, she rolled up the window and pressed on the accelerator.

Chapter 12

Friends Forever

The sun had long dipped below the horizon when she arrived in Lost Key around nine p.m. The stars twinkled brighter as if heaven had turned up the dimmer switch. She drove down a dirt road past several old cinder block homes and double-wide trailers, winding her Jeep around the curves and scrub brush. The foliage teasingly allowed glimpses of the shimmering waterway now dotted by the tiny lights of a billion stars. She reached the very end and turned into a driveway marked by a blue dolphin-shaped mailbox. The dolphin welcomed her with a smile and proudly displayed the number 117. *Lucky numbers.* She pulled up to the end of the lot. A pretty good-sized houseboat floated in a specially made dock. It resembled an old shack, yet sturdy, cozy, and inviting. The yellow glow of warm lights spilled through the windows. A mixture of plank boards and artificial grass joined together to create a generous outside deck about eight by ten feet, encompassed by a picket-fence railing that you'd find on any home in the suburbs. More plank floors and siding, topped off with a blue tin roof, comprised the rest of the houseboat. Though Bailey probably spent as much time here as her own home, this place belonged to her best friend.

"Hey, Keri!" she called out.

Her friend's head popped up over the picket fence. "Bailey! You're here!" she yelled and smiled.

"Yeah, it's me."

Keri waved. "Come on in."

Bailey walked past the wooden welcome sign hung at the entrance, where the deck connected to the boat. The invitation read, "*come sit a spell.*" Strings of lights adorned the railing complementing the stars glittering above. It looked festive and a little like Christmas. A palm tree sat contentedly in one corner wrapped in more lights. Large lazy lounge chairs, a small table, plus a few fishing poles and plants, completed the decor giving it a homey, living room feel. Bailey plopped down in one of the chairs, then propped her feet up on the deck railing. Keri reappeared from inside, wearing cutoff shorts and a cutoff tank top. She handed Bailey a margarita.

"I just made these. I thought you might be calling."

"You're the best." Bailey lifted her glass.

Keri clinked her glass to Bailey's. "We're the best." She closed the open book she had left on her lazy lounge and sat down.

Bailey caught a glimpse of the title—*The Pirates of Lost Key.* "A little fiction reading?" she jested.

"I keep telling you it's not fiction. This whole area has a fascinating *history* of pirates."

"Mmm hmm," she said, sipping her drink and rolling her eyes.

"No, I'm serious. Pirates used to hide their ships here. Some reportedly even buried their treasures in the shallow waters."

"Okay, maybe some pirate sailed by here a long time ago, but buried treasure? That's just myth. People have been searching for buried treasure here for a hundred years. No one has ever found anything."

Keri sat up, eyes gleaming. "Ah, that's not true. Legend tells of an old hermit who used to live out on the Point, in a house where the Tropical Palm sits now."

"Really? You mean where Max and Mary live?" Bailey knew they bought an old rundown shack and fixed it up. But she'd never heard this part of the story before.

"The same," Keri said. "Well, everyone knew the old hermit liked to go fishing at night. Then one summer, neighbors noticed he always came back with his boat riding low in the water from his catch."

"Yeah, so he caught some fish."

"No, heavier than that. The fisherman would haul big burlap bags from his boat into his house. They were so heavy he had to drag them. And the thing is, he never went out with a fishing pole, just a rope with a net attached to the end of it."

"What kind of fish you catch with a rope and a net?"

"Not fish, my friend. Treasure, ancient pottery and such, dating back a couple of hundred years to the time of the Native Americans and… pirates."

Bailey smirked. "Oh, come on."

"Go see for yourself. Lost Key Museum has some on display right now."

"So, what happened to the old man?"

She sat back. "His boat capsized during a thunderstorm. Some say it was foul play. Many believe there is still lots of treasure to be found right off that old point."

"Hmmm, interesting. But I think I'll stick with good old-fashioned hard work, rather than treasure hunting."

"I'm telling ya, there's lost treasure out there," Keri said.

"Yeah, right. I guess we don't have to wait for our ship to come in. It already has except it sank in the bay a couple of hundred years ago."

"Waiting for us to find it." Keri smiled and sipped her drink. Then she propped her feet on the railing and asked, "Soooooo… Mobile? How did it go?"

Bailey took a deep breath and told of her day. When she had finished her tale, Keri asked, "You had the same ad as they did?"

"Yep."

"That is so cool. You know what Aunt Lee is gonna say."

Then they both said in unison, "It's a sign."

The two friends sat for a bit under the bright stars sipping their frozen concoctions while Jimmy Buffett serenaded them on the stereo.

Then Keri said, "I know Mobile is your 'dream.'" Her mouth contorted as if she'd just bit into a lime. "But why would you want to leave all this? Life is easier, and you are part of this town and these people. You're already successful."

"Why did you say it like that? It *is* my dream." Bailey's eyes blazed, and she sat up, planting her feet on the deck. Keri sat up too, surprised by her friend's reaction.

"And what's easy about living here?" Bailey said a bit more loudly. "Every day is hard. Seems like every-where I go, something reminds me of them. Every day I worry who's gonna take Liam to t-ball practice. Did that floozy make sure they brushed their teeth? Or read them their bedtime story?" Bailey was close to tears, and Keri reached out to comfort her.

"Sorry," Keri said softly.

Bailey felt the comfort of her friend's concern. Then she saw the ring Keri still wore and remembered the tragic accident followed by the tsunami of grief that forever changed her friend. Her anger cooled as she met Keri's eyes. Squeezing her hand, she said, "I'm sorry too."

"I'm gonna miss you," Keri said, looking away as if trying to avoid that thought.

"You're my best friend in the whole world." Bailey squeezed her hand again. "We've been through a lot together. Nothing comes between us."

They toasted again, and both settled back comfortably in their chairs.

"I don't have much choice," Bailey said. "The company is for sale. I'm the only producing agent left."

"Maybe you could work for the new guy."

"No way," Bailey said with a huff. "He's too weird. What am I selling here anyway? Just airspace."

Keri choked on her drink, trying to suppress a giggle. "Airspace? Since when did the condos become airspace?"

Bailey waved off her comment and took another sip.

"You've always said that condos were a way for more people to have a home at the beach," Keri reminded her.

"Yeah, I know, but as I've discovered, they're not homes."

The conversation lulled, but neither rushed to fill the silence. The two enjoyed the unspoken connection between friends, a bond beyond words. They just enjoyed each other's company.

"I'm afraid I won't see you much if you go to Mobile," Keri said softly.

"Of course you will," Bailey said. "I'm only an hour or so away." Both knew the drive took almost two hours as Ann had said, but they could swallow the thought of it taking only an hour.

"I'll miss the drop-ins, though." Keri looked at Bailey, almost pleadingly.

"Oh, I'll be dropping by so much; you won't know I'm gone," Bailey said. Her mouth opened to say more, but Keri interrupted.

"Don't worry about it. I'm your friend. I'm here. Go for your dream! The change might do you good, a fresh start and all."

Bailey gazed into the night. "It's not just me I'm worried about. The Lost Key Realty I know will soon be gone. Margaret Jane wants to retire, but I don't think this guy she is selling to is on the level. The whole town needs a fresh start."

"Yeah, I hear ya," Keri said. "Things keep going like this, and all that will be left is oily dead marshland."

"Everyone will go to Destin," Bailey said.

"They already do."

"Yeah, but Lost Key has so much potential, and it has something Destin will never have…"

"Pirates?" Keri interjected.

"No, beautiful protected seashore, miles of it." Bailey's eyes gleamed when she spoke.

"It will be dead seashore if someone doesn't stop the spill," Keri said glumly. "Then it's goodbye pristine beaches, hello T-shirt shops and trinket stores. I'll take a natural sand dollar over a refrigerator magnet any day."

Bailey agreed heartily. "Unfortunately, some development needs to happen. I just want it to be the right kind of project that would work with the environment."

"Well, I hope you're right, my friend. I just don't know anyone who cares about this little patch of paradise as much as you do. You have always been its greatest champion."

They sat enjoying the usual night's chorus of crickets, frogs, and other nocturnal creatures. The electric bug lamp popped, having zapped another mosquito. Then a new sound intruded into the evening, the high-pitched hum of a machine. They listened.

Keri frowned and said, "Dang it!"

"What?" Bailey asked.

Before Keri could answer, an orange speed boat came roaring past. The three men aboard laughed as water splashed the girls. The whole houseboat rose and fell in the wake.

"Idiots!" Keri shouted. "That is so dangerous."

Bailey jumped to her feet, brushing water and margarita off her dress. "You know those guys?"

"They're locals. Those guys speed by once or twice a week."

"Seriously?"

"Yep, and I think the one steering, the cute blond, likes me. This is his warped way of flirting with me. One day there's gonna be an accident."

"Are you blushing?" Bailey asked. "You like him!"

"No, I don't even know him."

"Uh huh," Bailey chuckled. "Yeah, why should I leave this place. It's so upscale."

"Like that dress you're wearing," Keri teased.

Bailey tried to act mad, but could barely contain her laughter, as she glanced down at her margarita-stained-grandma-dress.

"To the redneck riviera!" Keri exclaimed.

"I'll drink to that!"

"I wouldn't do that." Keri laughed and reached for Bailey's glass.

Bailey stopped short of sipping the brackish beverage, her lime green- colored drink now tainted with the murky water of the Intracoastal Waterway. She covered her mouth. "Oh, my word! I almost drank this!" They both burst out laughing.

Keri grabbed the drinks and dumped both cocktails overboard, then went to pour some fresh ones. She called out from the kitchen, "How did you like Jade?"

"Oh! Jade is so cool!"

"I thought you two would click."

"She's like a goth hippie."

Keri burst out laughing again as she returned with two new margaritas that looked the standard lime green.

"Here's to goth girls!" Keri said, lifting her glass.

"Here's to redneck speed boat captains!" Bailey returned the toast.

They sipped.

Keri smiled warmly and said, "Here's to dreams."

Bailey held her gaze and beamed. Sometimes a look is worth a thousand words. Bailey relished the feeling of support and encouragement from her best friend.

Then she said the phrase that had become theirs over the years, "Friends forever."

As if the final note on the evening's concert, they clinked glasses.

Chapter 13

"Back from the Dead Red"

*M*orning came early the next day. Noon still felt like three a.m., which was about the time they had called it a night. Bailey hadn't drunk that much, only a couple margaritas; but for her, one was often the max. She awoke stretched out in a lawn chair under a blanket and smiled, knowing Keri must have covered her up. Though Bailey didn't remember falling asleep, she did remember strange dreams, of fiery places, of bulldozers clearing marshland, of Martin looking pirate-like. *Weird.* The smell of freshly cooked bacon aroused her from sleepiness. The grease popped, and the eggs sizzled. Bailey's mouth watered with anticipation.

"Morning, sunshine," Keri said

"Oh, my head," Bailey squinted. Both women were wearing the same clothes they had worn yesterday. Keri had on the same shorts but added her NOAA pullover and cap, and a pair of waterproof boots.

"The uniform of a Ph.D. marine biologist," Bailey stated.

"Yep, got to work just a little. The boss called and needed some help over at the Point, so I thought I'd give him a hand." She put a plate on the table, and Bailey stumbled to the chair and sat down.

"Total fun last night," Bailey said, crunching down on a crispy piece of bacon.

"Yes, totally."

"Mmmm, this… is… soooo… freakin' good!" Bailey said, tasting the eggs. "Thank you so much."

"You're welcome anytime." Keri buttered some toast. "You going in today?"

"Yeah, thought I'd check in for a little while anyway," Bailey muffled through a mouthful of breakfast.

"That's good because Margaret Jane called here looking for you."

"She called here?"

"Twice."

"What did you say?"

"I told her you were asleep on the deck. Long day, big night, and all that stuff."

"What did she want?"

"She said to tell you to get your you-know-what over there ASAP. She didn't sound happy, either."

"She said it like that?"

"Word for word. I'm quoting here."

Wow. Wonder what's going on. I closed the deal. "That's strange. Must be something off with the paperwork from the listing."

Keri looked up, "You didn't."

"No, I didn't."

Keri stared at Bailey.

"Really, I didn't give away my commission."

"Good girl." Keri returned to eating breakfast.

"In fact, he made a full-price offer with some incentives if the project succeeds."

"Really? Why would he do that? That's unusual considering the oil spill."

"Well, these guys were unusual. First of all, one looked like he just stepped out of a museum. Complete with long knee-high boots and puffy white shirt."

"In this humidity?" Keri said. "They must have been sweating like pigs."

Bailey looked away and smiled ever so slightly. "Martin did."

Keri stopped washing the dishes. She fixed Bailey in her sight. "I know that look. You attracted to him?"

She raised her eyebrows. "Well… he is rather good- looking."

Putting a hand on her hip, Keri said, "Didn't you say he was creepy?"

Bailey returned the same gesture with her eyes, "Well… yeah, and he gave me a headache."

She chuckled, and Keri shook her head.

"You're weird." Then she went back to washing dishes.

"You're just now noticing?" Bailey responded and took another bite. "That guy Stanley though, he didn't seem to perspire at all."

"Oh, come on, you gotta be kidding me."

"I couldn't see a drop of sweat. Stanley's hair didn't even move," Bailey said. "And not only that," she lowered her voice and leaned forward. "When I shook his hand… it was cold."

"That is weird," Keri agreed, then asked, "Why are you whispering?"

"I don't know." Bailey straightened. "They were super creepy."

"Well, they must not be from around here," Keri said.

"I've never seen them before. Nor heard of Acre Ron or Aceron... or whatever their company's name is."

"That is an unusual last name," Keri said.

"No, his last name is not Acheron; it's... oh what was it, kind of French-sounding... Delahaye! That's it, Martin Delahaye.

"Delahaye?" Keri's eyes widened. "Are you sure?"

"That's what he said."

Keri grabbed the *Pirates of Lost Key* book she had been reading last night. She flipped through, then landed on a page. "Here it is."

They looked at a picture of a lady pirate with fiery red hair, full cheekbones, and ocean blue eyes—a stunning artist's rendering. Bailey could only wonder how beautiful she must have been in real life. Then she gasped.

"I saw her!"

"Where?"

Bailey looked at her friend with a serious stare. "When Martin touched my hand, I saw this woman flash in my mind."

Keri's eyes peeled wide, and then she read the caption. "Jacquotte Delahaye was believed to be one of the most infamous and irresistibly beautiful female pirates. She had a reputation for being ruthless in the acquisition of her spoils, and quick to punish those who had wronged her. She earned the nickname 'Back From the Dead Red' when she faked her death to evade her pursuers."

"You think Martin could be related to this... Delahaye?" Bailey asked.

"If he is, then he is a descendant of real pirates." Keri radiated with excitement.

They both stared at one another.

"No way," Bailey said.

"I'm not saying anything. That would be crazy." Keri gestured defensively.

"You're messing with me," Bailey said. "You're not serious."

Keri snickered. "No, I'm not serious, I'm hungover." She cleared her plate from the table. "You got to admit though that it's pretty wild that his last name is the same as famous pirate lineage. Well, you're the one that saw him."

"I don't know what to think." Bailey took another bite of bacon.

"Ooh, maybe he has come back for lost treasure!" Keri teased.

Bailey gave her 'a look,' rolled her eyes, and then seemed somber.

"What?" Keri asked.

Bailey met her friend's eyes with a more intense glance. "I saw other things too."

Keri listened intently. Bailey trusted very few people with her 'visions.' Only Keri knew how long Bailey had been having them.

"I saw an old man with a small boat hauling in treasure."

"The old hermit," Keri said.

"Maybe. I also saw a woman. Her face was beautiful, but her head was bleeding. She looked like she had been killed."

Keri raised an eyebrow, and neither spoke. Hopefully, this flash was not an insight into future events but some strange creation of her subconscious mind. Yet both had learned over the years to hold open the possibilities of Bailey's 'visions.'

"And I said a name, Morales."

"Any idea who that is?" Keri asked.

"No, but it got their attention."

"I guess we'll have to wait and see," Keri said and touched her friend's arm.

Bailey nodded, relieved to have shared the burden of these images.

Finished with breakfast, Keri put her dishes in the drying rack next to the sink. "Well, I've got to go to work. We can fight the dread-pirate-Martin later!"

She donned an orange life vest and climbed onto her WaveRunner tied next to her deck. She laughed out loud and shouted back. "Call me!"

"Okay, will do, Dr. Keri. Cool ride you got there!"

Keri turned the ignition. Water sprayed from the back as the motor hummed, and she glided down the Intracoastal Waterway. Bailey savored the last of her coffee and listened to the boats buzzing across the water. She wanted to sit longer, but MJ had been trying to reach her.

I guess it's time to go in and see what's up.

She downed the last of the morning brew, and her head began to clear. She looked at the picture again. *Yeah, right. Martin, the pirate.* She chuckled. *You're losin' it, Bailey.*

Chapter 14

Money, Money, Money

A short drive led Bailey up to the intersection of Hwy 98 and Old Gulf Beach Road. From there, she could see her office on the corner. Just past the For Sale sign, sat a black sedan with dark tinted windows parked out in front. A small black flag affixed to the antenna flapped in the wind. Many locals sported small flags on their car antennas. Most of the time, they depicted the emblem of their favorite football team, or sometimes the American flag, and the occasional rebel flag from those who still yearned for a lost Dixieland. But she'd never seen a pennant like this one. It took several flaps in the wind for the symbol to become apparent— the image of a skull with a red bandanna. The mouth was turned in such a way to give it a fierce expression of rage. A single sword curved underneath the head. A red ribbon, matching the bandanna, tapered off the end of the handle. Tiny drops of blood dripped from the tip as if the sword had made a fresh wound. She inhaled sharply. The same image that had flashed in her mind when Martin touched her arm now fluttered in the breeze! She blinked just to make sure all the pirate talk wasn't causing her to see things. Just below that, flew another flag. Also black, this one displayed the image of an hourglass, the sands almost completely drained through. According to the emblem, the time had nearly run out.

Seriously? Who puts flags like that on a limo?

Then she saw the granite man! Dressed in black again, he stood next to the front door.

Bailey remembered their conversation from the other day. *"We take care of our own."* He had said. She wanted to turn around and go home.

No, wait, I can't. Get my you-know-what over there ASAP was the message. Are these men waiting on me? What if MJ needs help?

A car horn blew behind her.

"Okay, okay," she said, looking in her rearview mirror. "Can't you see there are weird people over there?"

I think I'll park around back. With the granite man out front, Martin must be inside.

She drove around to the far side of the office and parked next to MJ's car. She walked toward the back door leading directly to her broker's office.

Maybe they're in the conference room. I can sneak in and get a feel for what's going on."

She suddenly froze when she looked through the window.

They weren't meeting in the conference room but in Margaret Jane's office. MJ sat in her chair, back to the window, arms gesturing. Sitting across the desk, a sharply-dressed lawyer-looking man listened intently to whatever she was saying. Next to him sat Martin of Acheron. Bailey's breath quickened. Her headache returned.

"Whoa!"

Martin's eyes fixed upon her like a black hole in space, sucking in all the light and life around it. Bailey looked away, looked around. Her feet seemed sluggish as if she'd stepped in quicksand.

Margaret Jane must have noticed Martin staring because she abruptly turned and saw Bailey standing still. She got up and opened the door.

"Bailey, won't you come in here, please," she said, her tone calm and professional.

MJ moved more slowly and deliberately than the last time Bailey had seen her. Dark circles and puffy eyes only added to the stressed look on her face.

The air seemed to thicken and engulf Bailey's body. Her legs didn't want to move, each step lethargic and uncoordinated when she tried to walk. She felt the same as when she had signed the condo deal with Martin; then, her fingers seemed to have forgotten how to write. Slowly, her feet walked her into the office, as if against an invisible wind trying to keep her outside.

Once inside, Margaret Jane closed the door behind them, trying to hide the fact that she was leaning on the door handle for support.

"Mr. Delahaye, I believe you have met Bailey Evans." MJ gave her a stern parental like stare and quickly assessed Bailey's attire with a mixture of disbelief and disapproval.

Bailey had showered at Keri's but then put on her now-wrinkled, margarita-stained-grandma-dress. The same clothes she had worn the day before. She had no choice; that was all she had with her.

At first, Martin and the lawyer-looking companion gave no greeting, no reaction at all. They just sat. Then Martin stood and offered his hand. Bailey shook it. His hand was warm and sturdy, but elicited no visions.

"This is my attorney, John Stevenson," Martin said as the man stood.

The lawyer extended his hand dutifully. Bailey obliged politely. As they shook hands, her entire arm felt tingly, and she heard a high-pitched ringing in her ears. The ringing subsided as they broke contact. Bailey touched the side of her head.

"Still have a headache, Miss. Evans?"

"I just got one." She shot him a look.

Margaret Jane motioned for everyone to sit and then carefully walked to her chair, using the corner of the desk for support. She looked at Bailey with disappointment. Then she grabbed a large manila envelope that had been lying on her desk. Bailey recognized it as the one Martin gave her along with the signed contract. MJ turned the package on its end. Crisp, bundled stacks of money poured out on her desk. They looked to be stacks of ten and twenty-dollar bills.

Flabbergasted, Bailey walked closer, reached out, and touched the money as if checking to see it was real. *There must be several thousand dollars in that pile.*

"There are five thousand dollars, Miss. Evans, just as you specified," Martin said.

She turned to face him. "I specified? What are you talking about? I never said anything like that!"

"You most certainly did." He spoke matter-of-factly and fully confident of what he was saying. "You were specific about the amount of five thousand dollars, cash, preferably in mixed denominations."

"That's not true. I… I… I mentioned five thousand for escrow, but that is always a check."

"Yes, and I wrote you that check. You also asked for five thousand more as a retainer for your company's, how did you phrase it? Exclusive services."

"What? I would never…"

"You did. I remember it well," he said flatly. "You said your broker," gesturing toward Margaret Jane, "was fully aware of this; and that it was contingent upon signing the contract."

Bailey turned to her boss. "I would never do such a thing! You know that."

MJ said nothing, only gestured to the money fanned out across her desk.

"He told me to bring that envelope to you. Said it was something you and he talked about, umm… the information you had requested. He even said it was boring stuff like development plans and all that."

"Boring?" he scoffed. "This is my dream, Miss Evans. I find that remark insulting."

Focusing on Margaret Jane, Bailey said, "I had no idea what was in that envelope!" She closed her left eye and touched her temple.

MJ touched Bailey's arm. "You okay?"

"She was worse the other day," Martin remarked. "A couple of times, I thought she was going to pass out."

"I was not worse the other day! I'll be alright," Bailey managed to say, trying to focus her eyes.

Margaret Jane stood and said, "Gentlemen, would you give us a few minutes, please."

Oh, thank you. Yes, please, give me a minute.

They stood.

"My lawyers will be in touch," Martin said.

Margaret Jane started to escort them out, but Martin and his lawyer hurriedly scooped the money into the folder, flung open the door and left brusquely.

Chapter 15

Under Contract

*B*ailey managed to find her way to the couch. Margaret Jane remained in her chair but leaned forward, concerned.

"I don't know what's wrong with me." Bailey rubbed her temples.

"It's called a hangover, Bailey. Too many margaritas will do that to you."

"No, it's not that." Now rubbing her eyes. "I mean yeah, I had drinks with Keri last night, but this is something else."

"Care to explain the money?"

"It's just like I said." She lifted her head, eyes focused. "He gave me the envelope and told me to give it to you. He said that you and he talked about it and that it contained the information you requested. He didn't say anything about money. I promise. I was not feeling well, but I would never ask for extra money."

"I believe you," MJ said reassuringly.

Bailey lowered her head down into her hands. "Gawd that man gives me a headache."

"I can tell."

She looked at MJ. "No, I mean, he truly gives me a headache. It's the weirdest thing."

"Tell me what happened the other day. Mr. Delahaye? The listing?"

Bailey took a beat before answering. "He's spooky. I mean, you've seen him. He gives me… well… the creeps." She thought about sharing the discovery Keri made, that he might come from a pirate lineage, but then dismissed it.

"Bailey, this was a no-brainer," Margaret Jane said, shaking her head. "You were just getting a signature, for crying out loud."

"Yes, and I got the deal just like you asked. Even though these guys were really" …*super spooky pirate demons from hell*… "odd. We don't want him for a client. He's…"

"How many times do I have to tell you? Selling real estate is not about your feelings. It's business."

"It's more than a feeling. I overheard something."

That statement garnered her boss's attention.

"They were on the balcony talking when I arrived. Stanley, his associate, was quite upset, saying it's dangerous, saying that this whole thing is going to blow up in their face. When they realized I was standing there in the doorway, they got very uncomfortable, like I had heard something that they didn't want me to know."

Margaret Jane propped one elbow on the desk and rested her chin in her hand, listening more intensely. She huffed, then asked, "What else happened?"

Bailey took a breath. "Well, I focused on just getting the signature. I figured I was overreacting. Whatever they were saying was none of my business anyway. After he signed the contract, he gave me that envelope," pointing to the desk, "and said those were the papers you requested. It was unusual, but when I asked what was inside, he just responded that the envelope was full of boring business plans like I just said."

Margaret Jane scrunched her forehead intently, considering this new information.

"When I got to the parking lot, I met that huge oak tree of a man," Bailey gestured toward the front where minutes ago Martin's limo had been parked, "dressed in black and wearing one of those earpieces like some scary movie villain. At first, the man wouldn't let me pass. He didn't say anything or do anything else inappropriate except block my way. He was sending a message that they're in charge. Then he insisted on escorting me to my Jeep. He remained very polite. Then he said, 'We look after our own.' "

Margaret Jane looked even more concerned. "Hmmm, that is odd."

Bailey continued, "It didn't make any sense to me either, but I tell you it really bothered me. I figured I was just over-emotional."

MJ sighed. "Well, you can't be too careful about stuff like that. It's always best to trust your feelings when it comes to caution. We are fortunate that Martin is such an understanding gentleman. And not bad-looking either."

Bailey was dumbstruck. "Didn't you hear anything I just said?"

"Well, you know these big business types. They're all eccentric with odd behaviors and giant egos."

"Yeah, well, what about the deal you made?" Bailey asked.

MJ leaned back and looked puzzled.

Bailey pointed at the contract sprawled on the desk.

"That is a low offer for this company, and you know it."

"Not in the long run. This deal is lucrative over time. More than I would have gotten just selling the company outright."

"As long as he keeps his word."

"Well, that's why we have contracts, Bailey."

"I've just never known you to write them this way, with deferred payments. Keep the deals clean, you always taught me."

MJ nodded. "You're right, and that is always a good rule of thumb. But this is a deal of a lifetime, coming at the right time."

"Yes, isn't it, though? A little too convenient if you ask me."

"What's inconvenient is that you came back with $5,000 extra money. First, you give it away. Now you come back with too much!"

"I know it looks bad. But it happened just like I told you."

"Well, I worked it out. Fortunately, Martin was very nice about the whole thing. I gave him back the money."

"Nice? It feels like we are being manipulated," Bailey said.

"Nah, it's just a big misunderstanding."

"Do you really believe that?" Bailey asked, baffled.

"I've got no reason not to. We are officially under contract," MJ said, conveying a mixture of relief and uneasiness. "I need this deal to close."

"Yeah, but do you want to work with them?"

Margaret Jane picked up a stack of papers next to the money and held it up for Bailey. "What is this?" Then she plopped the documents on the desktop.

"Those are his contingencies," Bailey said. "I noticed you missed a few places that needed your initials. It's not like you to miss anything on a contract."

"Whether I'm one hundred percent or not, I'm sure I would have noticed this." Her broker plucked a single page from the stack and slid it across the desk to her top agent.

A tightness constricted around Bailey. Her heart began to race as she scanned the document titled 14-a. It spelled out a contingency clause that the final sale must also include an accepted offer on Lost Key Realty and the first rights of all its holdings, including lengthy legal details about rights and privileges of said holdings.

Bailey read the document several times and shook her head adamantly.

"As I said, I thought you missed this page. He talked about his grand plan for the whole area. It seemed odd to add something like this to the contract."

MJ leaned back in her desk chair. "Well, I've never seen this page. But they agreed to chalk the whole thing up to a misunderstanding as long as I also initialed Form 14-a."

"Did you?" Bailey asked.

"Yes, I did, since my company doesn't have any holdings anyway."

Bailey moved to the empty chair on her left across from her ailing boss. "Doesn't all this concern you?"

"According to them, you insisted he pay under-the-table money to close the deal."

"I didn't know what was in the envelope!" Bailey's lips pursed.

Margaret Jane stared at Bailey for a minute. "I believe you. But that envelope ended up here on my desk, and you delivered it. We're fortunate they are not going to push this legally. We could both lose our license over this. Why do you think he brought his lawyer?"

MJ leaned back in her chair. Her eyes darted around the room, avoiding contact with Bailey.

What? What are you not telling me?

Then MJ said, "You know the town's financial situation is dire. Well, it's worse than generally known. Lost Key is on the verge of bankruptcy. This development could save us." MJ looked away, evasively.

Bailey stared at her mentor and felt an intense dreadful feeling in her gut. "What is it? There is more, isn't there?"

Margaret Jane slowly returned her gaze to meet Bailey's. Her voice broke as she spoke. "You know I'm not well."

Bailey's mouth fell open. She had never heard her talk with such resignation.

"I know you've been tired lately."

"It's more than that. I'm exhausted. Something is wrong, and the doc s don't know what it is. I can barely keep my eyes open. They've advised me to work less or take early retirement."

Bailey touched her arm. "I didn't know."

"Of course not. No one did. So, you see, I need this deal to close. Developers aren't exactly lining up at the door." Then MJ gave her a look of hope on the verge of desperation. "If this works, then I could retire, take care of my mom, put my daughter through school, and help preserve this town I love."

Bailey sat back and slumped under the weight of this revelation, feeling helpless. Not only had some strange privateer invade her sanctuary, but now it seemed nature itself had conspired to help him take over.

Bailey sniffled. "MJ, he's not a savior. I've got a terrible feeling about these people. We don't need to be in business with them."

Margaret Jane regained some of her professional composure. "If we don't, then there won't be any business. Now, go home and get some rest."

Bailey started to respond, but Margaret Jane interjected. "That's an order."

Reluctantly, Bailey conceded. They stood. MJ opened the door.

Eddie approached, holding a piece of notepaper.

"He said his lawyer would contact you and wanted me to be sure to tell you..." reading from the notepaper, "that he's confident this will be a prosperous venture for all." He looked up at Margaret Jane. "Creepy guy. I mean cool outfit and all, but I don't get a Lost Key vibe about him."

"Me neither," Bailey concurred.

Margaret Jane shook her head. "Thanks, Eddie." Then she gently took Bailey by the arm. "Come on; I'll walk you out." They stepped outside into the bright Florida sunshine.

MJ touched Bailey's shoulder.

"Look, I know you love this scrub brush, swampy town more than anyone. It's cute, it's adorable, but change is here whether we like it or not. This deal is the biggest opportunity for our little company since I took over twenty years ago. If we don't work with him, someone else will. You understand?"

Bailey sighed. "But there has to be another way. Another buyer, at least."

"He's the one here," MJ said and took a deep breath before continuing. "Bailey, you can't appear to work here anymore."

"What? You're firing me?"

"No, I'm not firing you, exactly. I assured Martin and his lawyer that the money must be a misunderstanding and that you had taken an offer with another company in Mobile."

Bailey felt as if she'd been punched in the gut. "You *are* firing me."

"No, I'm trying to protect you from losing your license. His lawyer wanted to press it further."

Bailey folded her arms. "I was completely set up!"

"Look, Bailey, maybe Thomason Brothers is coming along at the right time. It's been your dream ever since I've been working with you. You've been here for several years, and many times you talk about going to sell those fancy homes in Mobile. Especially since... well, let's just say a change might do you good too. Here is your opportunity. Things happen for a reason."

"Yeah, maybe, but can't we find a better reason than selling out to that man?"

"Let it go. We are closing in a couple of weeks." MJ held her gaze on Bailey with sadness in her eyes.

"I hate to lose you," she continued. "You're the best agent I've ever had." Looking at the now-empty desks and then Eddie with his loud, obnoxious Hawaiian shirt and even louder clashing shorts and flip-flops. "By far," she added. "You are also good for morale. But you were meant for more than this, Bailey. I had no problem giving Ann a glowing reference. All I had to do was tell the truth."

Bailey blushed. "You're the best."

Margaret Jane studied her protégé. She chuckled at Bailey's windblown hair and wrinkled margarita-stained old dress. "Surely, you're not wearing that to work? Those clothes look like you slept in them."

Bailey pulled her lips inward, trying to suppress a smile. "Actually, I did."

MJ shook her head. "I must be the worst boss for the things I tolerate. All Eddie needs is a beer and easy chair. He's already dressed for laziness, and you come in here wearing the clothes you slept in."

"Hey, I'm off today."

"Well, if anyone drives up, just act like you're a customer."

Eddie had drifted off to sleep. His snore interrupted their conversation. Margaret Jane opened the door, wadded the nearest piece of paper, and threw it, hitting him square on the nose. He startled. "Wake up! This ain't your living room. I swear I don't know why I keep you around."

"Because his father owns the company?" Bailey said.

"I own the company. I just borrowed money from Eddie's father," Margaret Jane snapped. "Lost Key Realty has been in my family for three generations, or have you forgotten that."

"Okay, okay. Sorry."

"Get some rest. Then go show Mobile what Bailey can do."

They hugged. Bailey watched MJ slowly amble back inside, using the door frame and a nearby desk to steady herself.

As the door closed, she heard Margaret Jane say, "Eddie, change the 'For Sale' sign to 'Under Contract.'"

Chapter 16

Time's Up!

*I*s *Mobile my dream or my escape?* Bailey pondered as she drove toward her beach cottage. *I wish Martin were but a dream. Then I'd wake up tomorrow, and there would be no strange pirate-developer trying to buy my Lost Key.* Now, she wasn't sure she even wanted to go back to Mobile. The price seemed too high: leaving her friend Keri, the beautiful beach, her Tropical Palm family. *What was I thinking?* Besides, she'd have to dress up and get a new car. *Just twist the knife, why don't ya. I mean seriously*, she thought. *Maybe I could sell homes here where I live.*

But the Lost Key office was now under contract, too. Even the marshland was vanishing right in front of her eyes, covered in black slimy sludge and sold to a man who seemed at home in lower sludgy places. One undeniable fact, the Lost Key she knew would soon be truly lost.

Still, she had a gut feeling that going to Mobile was the next right thing. Now, because of Martin's deception, she had no choice. *He set me up good.*

Bailey felt soothed by the hum of her Jeep and the gulf air tossing her hair. Ann had given her the weekend to consider the offer from Thomason Brothers. She intended to take every minute of it. She crossed the bridge over the Intracoastal. Another mile and a half brought her home—a quaint two-bedroom beach cottage. She parked the Jeep and walked around to the beachside. She rarely entered through her front door and never locked the sliding glass back door. Why would she? Nothing bad ever happened in Lost Key.

The sun hung high and bright in the indigo afternoon sky, and the water looked inviting, as always. Not many people had the Gulf as their backyard, or a lawn made of white sand speckled with tall brown sea oats. At high tide, the ocean pressed within 25 yards of her back patio. As the waves crashed, her mind cleared. *That's what I need—a little beach time to get my bearings.* She strolled into her bedroom and began unbuttoning her shirt to put on her bathing suit. While she changed, she tapped the answering machine.

"You have seven messages," the mechanical voice said. Then they started playing.

"Hey, Bailey, this is your mom. I didn't hear from you yesterday. I just want to make sure everything is okay. Call me."

Beep…

"Hey Bailey, this is your mom again. It's been a couple of hours since I called, just want to make sure you're okay. Call me now. I'm getting worried."

Beep…

"Hey!" It was Keri. "How about an early dinner at the Shrimp Basket? I should be done here about four. Call you later. Maybe we can start some trouble." She laughed.

Beep… Silence… Then a click sound.

Beep… Silence… Then another click sound. *Someone must have the wrong number.*

Beep… "Bailey, it's your mom again. Where are you, hon? I'm getting worried…"

The doorbell rang. "Aahhh!" Bailey yelped. She left the answering machine running and managed to put on some shorts and a pullover beach shirt as she made her way to the front door and opened it.

"I have a special delivery for Bailey Evans," said a man dressed in black jeans and a black knit shirt. A bandanna covered his head, making it impossible to know the color of his hair, or even if he had hair. Mirrored sunglasses hid his eyes. Judging from the tone of his muscles and his brown beard, Bailey deduced he might be in his thirties.

"I'm Bailey," she offered.

The man handed her a single black rose wrapped in black tissue paper, garnished with a few sprigs, and a black card-sized envelope.

"This is for you."

"Who's it from?"

He shrugged. "I just deliver the flowers, ma'am." Then he smiled, exposing several brownish discolored teeth, and left.

For a moment, Bailey studied the rose. She had never seen a black one before. It was beautiful and yet mysterious, but it scared her.

They mean something bad, don't they? Who sends black roses?

She scanned the envelope for a name or return address but found none. She tore open the flap and removed the card inside. It, too, was black. An hour-glass symbol edged in yellow adorned the outside face of the card. The 'sand' in the hourglass was red. The red sand was either just starting to pour through or almost done depending on which way she tilted it. She opened the card. Hand-cut letters had been pasted to the inside, spelling the message: "Time's up."

"...Okay, well, call me as soon as you get this," her mom's message finally finished.

The machine beeped again... Silence... Then the faint sound of someone exhaling. A man's voice, slightly raspy, crackled on the speaker. "Your time is up, Bailey."

Bailey backed away till she bumped into the wall, her eyes fixated on the device.

Her head pounded; her heart raced. Her breathing became shallow.

She dropped the rose and the card. Placing her hand over her mouth, she backed into the wall again.

"There's no way! This can't be!" The room swirled as her vision blurred. She gasped for air. She flung open the door again. No one. The delivery man was gone.

"Nooooo, it's not possible!" she half-screamed. She jabbed her feet into her boat shoes, grabbed her keys, and ran out the back door as fast as she could. Hurrying into her Jeep, she cranked it and stomped on the gas. Gravel spewed as the vehicle spun out of the parking spot and backed onto Perdido Key Drive. Several cars skidded off the road, swerving left and right to avoid a collision. Horns honked in protest, but Bailey didn't care. Almost disregarding the clutch, she shoved the stick in first and stomped the gas again. The gears clanked and rattled. She heard the grinding sound of tiny shards of the transmission granulated at the forced change. Her mind raced like a horse scared out of the starting gate with no track to run on, no direction to guide it.

Oh, my God! Oh, my God! No! No! No! No! No! This can't be happening! Not again!

She drove erratically, barely able to see through her tears. The Jeep lurched forward as if it knew where to go. She headed back across the Intracoastal Bridge and then turned right at the first intersection, ignoring the red traffic light. The oncoming cars veered in all directions, barely missing her. Vehicles beeped, and angry drivers yelled obscenities. Bailey sped on, not looking back, no apologies. A mile down the road, she turned left at the corner of Flounders Restaurant and Island Road. She skidded to a stop in the driveway of the first house on the right, and jumped out, leaving the door open. A man was watering the palm tree out in the front yard.

"Hey! Don't mess up my driveway like that!" he yelled.

Bailey did not respond.

"Bailey?" he called after he noticed she was crying. "You okay?"

She didn't answer, just opened the door and ran inside. Irene, a dark-haired lady, mid-fifties, stood near the kitchen sink, washing a black pot.

"Well, there you are. I've been looking for you. What's the matter, hon?"

Bailey could barely get the words out. "Mom, he found me!"

Chapter 17

Signs & Symbols

*O*ver the next several hours, Bailey gathered herself. Time with her family and a visit from the sheriff helped, as did the home-cooked meal her mom fixed. After dinner Bailey drove over to Keri's place. She found her friend sitting in a lounge chair on her deck, nose buried in *Pirates of Lost Key.* Keri motioned to the empty chair. Bailey plopped down and exhaled a deep sigh of relief. On the deck of the houseboat, they solved most of the world's problems.

Keri laid her book in her lap. "What's wrong? You feelin' alright?"

"Got a creepy call today… and a strange delivery." Bailey relayed the recent scare to her friend.

Keri sat up, mouth gaped open, and looked at Bailey. She didn't even have to ask the question in her eyes.

"No, I don't know who it is," Bailey said. "But I have to admit that I thought it was the stalker again for a moment. It really freaked me out." She sank back into the comfy lounge as if she had been holding her breath for a long time and was just now letting it out.

"Well, yeah, of course, it did. It's freaky. Y'all go to the police?"

Bailey nodded. "Sheriff already came by."

"You okay?"

"I will be."

Keri looked away as people do when searching that invisible memory bank. "Wait a minute!" She began flipping through the pages of her book again.

"What is it?" Bailey asked.

"The card you described; it seems familiar." She flipped pages back and forth, then stopped. "Yes, I knew it."

She lay the book flat, turned it toward Bailey. "Is this the symbol you saw?" The picture on the page was an almost exact rendering of the hourglass symbol on the postcard. Underneath the logo were the words "Time's up."

"What?" Bailey picked up the book and held it closer. "No way!" She began to read. "Used by pirates to taunt their enemies, the hourglass symbol signaled an impending raid. It announced to their prospective victims that, quite actually, 'time was up.' Marauders were coming to plunder your treasures, perhaps kill you, and nothing could stop them."

Bailey sat the book down and stared at Keri, who was staring back. Then Bailey gasped.

"What?" Keri fixed her wide eyes on her friend with eager anticipation.

"I also saw this symbol the other day. On a flag on Martin's limo!"

The full realization of the conversation settled on the two of them. Keri stood, a look of excitement spreading across her face. It was the excitement of discovering something extraordinary in their everyday world—even though it was dangerous and unwanted.

Then Keri said, "Martin's a real, modern-day…"

"Don't say it," Bailey protested, but rather unconvincingly.

"It all makes sense." Keri had begun pacing. "I bet he even lives on a boat."

"This is just ridiculous," Bailey emphasized, but her eyes held a questioning look.

"Don't listen to me, then. Listen to yourself. You know something's up; you can feel it, even if your mind can't accept it."

"Are you saying that Martin is… well… a pirate?"

"You said he dressed like one. Plus, he's got a pirate flag on his car and using marauder tactics to intimidate you."

Bailey nodded. Keri made a good point. Martin both looked and acted like the real thing.

"It's not happenstance that the card matches that flag you saw on his car."

"You think he sent me the rose too?" Bailey asked but could already guess the answer.

Keri raised her eyebrows in a what-do-you-think kind of expression, then said, "And what better cover for a pirate than some normal occupations, like a merchant, or businessperson, or …"

"Developer," Bailey added.

"Exactly!"

"Seriously? Don't you think we are taking this a little too far?"

"Maybe, but you gotta admit this is too much to be a coincidence. Don't ya think?"

"Honestly, I don't know what to think."

"Then don't think… feel. What do your feelings say?"

"My feelings are the problem for me lately." Bailey resisted Keri's idea, but again it 'felt' right.

"I don't buy that," Keri said. "Problem is you are too slow to trust your feelings. You got great intuition, Bailey. I mean like psychic kind of good."

Bailey warmed at her friend's comment. "You're starting to sound like Aunt Lee." She chuckled. "Still, redeveloping a town seems an awful lot of trouble just to make a profit. Whoever heard of a pirate building stuff?"

Keri looked forebodingly at her friend. "The thing is, he didn't send that to the city; this is a message for you."

Bailey looked at the symbol and thought of the black rose. "You think he wants to hurt me?" Her heart pounded at the thought.

"He's already hurt you. He set up a conflict between you and MJ. He put the company in a compromising position. He sure seems to want you out of the way." Keri sat down.

"Well, he accomplished that," Bailey said. "MJ told me I can't work at Lost Key anymore."

"What? No! She fired you?"

"Not in so many words, but it amounts to the same thing. She claimed to be protecting me. Martin's lawyer was threatening to file a complaint."

"Oh, I'm so sorry, my friend."

Bailey puzzled. "But why would he bother? What threat am I to him?"

"I don't know. But you seem to be the only one in town asking questions, the only one who does not see him as some savior of Lost Key."

Bailey stared off into the night. As fantastical as these coincidences sounded, it felt real. *Is Martin a pirate? Really?* The notion of some would-be swashbuckler pillaging her town made her blood boil. How could she prove any of this? She'd be laughed out of town, or worse, committed to an institution. Her folks would think she'd finally snapped. Besides, she wasn't quite ready to believe this herself. MJ seemed okay with the deal, even relieved. But then MJ was not on her best game and getting more desperate each day. Then the thought occurred, if the rose and card did not come from Martin, that would be even worse because it meant someone else, some unknown stranger was targeting her. Either way, her safe refuge had become precarious, even dangerous. Except for Keri's houseboat, there seemed no place left to rest.

Bailey returned her gaze to the sand draining from the hourglass. The symbol seemed appropriate, for she could see no clear way to resist the invasion of Lost Key and the purchase of her beloved company. Martin's development was proving as uncontainable as the oil sludge seeping into the marshland. *MJ was right; maybe the Thomason Brother s' invitation is coming at just the opportune time.* It made logical sense, and it felt in her gut like the right next step.

Finally, she said, "I gotta move to Mobile."

"Absolutely," Keri agreed with no hesitation. "Get away from this whole place. Get away from… him."

"I'll rent out my cottage. It'll help cover expenses while I get started. That shouldn't be a problem. I mean, it's right on the beach."

"That will work." Keri nodded. "And why not? You sleep here more than at your place anyway." She chuckled.

Bailey's brow wrinkled as if she felt a sharp pain. "I miss this place already!

"Mobile is not that far," Keri said. "I'm over in the bay once or twice a week so we can still see each other. Besides, Bailey, home is something you carry with you, not a pushpin on a map."

"These days, I don't know where home is," Bailey replied flatly.

Keri sat on the edge of her lounge chair, then held up her hand for a high five.

Bailey scrunched her forehead and did not return the gesture.

"Come on; you can do this," Keri persisted with her intervention of optimism. "You have to do this."

"I don't know. It's all so much to take in."

Keri, still holding her hand up, leaned forward. "You got this, Bailey."

Bailey wasn't convinced, but she borrowed the confidence of her best friend.

"I can do this," she said, slapping Keri's hand.

Just then, they heard the hum of a high-pitched motor. A spray of brackish water doused Keri and Bailey as the same orange speed boat barreled past. The houseboat bobbed in its wake. Laughter trailed off as the watercraft grew smaller in the distance. Simultaneously, they made a gesture as if they were holding margarita glasses and toasting. Together they said, "To the redneck riviera!"

A zap echoed from the bug light.

Chapter 18

Leaving

The rest of the weekend, Bailey scraped together the best suit she could find, which was little more than a blue blazer, white slacks, and a light blue dress shirt. She borrowed the blazer from MJ, and this time, left her grandmother's dress at home. She also asked MJ for one more big favor: to borrow her car, a Honda Accord. The kinks and imperfections, the fading interior, all spoke of road experience. The car had seen some miles but still had some fire in the engine and tread on the tires. More importantly, it fit the Thomason Brothers Realty requirements.

She headed toward her parents' house one more time to say bye. As she approached their driveway, she noticed the doors of the Red Barn open. She saw Aunt Lee milling about inside of this Gulf Beach Road fixture. The Red Barn started as Uncle Jed's home garage for fixing and building race cars. After that, it had become a game room for local teens. Graffiti from Bailey's childhood still adorned the walls. At present, it served as a flea market. The latest conversion only meant that Jed had moved his cars out, along with the games, and Lee filled the space with racks of clothes and knickknacks, plus the variety of 'antiques' that folks 'dropped off.' Bailey still missed the days of the game room, playing foosball for hours on end. She pulled the Honda into the gravel parking lot and waved to her aunt as she got out.

"Hon, what happened to your car?"

"Oh, new company rules. Can't drive a Jeep and sell homes in Mobile. MJ let me borrow her car for a while."

"Tell them to go stuff it. Drive what you want," Lee protested. Then she hugged her niece. "Oh, I'm gonna miss you."

"Me too, you, Aunt Lee."

"Glad you came by." They walked inside the Red Barn to get out of the sun. Since it wasn't air-conditioned, the inside was almost as hot as outside. But the two fans at either end of the big room did their best to cool things down. They helped a little.

"I had a dream about you last night," Lee continued.

"Really? One of your premonitions?" Bailey asked. Unlike her mother, Bailey always found Lee's dreams fascinating.

They walked to the back corner and sat down at an old card table and two folding chairs, obviously donated. Lee took Bailey's hands in hers.

"You're supposed to go to Mobile, but that's not your final destiny."

Bailey frowned. "Is this your idea of a pep talk?"

"I would never discourage you from your dream, hon. You know that. I'm just saying. Mobile is going to prepare you for something, something big. I'm not sure what. But it has to do with Lost Key."

"Not you too, Aunt Lee. All that talk about staying here and how I shouldn't leave. Mobile is not that far."

"Did I say that? No, I did not. Now you listen to me, Bailey." Lee squeezed Bailey's hands tighter. "You're supposed to go to Mobile, but you're not supposed to stay there, at least not now. You will find something there." She pointed to Bailey's heart. "Something inside yourself."

Bailey was intrigued. "Really?"

"You said this new developer named his company Acheron?"

"Yeah, that's right."

Lee pulled a book from a shelf next to their table and opened it to a bookmarked page. "Do you know what the word Acheron means?"

Bailey shook her head. "No. Should I?"

Lee pointed to the open page of the book.

Bailey read. "The river of woe. River of woe? That's what it means? Look, there's even an illustration of some dark place with a river and bunches of people, they seem to be in agony or something."

"Exactly," Lee said, her eyes bright with excitement. "In ancient mythology, the river of woe, Acheron, is associated with the underworld. You know, hades, hell." She pointed to the illustration in the book. "These are souls waiting to cross over or escape, maybe."

Bailey looked at her aunt, somewhat astonished. "You're telling me that Martin named his company after an underworld place in hell?"

Lee leaned forward as if she couldn't wait to continue her story.

"Also, it says here the servants of Diablo guard the crossing of the river of woe." She showed Bailey another picture of the river. "Look at this. See how the artist depicted the people as suffering, some screaming, some crying out in pain?"

"Well, what would you expect if you were about to cross the river of woe," Bailey replied.

Lee pointed to the picture, then raised both eyebrows, eyes wide as she looked at her niece.

Bailey matched her expression. "Aunt Lee, I know what you are thinking, but he's just a developer."

"Maybe so, but I sense darkness about him. The Devil's got a hold of him."

"It's strange, alright. But Martin is just a man, not some guardian of an underworld river."

"Whatever he is, he's part of a storm that has arrived in our little town. Get away from him. Let the storm blow over. Then bring what you learn in Mobile back home."

Aunt Lee's instruction captivated Bailey. The eerie conviction in her voice and the calm assurance in her demeanor gave Bailey the chills.

"You're special, Bailey," Aunt Lee continued. "You've got the gift. Now it's time to develop it."

"Gift?"

Lee leaned closer. "Trust your feelings."

"I thought I saw you drive up," Irene's voice bellowed. She stood in the doorway, hands clasped behind her back. Something about her shadowy silhouette and the dust slightly swirling in the light only added to a sense of foreboding.

Uh oh, Bailey thought as she watched her mother stride into the room. *Speaking of a storm brewing.* She knew they would never end their sister-squabbles. It was the nature of their relationship.

Irene glared at Lee. "I've told you not to fill her head with all that voodoo nonsense." She spoke calmly but firmly. "She's got to keep her head in the real world if she is gonna make it in Mobile."

Lee, an eclectic, who believed in the spirits, tarot cards, and energy fields, bristled at Irene's comment, but arguing with her Christian, although non-practicing sister, was nothing new. Lee didn't really mind the word voodoo, except that was Irene's way of dismissing her beliefs. On the other hand, if someone didn't cut off the exchange early on, then a full-blown shouting match would likely ensue. The last one had resulted in them not speaking to each other for six months, even though they lived next door.

"Y'all, please don't fight today," Bailey said pleadingly. "I'm driving off in a few minutes, and I'd like to carry a different image of you two in my mind."

Her aunt, clearly irritated, looked away and huffed. Bailey's words landed.

"I can see you didn't give it to her yet?" Lee shot back.

"No," Irene said. "It's not time yet. She's not ready."

"Oh, hell's bells! What are you waitin' for? Right now is a perfect time!" Lee pressed her sister. "She's moving away, for crying out loud."

"Give me what?" Bailey asked.

"Oh, all right. Of course, I'm gonna give it to my daughter. I just don't want her thinking this has some kind of woowoo magic. She's got gifts all her own."

Did you just compliment me? Bailey thought, almost smarting off. Instead, not accustomed to praise from her mother, she smiled, relishing the moment.

Irene stepped toward them and brought her hands from behind her back. She deposited a small, dark, velvety looking box, made for jewelry, in the middle of the card table.

"Open it," she instructed her daughter.

Bailey held the gift respectfully, then gently pried open the lid. The box contained a simple, elegant silver cross with a delicate roped silver chain. Etchings of gold glittered along the edges of the string. Bailey wondered how in the world could somebody make this.

"This is just like y'all's! It's beautiful!" She pulled it out and held it carefully.

"This necklace has been in our family for a long, long time," Irene said. "It's a family heirloom, passed down from generations. It's very similar to ours but unique. There is no other necklace like it. And, as the story goes, this one was made just for you."

This time Lee's mouth fell open, and she looked with astonishment at her sister. Glancing at Bailey, she quickly pursed her lips together.

"For me?" Bailey repeated.

"One of your great ancestors claimed to have a vision of the future," her mother continued. "The vision revealed the number of descendants, specifically girls, that would be born into the family. After that vision, he made that exact number of necklaces. Each one is different—all with the instructions to gift them when the time was right. Of course, nobody could know how many daughters and granddaughters would be born, but it is a nice story. Somehow it has been part of our family tradition going back as far as I can remember."

"This is amazing!" Bailey exclaimed.

"It's more than a legend. It's a vision come true," Lee said.

"It's just a story, Lee. You know, as well as I do, there have been way more girls born into this family line than there were necklaces made."

"The necklaces were crafted for the ones with," Lee looked at Bailey, "the gift. She's got the gift."

"Now, Lee, you're gonna make me mad if you keep talking about this. It's a necklace." Irene gave her sister a warning look.

"It's more than that, sister." Then looking at Bailey, Lee continued, "It's a medium. It will protect you. It will even guide you."

Bailey glanced at her mom, then back at her aunt Lee. She never knew if what her aunt told her was true, but she loved hearing the stories and learning about these mysteries. Bailey smiled, relishing the moment. Even though she sensed that sparks could fly at any moment, she had never witnessed a nicer disagreement between her mom and Aunt Lee. Maybe that was because she was leaving.

"Well, one thing is for sure, it's lovely," Bailey said.

Her mom reached for the necklace. "Here, let me put this on you."

Maybe it was the power of suggestion, or just Bailey's desire to believe in magic, but she could swear that when her mother put the necklace around her neck, a warm tingling radiated up and down her spine.

Aunt Lee watched Bailey intensely. "You can feel it, can't you? You feel the power of this jewel."

Bailey smiled. "Well, actually, yes, I do feel something."

"Oh no, don't get your head all filled with nonsense," Irene said. "Just take care of it and wear it with pride." Then she looked approvingly and said, "It does look good on you."

"I'll take excellent care of it and wear it every day," Bailey said. "Home will feel a little closer."

Aunt Lee winked at her.

Bailey started to cry. She didn't want to move away anymore.

Lee hugged her.

"Home is more than a place, my dear. It's the people in your life," Aunt Lee said, complementing what Keri had told her the night before.

Irene's eyes watered. She too hugged Bailey. "And, you always have us—no matter where you lay your head. You just remember your way back. You hear?"

Bailey was too choked up with emotion to reply. She managed to nod her head. Over the next couple of hours, she also said her goodbyes to her Uncle Jed and Joe. In the south, leaving can take thirty minutes or several hours depending on how long you might be gone, and how many 'one-more-things' people tell you. One by one, she hugged everyone again and said bye for what felt like the hundredth time.

Finally, down the road she went, in a borrowed blazer, a second-hand shirt, and a used car, on her way to a new adventure. She only wished that it wasn't a pirate from hell pushing her along. *I guess the universe has a funny way of working*, she thought. Aunt Lee's prophecy echoed in her mind, *you are supposed to go to Mobile, but it's not your final destiny.* She clutched the cross around her neck, and to her surprise, she felt comforted. "Sorry, Aunt Lee, but I gotta make it work."

Chapter 19

Caravan

*S*he arrived at Thomason Brothers Realty, on Monday morning at about eight forty-five a.m.; fifteen minutes early for the start of caravan. Agents had already begun climbing onboard a brown, extended, luxury van just slightly smaller than a school bus, with high ceilings and a plush interior. Bailey stepped up inside and slowly made her way down the aisle, looking for a seat. Midway back, on the left side, she spotted Mandy and Michelle sitting next to one another. *How do they get such perfect hair?* Mandy had dressed in a blue skirt and a white, low-cut, sleeveless, silk blouse. The outfit looked tailor-made, and she wore it beautifully. Michelle wore a cute off-the-shoulder white dress, more suited for fine dining than touring homes. Mandy focused on Bailey as soon she stepped onto the bus. Bailey couldn't help feeling intimidated as Mandy's eyes traced every detail of Bailey's outfit as if examining her with a magnifying glass. At first, Mandy's expressionless gaze unnerved Bailey. *What, are you mad at me now?* She felt hot irritation rising. Then Mandy smiled mockingly and nodded almost imperceptibly. Michelle leaned over to her friend and whispered. Bailey couldn't quite make out what she said but overheard the word " Goodwill." Mandy burst out laughing extra loudly. Bailey stopped.

"Oh, hey, Bailey." Mandy giggled, acting as if she'd just noticed her. "Michelle just told me the funniest joke." She winked. "I'll catch you up later."

Michelle said, "Fancy outfit."

Mandy hit her friend playfully. "Be nice now."

Bailey stiffened, stung by the comment, and by the fact that they were clearly laughing at her. She wanted to lash out, say something cutting and witty, but she had never been that good at one-liner comebacks.

"Nice dresses, ladies. Where did you find those? Some magazine?" *Oh, what a stupid comment.* It was all she could think of at that moment.

Mandy stopped laughing. "This was a gift from my mother, Bailey. Sure, it's expensive. I'm wearing this today not to show off, but out of respect for this amazing company that I have the privilege of working for." She looked to the front of the bus, then down. She bowed her head and touched her forehead as if she had just gotten a terrible headache.

Really? You got to be freaking kidding me! "You phony, fake…"

"Good morning," a voice said behind Bailey. Instantly, everyone returned the greeting. Bailey turned to see Ann standing at the front. *Oh no,* Bailey thought, then sighed and looked away.

"Everything okay, ladies?" Ann asked.

Mandy sniffled just enough so that everyone would know she was upset.

"Yes, it will be alright."

Bailey stood speechless. Her stomach tightened; her jaw clenched. She shook her head. *Unbelievable! You set me up again!*

"Bailey?" Ann asked, "You gonna ride standing up?"

Everyone on the bus laughed.

Bailey slumped. "No, Ma'am."

A few rows down on the right, she saw Remy waving for her to come and sit in the empty seat next to him.

"Thank you," Bailey whispered as she sat down.

Ann continued. "Welcome to your first day. We will begin with caravan. It's a chance for you to see what's available, get a feel for the area, and the new listings on the market. The caravan is usually for all the company's agents, but today, this caravan is just for you."

She motioned to a young man sitting in the front of the bus. "Stand up, Lewis."

The man stood. He was shorter than Ann, a bit round with a disarming presence about him that made Bailey feel like she had known him all her life. His khakis, light blue shirt, and bright multicolored tie didn't quite match, but somehow, he pulled it off, adding to his playful demeanor. He waved. Everyone waved back.

"Lewis, besides lighting up a room with his ties," Ann said, resting her hand on his shoulder as the group chuckled, "also loves caravan. He is the one who creates the route, plans the stops, and keeps it all up to date. He will be your guide today."

Ann looked at Lewis. "I understand you have a very special caravan prepared for our new superstars?"

Bailey liked the idea of being a superstar. The word tickled her ears and ran down her spine with a warm shiver.

Lewis stood and addressed the group, answering, "Yes, ma'am. First, we're going to see some of the new listings. One of them just came on the market today. We'll drive around Mobile. You will get a sense of the different neighborhoods and communities. We'll finish our tour with the Holy Grail of homes." He paused with a mischievous smile as if everyone knew what he meant.

Bailey looked at Remy.

"It's better if you see it for yourself," Remy said.

Lewis continued. "Finally, on Friday, at the end of the week, you'll be treated to a special luncheon at La Petite."

Many heads nodded, and several cooed their approval.

Mandy clapped and said in a raised voice, "Excellent choice! We dine there often. Maybe Jean Michael will cook up a special surprise."

"Maybe," Lewis replied, his bright demeanor dimming a bit.

Bailey wondered whether they all might see another, less friendly side of Lewis if Mandy kept talking.

"Of course, she knows the chef," Remy whispered in Bailey's ear. "She probably slept with him."

Remy must not have realized how loudly he was speaking . The agents grew quiet, and heads turned toward Remy and Bailey. Mandy scowled as if she had some superpower in her stare that could incinerate anyone she chose. Bailey's eyes peeled wide. She couldn't restrain her smile. She covered her mouth, first with one hand, and then the other. A giggle escaped, then she leaned forward and laughed heartily.

Ann sighed and glared. That was all she needed to do.

"Sorry," Remy said.

Mandy turned back around, clearly disappointed that her death vision had not vaporized him.

"How could he know about you and Jean Michael?" Michelle asked.

Bailey saw the back of Mandy's head disappear as she sank in her seat.

Ann just rolled her eyes.

Lewis continued. "After our steamy lunch," he said with a wink, and everyone broke up into laughter, "we'll finish the week with a drive through Springhill.

Bailey's heart skipped. She whispered to Remy, "Springhill is the place with all of the elegant homes! Oh, I can't wait!"

Lewis proceeded. "Springhill is made up of Mobile's finest, most classic and lovely homes. We have a few listings there but would love a few more. Right, Ann?"

"We would love the whole neighborhood," Ann replied. "All of Springhill would be nice."

The recruits chuckled.

As Ann turned to exit, she paused at the door and surveyed the group one more time. "Enjoy your day."

With that, she departed. The driver closed the door, cranked the engine, and the journey began. Bailey noticed there was room for more and thought she had seen other candidates at the orientation last week. Just as they were leaving, another car came to a screeching stop in the parking lot, taking up two open spaces. A young woman sprang out of the driver's side, her hair not quite combed, trying to put on her other high-heeled shoe while running to catch the bus. Bailey recognized her from the orientation.

"Wait!" the woman yelled, then tripped. She scrambled back to her feet then cried, "Wait!" again, but the bus did not stop.

Lewis's voice came over the speakers. "Oh yes," he said. "One crucial tip. Be on time. Caravan waits for no one."

Remy said to Bailey, "We won't be seeing her again."

"Really? So, she was late. That happens."

"Yes, it does," Remy agreed. "But the unwritten rule is that if you are late to this first caravan, they usually don't invite you back. It's kind of a test to see who can cut it."

Bailey made a mental note to always arrive early.

The bus toured the places and homes Lewis had said it would. Bailey flipped through her map the office had given them, marking each new listing and jotting down notes to remind her of something about them. If the home was open and ready for a showing, they stopped and went inside. Some houses were small—only one bedroom, cute, efficient, and new. Others were older, twenty years or so, but mostly kept in good condition. Each one had a personality to it, or at least Bailey thought so. She could feel the house's essence, whether warm or withdrawn or even bitter from years of neglect. When Bailey walked into a home, it was as if she were transported somewhere, to another place, a place where only she could go, a place where she could sense the longing of the house. As if the walls and the foundation were speaking to her, she imagined them saying, "Find me my family with a dog." "I have a nice backyard," or "I'm perfect for a single mom." "I'll take care of a bachelor businessman." Bailey could look at, and listen to, houses all day long.

"Come along, Bailey," Lewis said more than once during the tour.

Bailey delighted in every presentation, and to go with a group, well, that was just heaven. Lewis not only sported a loud tie, but he also acted as MC along the way, telling jokes and even leading singalongs. Bailey joined with the group as they gave a lively and awful rendition of "Gilligan's Island." Like the SS *Minnow*, the caravan had set sail for the three-hour tour. Yet, Bailey couldn't stomach the thought of being stranded on a deserted island with Mandy. She shook her head, shrugging that image from her mind. *Focus, Bailey. You need something to jump-start your Mobile business, make a splash. You need to find that perfect home to sell.*

Chapter 20

The Unsellable House

"And there it is, ladies and gentlemen," Lewis said, "the Holy Grail of homes in Mobile. The house that no one can sell."

Bailey gasped and stared out her window at the magnificent structure. They had journeyed toward the downtown area, Old Mobile, the section where homes date back to the mid-1700s and early 1800s. The house that wouldn't sell sat on a corner two-acre lot. Large, ancient oak trees tinseled with Spanish moss shaded most of the residence and cooled the grassy lawn. The home presented itself as clean and well-maintained, only in need of minor repair work. The wraparound porch invited you to climb up and sit a spell. The ornate wood trimmings appeared to be antique but also in pristine condition. Some of the windows had that hazy shimmer from old original glass, seemingly so delicate it could shatter at the slightest touch, yet still standing firm after two hundred years. Bailey always pretended such old glass was a magical portal to see into the past. She imagined that if you looked at the right time of the evening, you'd be able to see those who lived there before, their lives unfolding, like an ancient viewfinder.

"I love it!" Bailey exclaimed, still staring, eyes wide with amazement.

"And that's the trap," Remy said. "They say you can't help falling in love at first sight. You are sure that something this lovely can sell and that somehow you are supposed to be the one to sell it. But no one ever does."

Bailey heard her friend but didn't respond. She relished this moment. As they approached, she couldn't find any real estate signs in the yard.

Then Lewis said, "You may have noticed there are no signs in the yard. Yes, this *is* for sale. No company in town has the listing. It's a FSBO —for sale by owner. We know the owner as Ms. Worthington. However, I've never seen Ms. Worthington nor heard of anyone who ever met her. A local law office downtown manages the listing and will handle the closing and the sale, if it ever sells, that is."

"Where does she live?" Bailey asked.

"Out-of-state, maybe even out of the country," Lewis answered. "Everything goes through the legal firm. We don't even get a lockbox on the door. The house is shown by appointment only."

The driver parked the bus along the wide street underneath one of the oaks. The eager agents poured out onto the lawn. Bailey swore it was ten degrees cooler under the shade. A tall, gray-haired man in a three-piece suit awaited them on the porch by the front door. The group gathered at the foot of the steps, and the chatter quieted. Everyone gave their attention to the distinguished-looking gentleman.

"Good afternoon," he said. The agents responded in kind. He continued, "Pleased to make your acquaintance." His accent sounded English, sophisticated, and confident.

Lewis ascended the stairs and turned to face them. "Meet Mr. Stockton. His firm manages the estate. A couple of times a year, especially when new agents begin, they invite us to visit and re-familiarize ourselves with this magnificent home."

The agents applauded. Mr. Stockton nodded, gracefully removed his hat, and bowed slightly.

Then he motioned with his arm and said, "On behalf of the family, please, won't you come inside."

The old boards groaned as each ascended the aged porch. The creaking echoed many footsteps before as if to say, 'I can handle many more.' Bailey felt warm and cozy, but not from the hot, humid day; rather, as if the house itself were radiating a proud heritage. She felt something else, too. She couldn't quite name it, a feeling of hope and a longing.

Surprisingly, the home was completely furnished. Though protected with tailor-fitted coverings, the furniture remained intact, and the inside kept clean. *Somebody maintains it!*

Bailey walked toward the couch, dying to get a peek at what must be a pristine antique. She started to pull one end of the slip covering but stopped at the sound of Mr. Stockton's voice.

"Please, allow me," he said. He gently peeled the sheet away, revealing a plush blue couch with dark hickory hand-carved wood in perfect condition.

"It's gorgeous!" Bailey said.

Others gathered to admire the ancient settee.

"Feel free to browse. Appreciate the rooms and décor," Mr. Stockton invited. "Though I implore you, please don't touch anything or remove any coverings. Thank you."

Everyone agreed. How could you not? The house commanded absolute respect. In Bailey's mind, the old sofa whispered of entertaining royalty and generals. The dining room brimmed with stories. She could almost hear the chatter and clinking of crystal and fine china, the laughter around the table. This place still teemed with life.

"Breathtaking, isn't it?" Remy said.

"I've never seen anything like it. It's amazing," Bailey replied, with a delightful vacant expression on her face, as if present in one world, while viewing another that only she could see.

"I'm going to sell it," they heard Mandy say. Her voice grated, interrupting Bailey's perfect daydream. "All my life I've dreamt of selling this house."

She voiced it loudly just as she passed. But she didn't wait for a response, dismissing Bailey like she was one of the ghosts in this estate.

Mandy approached Mr. Stockton. "I would like to meet the owner," she commanded.

Bailey couldn't explain why, but she felt that Mandy's words had no authority here. They sounded flat and lifeless.

"Oh, I am afraid that is out of the question," Mr. Stockton replied.

"Why?" Mandy pressed.

"It's simply not possible."

"Surely she comes into town now and then. Or better yet, I'll go to her. Where does she live? I don't care. I'll fly anywhere in the world. I *must* meet her."

He shook his head. "No, my dear, you won't."

Mandy frowned and pursed her lips as if holding back harsher words attempting to escape. It seemed she didn't hear 'no' very often. Bailey looked at Remy. They smirked, delighted that there was at least one place where Mandy couldn't control, one area that seemed beyond the reach of her family's influence and rich history.

What do you know, super girl's kryptonite. Bailey smiled.

"Do you know who my family is?" she said smugly.

An original vampire line? Bailey wondered.

Mr. Stockton remained unmoved.

"Are all the legal documents in order?" Mandy said slightly louder this time.

The other agents gathered.

"Mandy," Lewis cautioned softly.

She calmed a bit but persisted.

"It's just that, my dear Mr. Stockton, my family has been in Mobile for five generations, and we are very well connected. If you and the owner want to sell this majestic place, then I'm the best qualified to accomplish that."

"I'm sure you are Miss… Mandy, but it's out of my hands, you see. The owner is quite explicit in the care of this estate and how it may be sold." Mandy started to respond, b..t Mr. Stockton raised his hand. "I'm sorry, but the answer is no. The owner wishes to manage the sale in this way." Then he looked sternly at Mandy and spoke in a tone that conveyed a warning. "And yes, I assure you, all the documents are in *perfect* order."

Reluctantly, Mandy let it go, even though Bailey suspected that it was only for show. Mandy never let anything go. Mandy got what Mandy wanted except for now. Bailey loved the house even more.

"How much is the house?" one agent asked. "What's the asking price?"

The agents bunched closer.

Mr. Stockton cleared his throat. "The asking price is to find the right family."

"Excuse me?" Bailey said.

"Yes, the asking price for this house is to find the right family. Then they make an offer."

"We have to know how much the owner wants in order to find the right buyer, someone who can qualify," Bailey said.

Other agents nodded in agreement. Lewis smiled as if he had heard all this before.

"Have any offers ever been made?" someone asked.

"Oh, yes," answered Mr. Stockton. "Many, many offers over the years and from all over the world quite actually."

"What was the highest offer?" Remy asked.

Mr. Stockton thought, then said, "Ten million."

Gasps echoed around the room like popcorn in a microwave, followed by the rumblings of many concurrent conversations.

"Seriously?" Bailey asked.

"Yes. I am quite serious. A very distinguished gentleman from France offered ten million." He leaned forward. "And, most of that was a cash offer."

Again, exclamations and murmurings.

"The owner rejected that?" Mandy asked in disbelief.

"Immediately." He paused and spoke slowly. "He was not the right family. We have received many offers for many millions of dollars."

"Does she really want to sell the house?" Mandy asked, almost hissing as she spoke.

"Oh, yes." Mr. Stockton answered. "It is her deepest desire, but it must be the *right* buyer."

"But if she is never home, how does she know who's the right buyer?"

"I assure you, she knows. She knows. She has left one definitive sign that will tell our firm if we have found the right buyer. Her instructions are unambiguous. So far, in all the offers, we have yet to see the sign."

"Okay, so what's the sign?" Remy asked.

"I'm sorry," Mr. Stockton said. "I'm not at liberty to say."

Bailey saw Lewis mime Mr. Stockton's sentence word for word.

So, he has heard this answer before.

"You don't know," Mandy jeered.

"Oh, we definitely know. We are bound by the confidentiality of the agreement not to share it. It is the manner we will realize when to release the home." Then he looked at Bailey. "We are not just selling a house here. We are helping a family find a home." He looked around at the rest of the group. "A home for the right family."

"This is so bizarre," Remy whispered.

Mr. Stockton nodded. "Indeed."

The agents dispersed and continued their tour.

Remy leaned to Bailey and said, "This is ridiculous. Can you believe this guy? No wonder this house won't sell."

Bailey didn't respond. She stood, eyes wide, mouth open, staring at Mr. Stockton. She wondered whether she had heard him correctly. He noticed her stare and nodded respectfully. Then he winked.

Bailey smiled. "Did you see that? He winked at me. He's telling me something."

"Seriously?" Remy shook his head.

She looked at her colleague. "Didn't you hear what he said? We are not just selling a house; we are finding a home. That's my motto!"

"Bailey, this is the most ridiculous setup I've ever heard."

"He looked at me when he said it!" Bailey bounced up on the balls of her feet.

"Oh no, please don't fall for this. It's bogus. It has to be."

She placed both hands on Remy's shoulders. "No, it's not. I was supposed to meet this house. I know it." She could tell her new friend remained unconvinced. "I've got to see the rest of this place while we're here."

Lewis walked over to Remy as Bailey glided away into other rooms. "Looks like we have another name to add to 'the Wall.' "

Bailey finished her tour in a dream-like state before boarding the bus with the rest of the agents. She peered out the window with a giddy smile as the caravan rolled back toward Thomason Brothers. That's when Bailey saw her—an older woman staring back through a rippled living room window. The lady smiled wryly and winked.

"Who's that?" Bailey said, pointing, but the house was out of sight.

"What are you talking about? " Remy asked .

"The old lady. Didn't you see her?"

Remy shook his head.

Bailey gazed, frozen in a vacant stare. *It's another sign*, she thought.

"Bailey?" Remy said.

Her eyes remained fixed, seemingly not looking at anything, immersed in her happy home-selling fantasy.

"Hello, earth to Bailey?" Remy waved his hand in front of her.

She looked at her friend, smiled wide, and said, "I'm gonna sell that house!"

Remy shook his head. "Bad idea."

"Are you kidding me? It's a fantastic idea. Selling this home is the win I need."

"Bailey, nobody sells that house," he cautioned. "Don't get consumed with that house. It's not a win. You won't make the big splash you think you will. Many have tried before."

"How do you know?" Bailey turned slightly to face him, not smiling anymore. "You mean you've tried to be an agent here before?"

"No, but my good friend was a candidate. He was doing great. He had the most listings. Then he got cocky. He thought he could sell anything, even that house. It's a sinkhole, Bailey. You don't have your numbers up yet. Don't waste your time there." He nodded toward the front. "Besides, Queen Mandy would love to see you fail and fall flat on your face. Look, if anybody can sell the house, you can. But, Bailey, nobody has sold this house." He leaned closer, looking her right in the eye. "Nobody." He leaned back. "Some believe it's only a test set up by the Thomason Brothers. I mean, who markets a home this way anyway?"

Bailey sighed, frustrated at her friend's criticism. Then she thought, *He is only looking after me.* A feeling of gratitude replaced her irritation. She felt lucky to have a new friend like Remy. But still, Mr. Stockton held the same belief as she did. He sold homes, not houses, and he winked at her when he said it. Then, the appearance of the mysterious lady in the window erased any doubt. All these events were signs. An undeniable feeling came over Bailey. She had to do this.

"I appreciate you having my back," said Bailey. "But I'm telling you I know I can sell his house."

"That's what they all say. That's what my friend said."

Remy looked worried and frustrated that Bailey was not listening.

"But I'm the one who is supposed to sell it. Don't ask me how I know. I just do."

She caressed her cross with a playful spaced-out look on her face, wholly captured by the story and the majesty of that old house. The holy grail of homes was calling her.

Chapter 21

The Wall

ewis's voice boomed over the intercom as the caravan arrived back at the real estate office.

"One more stop on our tour today," he said. "Go through the lobby and turn right. We'll gather in the lounge."

The agents spilled out from the bus. As they were walking toward the front door, Bailey overheard Mandy say to Michelle. "I'm going to sell that house!"

"You go for it," her friend said.

"I'm the only one who can." She glanced back in Bailey's direction. As she turned away, Bailey swore she heard her giggle.

They entered the lobby and turned right, as Lewis instructed. After just a short walk, the hallway opened into a large room, the agent's lounge. Clusters of couches and cushy chairs offered a place to relax from a busy day. A coffee pot and a variety of snacks sat atop a refreshment table pressed against the back wall. An extensive map of Mobile, dotted with small pushpin flags, covered most of the space above the table.

Lewis gathered everyone closer. He pointed to a list of names running down the left side in alphabetical order. A flag, each one a different color, had been painted on the wall beside each name.

"Every agent has a unique color represented by these flags, and with the initial of your first name on them," Lewis said, and puffed out his chest as if he had just given a present.

Bailey found her name near the top of the list and saw a yellow flag, with the letter B, painted beside it. *Cool! Same color as my Jeep.* She noticed a deep purple flag with an M painted by Mandy's name.

Then Lewis gestured to the sizeable wall map next to the list of names. It seemed like hundreds of flag-pins dotted every neighborhood in Mobile.

"These are all the current listings of our agents," Lewis explained. "Your flag pins are the same color as the flag by your name.

Bailey scanned the topography and felt a rush of adrenaline. These were the players, the ones in the game. Then her eye caught a deep purple colored flag on the map, with the tiny letter M!

"Mandy's got a listing?" She realized she said it out loud. Mandy smiled wryly. *Crab Balls!* Bailey silently scolded herself. Revealing that Mandy occupied any space in Bailey's mind disturbed her more than seeing Mandy's flag planted on the wall.

Just then, Ann's voice echoed behind them. "You *all* have a listing. A gift from the company."

Ann walked toward the wall. Lewis stepped back, giving his broker center stage.

Bailey studied the other pin/flags on the map. Remy's little red one with an R had found a spot right up there, too. Then Bailey saw hers, yellow with a B. The thrill of seeing her first listing on the wall pushed out any of her earlier embarrassment. *Thomason Brothers knows how to inspire agents.* Bailey imagined her flags in every corner and every neighborhood.

"We love listings," Ann said, and the agents chuckled. "We love to see this map covered in a rainbow of flags."

Then Ann walked toward the adjacent wall. Everyone followed.

"What we love more are closings," she continued.

She gave them a moment to gaze upon the names and numbers of this wall. "Here, you see the current top producers, their number of listings, closings, and total production for the year. We update this weekly."

Bailey visualized her name at the top.

Ann motioned to the next adjacent wall, the one directly across from the large map. The agents gathered around. "Lewis, tell them about this area."

Bailey guessed there must be at least fifty pictures of agents, lined up vertically, a bar graph extended for each image marking months. Underneath, many of them had beginning and ending dates. Across the top, the title read 'The Worthington Estate.'

"It's called the Wall," Lewis began. Several chuckles peppered throughout the group. "It's kind of a memorial. This section is dedicated entirely to the house you just saw, the house which nobody can sell. See these pictures?" His hand traced down the agents. "These are all good agents who tried to sell this property. The thick black line out beside each name represents the number of months each one stayed with it."

Bailey looked at the top line. "Seventy-two months?"

"Yes, Corbett King," Lewis said. "Best agent the company ever had, till he got obsessed with trying to sell that house."

"That's six years," Bailey stated.

"Correct, and the last two of those years, Corbett dedicated all his time and energy to sell that house. He is the one who found the ten-million-dollar buyer. As you will remember, the owner said no to that! Said it wasn't the right family. Each year Corbett became more and more obsessed with selling that house. It ruined him. See these other dates under their names?" Heads nodded in acknowledgment. "That's how long they worked here. That is their status now."

Bailey surveyed the array of pictures of agents gone before. Except for the last three on the bottom, every name had both beginning and end dates and the words 'inactive' written beside them.

"They all quit over this," Lewis said. "It drained the life out of them."

"It's a memorial wall," she whispered to Remy.

"It is," Lewis said. "They are still alive, of course, but that house killed them as agents."

Bailey pointed up to another name. "What about this one in the middle? Stan Whitmore. His picture also has beginning and end dates, but the status reads 'active' under his name."

"He finally let it go," Lewis answered. "He is one of the few to walk away and save his career.

Ann said, "I understand we have a new name to add?"

"Yes, we do." Lewis picked up a piece of chalk and wrote Mandy at the bottom of the list.

Bailey gasped. *No way!*

"Here is the newest challenger to take on the Worthington Estate," Lewis announced.

People clapped. Mandy smiled and winked at Bailey, who fumed.

I'm meant to sell that house, not you. I'm the one. Bailey thought to herself.

"If you want to try and sell the house, just let Ann know, and we'll…"

"Add my name!" Bailey interjected.

She glanced at Remy, who shook his head and mouthed the word 'no.'

"Add my name," Bailey repeated.

"Very well." Lewis inscribed her name below Mandy's. "And Bailey, also."

The agents dutifully clapped in support of these two challengers.

"Thank you, Lewis." Ann stepped up front again. "Each of you has been assigned a work cubicle. An orientation packet and client contact information for your new listing are on your desk space. Read the information carefully. It outlines the tried and true path to lead a client to close. Also, as Lewis mentioned this morning, at the end of the week, you will get an extraordinary treat, lunch with Johnny, and the top producers of the company. It will be quite an experience, I promise you."

Enthusiastic hoots filled the room.

"All right, go get 'em!"

As the group dispersed, Bailey turned to Remy. "This is so exciting!"

"Yes, it is," he agreed.

"Remy, I'm gonna sell that house."

"Didn't you hear what Lewis said?"

"I've got a feeling, Remy. I can sell that house."

"You know Mandy likes to grandstand and posture. She's probably doing this to get your goat. She's baiting you, Bailey. She's got your number."

"She's such a bit… mean girl. You think she would do that?"

"I do! And yes, she is!"

As Bailey listened to her friend, she knew he was right. She heard Ann's advice echoing in her mind to get past Mandy. Get Mandy out of your head. Solve the problem. But Bailey knew, in that place of intuition that resides deep in her heart, she knew she could sell that house.

She turned to Remy. "I'm the one, Remy. I know it. I feel it."

Remy shook his head in disbelief. "'Well, I'm gonna get listings," he said. "I strongly suggest you do the same."

Bailey walked toward Ann's office. She did not like upsetting her new friend, but this feeling compelled her as forcefully as gravity pulled the waves ashore. When she got to her broker's office, she peeked through the doorway. Ann was sitting behind her desk. She stopped working and met Bailey's gaze.

"I'm going to sell the Stockton estate," Bailey said, matter-of-factly, as if it had already happened.

Ann peered over her glasses. Then she pulled them off and stared sternly.

"Very well, Bailey," she said flatly. "I hope you do." She donned her spectacles and went back to her work.

Chapter 22

New Clients and Friends

As she walked toward her cubicle, Bailey caught a chill. Ann's silence felt worse than a reprimand. *That's it? No encouragement. No "good luck, Bailey. Go for it." Not even a warning. But then Lewis already warned us.* Her boss seemed detached and cold. Bailey's assurance dipped, yet the house still summoned. *Maybe the universe is testing me, or perhaps I'm making this up.* Then her path became clear; why not let this be her test? Either she would accomplish what no one at the company had ever been able to do and sell the Worthington estate, or she would just be another name on the wall. Another ordinary agent, who thought they had some extraordinary sensitivity, only to discover it was merely wishful dreaming. Whatever the answer, she had to know. Selling that house became her solution. *Great, why don't you set the bar so high no one can reach it. Stay practical. I've got to sell some homes. Cover that map with yellow flags.* Her practical side won out, for now, but the intuitive, risk-taker part of her sighed. *Okay, I'll catch the whale later. Let's start with more clients.* She decided to take another look at the map and headed back toward the lounge. She wanted to visualize her success. When she reached the lobby, she saw Joy talking to a family.

"Just one moment, someone will be right with you." Joy held the phone in her hand, getting ready to page someone. When she saw Bailey, she put the receiver back in its hold.

"Well, that's great timing," Joy said. She stood and gestured toward the couple. "Bailey, this is Don and Ashly Antoine, and their son Andrew. They just moved to Mobile and are looking for a home."

The introduction snapped Bailey out of her future-planning mode. "Oh, nice to meet you, but I'm not…"

When she saw their little boy, she inhaled sharply, and a wave of emotion washed over her. She guessed he was seven years old. He had dark, shiny, wispy hair. When he smiled up at her, Bailey's professional demeanor dissolved. Images of another boy flooded her mind, vivid recollections of making cookies, decorating the Christmas tree, and laughing. She knelt in front of the family's son. She had to meet this child who looked so much like the one she had raised.

"Liam?" her voice broke.

"No, ma'am. My name is Andy."

She blinked. A tear escaped, but she quickly wiped it away.

"Of course, you are. You just remind me of someone I used to know."

She stood to face the parents.

"Hello, I'm Bailey." She sniffled as they shook hands. "He reminds me of someone I lost recently."

Ashly touched Bailey's arm. "Oh, my goodness. We are so sorry to hear that."

Don nodded and looked genuinely concerned.

Bailey stared at the boy. *My gosh, he is so…*

"I'm adorable," Andy said. "That's what my grandmother says."

They all laughed.

"Yes, you are." Bailey chuckled.

"Now, Andy, be humble," his mom managed to say though also chuckling when she said it.

"What's that mean?" Andy replied.

"Well, your grandmother was right," Bailey said, smiling wide. *I love this kid!* She pulled her eyes away from Andy and addressed the parents. "So, you're looking for a home? I'll be glad to help you. But you should know that today is my first day, and you'll be my first customers."

They looked at each other, then to Bailey. Don said, "Well, this is our first house."

"I'm new to Mobile," Bailey added.

"So are we," Ashly said.

"I like you," Andy said as he looked up at Bailey. His blue eyes melted her heart. She felt as if her whole self were a giant teardrop just barely contained. At any moment, she could burst into a happy puddle on the floor.

"Well, I like you too." Bailey knelt again in front of him.

Andy laughed, got red in the face, and hid behind his mom's leg.

Bailey stood. "Okay then, let's find you a home."

They followed her to one of the empty conference rooms. Now that she had clients, she gave the room a more critical view, making sure it was good enough. It passed her inspection. Mom and Dad found some comfy seats around the shiny oak table while Andrew played on the plush carpet driving his matchbox car on an imaginary adventure.

Joy stuck her head around the corner. "Y'all like a snack?"

Andrew immediately jumped to his feet, leaving the toy car parked in some make-believe location. Joy looked at the parents, and both signaled yes.

"That would be nice," Ashly said.

Joy stretched her hand out toward the boy. "Wanna come help me?"

The boy looked at Mom, who nodded her approval. He smiled and ran to Joy. They disappeared down the hall.

"Y'all enjoy your snacks," Bailey said. "I'll be right back with the paperwork, and we'll get started."

She found her cubicle nestled in amongst the others in the center of a large room. Her desktop had been neatly arranged with all the essentials—a pad of paper, pens, stapler, etc. A manila file folder lay in the middle, with a letter to Bailey on top. She opened it, delighted to see a welcome from Johnny and Robert. She would read that later. She flipped open the file and leafed through the pages. Contact information for James Morgan was on top of the stack, her first listing, courtesy of the company. She set the name to one side, making a mental note to set up an appointment. Fifteen to twenty pages, stapled together, constituted the remaining contents of the file. The cover page read, "Listing packet." The materials were indexed and organized. All the necessary forms were already there, including the step-by-step process of what to do next.

"Wow! They've got their stuff together."

She closed the file, grabbed a pen, and headed back to her first customers. She didn't want to keep them waiting too long.

When she returned to the conference room, she saw the family quietly enjoying their snacks. Andrew sat at the table next to Dad, the boy's complete attention captured by the second half of the uneaten cookie. Bailey joined them.

She opened the sales packet and began with the first step, the Buyer's Agreement. As Bailey read through each section, the Antoines seemed interested and impressed. She made a mental note to share the packet with MJ.

Soon they had worked through the details of the agreement. Bailey smiled, delighted with the support she already felt from her new company.

"So, do you have any questions?"

They looked at each other and shook their heads.

"No. Very nice job, Bailey," Don said. "I think we are in good hands."

Bailey beamed. "Terrific. I'm so excited for you. I saw a lot of new houses for sale, and I've already got a couple of ideas that I think you're gonna love." She closed the file. "I'll get this to our mortgage department, and they can begin the process of pre-qualifying you for your loan. That will give us a clear price range in which to search."

The couple stole a glance at each other before Don answered. "That will be fine."

Bailey sensed there was something more to that glance but decided not to probe. They were just getting started, after all. *Whatever needs to come out will come out,* she thought. "We can go look at a few homes right now if you like."

"Umm, thank you, but not today." Don looked at his watch. "Besides, it's getting close to dinner time."

Andrew, who had returned to playing under the table, popped his head up. "Can we go to Charlie Cheese? Please?"

His dad smiled and scuffed the boy's hair with his hand. "Sure."

"All right!" he said, closing his fist and shaking his little arm. Then he pointed at Bailey and said, "Can she come, too?"

Bailey smiled, then looked at Ashly and Don, grinning their approval.

Her heart swelled, looking into Andy's little blue eyes. "Okay, sure. Sounds like fun."

Andrew made a fist pump again. "All right!"

Even though she just met the Antoines, Bailey knew right then that this was no mere coincidence. They were going to become life-long friends. She already felt part of their family.

Chapter 23

Listings

*B*ailey arrived at Thomason Brother s the following Thursday around seven thirty a.m., eager
to find her lovely new clients their first home. As a
newbie, she didn't yet have a key to the office, but Joy
had offered to come early for a few days and let her
work free from other distractions. Bailey had spent
the whole week pouring through the available listings.
Still getting to know the Antoines, she wasn't certain
what kind of house they'd call home. However, she
was confident she'd 'feel it' when their home presented itself. *Little Andrew will be my sign. When he gives
his cute little fist pump, I'll know we've found the one.* She
warmed at the thought.

"Well, I'm surprised to see you here."

Bailey looked up to see Mandy dressed to the nines
and carrying a cup of coffee. Her warm feeling faded.

"Good morning, Mandy."

Mandy walked over. "Research for your new
clients?"

"What gave me away?" Bailey said with a hint of
sarcasm.

Mandy bristled slightly. "They're a cute couple. And
that little boy is adorable. I'm meeting my new clients

too, the Stevens," Mandy continued. "Funny, they also have one child, a girl."

Where are you going with this, Mandy?

"So, what price range do they qualify for?" Mandy asked.

"One hundred seventy-five thousand, give or take."

Why am I answering her?

"Oh, there should be plenty to choose from in that range."

"And how about your new family? What's their price range?" Bailey asked.

"Oh, a little more, but who's comparing?"

You are.

Then Mandy's eyes brightened. "I know some new homes that just came on the market. They might be a perfect fit for your first clients."

"Really? Got any paperwork on them?"

"No, none that I can give you. Like I said, they're brand new listings. There are three of them, close to each other." She grabbed a pen, a slip of paper, and wrote down the locations. "Here are the addresses. I've checked them out myself, very high quality."

Though a nice offer, Bailey didn't quite trust it. She didn't doubt the homes would be well built. Mandy seemed to have an eye for the finer things. But why was she being so nice?

"Thank you," Bailey said.

"Sure thing." Mandy winked and walked away.

The Antoines would arrive in about a half hour so Bailey didn't have time to preview these new listings herself. She looked up the addresses on the map; they were in the opposite direction of where she'd planned to go. *Hmm. Well, can't hurt to look, right?*

The Antoines arrived on time and eager to go. Andrew ran up to Bailey and gave her a little bear hug, and both giggled with delight. They piled into Bailey's car and began their house-hunting journey. Bailey couldn't help noticing how easily everyone fit in the Accord she had borrowed from MJ. Mom rode up front, while Andrew and Dad had a roomy back seat. *Ann, you were right. This is more comfortable for the clients than my Jeep would have been. Not as much fun though.*

"I'm so excited!" Bailey said. "Your home is waiting for you. All we have to do is find it."

"I can't wait," Ashly said, sitting up straighter.

"So, buying a house can be overwhelming. Here's how we'll make things easier. I've researched many homes for sale in your price range. Good news is you have a fair number of choices. I've brought you five that I feel you might like."

"Great!" Ashly said. "We don't want something too big, but we need a yard and at least three bedrooms and two baths."

"Yep, take a look at these." Bailey handed Ashly a stack of her choices. "Rank them as to which you like best. We'll start there."

She began to flip through them, passing each back to Don. They organized the pages as Bailey had suggested.

"We'll start with your top choice, and take them one by one," Bailey said.

"What happens if we end up not wanting any of these?" Don asked.

"I have more, but five is enough for one day."

After they had toured their top two choices, they gathered back in the car. Bailey held up the two listings side by side.

"Okay, out of these two, which one did you like the best?"

They all agreed, the first one. Bailey took the second one, wadded it into a ball and tossed it into the back seat. Andrew laughed.

"Now we go to the next house and see how it compares to your top choice," Bailey said.

Everyone seemed to like this system of elimination. The process produced a favorite and kept them from getting overwhelmed. Yet, at the end of the day, the Antoines still hadn't found 'the one.'

"That's okay," Bailey assured them. "Now we have a favorite to compare the next group against when we go out again."

She paused, studying her clients. They seemed confident in the plan.

"If you have a little more time, I learned this morning of three listings that just came on the market. My co-worker thought y'all might like them."

"Sure, let's take a look," Ashly said.

Bailey drove them out to the first address on the list that Mandy had given her. She spotted the other two on the same street. The neighborhood was brand new and still under construction, except for the three completed houses on the list. The homes stood large and sprawling, at least twice the size of any house they'd looked at so far.

"Wow! Are we gonna live here?" Andy asked.

"No, son. We're just looking," Don said, and shot Bailey a stern look in the mirror.

"Well, of course we like these," Ashly said. "But we can't afford this."

Bailey felt both embarrassed and angry. "Oh, I'm so sorry. I should have come to vet these myself."

I can't believe she lured me out here, knowing what they can afford.

Bailey felt ten degrees hotter when she spotted the three For Sale signs staked in front of the new houses. Each was adorned with a picture of Mandy, and the slogan 'Your home is waiting for you.'

What! That's my slogan on her listings!

"Bailey, you okay?" Ashly asked.

"Uhmm… yes. I'm so sorry to have wasted your time. Let me get you home."

"It's all right," Don said. "I'll look forward to the day we can afford one of these."

When they returned to the office, Bailey said her goodbyes to the Antoines and then stormed inside. She quickly spotted Mandy sitting in her cubicle. Mandy looked up and smiled.

Bailey marched over to her, drawing the stares of other agents as she approached. "Who do you think you are?"

Many didn't respond, and the room grew quiet.

"You knew my clients couldn't qualify for those houses. You just wanted to embarrass me and show off your listings! Then you steal my new slogan and slap it up on your signs! What is your problem?"

"Bailey," Ann's voice echoed.

Bailey turned and saw her broker standing in the doorway. She motioned for Bailey to follow.

Chapter 24

The Reprimand

"Sit down and close the door behind you," Ann said coolly.

Bailey closed the door and sat with her arms crossed.

Ann walked around her desk and took her seat across from her angry agent.

Still fuming, Bailey said, "Mandy set me up. She knew what my clients could qualify for and yet she suggested I show them those homes." Bailey sighed. "I should've checked them out myself."

"Yes, you should have," Ann said tepidly.

"She stole my slogan!"

"No, she didn't. As you know, that is also the company's new slogan."

Bailey closed her eyes and hung her head in her hand. "Of course," she whispered.

"Mandy is the first one to have new listings, so she gets to be the first one to use the new signs."

Bailey's confidence took a nosedive. She felt small, and worse, like an amateur. *Damn that girl is good. She orchestrated that perfectly.*

"I walked right into that one," Bailey said.

Her broker agreed. "Yes, you did." Then she leaned forward. "We can't have this in the office, Bailey. Not ever."

Bailey started to explain but Ann motioned for her to sit quietly.

"We can't have this," Ann repeated. Her tone was stern, and her words deliberate. "We all see something special in you, Bailey. You have potential, and I think more than that, you have gifts. But you can't get hooked like that. I don't know what's going on between you and Mandy, and I don't want to know. But you need to learn to deal with it. If she does something inappropriate or against the company's rules, then I'll take care of it. But if she's just pushing your buttons, then you need to handle it."

"I understand," Bailey said, kicking herself for letting Mandy get to her like that.

"No one gets fired here," Ann said. "They fire themselves. Understand?"

Bailey nodded, though not quite sure what her new boss meant, but definitely understanding the word 'fired.'

"Good." Then Ann added, "I know Mandy can be... well... Mandy. But, her being a pain in the ass does not excuse your behavior."

"Got it," Bailey said quickly.

"Even though Johnny is good friends with her family, Mandy will follow our rules. I promise you that. But you've got to find a way not to let her under your skin."

"Yes. I'll do better."

"Better is not good enough. Find a solution. We have a professional image to maintain. Thomason Brothers sets the standard in this town."

"Yes, ma'am."

Ann leaned forward. "You're not off to a good start, Bailey. You're distracted."

Bailey looked puzzled.

"Not only have you taken on the mission of selling the house that has ruined many an agent before you, but you're spending all your time on one client."

Bailey felt utterly exposed. Ann read her like an open book.

"You're right. About all that. I'm sorry…"

"Don't apologize. My job is to help you succeed. You're not on the path to success. You're here, but you're not. Part of you is somewhere else. Lost Key, maybe? You haven't found your perspective yet."

Bailey listened to her broker's words carefully, letting them sink in.

She nodded. "I hear you."

Ann leaned back again. "Good. Why don't you go on home? Take this weekend and regroup, gather yourself. Come back Monday focused and ready to go."

"Okay, thank you," she said flatly.

They stood, and just as Bailey was leaving, Ann smiled and said, "See you Monday."

Bailey nodded numbly and felt as if Ann were talking about someone else, some other candidate. Right now, she thought of not coming back.

Chapter 25

Mobile Bailey

ailey drove toward her apartment, thankful the day was over. She let out a long, slow yawn. What a strange first week, not what she expected at all, and with a crappy ending. But at least one ray of sunshine—she got her first clients and new friends too. Bailey thought of little Andy and how much he reminded her of Liam. An ache swelled in her heart; an emptiness filled her. She thought of her former life, her now ex-husband, and his two kids. *You son of a bitch. I raised those kids like they were my own. You had no right to take them from me.* She shook her head and wiped her eyes, taking another deep breath and exhaling slowly. She felt tired and drained. Yet, the last place she wanted to go was her run-down rent-by-the-week apartment. Tonight, Bailey needed a place that knew her name, that made sense. Immediately she turned her car toward Florida.

About an hour and a half later, she arrived at Keri's. Through the slats in the picket fence, Bailey could see that the deck was in disarray. One of the lounge chairs had been tipped over, and the palm tree lay on its side, the table turned upside down and shoved off in the corner as if someone had haphazardly thrown it aside. *Oh no!* She sprang from her car, yelling, "Keri! Keri, can you hear me?"

Keri emerged from the kitchen carrying a broom and dustpan. "Hey, I'm here," she said.

Bailey rushed to her friend. "What happened? Are you okay?"

Keri nodded as if on the edge of weeping. "Yeah, I'm okay. Somebody tossed my place." She looked around as if still trying to absorb this unwanted violation.

"Who did this?" Bailey asked.

Keri shrugged her shoulders. "Don't know. Sheriff thinks it may be some teenagers getting their kicks. As far as I can tell, they didn't even take anything."

Bailey peeked inside. Kitchen drawers had been pulled out with their contents dumped on the floor. The couch had been slit in the middle, and the stuffing spilled out in all directions. Bailey could see clothes scattered in the bedroom. *This is not the work of vandals.*

"Seems like they were looking for something," Bailey said.

"What could that be?" Keri asked, frustrated. "This kind of stuff doesn't happen in Lost Key."

Keri pulled the lounge chair upright, and stood the palm tree to its former position, pleased that the lights still worked. Then she said, "They didn't bother the blender. How about a margarita? I could use a drink, and it looks like you could too."

"Fire it up," Bailey said and plopped down in her familiar seat.

In a matter of minutes, Keri returned, carrying two freshly made drinks. She handed one to Bailey, then lounged back in the other chair. She sipped her cocktail and asked, "So, how's your day going? Hopefully better than mine."

Bailey sighed, "I blew it. I freakin' blew it today."
She recounted the entire week from the beginning, right
through the blow up with Mandy.

Keri sipped her drink, then said, "This Mandy girl
has your number."

"I know," Bailey said. "She just pushes my buttons.
It's like she knows how to say just the right thing so that
I lose it."

"She couldn't do that here," Keri said.

"What do you mean?"

"Well, here, you are in charge, you know your stuff.
You are known. You're Bailey! Sunshine Bailey. Over
there, that's her turf and her world, and it sounds like
she is well- connected."

"Yes, she is. She's already got three new listings,"
Bailey said. "Plus, Johnny is friends with the family."

Keri rolled her eyes and shook her head. "She is also
something else that you're not."

"What? Beautiful? Talented? Smart?" Bailey
retorted.

Keri sat up abruptly and glared at her friend. "I can-
not believe you just said that! I hate it when you do that
to yourself."

Bailey recoiled. "What?"

"Don't give me that bull. You know what. You put
yourself down. You believe all that crap that you heard
growing up."

Bailey averted her eyes, stung by those words.

Keri pressed her point. "You're beautiful, girlfriend,
and I don't mean in a Barbie doll way, but a real deep-
down goodness kind of way. You got it inside and out. Your
beauty goes more than skin deep. And you're smarter than

they'll ever be. And don't talk to me about talent." Keri's lips pursed, and her face grew a shade of red. "That whole condo project that you are so bored with wouldn't even be here without your imagination and creativity. You are the one who helped those developers see the idea. So, don't you ever put yourself down like that again."

Keri sat back and huffed, her eyes still ablaze toward Bailey.

"Sorry," Bailey said.

"Don't apologize to me, go look in a mirror and say that." Keri huffed.

They sat for a moment. Then her tone softened. "Look, all I'm saying is claim your value," Keri said. She crossed her arms in front of her heart and pointed at Bailey.

Bailey returned the gesture. "Love you, too. Thank you for being here, for believing in me."

"Always. Now, what was I going to say? Oh yes, Mandy's mean and you're not. She's got the home-field advantage. You can't play her game and win."

"What do you mean?"

"I mean, you've got to play *your* game, Bailey. Be yourself; that's what got you there in the first place."

Bailey thought about her words and let them sink in.

"Just be yourself. But in a Mobile kind of way," Keri added.

Bailey tilted her head and looked puzzled.

Keri searched for the right metaphor. "You can't be beach-Bailey. You know, find Mobile-Bailey. Mandy won't stand a chance." Then she sat back, lecture over.

"Mobile Bailey." Bailey leaned back and took a sip of her cocktail, pondering the concept. "Hmmm… who's that? I'm not sure those two words belong together."

"You had a tough week. Just don't overthink things, that's all I'm sayin'. Trust your goofy self."

Bailey lifted her glass to her friend, and they toasted. "Here's to being ourselves."

Then Bailey added, "Oh, the week wasn't all bad. I got my first clients!"

"Hello? You could have led with that news." Keri lifted her glass. "Congrats."

"Don and Ashly are this cute couple. They just moved to Mobile, and they have this kid, Liam…" she shook her head and blinked. "I mean Andy. He is just hard to describe, and something special for sure. You should see this little guy. He just melts my heart." Bailey noticed that Keri's smile had faded. "What?"

"Liam?"

"Oh, no worries, he just reminds me so much of Liam."

"I'm so sorry, my friend. What that man did to you was just plain wrong. It's not your fault, you know."

Bailey looked away and nodded. "Yeah, I know." The words felt hollow.

Keri sat up again. "Oh no, you didn't?"

"What?" Bailey feigned ignorance. "Don't look at me like that."

Keri let out a deep sigh. "You've already adopted them, haven't you?"

Avoiding her friend's piercing gaze, Bailey focused on the artificial palm tree, the signature plant on Keri's deck. "No, of course not. They're just clients."

"Mmmm, hmmm, that's what you said the last time, remember?"

"No, really, they are just clients. Strictly professional."

"Okay, we'll see if you keep your full commission."

"Yep, I will."

Then Keri grabbed Bailey's hand. "Come on." She handed her a life jacket and donned one herself. "Let's get outta here!"

"Yes!"

They jumped on Keri's WaveRunner. Keri pulled in the accelerator, and the front lifted as the craft lurched forward. The engine groaned and spat a long stream of water behind them as they sped down the Intracoastal Waterway. They laughed, leaving the worries of the day behind them as the sun was setting in front of them. The wind, the waves, and the friendship converged to make a superbly blissful moment at the end of a difficult day.

Chapter 26

The Future Site

Bailey woke the next day about noon, realizing she had fallen asleep again in the very same lounge chair on Keri's deck. After the impromptu ride, they had talked the night away. She couldn't remember exactly when she had dozed off. She stood and stretched. Bailey didn't hear or see her friend, and a rope snaked along the deck with no WaverRunner tied to it. *She must have gone to work*, Bailey thought. Her stomach rumbled. She strolled into the kitchen and found a note tacked to the refrigerator door by a colorful magnet shaped like a palm tree. She recognized Keri's handwriting.

Help yourself to any food in the fridge. Go be Bailey! XO XO.

She opened the fridge and scanned its contents—two boiled eggs, and some yogurt and fruit.

"Ewww, that's not breakfast." Bailey closed the door, showered, and headed toward the Tropical Palm. On her way, she stopped by Lost Key Realty, parking around back. There it sat all safe and sound—her Jeep.

"I'm right here, my friend." She climbed in the driver's seat. "Miss me? Well, I missed you. Don't worry; it's only temporary."

She turned the ignition, and the engine roared to life. Bailey smiled with delight. *I love driving this!*

A few minutes later, she skidded to a stop in the gravely, broken oyster shell lot of the Tropical Palm Café. Her smile turned to a somber, confused frown. Something was off. She could feel it as sure as she felt the sun warming her skin. She sat for a moment. Sadness enveloped her, but she didn't know why. It felt like... loss. Last time she sensed this at the Tropical Palm, an alligator had bitten someone. Even though a sign clearly warned folks not to feed the gators, they still did.

She peered through the window and saw Mary serving at the counter. Katie, holding her pad and pen in hand, waited tables. Now and again, Max's tattooed forearm slid a freshly cooked plate of food through the serving window. Everyone seemed okay, but something had shifted, and not in the right way.

That's when she glanced up in her rearview mirror. "What the heck is that?"

The plastic back window of her Jeep allowed only a hazy, distorted view. She opened the door and climbed out to get a better look. A sign, staked near the entrance to the parking lot, read 'Future site of Treasure Cove, Acheron Developers.' *What!* Bailey took a few steps closer, blinking several times, hoping it would disappear like some ugly mirage. A feeling of panic gripped her heart. She rushed inside, stopping in the middle of the diner, holding her arms wide open, staring at Mary.

"Well, look who's back," Mary said.

Bailey didn't move.

"Hey, Bailey," Katie added.

"Hey, Katie," she returned, her gaze still fixed on Mary. She put her hands on her hips, defiantly.

"Uh, oh," Katie said, glancing up at Mary, then continued tending tables.

Mary motioned for Bailey to take her usual spot. "Come on in, hon. Have a seat while there's still one to get."

Bailey huffed and took her usual stool at the counter and waited impatiently for an explanation.

Mary flung her dishtowel over one shoulder and brought her attention to Bailey. "We had no choice," she said.

Bailey had never heard such a tone of surrender in Mary's voice. It unnerved her. Max came out of the kitchen, wiping his hands. Bailey looked at him pleadingly with a *tell-me-this-isn't -true* look in her eyes. He answered her unspoken query with a gentle nod of his head then looked away.

Questions swirled in Bailey's mind. *How can this be? Something is not right here. Are they in some financial trouble?*

"Of course, you have a choice," Bailey finally said. "This is your property. They just can't take it away."

Mary and Max exchanged glances. Mary said, "Well, that's where you're wrong, my dear. It's not our property. Never has been."

"What? You don't own the Tropical Palm?"

"It's our building, our business, but the city's land," Max clarified. "We've always been here because the powers that be have been gracious. This land is a portion of the Lost Key marshland, technically speaking."

"No, that can't be." Bailey shook her head, like trying to shake unwanted water out of her ear.

"Afraid so," Max said, resigned. "When that Martin fellow purchased the marshland, his cronies came and informed us that we would have to vacate to make room for a redevelopment project."

"But he hasn't bought the marshland. I know he wants to develop it, but he can't buy it without the town's approval.

"MJ explained it to us," Max continued. "There's an addendum that says when he buys the company, he also gets all its holdings." His eyes scanned the diner. "Which includes this place."

"That doesn't make any sense. MJ would never do that."

A wave of nausea hit Bailey. *Was this part of the addendum? Something I missed?*

"I can't believe this!" she said.

"Believe it," Max echoed.

"I have to say, he was nice about it, but he wasn't asking permission," Mary added. "They staked a sign out front and told us we got thirty days to vacate."

"Offered us something for our trouble. Not much, but better than nothing, I guess." As Max said this, his face looked as if he'd just eaten spoiled fish.

It didn't sit well with Bailey, either. She felt a knot in her stomach. "How could MJ allow this?"

"It's not her fault," Mary said. "She called and apologized. Said she'd help us relocate, but really, we're too old and tired for a new start." She paused. The next words were almost inaudible, and she could barely say them. "We just didn't want to go out this way."

Max banged his hand on the counter and then took a deep breath. "It's my fault. I should have figured a way to buy this outright a long time ago."

Bailey's heart ached. "Why didn't you at least call me? I could have helped you. I would have gone to bat for you both!"

Max touched her arm, reassuringly. "We thought about it. I almost picked up the phone a couple of times. I didn't want you to find out this way. But Mr. Martin is using MJ exclusively. And we have no claim on the property."

"Besides, we knew this would just break your heart," Mary added.

Bailey took a breath. The hurt eased. "I understand that part. Thank you."

Max squeezed her forearm gently. "Also, we didn't want you to worry. You've got enough going on right now. We'll be alright. Focus on that big dream of yours."

"Well, losing the Tropical Palm, you two losing your home, your livelihood, that's not part of my dream."

Mary hugged her.

Bailey pushed away from the counter. "No! We're not going down without a fight!"

"Now, Bailey, where are you going?" Mary asked.

Bailey, already heading for the door, said, "I've gotta do something about this. I can't just stand by and let…"

"Bailey!" Max snapped.

She stopped short of the exit, and conversations in the diner hushed to a whisper. Everyone took notice of Max's unusually sharp tone. He walked over to Bailey. Then he looked around. His gaze commanded the patrons to mind their own business. They obeyed, and chatter resumed. He cradled Bailey's elbow, gently leading her outside.

"Don't tangle with this fella," Max said.

"I ain't afraid of him," Bailey fired back.

Max's eyes narrowed. He looked at her with a steely thousand-yard-stare she'd never seen before. "You should be." His gaze added an exclamation point to his sentence.

"Okay, Max. I hear ya."

He leaned closer. "I've seen the best and worst of men. There's something cold about him, Bailey. He's damaged goods. You stay clear, you hear?"

Bailey nodded and shuddered. Max had never spoken to her this way, nor ever given this kind of warning before.

"I don't like him," Max added, "but he might be just what this town needs, just what MJ needs. We'll be okay." Then he hugged Bailey and went back inside.

Bailey climbed into the driver's seat, fighting back her rage and losing. *I can't believe this is happening! Why didn't MJ tell me? How can I go back to Mobile when the people I love here in Lost Key are in trouble? How can I sit back and do nothing?* She needed more answers. All she could think about now was to get to the office. *MJ owes me an explanation.*

She glanced at the rearview mirror again and saw the project sign posted directly behind her. She looked back at the café. Max, Mary, and Katie were all watching her from inside. Then Bailey smiled mischievously and cranked the engine. She slammed the gears in reverse and stepped on the gas. The Jeep sprang backward, spraying gravel and crushed oyster shells in its wake. Instead of turning around to exit, like she typically would, she continued backing up in a straight path. Bailey heard a loud thud, then cracking, and felt a shake as her vehicle plowed right over the horrid sign. She skidded to a stop, shoved the gear into first. As she drove away, she gave one final glance to her friends, her family, and the café. Like living window decorations, arms waved, and people clapped. Katie's eyes were wide in delight and disbelief. Mary held her hand over her mouth, concealing a big smile. Max twirled a dish towel over his head in celebration. Even from the edge of the parking lot, she heard the faint sound of cheering.

Chapter 27

14-a

ailey gripped the steering wheel tightly and clenched her jaw. *I can't believe this! What is happening to my Lost Key!*

She sped down the winding road, swerving like a tiger chasing its prey. Small shards of shell pelted the front of the office when the Jeep skidded to a stop outside of Lost Key Realty. Bailey burst out, slamming the driver door behind her and leaving the vehicle parked almost sideways. She shoved open the front door, and it cracked into the desk behind it. The little bell hooked on top flew across the room, smashing into the wall. The makeshift doorbell worked well, alerting the office whenever a customer entered, but it couldn't withstand hurricane Bailey.

Eddie looked up. "Whoa… Bailey, you alright?"

She said nothing. Her eyes fixed on MJ's office. Without knocking, she flung open her boss' door. Surprised, MJ stood, meeting Bailey's fierce gaze with her own, then said, "The Tropical Palm."

Bailey's face flushed a deeper shade of crimson. Tears rimmed in her eyes. "How could you?"

"Now, Bailey, please."

"How could you, MJ?"

"I didn't know! Okay? I messed up!"

"What?"

"I didn't know the property was part of the company's holdings."

"How could you not know that?"

"Did you?" MJ shot back, then placed one hand on the desk to steady herself.

Bailey glared at her. *Well... no.* But her anger still boiled over and had to land somewhere. MJ was the closest one. "How could you let this happen?"

"I'm sorry, Bailey. The details had been buried in the description. The powers that be, way back then, negotiated a deal allowing Max and Mary to open the Tropical Palm on that spot. It's been so long ago, no one ever knew. According to the original surveys, the preserve includes the property the diner is sitting on. The renderings were changed when the town first voted to make that marsh you love protected wetlands." She motioned to her couch. "Come on, at least sit down."

"I'll stand." Bailey crossed her arms.

MJ slumped slightly as if the thought of standing were like adding extra reps on a workout routine. She steadied herself with both hands before proceeding.

"They drew the plans almost forty years ago. Back then, Max and Mary were good friends of the mayor, old Navy buddies, and all that. Max's buddy did him a favor. He intentionally skewed the surveyor's lines so that particular plat of land wasn't designated as a preserve, and then they could build on that property."

"So, Max and Mary were in on it?" Bailey asked with a pleading look in her eyes, hoping it wasn't accurate.

"No, they weren't in on it," MJ replied. "He never told Max what he did. They knew after the fact, after the vote. The mayor kept it secret to protect his friend, thereby giving Max plausible deniability. If anyone found out, he could just claim it was a mistake on the drawing. The mayor even made this real estate company the official owner of record. When it came time for a vote on zoning the preserve, they presented all the facts, but the good town folks just looked at the drawing. No one read the description."

Bailey finally sat on the couch as if the weight of this revelation were too much. MJ walked over and sat next to her.

"Just before the mayor died, he shared it with them, and the city council," MJ said. "I guess he wanted to clear his conscience, final confession and all that. Max and Mary have only known for a few years. This town loves that old diner, and those two who run it, so much that the council voted to change the legal description on the plat to protect Max, Mary, and their diner."

"But this company has been in your family for three generations. How could you not know?"

"Well, if my father knew he never told me. I never heard Grandpa talk about it either, and he loved to tell all the old stories of this company."

Bailey shook her head. "Still, how can Martin just put up a sign that says the future home of whatever? Who gave him that right?"

MJ gazed at Bailey. "You did. When you signed the addendum."

"What? But that's not possible. I would never have sold the Tropical Palm."

MJ handed Bailey page 14-a of the addendum. "As you can see, it reads the offer on the condo is contingent upon an accepted offer for this company and all its holdings. Buyer can take immediate possession of the property and its holdings upon signing this contract."

Bailey read the words, then looked back at her former boss. "Yeah, so?"

"Like I said, Lost Key Realty holds title to the land on which the Tropical Palm sits."

MJ looked down and away.

"What?" Bailey asked. "Is there more?"

As if she had to summon great courage and effort, MJ brought her gaze to meet Bailey's.

She took a slow deep breath and said, "The deal includes the marshland where Snaps lives."

"What the hell!" Bailey yelled as she sprang up to her feet. "That's not possible! Those are part of the protected preserve!"

"Not that particular patch of marshland," MJ said calmly. "The former mayor worked out that deal too. He convinced the town, which was a lot smaller at the time, to go along with it. It was done all in the name of protecting his friends and that parcel of land. Again, I never heard about that till now."

"So, the town doesn't have to vote on it?"

MJ shook her head. "Nope. That was taken care of a long time ago. The town hall meeting is for information; no vote is needed. He wants me to advocate just to help sell it. I think he is not even going to show up."

Bailey exhaled a deep breath like the wind fading from a sail. She sank back into the creaky couch. Not only was Martin taking the places Bailey loved, but she helped him do it. She held her head in her hands. "What have I done?"

"We both did this. I signed the contract too." MJ tried to console Bailey. "Listen, when I verified this news, the first thing I did was sit down with Max and Mary. They don't like the way this is happening, but they are ready to let go. The Tropical Palm needs repairs. They're tired, and the whole town seems worn down. Sentiment for the preserve has waned over the years. You care about that more than anyone. We can find a new home for Snaps."

"Are you saying you want to go through with the sale?"

"I have to. I need this one. Besides, it's time. Time for me to step out of this business."

Bailey shook her head and grabbed her stomach. She wanted to vomit. "I don't know if I'm ready to let this go. Now that it's happening, I don't want it to end."

"It's an okay offer, all things considered. Not what we thought we'd get, but with the oil mess, it's good enough."

Bailey could find no way to make this news digestible. Another wave of nausea settled in her stomach.

"A development will be a much-needed shot in the arm for the economy," MJ reasoned and sounded like she was trying to convince herself.

But Bailey wasn't comforted, and from the look on her friend's face, she wasn't either—more like resigned.

"Do you trust him?" Bailey protested a final plea.

"I trust the contracts. Martin is a bit odd. But sometimes it's the odd ones who get it done."

"You think he will leave it marshland?"

"Probably not. This oil has ruined it. You know it will never be the same. Even if it recovers, it will take years, and the town will be bankrupt long before then. We need to sell it. Who's going to buy oil-contaminated wetlands, which will soon really be only wastelands."

Bailey sparked. "So, we discredit Acheron Developers, and find another one to take his place, one who would preserve the marsh."

"This ain't politics, Bailey. We can't launch some smear campaign. That's not only illegal but immoral. Legally, Acheron Developer, Inc, is the buyer. The town folks don't get to vote on that."

"Yeah, I hear ya." But she seemed only to be half listening.

"Bailey," MJ said, "Don't mess with him. Martin's been nice so far, but he's lawyered up. We are not going to win this one."

Bailey's eyes were fixed and stoical. *Nice? Really?*

"Did you hear what I just said?" MJ continued, "The marshland won't survive the oil anyway. Besides, aren't you moving? Your future is in Mobile. Go live your dream."

MJ's words landed flat. Bailey suddenly realized how attached she was to this smelly old office, and how much the folks at the Tropical Palm were like family. She also saw more clearly how this was a no-win scenario. Yet something still didn't feel right down to the pit of her stomach. She felt the grief of losing part of her home, but it was more than that. For reasons she didn't quite understand, she couldn't accept the situation.

"How could Martin know all this?" Bailey asked.

MJ shook her head. "I don't know. But he did his homework, that's for sure."

"Yeah, but it's not the kind of thing someone sails into port and learns. It's almost like you'd have to have a history with Lost Key."

"Or you could do some thorough research down at the county records. It's all there."

"Maybe." Bailey remained skeptical.

MJ looked pensive. "Well, there's something familiar about Martin."

"You know him?"

MJ's face remained thoughtful. She took her time answering. "No. No, I'm sure I've never met him. But there is something. I can't place it. I'm just tired, I guess."

"You know I had the same feeling, like I'd met him before."

"Aw, probably just one of those familiar faces," MJ said dismissively.

"But why make Tropical Palm part of a hidden addendum? Why not just make Max and Mary an offer?"

MJ shrugged.

"It's like he wants to make sure he got that particular piece of land. What's so important about that spot?" Bailey mused.

"I don't know. It's been the Tropical Palm for years. I think before that, it was just a piece of marshland with an old, dilapidated, abandoned shack on it," MJ said.

"Really? " Bailey reacted to that bit of new info. "Who owned the shack?"

"I don't know. My grandfather told stories about an old hermit fisherman who lived out there."

Bailey wondered if this were the same hermit Keri mentioned earlier.

"Still, what does he gain by making this part of the deal?" Bailey asked.

"Well, for one thing, it ensures he gets the land. Another is that it permits him to take soil samples."

"Yeah, I saw that too. I didn't think people bothered with that."

"He wants to test the ecological effects of the oil spill. Kind of like an inspection when buying a house, only this time, the local environment is inspected." She put her hand on Bailey's shoulder. "Don't overthink it."

Bailey sighed. "Yeah, maybe you're right." Then she looked around. "I'm gonna miss this place."

MJ put her arm around her distressed friend. "Things change. But it will be alright."

"It doesn't feel alright. Something's wrong here. I know it." *And it's my fault too.*

"This is not something you're gonna feel good about. Just try to accept it and move on."

The phone rang. It took several rings for MJ to make it back to her desk.

She answered. "This is Margaret… Oh, hello Martin… what? Well, I don't… yes certainly…" then a click sound. She hung up the phone. "Well, nice talking with you, too." She grinned at Bailey. "That was Martin. It seems someone ran over his 'Future Site' sign at the Tropical Palm. You wouldn't know anything about that, would you?"

Bailey averted her eyes and pursed her lips, trying not to laugh. "Nope, not a thing." She stood. "I think it's time to go back to Mobile now."

MJ handed her a note with a name on it. "Here, this is from Ann."

"Ann? You mean Thomason Brothers Ann?"

"Yeah, one-in-the-same. Ann called yesterday. Said she had a good feeling about you."

"Still? After the week I had?"

The note had a name, Nathalie, and a phone number. "Who's this?"

"A fancy stylist."

Bailey frowned.

"Now, before you get your back up, Ann is just looking out for you. It's a big deal for her to recommend you. This hairdresser is someone she likes and uses personally. Just check it out. Who knows, you might even have fun. Also, you can't look professional in my old blazer, or your grandmother's dress."

"Hey, how did you know it was my grand... I like that dress."

"Here." MJ handed Bailey another note. "She gave me the name of a clothing store also."

Bailey read the note. "Yeah, she gave me that one too."

MJ handed Bailey another envelope. "Your outstanding commission checks are ready, plus, I added something extra to help you get on your feet."

"Thanks, MJ."

MJ chuckled, shaking her head. "Go get 'em, Bailey."

Bailey paused at the door. "Sorry about your doorbell."

MJ waved her hand dismissively. "It didn't ring much anyway."

Chapter 28

Mobile Dreaming

*S*unday morning, Bailey headed west. As she began to cross the long Mobile Bay bridge, the sun shimmered off the water, and a melancholy mood crept over her. The life she knew, the life she loved in Lost Key, had eroded before her eyes. Like Old Gulf Beach Highway, it needed protecting and repairing, except no crew would be coming to save it.

Why am I going to Mobile? Someone's got to stand up to Martin.

She entertained the idea of turning around, driving back, and challenging the privateer. But she pressed on. Like the sparkling reflections on the water, Mobile shined in its unique way, beckoning her, calling her toward her emerging new life. Today felt like more than just crossing a bridge, but a path of transition from one life to the next.

There was nothing she could do for her beloved oasis. If she did stay, she'd have to open her own office, because there's no way she would work for Martin. She thought of Max and Mary, then of Keri and MJ. She tried to reassure herself that they would be all right. They had told her not to worry. She took some comfort in knowing that her friends and family wanted her to succeed. They would love nothing more than for her to become a superstar at

Thomason Brothers. Yet, Bailey felt a strange mixture of both surrender and openness. She felt sadness for losing what she knew, but also the thrill of what lay ahead.

She realized that the only way to embrace the adventure awaiting would be to let go of the life she had lived. It could never be the same, not with the oil polluting the cove, not with the company sold. She clutched her cross. Now she understood in a more profound way that one can't willfully let go, it's a spiritual thing. Letting go meant hanging on to a higher power and trusting that power has your back. Things always happen for a reason, her Aunt Lee had told her.

"Well, I hope you're right, Aunt Lee," Bailey said. Her aunt had also said Bailey was supposed to go to Mobile, but it wasn't her final destiny.

She held tight to the elusive hope that all this was somehow for the better. *What if these events were parts of a divinely orchestrated play?* She wondered. Right now, this looked more like a sad tragedy. Whatever the outcome, she had to see it through to the end.

Bailey rolled down the window, and the bay breeze rushed in and enveloped her like a warm, wet blanket. Sometimes that blanket could be suffocating. During the dog days of late summer, one started sweating as soon as they stepped out of the air-conditioning into the steamy bayou. Still, it was her blanket. It felt comforting and warmed her right down to her bones.

The Mobile skyline rose from the horizon, and she took the exit for the old Bankhead tunnel. Built before the interstate, this used to be the only tunnel that took traffic under the Mobile River. The once fresh, modern style now looked tired with its moldy dated tiles and exhaust-stained ceiling. It needed much more constant maintenance than the newer tunnel. Yet, this old passageway delivered you right into the heart of downtown Mobile.

Lazy oaks and French-style buildings greeted her as she emerged from the underwater roadway. Black wrought iron railings wrapped around the second story balconies of some buildings, giving them a New Orleans-like feel. The old Battle House Hotel, a favorite of Andrew Jackson, still held its ground only a couple of blocks to her right. The new convention center sprawled behind her. She drove west on Government Street under the canopy of the old oaks. Once again, the covering of branches felt like a comforting hug. These gnarly majestic trees, dense with moss, provided the best welcoming committee the city would ever have, and Mobile knew it.

She turned right in the direction of Bienville Square, one of her favorite places to visit. This patch of landscape claimed several blocks and formed a giant downtown refuge. Soft, green grass and more sprawling oaks completed the comforting touches of this lush oasis. A gazebo sat off-center with white, welcoming benches.

Bailey slowed and turned right, traveling along the park. She pulled into a space in front of Dell's popcorn shop. The sign boasted that the shop had been open for business since 1923. She never researched that fact. Part of her didn't want to find out anything different. One thing Bailey knew for sure—it had the best popcorn anywhere in the southeast.

"Bailey!" a man behind the counter said. He wore a red and white candy-striped apron with a matching rectangular- shaped paper hat. "Good to see you again, been a while."

"Hey, Dell," Bailey said, smiling. "Yeah, I've been busy."

"Want your usual?" the man asked. Dell, formally addressed as Dell V, carried on the family legacy of his great, great grandfather, Dell Sr., the founder of the shop. Some folks grow eager to leave Mobile as soon as they can. Not Dell V, he knew right where he belonged. He got a case of wanderlust once and took off to see the big full world. His first and only stop landed him in New Orleans during Mardi Gras. Del took one look at the bizarre cast of drunken characters parading down Bourbon Street, turned around, and came right home. He had been in Mobile ever since.

"Yes, that would be great!" Bailey answered.

First, Dell scooped a little popcorn into a small bag, then topped it with a bit of their homemade melted butter, then more popcorn and more butter.

"Here you go." He handed the bag to Bailey.

"Perfect," she said. "And nuts?"

"Ahh, of course." He scooped a small bag of roasted peanuts still in the shell. "The squirrels will be glad to see you."

"I've missed them," she said.

She paid for the popcorn and peanuts and walked out into the park. Half a dozen grayish squirrels appeared as if they had seen her coming. She sat under one of the big oaks, grabbed a peanut, and extended her hand. A squirrel approached casually and, with its tiny claws, gently took the prize from her fingers. More squirrels appeared, as though the word had spread by animal telepathy. She repeated the ritual a dozen times. Bailey never grew tired of this routine. She didn't have to shell the peanuts; the squirrels were experts at that. Bailey leaned against the tree, watched the people, fed the squirrels, and ate the world's best popcorn.

Slowly, a kind of meditative peace came over her. Like looking through a time portal, modern buildings faded, new cars transformed into horse-drawn carriages. People paraded before her, not in the present-day casual clothing of jeans, shorts, and tennis shoes, but rather in the elegant attire of long ago. Women dressed in flowing gowns, twirling delicate umbrellas propped on one shoulder, shading their heads. They strolled unhurriedly as if their purpose was to adorn the square with beauty and elegance. Men sported suits, ties, and top hats.

For a short while, Bailey remained transported into her nostalgic dream. She simply loved Mobile in all its former fading beauty, and in the timeless beauty that endured. Bailey didn't know nor care how long she daydreamed. She might have stayed in Majestic Mobile indefinitely, except she felt something touch her leg. One of her bushy-tailed friends had come looking for more treats. She showed it the empty bag.

"Sorry," she said, delighted that a squirrel tugged her pants. It sniffed then looked at her. With the popcorn gone and squirrels fed, Bailey stood, brushing the grass from her pants.

"Well, time to go, my friends." She wadded up the empty bag and scooped up her purse, accidentally spilling its contents onto the lawn. As she corralled her personals back into her handbag, she noticed a slip of paper on the ground.

"Nathalie," Bailey read. There was a phone number written under the name. *Oh, yeah, this is the note I got from MJ; the recommendation Ann gave for a stylist.* Unex-pectedly, Bailey felt intrigued at the idea of an after-noon at the salon.

Another squirrel seemed to be staring at her.

"That's what I need, a makeover. What do you think?" Bailey said to her furry companion. "Time to start new. I'll show them who Bailey is. I'll show them what Bailey can do."

Chapter 29

Bailey 2.0

The following Monday, a midnight blue British sports car turned into the parking lot of Thomason Brothers Realty. The deep, rich hue cast a hypnotic spell and stopped conversations as it glided past the porch and into a parking space. The door opened, and the driver began to emerge. As she stepped out of the car, the slit in her new skirt parted, running a third of the way up her tan, muscular leg. With all the grace of high society, she exited, locked the door, and began walking toward the entrance. Her long beige skirt stopped just past the knee. Formfitting, it wrapped around her waist, perfectly accenting her athletic figure. A white, silk, short-sleeved blouse was tucked neatly in the waistline of the skirt. The delicate shirt looked tailor-made just for her. She had left the top button undone and completed the outfit with a soft, understated gold chain.

She didn't just wear the outfit; she commanded the style. Her shoulder-length hair had been delicately layered and bounced as she walked. It shined as if infused with pure light. She promenaded confidently toward the office front door, taking each stride with the calm assurance of a woman who knows her purpose. Agents, who had been milling about in the lobby, now looked out the window as she drew their focus. Others also paused from their conversations as if compelled to behold this living work of art.

Johnny and Robert stood on the porch, talking to a handsome young man who carried a large drawing that looked like an advertisement.

Robert spotted her, did a double-take, and said, "Bailey?"

Bailey smiled and nodded gently. Then she glanced at the drawing the young man was holding and recognized it as the same one they showed her during orientation. She could make out the words *your home is waiting for you.* Out of the corner of her eye, Bailey glimpsed Mandy and Michelle, gawking at her through the lobby window. She winked at them and smiled.

It seems I've got everyone's attention now, Bailey thought.

Ann appeared in the doorway, smiled, and raised one eyebrow. "Well, good morning, Bailey. I love your outfit!"

Her words snapped the men out of Bailey's enchanting spell.

Johnny realized he, too, had been staring. "Yes, very sharp, Miss Evans."

"Thank you," she replied as if so accustomed to hearing compliments that she expected them. Actually, she was not used to the affirmations, but for the first time in her life, she felt gorgeous. She sauntered toward them like a model strutting down her exclusive runway.

"And I love your car, too!" Robert added.

"Thank you. It seemed fitting for someone who is going to be your top agent." She said it as if it were inevitable.

The men chuckled with delight.

"You bought a new luxury convertible?" Johnny asked.

"Leased it. Business expense."

The brothers nodded respectfully.

Johnny motioned to the young man next to them, who still stared wide-eyed.

"This is Mark."

"Hi. I'm Mark Sketcher." He fumbled for a moment with his large posters before getting his hand free to shake hers.

"Bailey Evans, a pleasure to meet you."

When they shook hands, Bailey felt a warm electric tingle run up her arm. She giggled and thought to herself, *What? Am I in a movie?* His dark hair and ocean blue eyes instantly captivated her. Judging from his tanned arms, face, and neck, Bailey concluded he must live at the beach or spend a lot of time outside. She also felt a sense of déjà vu. He seemed familiar, yet she couldn't quite place where or if she had seen him before.

"You two know each other?" Johnny asked.

Bailey realized she had also been staring. "Oh… no. No, can't say that we do."

"No," Mark agreed, "but I'm glad to make your acquaintance now."

"Me too." Bailey smiled again.

"Mark," Johnny said, "this is the young lady we were telling you about."

"Oh. You're the one who created the ad like this one," Mark said, his eyes sparkling as he motioned to his poster board.

"Yep, that's me." Bailey bounced on her toes. "So, you're the one who created the new ad initiative."

"Yep, that's me," he mimicked. "Maybe we could grab a cup of coffee sometime. I'd love to hear about how you came up with your idea."

"Sounds wonderful. Any time!"

Mark turned to Johnny and Robert. "I'll get to work on that right away." Then he departed.

Robert said to Bailey, "Nice to see you again. I'm glad you're back."

Bailey beamed. She looked at Ann, who winked and went back inside. Bailey caught another glimpse of Mandy and Michelle as they walked toward the caravan bus. *If her eyes were daggers*, Bailey thought.

Then she muttered out loud, "That girl just doesn't like me at all."

"She likes you even less now," Remy said. He had been walking by to get on the bus and stopped next to Bailey. Noticing the puzzled look on his friend's face, he continued. "Mark, that handsome young man you were drooling over…"

"I was not," Bailey protested.

"Oh, come on, Bailey, you were in Lala land. If Ann hadn't interrupted, I think you two would *still* be staring at each other."

"Stop it. The last thing I need is to get tangled in some relationship," Bailey said, trying to ignore her obvious attraction to Mark. "So, what's that got to do with Mandy? Is she jealous now because I turned some other guy's head? 'Cause I got a man to look at me and not her?"

"Not just any man; Mark used to be her boyfriend."

"What?" Bailey looked disappointed. She felt her excitement dwindle. Suddenly prince charming wasn't so perfect after all.

"Word is that he dumped her."

"Really?" Interest flickered within her again.

"Usually Mandy is the one doing the dumping. She uses a guy for a while, and she gets bored, which ain't very long, then she breaks up with them for some whimsical reason, sends them away, and she's off to the next one. She's got a ton of men in her wake. At least Mark had the sense to let her go and not look back. I think that's what bugs Mandy the most. The men she dumps usually crawl after her for a while like some whipped puppy dog. Pathetic, really."

"You ever fall under her spell?" Bailey asked.

"No. I'm not her type."

"Her type?"

"Yeah, good-looking or rich, or both. Oh, I have some family history here, but Mandy, she wants more. She always wants more. She wants everything. And now, my friend, she wants to take you down. That's plain to see."

Bailey didn't like that news. She didn't like conflict. Though Bailey wouldn't pick a fight, she also wouldn't back down from one. If pushed, she would push back alright.

"Just watch yourself, Bailey. She's well-connected, and she doesn't fight fair."

"Thank you," Bailey said.

Remy averted his eyes. She watched him curiously.

Half smiling, he said, "Mandy's not your real problem."

"Oh really?" Bailey said, slightly annoyed.

"You're like a centipede," Remy continued.

"What?" Bailey said.

"I mean no offense. But you ever wonder how a centipede walks with all those legs?"

"No, I can't say I've given that much thought. What are you talking about?"

"Hear me out on this. If a centipede had to think about each and every step with those legs, it would never get anywhere."

The bus cranked as the caravan prepared to leave. Bailey's brow wrinkled trying to understand what Remy was talking about.

"All I'm saying is that a centipede, in order to get anywhere, has to not think about it. It has to walk on instinct. I already know you've got some of the best instincts I have ever seen."

"Thanks, but what's that got to do with a hundred-legged bug?"

Remy stepped closer. "Trust your instincts, be yourself. Don't try to walk like her." He nodded in Mandy's direction. "Be Bailey."

She crossed her arms, uncomfortable now in her new outfit. Though taken aback at first, Bailey realized that by luck or divine design, she had made a genuine friend in Remy. She smiled, and said, "Learned all this from a centipede, did you?"

"Nature is full of wisdom; all we have to do is look."

She chuckled. "So, don't even think about it, huh?"

"Right. Go barefoot."

"Excuse me?"

"You know, it's a metaphor. What if the centipede had to wear shoes?" They laughed. "That would be a nightmare."

"I like the idea of 100 pairs of shoes, but all the same? And putting them all on before leaving . It would never get out of the house."

"Exactly. Go barefoot."

"Remington, you're strange," Bailey said.

"Must be the company I keep," he muttered.

Bailey put her arm around Remy and said, "You're a good friend."

Remy blushed. That's when she noticed the rather large wet spot under her arm. "Oh, my God!" She jerked her arm away.

"It's all right; you don't smell."

"How come no one told me?"

"I didn't notice anything till you put your arm around me."

She held up her other arm; another wet spot! She felt exposed as if the stains were bright signs flashing low country gal, not high society agent. Runway model Bailey dissolved back into beach Bailey.

"See that," she said, pointing to her underarms. "It's gross. I can't have that."

"How can you not? This is Mobile. It's like living in a steam bath."

"Tell them to hold on; I'll be right there."

"Hold on? Hold on?"

Bailey was already running inside as fast as she could in a tight-fitting skirt.

"They don't wait, Bailey. You know that." He shouted after her, "The caravan waits for no one!"

She had already disappeared through the doorway.

Ann was standing in the hallway when Bailey came barreling around the corner, almost bumping into her.

"Problem?"

Bailey lifted her arms.

Ann's eyes opened wide. "Come with me." They went into Ann's office. "Here, let's see." She started opening drawers, first the top left, then the one underneath. Finally, in the bottom drawer, she found what she was looking for—an unopened pack of mini pads. She handed them to Bailey, who looked dumbstruck at the packet of pads, then at Ann. Her expression said, 'you gotta be kidding me.'

"It's an old trick and only an emergency solution." Ann tried to be professional but could not contain her grin.

Bailey blushed.

"Don't sweat it," Ann said, and they both laughed. "They do make real underarm pads. You will want to get some. Most drugstores carry them, and every good department store will have them for sure."

"Thank you."

"You're going to miss caravan if you don't hurry."

How can I go out like this? I can't." She rushed off. A few minutes later, she emerged from the bathroom wet spots fading now thanks to the blow-dryer that Ann also found in her bottom drawer. The mini pads were in place under her arms. Though not designed for this creative sweaty solution, at least the pads were discreet. Bailey decided that she was going straight to the store to buy the real ones Ann recommended.

She reached the lobby only to see Remy looking at her through the window as the bus pulled away. Her heart skipped a beat, and she wondered if she would have a seat next time—nothing she could do now.

Joy was not at her desk. She realized she now had several hours on her hands. Just then, she caught a glimpse of herself in the full-length mirror that hung on the back wall. Slowly she turned, admiring her new look. The blouse, the skirt, the shoes all fit perfectly. The underarms had dried completely now too.

"Hmm." She nodded approvingly and blew her mirror image a kiss and said, "Oui."

Even as she was admiring her new style, however, an unexpected feeling surfaced. Curiously, she found herself missing her old boat shoes, cargo pants, and breezy beach pullover. Clothes are more than fashion, she had heard Nathalie say. They are a statement about you.

Just then, a familiar voice pulled her away from her reflection.

"Who's that stunning beauty?" Joy asked, appearing in the doorway, back from whatever errand she had been running.

Bailey put on a southern voice. "Why, this old outfit? Just something I threw together."

Joy smiled. "Well then, a very nice toss, madam."

The front door chimed. Mark had returned.

"Well, hi!" he greeted almost over-enthusiastically. "I didn't expect to see you so soon. I... I... um... just forgot one of my ads and had to come back for it."

"Oh," Bailey said, "nice to see you, too." She found herself almost gawking at the handsome young man.

"I put your case in the conference room," Joy said to Mark and pointed. "First door on the left."

He hurried to retrieve the item.

Joy smiled at Bailey. When Mark was out of sight, she said, "Nice catch."

"Who, him? Oh, no, I... I um... well, there is no, like, we. I don't mean it like that. I mean, um, you know, I just met him only a few minutes ago."

"Really?" Joy grinned. "You could have fooled me."

"Oh no, um no, I don't know anything about him, really."

Mark reappeared with this poster. "Found it."

"Well, um, I guess I'd better be going." Turning to Joy, he said, "Thanks for your help."

"Any time."

Now back to Bailey. "Again, nice to meet you."

"You too."

He gestured goodbye and started to leave, then stopped at the door and turned back toward them. "Say, Bailey... You wouldn't happen to be free now, would you? Want to grab that cup of coffee?"

"I'd love to," she answered immediately, despite her recent protest not to start any new relationships. She waved bye to Joy and accidentally knocked over a round cylindrical container sitting near the edge of her desk; about a dozen pens and pencils scattered in all directions over the floor.

Bailey's eyes widened, and her face turned a shade of crimson. "Oh no, I'm so sorry." *So much for first impressions.*

Both she and Mark scrambled to help pick up the wayward writing instruments, but Joy waved them off. "I got this. Don't worry about it; it happens all the time. I need to move my pencil holder." She winked at Bailey.

Bailey figured this probably never really happened that much, but she sure appreciated the gracious covering.

"So, where would you like to go?" Mark asked.

Bailey mused. *Anywhere; no, nowhere. I don't need to be starting a relationship right now. What relationship? You're just having coffee.* "I don't know. What is your favorite place?" she finally asked.

"Hmmm well, let's see…" Mark pondered.

Joy picked up one of the pencils and wrote on a small piece of paper. "Here. Try this place." She handed the paper to Bailey. "It's wonderful."

"Seize the Day Café," Bailey read out loud.

"I've heard good things about that place," Mark said.

"They have French press coffee," Joy added.

"Sounds perfect."

Bailey smiled and mouthed a silent 'thanks.' "I'll be back in a short while."

"Have fun," Joy said.

Bailey's mind swirled, and she brimmed with excitement. *Breathe.* She told herself. *This is just coffee, just business. This is not a date.*

"My car is right over here," Mark said.

"Your car? You're driving?" Although Bailey's mind had quickly explored many ideas for conversation topics and questions to ask, she never considered riding in his car. She felt uncomfortable at the thought and hoped he hadn't noticed. She didn't want Mark to take it the wrong way. Yet, she didn't know this person, and it was never good to just jump in the car with a stranger. Then again, Johnny and Robert had introduced him, so the chances of him being a mass murderer were practically non-existent. But then you never really know.

"Bailey? You okay?" Mark asked.

Bailey had stopped on the porch just outside the door. She didn't know how long she had been standing there pondering these scenarios.

Well, so much for second impressions too, she thought.

"Oh yes, I'm fine," she finally said. "I just realized I'd better drive separate. I have an appointment later, you know." It was a pretty good fib. She almost convinced herself.

Mark shook his head but smiled slightly. "No, I didn't know that."

"Oh, no, what I meant was…"

Mark raised his hand. "Just kidding. No problem, Bailey. Works for me too."

"Okay, I'll meet you there."

"Perfect," he said. "See you in a few."

Bailey opened the door of her new car and slid inside. The convertible purred to life as she started the engine. After a short drive through Springhill, admiring some of Mobile's most luxurious homes, she pulled into the pebbly parking lot of the Seize the Day Café.

Chapter 30

Seize the Day Cafe

The car glided into an empty spot, fourth space from the door. Bailey secretly believed that she had the power to manifest the ideal parking space. She knew, somehow, she had created this perfect slot on her drive to the café. However, she didn't account for the longer and heavier convertible, needing more room to park than her Jeep. Before she realized it, the front end nudged across the narrow sidewalk and crashed into a small planter fresh with spring flowers.

"Oh no!" she said.

She quickly reversed the car, so it wasn't blocking the walkway to the front door and pushed the gear shift lever into park. She scurried around the front to assess the damage. Despite her thorough scan, she could find no evidence of an accident. The car looked undamaged. She breathed a sigh of relief, glad she had purchased the extra insurance option. *Whew! Impressive.*

However, embarrassment flooded Bailey when she saw that the hand-crafted, rectangular planter had held its last flowers.

Mark walked up. "Whoops."

"I better let the manager know." *Great, that will surely impress him now, Bailey*, she mumbled to herself.

Dark clouds gathered, cooling the heat of the Mobile day and threatening a downpour. Thunder rumbled, promising to make good on that threat.

"Looks like rain coming," Mark said.

"You think?" Bailey shot back playfully.

They strolled up the steps and went inside. The aroma of fresh ground coffee greeted them. It was clear the Seize the Day Café used to be an old house. The downstairs had been transformed from a large living room into a cozy assortment of tables and chairs, with wooden bookshelves. Various conversations converged in a low hum. Folks seemed respectful that some people came here to read, wanting a quieter place, and somewhere more "hip" than the library. They quickly spotted the ordering counter off to the right and back just a bit. Delicious goodies and tasty treats sat on delicate doilies in the glass countertop case. Bailey's mouth watered at the thought of biting into the lightly glazed cream cheese pastry. She resisted the temptation.

"My treat. What'll you have?" Mark offered.

"Café Pecan Mobile, French press, of course."

"Excellent choice. I'll have the same."

"I'll go find us a table," Bailey said.

Outside on the porch, a young girl was just packing up her papers and finishing her work. Bailey hurried to claim their spot.

Shortly after, Mark brought the drinks.

"I thought it would be nice to sit out here," she said. "You mind? The rain will cool things off."

"Perfect. Nothing like the scent in the air just after a summer storm."

Bailey could already smell the approaching rain. Mark sat down and placed her coffee on the table in front of her. After a couple of minutes, they slowly pressed down the mesh plunger, creating a perfectly brewed cup of hot Café Pecan Mobile.

She lifted her mug to toast. "To the rain," she said.

"May it pour."

They clinked their mugs.

Pour it did. Hard at first, then slow and steady. The rain cooled the hot air and plinked steadily against the coffee shop's tin roof, soothing and relaxing. Bailey felt the urge to take a nap. They sipped their gourmet coffee under the cozy protection of the awning. *I could sit here all day*, she thought.

"You look familiar to me." She squinted at Mark.

"Hmmm," Mark said, finishing a sip.

"I have this strange feeling like I've seen you before. Where do you live?" Bailey asked.

"West Mobile," he answered. "I got one of those new apartment homes. No maintenance. You?"

"Over by Grelot. I'm in an apartment right now, great neighbors, but I've got my eye on a new subdivision, Hillcrest Crossing. It's a new concept. They call them patio homes, looks like a good idea."

"Yeah? Maybe you can show me someday," Mark said.

"Any time." Bailey winked.

Mark's face flushed a soft rose red.

Bailey raised her eyebrows and smiled playfully.

He smiled back and looked away briefly. "So, what a coincidence, huh?" he said.

"You mean bumping into each other?" Bailey asked.

"Yeah, that, but I mean the ad. I mean, really, how cool is that? We had the same idea."

"Yeah, that is wild. Maybe even…" She looked up as if searching for the right word; then her eyes met his. "Serendipitous."

He nodded, seemingly pleased at the idea of this being more than coincidence. "So how did you come up with it?"

"I'm not sure how, really. It's just something I've always felt." Bailey looked off in the grayish clouds. She felt comfortable talking with Mark. "I find myself kind of bored with selling condos. What I discovered is that I like connecting people with houses."

Mark nodded. He seemed fixed on her every word, and his attention felt like a refreshing drink of water on a parched day. He seemed genuinely interested in her ideas and what she had to say.

She continued. "When people come to buy a condo at the beach, they don't have the same feeling as when they find a house. I got a call one day at the office. I was on floor duty, something I hate."

She realized from the puzzled look on Mark's face that he did not know the inner workings of a real estate office.

"Every agent takes a turn sitting at the front desk, answering the phones and greeting any walk-in customers. That's floor duty. I hate floor duty because it's often boring, and not much business ever comes from it, at least in sales. When I'm tired, it's okay for the same reason— not much to do, except this one time. I got a call from an elderly lady named Martha. She called and wanted to find a house, not a condo but a house. At first, I tried to give this buyer away because, at the time, I focused exclusively on selling condos. Condos are much quicker and more lucrative. But none of the other agents were available, and she just sounded so sweet and in need of help, so I took her on as a client. I set up a meeting. When I met her, I was immediately glad I did. There was just something about her. She was kind and wise, an adorable lady. But right away, I realized she wasn't going to buy an expensive house. She couldn't afford much. It was a royal pain getting her to qualify for a mortgage, let me tell ya. I think the mortgage company finally granted her a loan because they took my word that she would be all right."

Mark sipped his coffee, keeping his attention focused on Bailey's story. "Impressive," he said. "You must have a good reputation."

"Thank you." Bailey beamed. "Yes, I do, or at least back there, I do. Nobody knows me here yet."

"I'm sure that won't take long." He said it so sincerely, so matter of fact, that this time Bailey blushed.

Smiling, she resumed her story. "So, we were looking for houses, and there wasn't much to pick from, at least none that I thought were a match. Then we went to this one on Waterford Way. Isn't that a great name?" Bailey asked, and Mark nodded his agreement.

"Waterford sounds fancy, but it isn't. It's one of the dingiest streets in the area. Not dangerous mind you, just kind of run down and shabby. The fanciest thing about the place is the name of the street. Anyway, the house was hard to sell, small houses always are, but this one was also in a tough location, and needed a good bit of fixin' up. Then I learned that the houses on that street had a reputation of being hard to sell. Other agents stayed away from Waterford Way. I also found out that I wasn't the first agent to try and sell this home. Others had tried to sell it, but none succeeded. Some thought it would never sell." Then her eyes gleamed. "But I tell ya, she loved it the minute we turned into the driveway. When she stepped through that door for the first time, she stood taller and smiled from ear to ear. It was like she was coming home after a long time away. She even said out loud. "Yes! This is perfect." I remember how much joy I felt watching her light up. This may sound crazy, but I swear the house lit up too."

She paused, looking at Mark, considering whether to tell him this next part or not. Then she leaned in, and Mark leaned in as well, eager to hear more. She spoke in a softer voice. "When we walked through the front door, the light came on!" She could tell by the puzzled look on Mark's face that he did not yet grasp her meaning, so she made her point clear.

"The light came on all by itself!"

Mark sat straight up and said, "No way!"

"Way!" Her eyes opened wide as if to say, can you believe that?

"They came on all by themselves?" he asked a bit more softly.

"Yes! At least the foyer lights. All by themselves. I'm not making this up."

"No one flipped a switch?"

"Nope."

"What did y'all do?"

"Well, Martha and I looked at each other for a minute. We didn't say anything, but we knew. Then she just smiled and said, "I'm home!"

"That is amazing!" Mark shook his head, mouth gaping. "That is incredible. You sold the home that no one could sell. On a street that other agents avoided."

"Yeah, I suppose I did." Bailey agreed. "But more than that, I felt sooooo good. My heart filled up with joy. I just wanted that experience again. I even cried. Martha was so grateful for my help. I knew right then I didn't sell you a house. I helped you find a home. I mean, the place didn't even have a refrigerator, and she didn't have one either. But that didn't bother her."

"That is quite a story, Bailey. Truly inspiring. You've changed my picture of real estate agents and real estate."

She lifted her mug. They toasted.

"I know real estate agents get a bad rap, and sometimes it's deserved, but I just see this business differently."

"So how did Martha find a refrigerator?" Mark wondered. "Those things aren't cheap."

Bailey slouched back and looked away. "Well… it just kind of worked out."

"What? Is there more? Don't hold back now. Tell me the rest of the story." He leaned in again, putting his elbows on the table.

"Okay, but I'm not bragging or anything."

"Okay," Mark said.

"I took my commission check and bought her a new one."

They gazed at one another in silence. Then Mark shook his head slightly with a look of admiration on his face. "What a wonderful thing to do, Bailey, sincerely."

Bailey's cheeks turned pink at his praise.

The rain fell gently, and the porch held them in its cozy spell.

"So, your turn," Bailey said. "How did you come up with the slogan for Thomason Brothers?"

"Well, my story is not nearly as exciting as yours. I just kept thinking, what do people long for? I get Thomason Brothers wanting to be more than just a company; striving to be almost a family."

"Yeah, I felt that, too," Bailey confirmed.

"I see the competition pride itself on selling your house more quickly and for more money than the others. I get that's part of the business. You have to sell houses to keep the doors open. But what would capture 'the more,' the distinctiveness that sets them apart? A house is one of the most significant purchases a family can make in their lifetime. It's a place to belong, to have roots and connections. It's home. That seemed to me to be what Thomason Brothers is trying to do. Sell you a home. That's what Mobile is all about. Home is that place you're loved and accepted, and where you belong."

Bailey noticed that she loved the way he talked. Watching Mark form his words was... delicious. She relished his every syllable. She sipped her beverage.

"That is lovely, Mark." She also liked what he was saying. As far as Bailey was concerned, he was describing heaven. "Too bad not everyone has such a place," she added. The soured look on her face revealed there was more to tell, but she didn't go there, and Mark didn't pry.

"No," he said. "I believe we are all in search of that place, long for that place. Everyone needs a home."

Bailey's cheerful affect grew somber. The course of the conversation had taken a painful twist.

"So, you like my ad?" he asked.

"Oh yes, very professional, and I like the theme, too."

"You know that wasn't my original design."

Bailey tilted her head.

"You want to see my favorite ad?" His expression looked boyish and playful as if he had some fun secret to share. "It's what I came back to the office to get. I had turned it in along with the one you saw, the one they chose."

Bailey's eyes sparkled again. "Sure! Don't hold back on me now," she said, mimicking him.

Mark ran to the car, dodging the rain as best he could. He retrieved a leather folding case from the rear seat and zig-zagged back to the porch, trying to avoid the puddles but to no avail. Mark picked up his napkin and wiped the water off his leather case. Then, gently, he placed the shoulder bag on the table and opened it, revealing a drawing. Protecting it, so that nothing spilled on it, he turned it toward her. *This work is really important to him.* Then he stood, smiled, and gestured a voilà with his hand. Bailey expected to see a photo of a house. Instead, she saw a colorful, animated drawing. The house had personality, seemed playful, like something out of a storybook. Even the tree was smiling, as if a character in this wonderland.

Bailey stood and gasped, opening her eyes wide to take in the picture. "This is beautiful! I just love it!" The words came out unfiltered and spontaneous.

"Really?" Mark said, delighted at her reaction, and maybe just wanting to hear it again.

"Yes! Really! It's so playful and cozy and inviting. Oh, I could live here!"

"Yes!" Mark said, raising his hands in the air briefly. "That's just the effect I was going for, that is exactly the response I was hoping to see."

"I feel like even the tree wants to provide shade for me, and it would move to wherever I was sitting."

"Exactly!" Mark said excitedly. "You get it!" Then he looked at her. "You get me."

"It's wonderful. So, the brothers didn't go for this one?"

"No," he said, folding the drawing carefully and tucking it away in the protective case. "Ann wanted something more professional. Which is fine; that's okay. My job is to give my clients what they want. But I just couldn't help doing something different and unique. Something that is me."

They both sat down.

Bailey said with her mouth still open in amazement, "Well, it's just stunning."

"Thank you. You know I didn't set out to create ads."

"Oh?"

"No, I still dream of being an artist."

"With talent like that, you could. You could live that dream, Mark. This," pointing to the case, "this is a work of art! I would buy it!" She smiled, surprised how much she liked his renderings.

"Thanks," he said. "But I have to pay the bills, you know. They don't call us starving artists for nothing."

"I know. We got to eat!"

"Yes, and buy exotic French press coffee," he added.

"Absolutely, can't live without it."

The rain let up, offering a natural break in their conversation. What a perfect time, too. Everything was just right.

"Well, I guess I better get to work," Bailey said.

"Yeah, me too. I enjoyed our coffee, Bailey. Thanks for showing me this place."

"You're welcome, but actually, it's my first time here too."

"Cool. More than this, though, thanks for sharing your story and letting me share mine."

"The pleasure's mine."

There was a moment of awkward silence when Bailey was not sure which way to go. *Aren't you going to ask me out again? Or should I? Maybe I should be the one…*

"You want to grab dinner sometime?" Mark asked.

She paused, then said, "No."

Mark's head moved back slightly, and his cheeks flushed. Before he could speak, she said, "I don't want to *grab* dinner, but I'd love a longer dinner with you."

He chuckled and nodded. "Absolutely. Friday night?"

"I look forward to it." She winked.

She floated back to her car, oblivious of the rain. When she sat down behind the driver's seat, she glanced at the rearview mirror and chuckled. Her silk blouse was spotted from the many droplets still falling gently from the sky, and nothing ruins a hairstyle quicker than the humidity of the bayou. She brushed aside a strand of hair with one hand. She looked like she'd just come out of a steam bath, but surprisingly she felt giddy, energized, alive. What excellent coffee and conversation.

Even the afternoon storm couldn't rain on this parade. Just then, her new cell phone rang. It was Keri.

"Hey, how's Mobile?" she asked.

Bailey glanced out the window and saw Mark climbing into his car. "Oh, we're all sunshine here."

"Really? 'Cause the weather says you're getting a lot of rain…" then Keri paused. "Okay, what's his name?"

Bailey laughed. "We just had coffee, that's all."

"I want details, girlfriend, and soon."

In her most southern melodic voice, Bailey said, "Why, I don't know what you're talkin' about." She giggled.

"Yeah, right." Keri returned the laugh. "Hey, listen, Jade just called. Her message sounded kind of funny, not like herself at all. I called back but got no answer. Can you do me a big favor and go down to DMC, check on her, and pick up the test results?"

"DMC?"

"Oh, sorry, the Dauphin Island Marine Center."

"I suppose that is on Dauphin Island?"

"Well… yeah… the place you went before."

"I know where it is; I'm just messing with ya. Of course, I'll go pick it up," Bailey said. "But can't Jade just fax it to you? This is the '90s, you know, the age of technology."

"I'm a field agent, so I don't have a fax machine. The government does not want official documents faxed just anywhere. Jade's doing me a favor anyway. So, you're my fastest option."

"You got it, no problem."

"Thanks a million. And I want to hear about who is making you smile in the rain."

Bailey smiled. "Talk to you later, my friend."

As she backed the car away, she again saw the remnant of the flower container she had destroyed about an hour ago. Thankfully the manager was gracious when Bailey confessed to the accident, assuring her not to worry about it. Instead of feeling embarrassed, she laughed.

Chapter 31

Chased

Bailey could reach the DMC in less than an hour, and a quiet drive in the afternoon rain felt appealing. Missing caravan because of her underarm fiasco left her day free. She didn't have to be anywhere until eleven o'clock tomorrow morning when she planned to show houses to the Morgan family, her initial listing provided by Thomason Brothers. She figured they would surely be a friendly client and a solid sale. Today, however, Bailey wanted to bask in the afterglow of her delightful conversation with Mark; and of course, she'd take any opportunity to go to the beach.

She reached the DMC near four thirty p.m. The rain had subsided, and the sun peeked out as it pushed the storm clouds out of the way. The late afternoon light painted the sky with a mixture of auburn, purplish hues. Steam rose from the wet, cooling pavement. She quickly found a parking space in the half-empty lot of the estuary. She climbed out of her car and stood a minute. Bailey's heart longed for home. She drank in the sunset like a tall cocktail. It fully intoxicated her soul. She inhaled deeply, let out a long slow breath, then headed for the front door. After four p.m., admission was free, so Bailey walked past several displays until she found an attendant.

"Welcome to the Dauphin Island … oh hi, I remember you." The young woman's greeting remained as warm and friendly as last time. "Welcome back."

Bailey wondered if the gal ever had a bad day. How could anybody be this cheerful? "Hello again, I'm trying to find Jade."

"She's not here. Left early today."

"Do you know where she went?"

"She lives in the dorms, but I think she headed home or something."

Although Bailey had stayed with Jade at her dorm room that first visit, she realized Jade had never mentioned where she called home.

"Where is her home anyway?"

"I don't know… Mobile? Or was it Dothan?" Her eyes darted back and forth as if searching for an answer.

"Can you give me a phone number or address?"

The girl frowned. "No, I'm sorry that's not permitted. I don't know it anyway, but you would have to ask our personnel department."

Bailey pursed her lips, then said, "Okay, fine, did she leave a package for Keri? She was running a test for her."

The hostess's face lightened, "Oh, that's right, you're a friend of Keri's. She's the best. Sorry, but I don't know of any package or anything. You could check with the main office." She pointed. "It's just around the turtle display."

Bailey found the administrative office just where the attendant said it would be. They didn't know of any package left for Keri or any other test results left by Jade.

When she asked for a phone number or address, the receptionist retorted, "Look, it's like I told the other two gentlemen. We don't give out any personal information on our employees or students living here. They didn't like my answer, but I'm not about to give away someone's private, personal information to strangers."

"Someone else was here? Asking about Jade?"

"Yeah, just a couple of hours ago. One of the men said he was Jade's uncle and wanted to see her. When I went to get Jade, she got very upset. Said her uncle died a few years ago, and she didn't know who those men were. Then she took off."

"Did you call the police?"

"I threatened to, but the men got polite and said they had made a mistake and left. A lot of strange people in this world," she said with disdain.

An image of two strangers dressed in black flashed in Bailey's mind. Strange, but she couldn't make out their faces, despite the sharpness of the picture. She knew their visit was not a mistake. "Thank you," she said distractedly.

"Sure thing. Be careful out there."

Bailey left, got into her car, and pulled out of the parking lot heading back to Mobile. She couldn't shake an unsettling feeling that something was very wrong. *Why would Jade leave like that if she knew I was coming to meet her? Where did she go? Who were those men pretending to be her uncle?*

She rolled her window down once more to savor the salty humid air. She had nowhere else to be today, so it didn't matter if her hair had that wind-blown look. The rain had already soaked it back at the coffee shop anyway. She drove slowly away, relishing the cool of the evening twilight. She didn't notice that a black sedan had pulled out behind her. She turned right onto State Road 193, tracing her path back along the Dauphin Island Parkway, the only way on or off the island, except by boat. Dusk proved an especially lovely time for this drive. Several bridges stretched long and lazy across the canals and marshy islands. The last glow of the setting sun glistened on the watery horizon. Finally, the bridges deposited her onto even longer stretches of a deserted highway. Thick scrub brush and sandy soil replaced the liquid landscape. Puddles of recent rain randomly blotted the hot road, the last remnants of the afternoon storm.

She flicked on her headlamps, then adjusted her rearview to dim any car lights behind her. Soon she noticed two bright ovals approaching from directly behind. They grew larger in her rearview mirror till the whole back window seemed one blinding reflection of light. She expected the car to pass, but instead, it stayed about ten feet behind, matching her speed.

"Oh, come on. Really? Just go around already." She slowed, hoping the car would get the hint. Instead, it closed the distance even more. Again, it matched her speed. *Why won't they just pass? Hello! That's why I slowed down.* She stuck her arm out the window and signaled for them to drive around. She waited for the blinding glow filling her rear window to sweep left as they accepted her invitation, but the light intensified, and the car crept even closer.

"Seriously? I can't believe you put your brights on!" *Fine, I'll pull over then.* Bailey flipped the turn signal indicating her intention even though there was no spot to stop, no turn to take, only straight dark road ahead. *What am I thinking! I can't pull over here, in the middle of nowhere, with a strange car chasing me.*

A loud horn shrieked from behind as if the car itself were yelling 'get out of my way.' The screeching was relentless, sometimes coming in small bursts, at other times prolonged. For Bailey, the sounds seemed like the blast of a freight train.

"Okay, if that's the way you want to play! Let's see you chase this!" Bailey pressed the gas and increased her speed. At first, the lights faded as the sports car accelerated. Then, again, the mysterious car closed within a few feet from her rear bumper, their lights still shining bright and full. She squinted once more in the mirror, hoping to make out some detail of the vehicle, but all she could see were two blinding beams.

The terrifying realization gripped her. *Oh, my God! Are they chasing me?* The answer was evident. *Yes, they are chasing you!* There was only one place to go, Tillman's Corner, 10 miles north. Instinctively, she stomped on the pedal again and leaned forward. Her heart raced as fast as the pistons in the engine. Her mind began to spin wild imaginative tales. She wondered what these people could want. She thought of a recent news story of Sandy, a female real estate agent who had gone missing.

"What if these are the same people?"

Her breathing became shallow and rapid; her eyes darted swiftly back and forth. The sun had fully set now, and each minute, the darkness thickened, like an eerie, soupy, gel. The road ahead seemed like a revolving tunnel in a horror house. Her vision blurred. She leaned her head slightly out the window, to let the warm wet breeze blast her face. It helped. Then it began to rain again.

Not good. She sped up, holding onto the single goal of reaching Tillman's Corner safely, getting to civilization where there were people and… lights. Fifty, sixty, now seventy. Her car raced onward. Briefly, like before, the lights receded in the rearview mirror, but only to draw closer again. The sleek convertible glided along the highway, giving her a measure of assurance. Thankfully, it was a long straight stretch of road. She prayed some animal didn't dart in front of her. She nudged the gas pedal to the floor. Seventy-five, now eighty miles an hour. She just might make it. She felt a strange exhilaration from fear, adrenaline, and the 450-horsepower engine surging under the hood. *Screw you*, she thought. *I'm not going to be some headline today.*

Then, unexpectedly, the steering wheel began to vibrate. At eighty-five miles an hour, the vibrations grew worse. The whole car shook, then began to shimmy from side to side. *Damn tires must be unbalanced*, she thought. Watching her Uncle Jed rebuild race cars had taught her that much.

Reluctantly, she let off the accelerator; otherwise, she might have lost control. The car slowed back down to eighty, then seventy-five. The ride smoothed out, but the mysterious car closed rapidly. Only this time, it did not hang a few feet behind. Instead, it smashed right into the back of the rear bumper.

Bailey let out a yell as she fought to keep it on the road. Her car swerved left, then right, and straightened again. Her skin tingled with terror. There was no place to go, no way to hide from the howling light. Bailey's head jolted back hard against the headrest as the car smashed the rear more forcefully. Shattered glass from a smashed tail light clinked, and the sports car swayed, this time veering off the right side of the road. Dazed, she tried to regain control, but overcompensated, driving across the road and slightly off the left shoulder. She fought the wheel and finally managed to straighten it again. Suddenly a truly horrifying thought pushed out all the rest. *I'm not going to escape.* The next impact would certainly push her off the road altogether. If they forced her into a swampy section, who knows how long before anyone would find the wreckage. She would be food for the gators, or worse, slowly digested by the bayou as her body decomposed. *And in my new outfit too.* She chuckled at how strange it was even to consider her outfit at a time like this. Who knows what people think when facing their demise?

Just then, Bailey felt a strange sensation. The cross her mother had put around her neck began to warm. It felt oddly comforting, especially at this moment. Was this a message that she would be okay? That she would find a way out? Or was this a divine message that an angel awaited to escort her from this world to a heavenly place free from mysterious car monsters chasing her in the night? That she would be all right, but not in this life. It had to be the latter, for escape seemed impossible. Bailey's swirling thoughts landed on one final act. *I'm not gonna die afraid.* She reached down and unclicked her seat belt, feeling this a kind gesture to herself. *If I have to be swallowed by the swamp, I'm not gonna be awake for it.* Finally, what she believed would be her last gesture, she lifted a middle finger in defiance of the bright death and waited for the end.

Then she saw the sign directly ahead, Tillman's Corner 5 miles. Five miles, she just had to make it five more miles. Bailey figured to travel that distance in five minutes or less. Hope leaped within her. *There is a way out!* With a renewed determination, she refastened her seat belt, gripped the steering wheel, and stomped on the gas again, accelerating to eighty miles an hour. The vehicle shook and vibrated, protesting the speed, but Bailey held fast. Eighty was as far as she dared push it without knowing the car better. The mysterious pursuers maintained the chase, still hanging a few feet off her rear bumper. Five minutes seemed like an hour, but then suddenly, the brush and trees receded, and the motor car emerged from the foliage speeding toward the highway ahead. Bailey saw cars coming from the opposite direction. The glow of the shopping centers shined like lights at the end of a long, scary tunnel. The bright ovals in her rearview dimmed and shrank as her pursuers drew back, assuming a more appropriate position for highway travel. Apparently, they didn't want to draw attention to themselves.

Bailey pulled into the large parking lot of Larry's Home Improvement up on the left. The car still followed. She stopped next to the entrance in the section that said no parking, drop-off only. The pursuers stopped in an almost parallel position at the far end of the parking lot near the exit. Through the drizzly foggy haze, she could see that the car was a black sedan. The tinted windows blocked any view of who was driving or if there might be a passenger.

Bailey jumped as she heard a tap on her window. A young man with intense eyes stared at her from under a rain hoodie. LHI was embroidered across the front of his poncho. He worked there! *Oh, thank you!* she thought as she rolled down her window.

"Ma'am, you can't park here," he said.

"I know I know; it's just that… that car…" Bailey turned to point to the sedan, only to see it pulling out of the parking lot and driving down the highway.

The young man looked back at Bailey and asked, "You okay, ma'am?"

What the hell is going on? The answer felt close, yet just out of reach.

Finally, she turned back to the young man and managed, "Yes, I'm okay. Thank you."

She rolled up the window. *Breathe*, she told herself, inhaling slowly and deeply. *Just breathe*. Her heart rate slowed, and her mind quieted. Home sounded good; it was only a short drive away to her Hillcrest Apartments. She wondered if she were the victim of some random rednecks having their twisted fun. But she couldn't be sure, so she decided to take extra precautions. Instead of driving directly home, she took several detours, frequently checking her rearview to make sure she wasn't followed. She stopped at a convenience store just to be doubly sure and even flirted with the attendant to stall for time. All seemed clear, no sign of the black sedan. The drive that should have taken ten minutes lasted forty-five. Even if she was just paranoid, the peace of mind was worth the extra time.

Just then, her new cell phone rang. It was Ann. Bailey relayed the whole story of the drive home, relieved to tell someone about the experience.

"Yes, I'll rest, I promise… Okay, I'll call you as soon as I get home… Okay, thanks, Ann."

She felt drained and shaky, almost lightheaded. *Take your time. You can get home.* A glass of wine, an old movie, and a hot bath were her prescription now.

A few minutes later, Bailey arrived at Hillcrest Apartments. She parked in her assigned space. The rain had begun to let up but still fell steadily, the storm showering her as soon as she stepped out of her car. Exhausted, she lumbered up the stairs leading to her apartment. She could already taste the cabernet and feel the warm bath. The stairs seemed unusually high this evening. Her legs felt heavy and waterlogged, and each step required more effort than the one before.

Reaching the top, she paused to catch her breath and noticed a light shining through the curtains next door. *Good. Valerie is home. Maybe she has cooked up something yummy.* She felt fortunate to have such a caring neighbor. Even though Bailey had just moved in, Valerie often dropped by with a dessert or invited her for dinner. She looked after her neighbors, a self-appointed second-floor mother. Bailey's hand shook slightly as she opened her door. Once inside, she kicked off her shoes and scrunched her toes into the comfy carpet.

"Ooohh, that feels good," she said, nestling her achy feet further into the soft flooring.

The phone rang. *Mmm, must be Ann again, making sure I got home. How cool she's checking on me.* She picked up the receiver. "Hey, Ann. I just got…"

"You owe me an apology, Miss Evans. And a new sign."

The voice was unmistakable and sent an icy chill throughout her body.

"Martin?" Her lip quivered as she said his name. Any calmness she had recovered after the car chase was now gone. She leaned against the wall, body trembling. "What… how… did you get this number?"

"In the company directory, of course. I'm a businessman, Miss Evans, not a stalker."

"I don't know who you are." Images flashed across Bailey's mind. She saw a pirate-like figure holding a bloody sword, and people screaming next to a river.

"Oh, I think you do," Martin said coldly.

Her pulse quickened, and she felt a pain in her right temple. His words landed like heavy rocks. She slumped, fighting to stand.

"I'm a developer," he added. "A privateer."

"Why are you calling me?" she managed to ask, her voice raspy.

After a pause, she heard a deep sigh before he spoke. "Stop interfering with my project!"

Her entire body tensed at his last sentence. He spoke with such command, such anger, a more massive rock on her shoulders.

"What are you talking about…"

"Time's up!" he interrupted.

"What? What did you say?"

Her knees buckled as she struggled to maintain her balance. Nausea stirred in her gut. Her vision blurred. She blinked, but it didn't clear. She felt trapped on the phone. She didn't want to listen a moment longer but couldn't hang up.

"Stay away from my project," he repeated. "Time's up!"

The conversation ended with a loud click, followed by a dial tone. Bailey breathed deep but couldn't seem to catch her breath. The room spun like a ride at the amusement park; only this wasn't fun. The once-hard walls moved in placid wavy lines. She groped for the table near the entrance but grasped only air. The light started to fade to a silver-gray. She knew she was falling; then all went dark.

Chapter 32

Step It Up

ailey awoke to the bright sun beaming into her bed-room. She sat quietly at that moment just after one awakens and before the mind floods with the day's worries. A feeling of déjà vu came over her like she knew this space. Bailey sensed a familiarity, a homeness. Then, the memory of Martin's creepy call jolted her awake. Scanning the room, all seemed normal, safe and quiet now. *How did I get to my bed?* The last thing she remembered was the sensation of falling. The phone still dangled off the hook and made an annoying buzzing sound. *Okay, it wasn't a dream, he really did call.* She realized she was still wearing her tan skirt and white blouse from yesterday, wrinkled from the night's sleep. She replaced the receiver to quiet the off-the-hook noise. She looked in the mirror. Her hair flared out in a dozen different directions. She chuckled. The just-woke-up–wrinkled-clothes–early-morning look conveyed a mischievous, slightly improper side of her. She liked it. As she brushed a strand of hair aside, she noticed a slight tremor in her hand. She shook it, but the tremor persisted. Then she glanced at the clock—eleven thirty a.m.!

"Oh, no! No! No! No! No! Tell me that can't be right." She checked the stove clock in the kitchen; it displayed the same time. Bailey had slept right through the morning.

"Dammit! The Morgans! I'm supposed to meet the Morgans at Timber Creek in half an hour!" She checked her pager. There were five messages from the office. "Oh, crab balls! They're looking for me." She called in. Joy answered the phone.

"You have some visitors here," Joy said. "They've been here about a half-hour."

"What? Please tell them I'm so sorry. Tell them I'll meet them at Timber Creek."

"Is that her?" a man's voice bellowed in the background.

"Yes sir, I've just gotten through."

"Let me speak to her."

"Well, I don't think—" Joy was cut off in mid-sentence, her voice abruptly replaced by the man's voice.

"Miss Evans, are you there?" he said.

"Yes, Mr. Morgan," Bailey managed to say. "I'm so sorry. I got caught up in my last meeting…"

"I don't want to hear it! We've been waiting for over half an hour. I don't know what kind of business you're running, but my time is valuable, and I don't like to be kept waiting."

"Yes, sir." She wanted to apologize further, but he kept talking.

"This is lousy customer service, and if you can't keep your appointment, how can I trust you with something as important as helping us find a new home for our granddaughter? How do I know you'll get the mortgage papers, right?"

"Mr. Morgan, I'm so sorry; I can be there in 15 minutes."

"Don't bother. We shall take our business elsewhere."

"Mr. Morgan, wait… Hello?" But there was no answer.

"They're gone," Joy said. "I'm sorry, Bailey."

"Don't let them leave. I'll be right there!" Bailey urged.

"I'll do what I can," Joy pledged, "but you better hurry."

"Okay, thanks." Her heart raced. She stepped into her shoes, ran a comb through her hair, and straightened her skirt and blouse. Grabbing her keys and purse, she ran out the door.

Tires squealed as she turned onto Grelot Road. She drove right past two stop signs and ran one questionable yellow light just turning red as if they were only suggestions. She reached the office at eleven fifty a.m. and parked crookedly next to the front door. She'd barely turned off the ignition before bolting out the car, leaving the door wide open. One minute might make all the difference. She flew up the steps and through the entrance, then looked at Joy, who was sitting behind her reception desk.

Joy shook her head. "Sorry, they left a few minutes ago."

"Damn it!" Bailey stomped. She wasn't mad at Joy, but at herself. *How could I let this happen!*

"Sorry, Bailey. I tried…"

"I know you did. It's not your fault, it's mine." She sighed deeply. "I'm gonna go find their number. It's in my folder. Maybe I can get them back." She started to walk toward her cubicle.

"Um… you may want to talk with Ann about that," Joy suggested.

Bailey stopped. "What do you mean?"

Joy looked away, then made eye contact again. "Just talk to Ann."

Bailey walked to her boss's office and found the door open. She saw Ann sitting behind her desk, focused on some paperwork. Bailey knocked.

Ann looked up and arched an eyebrow. "You look like you slept in those clothes."

"Um… well, actually—"

"Are you okay?" Ann interrupted and gestured toward the couch. Bailey sat down as Ann stood behind her desk.

No, I'm not okay. But you better say you are. You're okay. You're okay. "Yes, I'm okay," Bailey managed to say.

Ann looked worried and unconvinced. "Okay, then. That's the most important thing." She sat down in her chair before continuing. "Bailey… you've got to get yourself together. I don't know what's going on with you, but pull yourself together."

"I'm so sorry."

"Sorry doesn't cut it," Ann answered abruptly. "Fix the problem."

"I'll make it up to the Morgans," Bailey promised.

"No, you won't. Johnny gave you that one, but you didn't exactly shine, did you?"

"No, but I can get them back, I know I can."

"No, you can't. Besides, there is no need to. The family is still with Thomason Brothers; Johnny talked them out of leaving. I think Mr. Morgan is a pain in the you-know-what, rude, and arrogant. But he's a friend of Johnny's and a valued customer. He buys and sells a lot of homes, and when he does, Johnny shares the listings with new agents." She paused, then said, "Johnny gave your listing to Mandy."

"Mandy! No way!" Bailey stood, her face red, eyes fierce. She caught Ann's gaze and sat back down.

"Mandy was available, you weren't," Ann said matter-of-factly. "Step it up, Bailey. My advice—do whatever it is you need to do but get it together." Then she took off her glasses. "And get Mandy out of your head."

"Yes, ma'am."

Ann donned her glasses and returned to her paperwork, dismissing Bailey with a wave of her hand.

Chapter 33

Letting Go

Stay calm, Bailey told herself as she drove the Antoines from the last showing. After hours of research and several days of showing houses, the rejected listings piled in her backseat like an unwelcome hitchhiker. *Go ahead and give these nice people to Mandy. They deserve a real agent.*

Dad sat in the right rear passenger seat, edged over toward the middle, with Andrew next to him. Ashly rode up front with Bailey, quietly looking out the window.

"Don't worry," Bailey said. "The Thomason Brothers' system works. It's proven."

She didn't know if it would work. So far, nothing had worked for her. But she believed in the company, and that sincerity came through.

"The most important thing is to find y'all the right home. It's out there. We just need to keep looking." She felt like a cheerleader trying to give hope to the home team desperately behind and late in the game. Even if she didn't think there was any hope, she still had to act like a miracle was coming with the next play. Bailey knew she was reassuring herself as much as the Antoines. *You couldn't even handle a freebie from the company. What makes you think you can take care of this lovely family?*

She looked in the rearview. "Okay, Andy, hand us another one."

He grabbed a paper and passed it up front to his mom. "This is all that's left."

"One? Really? You sure?" Bailey gulped, trying to conceal her concern. *Did we go through all the listings already?*

"Yep. No more."

She glanced at Ashly, who nodded yes and began studying this new one. She gave Bailey the address.

"Okay. We'll check this last one out and see how it measures up against your current top choice."

Per the company's system, she matched them with potential homes, bringing the top possibilities, and visiting each one. Although seeing five houses per day was their average, having a lot of listings didn't make their decision easier. They just became more confused. Their top choice seemed to change every other round. *The system is not the problem. YOU ARE. You're a crummy agent!*

"Mom, there are a bunch of papers back here," Andrew said.

Bailey glanced at his image again in the mirror. His dark hair, blue eyes, and boyish southern charm had won her heart at first sight. *Now hush, dear,* she thought. *Don't point out the ones that didn't work.*

In the short time she had known them, Ashly, Don, and Andrew had become more than clients. They already felt like family. The Antoines were young. She figured they didn't have a lot of credit history, and this was a tight market. *They need a break, and I'm gonna give them one.*

"We'll find that home. I promise," Bailey said adamantly. *Then get them a new agent!*

Ashly rode, pensively staring out the window, then said, "Bailey, we can't keep asking you to do this. We can't keep taking so much of your time."

"Nonsense. I want to do this. I'm on a mission now." Bailey scrunched her brow and focused her eyes. She gripped the steering wheel tight and leaned forward, as if by sheer willpower she could command the real estate gods to show them their perfect house. It also hid her shaky hand. However, her defiant lean-to transformed into a slight slumping as her willpower waned.

Don spoke from the back seat. "Ashly's right, Bailey. We have been through, what is it now, fifteen, twenty homes? We don't know what we want, and we don't quite know what we can afford. This outing is our third time looking now. It's not you, Bailey, it's us." *It is you.* Her inner critic interjected before Don finished. "We may just have to rent for a while."

Ashly looked resigned. Bailey knew that look and empathized with her new friend's longing. She knew if she didn't find their home soon, they would give up. Somehow that only strengthened Bailey's resolve.

"Bailey," Don said softly. She saw his eyes in the mirror, looking back at her. "Let's call it a day." She started to protest, but he shook his head. "You did your best. Thank you for that. Time to go home."

Ashly remained silent. Her eyes glistened, and her jaw clenched.

"Okay," Bailey conceded and gave one more cheer. "Yes, let's call it a day. We can take a fresh run at it again… tomorrow."

"We'll check our schedules and get back to you."

Oh no. I'm about to lose these buyers. Well, can you blame them? It's been super frustrating. Maybe it's time for you to quit, too. Bailey shuddered, attempting to derail this train of thought. Now was not the time to go down the negative-thinking, beat-herself-up road. But that train had already left the station.

The engine purred. The hum of the tires gripping the road filled the silence in the car, as Bailey drove them home.

"Do we have to go home?" Andrew pleaded.

Don touched his son's hair, gently comforting him. The words were slow to form at first, but he finally managed, "Just for a while longer."

A short while later, on the edge of Mobile, she arrived at their destination. Graffiti smeared the sign at the entrance to their apartment complex. 'Bracken-wood' Estates had been spray-painted to read 'Broke-wood' Estates. A half-fallen gutter poured rain down to the grass next to their building. The large puddle had carved a channel to the parking lot. Home for the Antoines was the cheapest apartment complex in Mobile. It had started as a decent development, but the owner didn't care about the tenants or property, only the profits. His greediness deprived the place of much-needed care. He maintained the property at or below minimum standards. Over time, the complex had attracted a more desperate, jaded clientele. Ashly had told Bailey they often heard yelling through the walls when the neighbors fought.

The tires crushed a used syringe as she pulled into a parking space near their door. No wonder Andy didn't want to go home, neither did Don nor Ashly. Bailey didn't want to leave them here, either.

She turned off the engine. It began to rain again.

There's got to be something better than this for y'all to live in! I know there is and I have to find it. Her inner critic scoffed.

She unbuckled her seat belt and turned to face Ashly, and so she could better talk over the back seat to Don and little Andy. "You will find a home. I promise you."

Rain splashed on the windshield and plinked off the hood and roof.

Don took on a serious look. "There is something you need to know," he sighed. "I had to file bankruptcy a few months ago. I lost my last job due to cutbacks. Then our son got sick. It took all our savings to get through that."

Andy hung his head when he heard this.

Don lovingly put his arm around his son. "And it was worth every penny."

The boy smiled and leaned onto his dad.

"I just got this new job here in Mobile," Don continued. "It's a good position, but I'm just starting. I'm sure that will affect our qualifying for any loan. I should have told you sooner."

"But you've already been pre-qualified for a mortgage," Bailey said. "It's not as much as we hoped, but you can still find a good home in your price range."

"The problem is that we don't have the down payment. I thought my parents could help, but Dad called earlier today and said there's still a chance, but it's not looking promising. I guess I'm just holding on to hope. I'm sorry, Bailey."

Bailey met each of their eyes. *So that's the rest of the story.* She nodded understandingly. She knew there was something unspoken exchanged between them in that glance they gave one another back in the conference room. This news also explained their solemn mood today, as they had been less animated than usual. A single tear ran down Ashly's cheek, while Don looked resigned but courageous, a father facing reality head-on. Andy played with his car, running it across the seat.

Moved by their honesty, and a bit relieved, Bailey said, "I'd thought you were upset with me, that I was letting you down."

Ashly touched her arm. "Oh, not at all."

"I'm the one letting you down," Don said, taking full responsibility, even though everything that had happened was out of his control.

"Thank you for sharing what is going on with y'all." Her heart swelled with affection. *God, I love this family.*

Bailey took a slow deep breath. With a calm assurance and a wellspring of new conviction, she said, "We will find you a home. I know it."

"We can't keep asking you to show us houses," Don said flatly. "That's not fair to you. We'll have to let go of our dream for now." He reached over the back seat and placed his hand on Bailey's shoulder. "You're welcome in our home anytime, wherever we are living."

Then the Antoines said goodbye and hurried inside.

Bailey drove back to the office, frustrated and annoyed. The light shower had turned into a steady downpour by the time she arrived.

Joy greeted her as she ran inside. "Ann is waiting to see you."

Really? Wonder what that's about. "Okay, thanks." Bailey's stomach tightened as she reached Ann's office. She was learning to trust her stomach's premonitions. She slowed her pace a bit, to see if any insights would come. But no, just a feeling that this would not be a pleasant meeting.

Ann motioned for Bailey to come in and sit down. She laid her glasses on the desk, walked around, and sat in the chair across from Bailey.

"Have you been with the Antoines all day?" Ann's tone conveyed no pleasantries, all business.

"Yes, we're getting closer—"

"Bailey, I know that you like this family," Ann interrupted. "But you have let yourself get too close to your client. You've attached to them like they're long- lost friends. How much time did you spend with them this week?" But she didn't wait for an answer. "You're not their friend. You're their agent. Be their friend later."

"I know I can find them a house," Bailey protested.

"How many houses have you looked at with them?"

"Only about twenty… five."

Ann raised her eyebrow. "How many houses have you vetted to get the list down to 25?"

Bailey thought of the long hours she had spent canvassing the listings and making calls on behalf of her one client, the Antoines.

"You know, not that many."

Ann just looked at her.

"Okay, well, a lot."

"You've lost perspective. MJ said to watch you for this. It can happen to any of us. When I saw that little boy Andrew, my heart melted too. I understand your feelings, but you've got to stay professional. That's why they're hiring you."

"I know, I know. It's just that if you saw where the Antoines lived, Brackenwood Estates…"

"Oh, no!" Ann rolled her eyes and sat back, taking a breath. "That's the worst place in Mobile." She quickly returned to professional mode. "Still, you're not doing them any favors. You can't rescue them. You can't fix this."

"I just had to try."

"Understandable," Ann acknowledged, "and I'm not without sympathy myself. But this is consuming you. You need to put listings on the board. You haven't built any momentum yet, and you lost the starter listing the company gave you."

That comment stung, but Ann wasn't trying to be mean. She was trying to teach a hard lesson.

"We are not welfare agents; we can't be. My advice— let the Antoines go."

"I understand."

Again, Ann raised one eyebrow in a questioning look. "It's your business to run, Bailey, but it's my job to look out for you and watch your back. That is all I'm going to say about it. You'll do what you have to do." She paused, then said, "Good luck."

Ann stood, concluding the meeting. Bailey knew her broker was just doing her job. She even admired the way her boss could both have compassion and yet remain the supervisor. But Ann's cool, detached tone unnerved Bailey. *Is she losing confidence in me? Can you blame her?* A deep feeling of unsettledness crept over her. This new job was not going well. In just the first two weeks, she'd lost a free listing to Mandy, her majesty, who seemed determined to undermine her every move. And the Antoines, her only real clients, had no money for a down payment. Added to this plate-full of worry, her new friend Jade was inexplicably unavailable. Strange men had chased her, and some mysterious pirate-guy was stealing her town! *How did my life get so complicated?* She consoled herself with the thought that at least her personal life looked promising. She couldn't wait for Friday and her date with Mark.

Chapter 34

Missing

Mark and Bailey headed toward the Sunset Grill for their Friday night date. This local restaurant boasted of the best fried-fish platter on Dauphin Island. During the drive down, Bailey told Mark of the recent events, including the car chase and the cryptic message. He listened intently, occasionally nodding as if committing to memory every detail of her story.

"… and then there's… Magnolia Mandy. She thinks she's better than everyone else because she grew up here. So what if her family knows… everyone? She drives me crazy. But she can sell. I'll give her that."

Mark's expression turned blank at the mention of Mandy. Bailey sensed his awkwardness. Then she remembered that Mandy and Mark had once been an item. She decided not to talk about her anymore. Mandy wasn't welcome on *this* date.

Bailey continued, "I think my broker is getting frustrated with me."

"Ann? Really?" Mark asked.

Oh good, you're back with me. "Yeah, lately she has been, I don't know, cooler. Not as friendly."

"Well, she is your boss."

"Yeah."

"And Thomason Brothers is in the real estate business."

"True."

"How is your production?" Mark asked.

"Terrible. I'm way behind compared to the other agents. It's just that so much has been happening. This move has been more of an adjustment than I realized."

"Not to mention, trying to move here, start a new job, and with all that is happening in your home of Lost Key."

"Oh, I can hardly think of that. I just want to cry."

"That's a lot for anybody, Bailey. Maybe you just need a little time."

She smiled and touched his hand. "Been looking forward to this evening, though."

"Me too. I think you're going to love the food at the Sunset Grill."

"Thanks for starting our date sooner," Bailey said.

"No problem. Just sorry about the reason." He smiled.

She nodded. "Keri sounded really worried when I talked with her earlier today. She still has not heard from Jade. I'm worried too."

"I sure hope she is okay. We'll stop by the DMC on the way."

"I appreciate you taking the time. I just gotta check and see if anyone there has heard anything."

"Absolutely."

They arrived at the Dauphin Island Marine Center around four p.m. At that hour, the parking lot was nearly empty. Mark easily found a spot close to the door. As they went inside, the attendant, Jennifer, greeted them. Her perky, welcoming manner seemed more forced today. *They must not have heard from Jade yet either.*

The attendant led them back to the personnel office and introduced them to a woman in a rumpled business suit with frizzed black hair. Long years of worry and stress had lined her face into a permanent expression of concern. Stacks of papers covered her desk in no discernible pattern, and the lady sitting behind it seemed like an overwhelmed captain barely in control of the ship. After the introductions, she answered Bailey's question.

"No one here has seen or heard from Jade for several days. We just filed a missing person's report with the Mobile Police department today."

Bailey's mouth fell open, and her worry intensified. "You don't think something happened to her, do you?"

"Well, something is not right," the woman retorted. "How do you know Jade?"

"Through a mutual friend, Keri," Bailey answered.

"Dr. Keri Macintosh from NOAA?" the woman asked.

"Yep, that's her."

The woman's concerned expression softened. Bailey could still see the wrinkles of the worried look, clearly her more natural state. "Keri is a great person." Then she chuckled. "She found her lost treasure yet?"

Bailey returned the laugh. "No, ma'am."

The lines on the woman's face sharpened again. "I need to take down your contact information. We've been instructed to notify the police if anyone came looking for Jade."

"Certainly, I understand." Bailey gave her the information she requested.

"You say you were picking up something Jade left for you?"

"Yes. Well, I mean, Jade didn't leave it for me, but for Keri."

The woman nodded as if this wasn't the first favor Jade had done for Dr. Keri.

"Sometimes, she will research a project for Keri. Do you know what she was working on? Was it a report of some kind?"

Bailey wasn't sure how much to disclose. This testing was an off-the-books kind of favor, and she didn't want to get her new friend in hot water. But more importantly, Jade was missing and could be in real trouble. The more information, the better. It might even help the police find her.

"Keri had sent over a sample from the oil spill in Lost Key. She said it was routine and hoped Jade could run a quick analysis."

The lady frowned. "Oil spill? I haven't heard anything about that."

"Well, Keri said it seemed pretty localized, mostly affecting Lost Key and the immediate surrounding area."

"A localized oil spill. Huh… that's odd."

"That's just what Keri said."

The lady scratched her head and rifled through a stack of papers on her desk. "There's no mention of this in Jade's notes."

Bailey looked puzzled.

The lady continued, "We don't normally run such studies, but Jade is exceptionally gifted, and Keri's a friend. Since it is an oil spill analysis, Jade would have kept notes and copies and turned the results over to NOAA and the Florida Dept of Natural Resources. It's standard procedure. There is no record of that analysis."

Bailey said, "Maybe Jade never finished it."

"Or, maybe she did. Maybe she found something that put her in danger," the manager said. The implications of that statement paused the conversation. The worried look deepened even more on the woman's face.

"In danger, really? You think so?" Bailey asked, even though her recent car chase pointed to the worst-case scenario.

"The devil can find you anywhere," the lady said matter-of-factly.

"What did you say?"

"Just an expression." She waved her hand dismissively, then added. "I'm a person of faith; evil waits for opportune moments."

Bailey's cross felt warm again. She wondered if something otherworldly was going on here, but quickly dismissed the notion.

"Thank you for sharing more of the story," the manager said. "I'll get this info to the police. I've got to close up this place now." She stood and extended her hand.

"I sure hope it helps," Bailey said, as they shook hands.

"You be careful out there."

"Thank you."

Walking back to the car, Mark said, "Wow, that doesn't sound good. I hope your friend is okay."

"Yeah, me too." But 'peace of mind' eluded her. These events amounted to more than just her taking a couple of sick days off work. Jade might be in real trouble.

"I guess we've done all we can do," she stated, looking at Mark with a question in her eyes.

"For now, at least," Mark replied. "All we can do is wait."

Waiting. Waiting was the last thing Bailey wanted to do. She had to do something. But what? She sighed. Her stomach tightened again as her mind pondered the horrifying scenarios of what might have happened to her new friend.

As if reading her thoughts, Mark said, "Hey, how about we take a walk first, then eat a little later?"

"That's a great idea," Bailey said, nodding in agreement. "I couldn't sit still now anyway."

They pulled out of the lot and drove toward the end of the island. At a discrete distance, a black sedan followed.

Chapter 35

The Men in Black

Very few settings, if any, are more romantic than that sandy gulf beach at sunset. They strolled as the fading light painted the sky and clouds in violet-indigo hues. The Gulf turned a deep blue topped with tiny whitecaps. This evening, however, apprehension, not romance, colored Bailey's mood. *Where was Jade? Has something terrible happened to her? Is her absence connected to the report?*

Mark reached for Bailey's hand. She recoiled as if by instinct. Mark looked surprised and a bit disappointed. *He'll just hurt you,* she thought. *'No, he won't,' argued another, deeper voice within.*

She quickly grabbed Mark's hand with both of hers. Despite her fear that she might not survive another heartbreak, somehow, she trusted him.

"It's okay," she said, her heart thumping with both excitement and apprehension.

Mark gently grasped her hand, his fingers interlacing with hers. Bailey felt exhilarated and comforted at the same time. She tightened her clasp, and they exchanged a glance and a smile. She tilted her head back slightly, inviting the warm, humid breeze to caress her face and toss her hair. The air felt as heavy and hot as the longings of the heart. She stopped thinking, let go of the concerns swirling in her mind, and just enjoyed this moment. She even ventured to close her eyes and allow Mark to 'walk her.' At first, she held her eyes shut only for a few seconds, then a few more. She clutched Mark's hand, letting him be her guide. She was surprised how good it felt to let go of control, of worry, even for a moment. She couldn't remember the last time she trusted any man enough to hold his hand and walk alongside him, and never with eyes closed. Her entire body felt more relaxed as if sighing with gratitude. Fret and worry receded, replaced by a serene feeling as she listened to the sounds of the waves crashing and the seagulls calling. The sand squeaked beneath her feet, and occasionally, the ocean lapped her ankles. They strolled hand in hand along their enchanted shoreline, enjoying the bliss of this momentary escape.

Far too soon it seemed, they reached the end of Dauphin Island, the point. Bailey opened her eyes. The waves of the Gulf crashed on their left. She wished she had a catamaran right now. If they ventured right, they would enter the channel separating the island from the mainland. With no place left to walk, they turned toward one another. Bailey reached for Mark's other hand. They stood facing each other, holding hands. Bailey stared at his full lips and wanted to lose herself in a fairy-tale kiss, another feeling that had not visited her for a very long time. Her prince leaned in as she tilted her mouth to meet his. That's when she saw them. Bailey stopped abruptly and squeezed Mark's hands.

Her attention focused inland. "Who are they?" she asked.

Mark looked but didn't answer.

Bailey's internal alarms rang loudly. The two men, dressed entirely in black, stood about 100 yards from them. They didn't look like beachgoers, nor did they seem like just two friends out on a casual after-dinner drive. The strangers were watching them. Bailey's breathing grew shallow and pithy.

"Let's just go around those guys, shall we?" She pulled Mark.

"Good idea," Mark said, keeping his focus on the strangers.

Crab balls! We were just getting to the good part. Bailey huffed. They walked toward the channel side of the point to avoid an encounter. The men in black moved toward them at an angle, closing their distance at a brisk, steady pace. Bailey clung to a desperate fantasy that maybe they were tourists in great need of directions. However, tourists never wear black to the beach, and these men didn't wave nor call out. They just pursued. Mark and Bailey quickened their steps as fast as they could just short of running. The men moved more swiftly as they were still walking on the pavement. That advantage would soon end as the hard ground turned to sand, but not before they closed the gap even further. Bailey quickly looked for another way past them. There was nowhere to go. The advancing strangers cut off their path, blocking any escape route. And worse, she couldn't see anyone else around. The beach was deserted, with no help in sight.

I wish I had my new cell phone, Bailey berated herself. Worry escalated to panic.

"Oh, my God. Oh, my God!" Bailey repeated. She gripped Mark's hand like a vice. "What if they are the same men who followed me?"

Mark said nothing, but his eyes were darting back and forth as if looking for something, someone, any kind of help.

"There!" Mark pointed to a small boat on the shore just up ahead. The craft sat tilted toward one side, anchored to the beach with a short rope attached to a brick. It looked more like a decoration than a working boat. Judging from the chipped wood and faded paint, it appeared that someone had left it to rot. They would have never considered using it any other day, but right now, this was their ride. The only way to escape the two approaching men was to get off the point. That meant either swimming or in a boat.

As soon as Mark pointed to it, he said, " Whoops." In showing Bailey the boat, he had also given away his escape plan to the approaching men.

Bailey judged they were about equidistant from the craft. It was a matter of who would get there first. Almost instinctively, as if their minds were linked, they let go of each other's hands and ran. Simultaneously the men ran after them. The heavier of the two fell behind, but the other one kept pace. He had big, broad shoulders and moved as one accustomed to exercise. He showed no signs of slowing. They would probably get there before him, but not by much.

"We're not going to have a lot of time!" Bailey shouted.

"I know," Mark said between breaths.

When they reached the boat, Mark grabbed the brick make-shift anchor, threw it on board, and yelled, "get in!"

Bailey fell into the dinghy. Mark pushed them away from the shore. His pace slowed as the water crept higher, over his ankles, then to his knees, allowing the lead pursuer time to catch them. Bailey heard the splash when the second pair of feet hit the water. The boat tilted as Mark grabbed the edge and began to pull himself up. Bailey sat up just in time to see two large arms grab Mark from behind, trying to pull him back into the water. Mark's eyes opened wide in surprise. The man wrapped one arm around Mark's waist and curled the other around his neck. He positioned the crook of his elbow just under Mark's chin, his bicep bulging under his wet black shirt like a mighty creepy sea serpent. Forced to let go of the boat's side, Mark grabbed the attacker's elbow pulling hard, trying to loosen his python-like grip. Bailey watched horrified as Mark's eyes bulged, and his face reddened. She heard his eerie gasps for air. Holding tight, the man turned his body sideways, rolling them both underwater. For a few seconds, they disappeared under the murky brackish channel. Suddenly, water splashed right next to the boat, as a foot broke the surface. One of them was kicking, but she couldn't tell who. Then both emerged. Mark remained locked in the man's grip. The two men struggled only a couple of feet away from the port side of the boat. Bailey's heart leaped to her throat when she looked at Mark's eyes. His stare seemed distant, vacant. He squinted as if fighting to hold them open. His face had turned an icy bluish color. *Oh no! He's losing!* His attacker gasped also, and Bailey realized that he had only come up for air. She knew Mark would not survive another submersion.

She searched for some solution. Then she spotted an oar lying in the bottom of the boat. She grabbed it with both hands as strength coursed through her. The paddle felt light and yet solid. She stood tall. The boat bobbed and rocked in the choppy waters, yet somehow, she remained perfectly balanced, bracing herself, each foot against the sides. She lifted the oar high, then swung with all her might. Her swing felt powerful as if gravity itself was energy she wielded. The wooden weapon found its target. A loud crack echoed as the oar connected with the back of the assailant's head. He cried out and let go of his death grip as he put his hand on the back of his skull. Mark elbowed the man's ribs. Bailey wondered how he even had the strength to do that much. The assailant yielded and floated away, coughing and disoriented. Bailey stood tall and triumphant in the boat, holding a paddle over her head. Then, she realized the reprieve would likely be short-lived.

"Get in!" she yelled and reached for Mark.

Mechanically, robotically, he flung his arms over the side, first one then the other. His limbs thumped against the wooden craft like waterlogged futons. He tried to pull himself aboard but only rose partway out of the water before sinking back down. Bailey grabbed him with one hand under his shoulder, and the other pulling his pants from the back waistline.

"Come on, Mark! Stay with me!" She yanked hard, and finally, Mark rolled himself into the boat. He lay on his back, gasping, eyes droopy but no longer bulging quite as much. The larger man had reached his wounded companion staggering back onshore. The assailant still held one hand to the back of his head. Blood trickled through his fingers from the gash Bailey had inflicted.

The larger, slower man yelled at his partner. "What are you doing! We're only supposed to scare them! Not hurt them!"

The wounded man wobbled to his feet, pushing his companion away. The boat had drifted farther away from shore. Bailey sat down and paddled as fast as she could. The distance between them and the danger rapidly increased. The men stood and stared at them for a moment, then hurried toward their car. Bailey continued to paddle with all her might, as the small craft turned the corner and headed up the channel, finally out of sight of their attackers. Convinced they might be safe, at least for now, she fell back panting, limbs limp at her side.

Mark, more alert now and eyes brighter, stared at Bailey-turned-Wonder-Woman. His face expressed a look of amazement and bewilderment that conveyed both 'Who are you, Bailey?' and 'What have you gotten yourself into?'

Bailey raised her eyebrows as if to say she was just as surprised by her recent heroics.

"Can we go eat now?" Mark finally said with a chuckle.

Chapter 36

Row, Row, Row Your Boat

Bailey sat back and watched Mark row them forward along the channel. She caught herself staring. His soaked shirt revealed a muscular chest and toned abs flexing in concert with each stroke of the paddle. The heat of the Mobile night surrounded them like a sauna. His clothes wouldn't dry out anytime soon, which was just fine with her. The moist, hot air, the cadence of the night creatures, and the moonlight sparkling on Mark's wet forearms felt like catnip to this girl from the Gulf. Mark noticed her gawking and smiled. She quickly glanced away, suppressing an embarrassed smile and hoping the dim light of dusk would hide her blushing cheeks.

What am I thinking about at a time like this? Some creepy guys are trying to get us, and our only escape is this old rowboat. Admiring Mark's abs would have to wait, as would that kiss, apparently. But she knew it would be worth it.

The water remained perfectly still except for the ripples as the boat glided along. The paddle swished, and the vessel lurched forward. Mark's pace slowed since their pursuers were no longer in sight. Even if they were running alongside the bank, thick brush and undergrowth created a barrier between the channel and the island, and the darkness made it impossible to see through from either side. The only breaks in this natural wall occurred whenever they encountered a house or a dock. Every home they saw seemed forbidding—no lights in the windows, no signs of life inside, probably because most of the houses along this stretch belonged to the more wealthy who used them as a weekend getaway.

The bad guys were still out there, lurking. Bailey shivered at the thought of them waiting behind some dark corner. She suddenly felt exposed and vulnerable.

Bailey said, "Maybe we should break into one of those houses and call the police."

Mark shook his head. "That occurred to me too, but I don't think they would believe us. What would we say? Two strange guys are chasing us, so we had to bust your window? They keep a watchful eye for break-ins down here."

Bailey looked puzzled. "Well, yes, exactly, that's what we would say." She couldn't hide her slight agitation. "Because two guys *are* chasing us. One of them tried to drown you!"

"I know, I was there!" Mark fired back. Immediately he closed his mouth as if he just revealed a side he'd rather not show. He took a beat, composing himself before continuing. "It's just that break-ins are common in these houses, usually by young couples looking for… um… privacy."

"Oh. No way."

"Way."

"Still, at least we'd be safer than out here." Bailey sensed something else about Mark's resistance to go to the police. She wondered why he seemed hesitant. Hiding in a house struck her as their best option. She didn't press for an explanation, hoping patience would coax an answer from him. They glided in silence.

Then Mark said in a softer, lower voice, "I don't know where those men are. Okay? They can't get to us in the boat, but if we put in at the wrong house and they are nearby… also, many of these owners turn off the water and phone services while they are not here. It's a crapshoot if we hit the right house with both service and no bad guys."

He looked apprehensive, then he turned his head and spoke again in that softer, vulnerable voice. "Bailey, the man who tried to drown me… I can't take him. He's too strong."

His words felt as heavy as the humid air around them. The thought of Mark fighting for his life caused a pain in her heart. The near-death experience seemed to open an emotional wound for Mark, a laceration to his confidence. She recognized the look of fear on his face, and she felt afraid too. Her heart swelled with compassion and warm affection for him. Though his esteem as a man had taken a hit, Bailey saw him as courageous. She recognized the sheer strength it took to reveal his fear to her and acknowledge his defeat.

She reached out and touched his arm. "Maybe you're right. I do feel safer in this boat. Let's keep paddling for a while. We'll figure it out."

He looked at her tenderly, and Bailey could feel his appreciation for her understanding. He didn't need to say anything.

"Well, you're right, too. We have to go somewhere," Mark said. "We can't just keep paddling along the channel."

"No, we can't." Although part of her hoped they could stay in their cozy craft for a while longer. Then she sat up a little straighter. "Oh, no!"

"What? What is it?" Mark focused intently.

"There is an intersection where the road crosses the channel." She was on edge again. "I remember it because I was struck by the view when I drove across. They could catch up with us there! It's a long drive but, with a car, they could get there first."

"Crap! We're not safe in the boat either," Mark said, frustrated. He breathed more rapidly. "Okay, okay, let's think. If we get there first, where would we go? We can't just keep paddling out into the bay."

They pondered the situation. There seemed no safe way off the island. Maybe hiding for tonight might be the only option—row the boat ashore, and take their chances on finding a safe house. Then they looked at each other and simultaneously said, "The ferry!"

The Mobile Bay Ferry escorted cars and passengers daily from Dauphin Island to Fort Morgan. Could they reach it in time?

Mark glanced at his watch. "It's eight forty."

"The last ferry leaves at nine," Bailey exclaimed. "Paddle!"

Neither said it out loud, but the math didn't add up. Twenty minutes in a rowboat, with only one oar, they would never make it in time, even with two people taking turns rowing. The physics were impossible.

Still, they rowed. After several minutes, Mark finally leaned back, panting heavily, exhausted. He handed Bailey the paddle, rechecked his watch, then let his arm drop as if he just lifted a ten-pound weight. His hand twitched, either from exhaustion or nerves.

"We're never going to make it," he said.

Bailey paddled frantically. "We have to make it."

But she doubted her own words. She paddled more frantically, drawing on a deep well of frustration and fear. She rowed, first the left side, then the right, stabbing the water with the oar then pulling back hard as she could. Three strokes on the left, now right, then, as she shifted the paddle from one side to the other, it hit the edge of the boat with a loud clang. The sudden jolt knocked it loose from Bailey's hand and sent it flying forward just off to Mark's left. It hit the water with a slap and began to drift away.

Bailey yelled and reached for it, tilting the boat to one side. But she wasn't even close.

"The paddle! Grab it!"

Mark quickly extended his arm and grasped the floating oar, but as he pulled himself upright, he knocked his hand against the edge of the boat, jarring it loose. He stretched across the water again as far as he could. This time his middle finger touched the tip of the oar and inadvertently pushed it farther away beyond his reach.

"Dammit!" All he could do was watch as the wooden blade floated away, disappearing into the darkness behind them. The momentum from rowing and the slight current carried them onward.

"I can't believe this night!" Bailey yelled. "Aaaagggggghhhh! Crab balls!"

Mark scrunched his forehead, and half smiled, looking at Bailey as if he adored her even more for her strange expressions. Then he chuckled and said, "I guess we're up the creek without a paddle."

"You can make jokes at a time like this?" Bailey said, astonished and slightly peeved. She tried not to smile. Then she chuckled, too. "Okay, that's funny."

"Sorry, Bailey, sometimes I think the funniest things when I'm stressed."

He stared at the water as if trying to see where the paddle might have floated. Bailey squinted against the night but saw no sign of it. Mark sat up and looked around.

Bailey knew what he was thinking. "Don't go after it."

"But we gotta have it. Besides, it couldn't have drifted far."

"There's gators in these waters, and moccasins, too. It's a hot night. They'll be out and about."

"Believe me, I don't want to get in this water," he said. "But what choice do we have?"

Bailey squinted and pointed up ahead. "I think I see it."

Mark turned to get a look. "Where?"

"Just up on the right. See it sticking out?"

A long dark shape protruded by the reeds near the bank.

"Oh, what luck," Mark said as they began to paddle with their hands toward their missing oar.

When their small boat got close enough, Mark reached for it.

"No, wait!" Bailey said, but it was too late. As soon as Mark grabbed the object, it moved, whipping violently at Mark's touch. A greenish bumpy scaled head abruptly surfaced, eyes bulging.

"Gator!" Bailey yelled.

Its broad, rounded u-shaped snout opened wide, bearing its sharp pointy teeth. The gator hissed and turned toward them. Instinctively, both recoiled. The momentum of shifting their weight simultaneously to one side proved too much for the small craft. It tipped, dumping both of them into the water.

Bailey broke the surface, eyes frantically searching. "Where is it?"

"I don't know," Mark yelled as he treaded water a few feet away.

Bailey's heart pounded with enough energy to power an outboard motor. It wouldn't do any good now, as their craft had turned upside down and was already half-submerged.

"There it is!" she yelled. Two bulbous, periscope like eyes glided toward them, gently swerving left to right. It approached with the cross-eyed vacant look of a mind-less eating machine.

They paddled on their backs, afraid to take their eyes off the advancing creature. It would have been faster to turn over and swim for it, but Bailey knew that you couldn't out swim a gator. Maybe she could kick it away when it tried to bite.

Just then, a bright light shined upon them from a nearby cove. The creature's eyes glowed white. Seem-ingly disoriented, the gator stopped and swam away. They could now see its full length, about ten feet from tip to tail.

Then a voice behind them said, "Would you two quit making so much noise?"

Chapter 37

Saved by a Cricket

The voice sounded familiar, but Bailey couldn't quite place it. When the light lowered, she could make out the shadowy silhouette of a man sitting in a small chair on the front of an old boat. It resembled a bass boat, though definitely not like the ones in the store. This one looked homemade, complete with the scrapes and dings of many fishing adventures.

Bailey blurted out, "Mister, we need your help, there are these two guys…"

"Bailey?" the man said. "Is that you?"

She paused, surprised that the stranger had called her by name. Again, his voice seemed familiar.

"Do I know you?"

The man swiveled his chair slightly and pressed a pedal on the floor with his foot. An electric trolling motor hummed, and the water rippled as the boat silently glided toward them. He pulled alongside. He wore an old green fishing vest over a shirt and a dirty camouflage ball cap with the phrase 'I'd rather be fishing' embroidered across the front.

"Cricket!" Bailey splashed with excitement, then quickly stopped as to not attract any more predators. "Cricket! I can hardly believe it! What are you doing here?"

"I'm fishin'." He looked at Mark, then back to Bailey. "What are *you* doing here? And what 'n heaven's name y'all doin' in the water?"

The fisherman helped them into his boat—only slightly larger than their sunken one.

"Mark, this is Cricket, a longtime friend from Lost Key."

"Very, very pleased to meet you." Mark shook his hand vigorously.

Cricket looked at him curiously. "Anybody ever told you it ain't a good idea to grab a gator's tail?"

Mark chuckled. "Of course. I thought it was our paddle."

"Figured as much. I thought I'd better scoot over here and see if y'all needed any help.

"When Cricket is not fishing, he runs the car wash," Bailey explained. "Oh, Cricket, you're not gonna believe what has happened to us this evening."

They explained the situation to their fisherman friend, who listened intently, shaking his head from time to time. He shined the light toward their boat, now almost entirely submerged.

"Well, y'all ain't goin' anywhere in that thang." He glanced at his watch and said, "I know Cap'n Ron, who runs the Ferry. It's a slow tourist weekend. So, he'll likely leave a bit early. Your best bet is to get to the police station. Though I betcha there's only a skeleton crew, one maybe two people on duty." He rechecked his watch. "They may even be on their rounds by now."

"You know their schedule?" Mark asked.

"I've been fishin' here for a while. We'll start with the police station, but at least I'll get y'all out of here to a safer place."

"Oh, thank you so much, Cricket," Bailey said. She hugged him and sat on the deck toward the front.

Mark made his way to the middle. Then he said, "My car! I left it at the beach."

"Police will find it." Cricket lifted the trolling motor out of the water. "They patrol this island thoroughly."

"It will corroborate our story," Bailey added.

"Good point," Mark said and sat down on the bench that ran across the middle. "I sure don't want to go back there now. Better to wait till tomorrow."

Cricket planted himself in the very back, next to the main engine. He motioned for Bailey to sit on the boat's floor so as not to block his view. The refurbished boat had been designed for only two passengers comfortably. "Let's get out of here then," he said.

One pull on the starter cord, and his outboard motor shook with a steady rumble. He turned the throttle of the small engine as far as it would go. It whined, spat out a stream of water, and the craft lurched forward.

Mark turned toward Cricket. "Hey, you want me to shine the light out in front like a headlight?"

Cricket shook his head. "No. Might give our position away to those guys chasing you. The engine is gonna be loud enough. We don't need to shine a light for 'em too."

Mark nodded.

"Don't worry," Cricket said, "I know these waters better than the back of my hand. I can navigate this channel in my sleep."

He steered the craft expertly through the winding channel as if driving from memory down a path he'd traveled many times before.

Bailey peered but couldn't see more than twenty feet in the pitch darkness. She thought she heard Cricket chuckle with delight over the high pitch of the engine. She looked back and saw he had a smile pasted across his face. They rounded a turn that opened into a broader, straighter stretch. Up ahead, they could barely make out a bridge that crossed the channel. Beyond that, the passage poured into the bay. They were on the home stretch. Bailey could see the path ahead now. The foliage parted, and the full bright moon hung low in the sky like God's nightlight.

Mark called back to Bailey, "There's the bridge up ahead. We'll go under that and then to the station."

Just then, a black car began to cross the bridge. It slowed to a stop halfway across. Two shadowy figures emerged from the vehicle. Even silhouetted against the moonlight, Bailey knew who they were.

"That's them!" she pointed. "Those are the men chasing us."

Cricket nodded that he understood. The boat sped forward. One of the men, the slimmer one, reached behind him and pulled an object. Bailey couldn't quite make it out, but it fit in his hand. He raised his arm toward them. Moonlight reflected off a smooth metallic surface.

"Oh no, that's a…" They heard three distinct sounds 'pop, pop, pop,' followed almost instantly by the swish, swish of two bullets hitting the water, and a loud clang as the third glanced off the boat.

"They're shooting at us!" Cricket shouted. All three ducked.

Mark said, "I can't believe it! They're actually shooting at us!"

Again, they heard a pop, pop, followed by a swish and then clank. The last bullet didn't glance the boat; it hit directly. Water poured in from the new hole.

"We are taking on water!" Mark sat up.

"Stay down!" Bailey yelled.

"Dang it to hell; they shot my boat!" Cricket yelled.

He swerved left, then right, then right, left, right, making them harder to hit. Bailey's breath grew shallow and rapid. Her eyes darted back and forth, searching for some point of reference, some safe fixture to anchor herself. A wave of nausea stirred in her stomach.

Mark reached for her arm. "Hang in there."

Bailey said, "What else am I gonna do, go for a swim?"

Mark yelled back at Cricket, "You gotta pull over. We can't keep going to that bridge. We're sitting ducks!"

"I know a shortcut, hold tight." Cricket showed no intention of stopping, nor of turning around.

As far as anyone could tell, there were no shortcuts, only thick brush on either side. Their fisherman friend continued to weave and swerve the boat like a mad captain. Bailey expected more shots, but they didn't come. She glanced up and saw the two men arguing. The one with the gun pushed the other one away. Then he lifted his hand, aiming for another round of shots. This time they were a lot closer.

"Get down! He's going to shoot again!" Bailey screamed. They ducked. They waited for the popping sounds, or the swish, or worse. Suddenly, Cricket took a hard, right turn and headed straight for the bank at full speed. Bailey's eyes fixed wide in disbelief. She screamed.

Cricket yelled, "Whoo-rah!"

They hunkered down and braced for impact. But instead of hitting the embankment, miraculously, the boat kept going. Branches scratched and screeched against the metal hull as they penetrated the underbrush. The shortcut seemed more like a gauntlet guarded by a monster with a thousand fingers grasping for its prey. Only the worthy could pass. Abruptly, the piercing sounds of nature against aluminum stopped, and they seemed to weigh nothing at all. Bailey floated ever so slightly off the bottom of the boat. Then they hit hard with a splash. Everyone jolted and grunted. Bailey's head smashed against the metal seat. They had burst through the other side of the thicket and became airborne for a few seconds before they landed in the bay.

Cricket let out a hearty laugh. "That's what I'm talkin' about!"

Bailey looked back and saw the bridge receding in the distance, with two men staring at them. Cricket steered right again, guiding the boat around the bend. Up ahead of them, the ferry was just pulling away. They all waved their arms and screamed. "Wait! Over here! Wait!"

The ferry slowed, and the refugee boat pulled alongside.

The captain came out. "Cricket, is that you? What the world are you doing?"

"Just fishin'," he said. "Only tonight I caught these two swimmin' with the 'gators. They need a lift somethin' fierce."

The captain raised an eyebrow on his sea-weathered face. "Looks like you do too, my friend."

They all noticed the water rapidly filling the boat. The flow came in from a second breach, a much larger hole in the hull's bottom right.

"Dang it to hell!" Cricket exclaimed, slapping his cap on his knee.

"Looks like that other bullet didn't bounce off," Bailey commented.

"No, that hole is too big to come from a bullet," Cricket said. "I think maybe one of the branches must have poked through an old rust spot."

"Bullet?" the ferry captain asked, helping them climb on board. "You mean somebody was shooting at y'all?"

"Afraid so, my friend."

Quickly they climbed onto the ferry, then watched as the old fishing boat slowly faded underwater. Bailey felt Cricket's heart sink with it. She put her arm on his shoulder.

"So sorry."

"You're gonna need a new boat," the captain said.

Cricket sighed, staring as his floating companion disappeared into its watery grave. "Me and her been together a while. I just got her good 'n broke in. And that engine was new!"

"Well, at least you're safe. Welcome aboard," Captain Ron said.

"We should call the police," Bailey said. "I mean, those guys tried to kill us."

The captain frowned but remained calm, methodical. "Ma'am, you're bleeding."

Bailey touched the right side of her head where it had connected with the hard metal. Then she looked at her fingers, now stained red. "I guess I hit my head harder than I thought."

The captain motioned to a crewman.

"Anyone got a phone?" Mark asked.

"We got a radio, and we'll call the Coast Guard." Then the captain turned to the crewman. "Grab the first-aid kit and get on the radio. We need to let them…"

He stopped mid-sentence as his eyes peeled wide, his face a look of shock and disbelief. Everyone turned to see a bright ball of fire raging in the distance just down the shoreline. The flames flickered wild and angry, challenging anyone who dared to come near. They all walked to the railing and strained to get a better view.

The captain spoke again to a young man in uniform. "Get on the horn and tell the Guard we got a fire at the Marine Center."

Chapter 38

Safe

"You mean the Dauphin Island Marine Center is burning?" Bailey asked.

The captain nodded. "It's after hours, so hopefully no one's there."

Everyone watched mesmerized as the hot, insatiable flames cast a hypnotic spell. Just a few minutes later, they saw the flashing lights of fire trucks and a rescue vehicle. Bailey felt both relieved and impressed by the quick response of the emergency departments.

Mark leaned closer to Bailey. "You don't think those two goons did that, do you?"

"I don't know what to think anymore." She stared at the fire, clutching her cross. *I hope no one was hurt. Jade, wherever you are, stay put. This 'accident' shouldn't have happened.*

The crewman returned a little out of breath and carrying a first aid kit. "Coast Guard on the way, sir! The fire department is responding, too." Then he whispered something into the captain's ears.

The captain nodded and muttered, "Good work, son, let's pray no one's hurt." He turned to the passengers. "Okay, everyone, we've got seating inside upstairs with plenty of windows and warm coffee. Make yourselves comfortable; we'll be at our destination in about 30 minutes." Just to his new passengers, he said, "The authorities will be waiting for you on the other side. They'll take your statements there. You're safe for now."

They thanked the captain again, then went upstairs. The chairs were a welcome relief. The crewman cleaned and dressed Bailey's wound while Mark brought them all some coffee. Bailey took a drink, and the hot beverage warmed her body. Her mind searched for answers but still couldn't make sense of these events. She felt numb, unable to accept what just happened.

"Were they really trying to kill us?" she said in disbelief.

"That man would have drowned me if you hadn't conked him over the head," Mark said.

"Yeah, I'd say they were trying to kill us," Cricket added. "I got bullet holes in my boat to prove it."

"I overheard one of them yelling at the other that they weren't supposed to hurt us, just scare us," Bailey said.

"Well, it worked." Mark sipped his coffee, his tremors less noticeable now.

"I saw them arguing again on the bridge before we took Cricket's shortcut. Do you think he was shooting at the boat, and not us?"

"He'd have to be a pretty good shot to pull that off," Cricket said.

"Yes, but... why? Why chase us at all?" Bailey wondered. "Who are we to them? Who are they, for that matter?"

No one had any answers.

Cricket gazed at the fading ball of fire onshore. "It's a shame that place is going up in flames. Lots of kids will be disappointed. Good people work there. DMC has been a staple on that island. But, if I know that community, they'll build that thang back, no time."

"What if it's not an accident?" Bailey said. "I just don't have a good feeling in my gut about this one."

"I don't either," Mark said. "How could we? Someone just tried to end us."

"Anythang could have started that fire," Cricket said. "Faulty wire, maybe someone left one of them test tube burners on. Who knows?"

"Why would anyone want to torch the Marine Center?" Mark wondered aloud.

"Some people 're just broke inside," Cricket reasoned and sipped his hot beverage.

"But what if it does have something to do with those guys that were chasing us?" Bailey said.

"Okay," Mark said. "So, who are those guys, anyway?"

Cricket spoke up. "I never really got a clear look at 'em, but I started seeing strangers just a few weeks back."

Bailey and Mark focused on him.

"I've been fishin' these waters regular for several years. I know every sound, every movement. I know when somethin' ain't right, or someone don't belong. Been noticin' strangers driving a car, but they never did nothin'. Or at least not that I could tell. Certainly, nothin' I could tell the police about. First off, I figured they might be lookin' for a place to live. They sure don't seem like tourists, though."

"Well, we're fortunate you were there tonight, Cricket." Bailey hugged him again. "You saved us." Then she asked, "It's a long way from Lost Key. You come to fish here a lot?"

"I've got many fishing spots, Bailey. Been comin' here lately since the oil done messed up Lost Key. Fishing there ain't good right now."

"That's it!" Bailey sparked. "What if... what if it's about the oil?" She could tell that neither of them followed her reasoning. "What if they work for Acheron? What if they are Martin's minions?" She thought for a moment. "Of course, that has to be it."

Still, she got blank stares from both men. She stood and began pacing.

"Okay, follow this. My best friend Keri works for NOAA. She sent some oil samples for testing to the Dauphin Island Marine Center. It's a matter of routine. The samples came from the oil spill that has been polluting Lost Key. She was waiting for Jade to get back to her. I went down there to pick up that test result."

Mark said, "If we hadn't been shot at tonight, I might say you're reaching. But it makes sense. Except we have no proof. And it still doesn't explain why they are targeting us."

"Unless they think we know something? But what?" Bailey mused.

Mark shrugged.

Cricket gazed into the distant night like he was tracking down a memory. "You know, come to think of it, I saw some strange things back in Lost Key since the oil showed up." He looked back at Mark and Bailey. "Lately, I've seen two other fellers fishin' in a boat, mostly at night. Their boat moved slow and silent, no lights. I figured they got a trollin' motor like me. The thing is, they were a little far out, you know, a little too far offshore to catch anything good, especially at night. Everyone knows that."

Bailey nodded even though she didn't know what Cricket meant. He continued. "The fish like to stay up near the reeds in the bank, at least the ones I fish for. Another thing, I thought odd that their fishing poles were just layin' in the boat and stickin' over the side. They should be propped up when trollin'. If a fish did strike the bait, they'd pull that rod right out of the boat before they knew what hit 'em. And here's the kicker, they seemed to be going back and forth across the mouth of Lost Key Cove, which made no sense at all. Then they hurried off quietly as they came. Seen them guys a couple of times now. Always at night."

"That is odd," Mark said.

"Ah, tourists. They don't know what they're doing. Not too friendly either. They'll probably be leaving soon. But between them and that black crud polluting everythang, I figured in the meantime I'd just come over here and visit my Dauphin Island spots."

Bailey's intuition told her Cricket's story was important. She knew he just gave her a key piece of the puzzle but didn't quite know where it fit. She grasped her cross and felt a warmth radiating.

Mark said, "What? What is it, Bailey?"

"Hmm, I don't know yet. But…" She shook her head. "I don't know yet."

The captain walked up to them. "Good news. They got the fire contained at the Marine Center. And no one was hurt."

"Oh, thank goodness," Bailey said.

"The fire chief said it looks like it started in one of the labs. So, it could have been a faulty burner or something. They won't know more until after the investigation."

Bailey looked at Cricket. He shrugged.

The captain continued. "The tourist part of the lab seems okay, just a bit of smoke damage. Firefighters caught it early, so the DMC should be up and running in a week or so. They just won't be doing any research for a while. We also notified the sheriff's office, and they'll be waiting to take you three home when we dock in about ten minutes."

"Thanks, Captain." Cricket, Bailey, and Mark responded almost in unison.

"Anytime. Glad y'all are safe."

Chapter 39

What the…?

*B*ailey woke the next morning, the sun a quarter way up the sky. *Must be ten or later,* she thought, realizing that she'd fallen asleep in the lounge chair on her best friend's houseboat like she had done many times, and that Keri had again covered her in a blanket. She felt grateful for her friend. Bailey moved gingerly, her shoulders and back ached, and her forehead throbbed where she had hit the boat seat. Her whole body felt sluggish and heavy. She only had a few sips of drink last night, so this was another kind of hangover—the one you get from being chased by bad guys, almost eaten by an alligator, and from dodging bullets, when all you wanted to do was walk on the beach with your date.

Keri appeared in the doorway wearing her ball cap, official navy blue shirt, and tan shorts of NOAA. "Well, look who's up."

"Oh… not really." Bailey pushed herself up, surprised by how much effort it took just to accomplish that.

"I'm so glad you're okay." Keri's statement sounded like a question. "You need some rest now."

"Yeah, I'm gonna hang out this weekend… go to the Tropical Palm… drop by the old office and say hello to MJ."

"And?" Keri prodded.

"What? Oh, yes, rest."

"And go see Mark, let him make you a po'boy."

Mark had promised to make Bailey his famous fried shrimp po'boy sandwich.

Bailey winked. "You know it."

Keri grabbed her life jacket and headed for her WaveRunner, "Well, I gotta go to work. Mi casa es su casa!"

Bailey put up her hand, and Keri high-fived it as she passed.

"Oh, hey, I need to borrow your truck!" Her car was still in Mobile.

"Sure thing. You know where the keys are." Keri pressed the ignition, and the engine sparked to life. She pulled back the throttle, and the small craft lunged forward, speeding her down the Intracoastal.

More awake and hungry, Bailey showered, then changed into some spare clothes she kept at Keri's. She called her mom to let her know all that happened and promised to see her later so that she could hang up. Then she got in Keri's small, old pickup truck and drove toward the Tropical Palm. Her mouth watered already at the thought of crunching down crispy hash browns. She could almost hear the bacon popping and the eggs sizzling on the grill. She rolled down the window to let the hot, humid air bathe her skin. It felt good to be in Lost Key; it felt normal. The seagulls, the palms trees waving under a deep blue sky, and even the cadence of the bugs along the marshy waters were the comforts of home. All her senses drank it in, recharging her Bailey batteries. She chuckled, relieved that Lost Key still had this rejuvenating effect upon her. Yet, an uneasiness had settled upon her over the past few days, and it wouldn't leave. The monsters were real and getting closer to home.

Her shoulders loosened. She felt safe and anonymous, driving Keri's truck. Any bad guys pursuing her would be looking for a bright yellow Jeep, not an old faded blue Chevy pickup. That made her friend's vehicle invisible to the strange stalker's radar. She shook her head, recalling the events of last evening. *Who were those guys? I can't believe I got shot at.* In her mind, she saw the shooter again, taking aim. *He had us right in his sights at the end. Why didn't he fire? Was he only trying to scare us? Well, it worked!*

About ten minutes later, stomach rumbling, she arrived at the Tropical Palm. A new 'Future Site of Treasure Cove' sign by Acheron Developers replaced the old one she had driven over last week. She smiled and thought about plowing down this one, too. But then something in the distance caught her attention. She stared out the window, astonished. A good-sized yellow backhoe sat anchored at the far end of the parking lot. Though idle now, it had already scraped a pile of earth next to it on the left side. Clods of dirt clung to the teeth where the beast had chewed its gaping hole in the land, the Tropical Palm land. The truck slowly drifted to a stop in the middle of the parking lot, Bailey's attention captivated by the monstrous machine.

"What the ...?" she exclaimed.

She climbed out for a closer look. The hole was about three feet by four feet, and about four feet deep. It was near the bay's edge, and water had begun to fill the cavity as the tide crept higher. Bailey couldn't figure the purpose for such an odd dig, but her inner alarm bells rang loudly. Whatever reason would be given, she already knew it wouldn't be the real one. Her stomach rumbled again. Bailey ambled inside, so preoccupied with this new development that she left the truck parked in the middle of the lot.

"Hey! How's my Bailey!" Max shouted from the grill as soon as she opened the door.

"Hey, Max! Better now." She sauntered up to the counter and bounced onto her favorite stool like it was her home kitchen.

Mary poured her some coffee and hugged her. "Welcome home, girl."

"It feels great to be here."

"Enjoy it while you can, hon. We ain't going to be here for too much longer."

"Yeah, I saw the new sign just now." Then she motioned her head toward the window. "What's with that thing?"

"Get this," Mary said, raising one eyebrow, "he says it's for collecting soil samples."

"With a backhoe?"

"Exactly." Max's voice echoed from the kitchen. He peered out the serving window at Bailey. "It's more like he's looking for something if you ask me."

Bailey nodded. "Yeah, using a backhoe for soil samples is like Keri using a barrel to collect a water sample."

Max winked and made a clicking noise then went back to cooking.

"Isn't there anything you can do—we can do? Let's fight this." Bailey already knew the answer, but it felt good to ask the question.

Mary set a place mat in front of Bailey and arranged a napkin and utensils beside it. "I wish we could, hon, but legally there's not much we can do about it."

"MJ told me the story."

Mary seemed relieved not to have to explain that part. Then she said sadly, "It's like we were never meant to be here in the first place."

"Or maybe you were," Bailey countered. "Maybe that's why it happened the way it did in the first place."

Mary patted her arm. "I like that."

"I believe it," Bailey emphasized. "Everyone in town loves this place. That's why no one ever did anything to correct the lot lines or change the zoning."

"Because no one knew, at least not till this Martin fella."

"No one knew, because you are supposed to be here," Bailey said emphatically, surprised how much she sounded like her Aunt Lee.

She felt the strong arm of Max hug her shoulder. She leaned into his grandfatherly embrace, as he set a piping hot 'Bailey Special' down in front of her.

"Well, all things come to an end, too, sweetheart," Max said. "Don't get me wrong; I was mad. I don't like this pirate one bit."

Bailey almost choked on her food. "Pirate? Who said anything about a pirate?"

Max smiled. "Well, that's what I call him. He's plundering my diner. Now he's even digging holes like he's looking for buried treasure."

Mary just shook her head in an isn't-he-adorable kind of way.

Then Max's face looked forlorn. "I just feel grateful to have had this place for so long. Honestly, I never got comfortable carrying that secret around. I'm glad it's coming out in the open. I wish this all had a better ending, but that's life. You don't always get what you want." He jostled Bailey's shoulder. "But you just know this, Bailey; you always have a place to come home to. It may not be here, but we'll cook you breakfast in our house."

"Any time," Mary added.

Bailey smiled. "I love y'all, too."

Then she saw the blank space on the wall above her head where the picture of the treasure map used to hang.

"What happened to your map, Max?"

"He took it."

"What!"

"Said it was his now."

"He can't do that. The deal hasn't closed yet."

"It's okay. You know I found it in that old shed out back."

"But you love that old map. Finders keepers."

"That's funny. Martin said something similar. Whatever anyone finds on this property is his now or something like that."

"This guy is unbelievable, a mental case," Bailey said.

"Aahhh, eat your breakfast before it gets cold. I made it special for ya." Max tossed his dish towel over his shoulder and headed back to the grill.

Bailey took a bite of hash browns. They were every bit as delicious as she imagined them to be, and her stomach warmed, grateful to finally have food in it.

Mary began clearing the leftover dishes from the last patron a couple of seats over. "The oil spill sure made a perfect opportunity for a man like Martin. It practically handed him the marshland. Of course, he has to be willing to clean up the slimy mess."

Bailey's chewing slowed as she listened. *That's just what I thought. The timing of this is super convenient for him.* Images flickered in her mind. She saw brief but disjointed mental pictures of men trolling in a boat, a shadowy figure leaning over some files researching, Martin's face surrounded by flames. *Na. Come on, Bailey, you're just tired.* She tried to dismiss the strange visions as random weird thoughts; then, she realized she had been fidgeting with her cross. Somehow, she just knew these flashes revealed more pieces of the enigmatic puzzle. She shook her head and took another savory bite of breakfast. Like the lenses on a long-exposure camera, her eyes slowly surveyed the diner, attempting to imprint this moment forever. She took extra care to notice all the sounds, all the decor, everything that made the Tropical Palm special. She was not sure how many more meals she'd have here, not sure if this was the last breakfast. *Okay, Bailey, enough. Let's get on with the day.* She finished her coffee, paid her bill, and hugged Max and Mary.

Chapter 40

Who is Mr. Delahaye?

With the truck idling, Bailey sat behind the wheel, looking at the worn multicolored office that used to be a bar. The falling-down gutter and fading paint job adorned the building like the familiar outfit of an old friend. She chuckled, turned off the ignition, and stepped out into the hot afternoon. The bell jingled as she opened the front door and went inside. The only sounds above the oscillating fan were the familiar snores of Eddie.

She shook her head. *Yep, no place like home.*

MJ hurried out of her office, arms open, and hugged Bailey tight. "The prodigal daughter has returned." Then she crooked her head to one side. "You okay? You don't look like you feel so good."

Bailey shook her head. "I don't."

"Come on in my office." Then MJ crumpled up a piece of paper and tossed it at Eddie. The wad found its target. She had become skilled at these napping-paper-tosses. "Wake up! This office ain't your living room."

Eddie stirred and began shuffling some loose forms on the desk, pretending he had been working.

MJ closed the door behind them. They sat on her couch as Bailey told the whole story again. As MJ listened, her expressions changed from surprise to disbelief and then shock with each revelation of the winding tale. Recounting her experience, Bailey realized how much she had been through these last couple of weeks.

MJ fetched a glass of water and gave it to Bailey. "Any word from the police?"

Bailey took a refreshing drink, using both hands to steady her grip. "No, not yet."

"That's a rough start, to say the least."

"Ann's already getting frustrated with me. I can tell."

"Well, none of this is your fault. But at the end of the day, real estate is a business."

Bailey took another sip, ready to talk about something else. "Speaking of business, how are things going here?"

MJ struggled to her feet and sat on the edge of her desk. "Well, the deal is still on. We are closing next week."

"You don't sound very excited."

"I guess I have mixed feelings. The money's okay, but I'm going to miss this place, and the Tropical Palm. I'm sad about the changes in Lost Key."

Bailey nodded quietly. She shared the feeling. "Is the town hall meeting still happening?"

"Tuesday night."

"Have you seen the backhoe at the Tropical Palm? Since when does one dig a ditch to take a soil sample?"

MJ rolled her eyes. "Since when does Martin do anything normal?"

"Max thinks he's looking for something."

MJ smiled. "He probably thinks he's a pirate."

"Yep."

"Hmm," MJ leaned her head curiously. "Well, if he did find something of value, he could now claim ownership."

"He already took Max's treasure map."

MJ looked surprised. "That's presumptuous. Why would he do that?"

"I don't know, giant ego, I guess."

Again, her former broker's face took on a puzzled look. "You know, I still can't figure out how Martin knew about the zoning. I didn't even know that we hold title to the land the Tropical Palm is sitting on. That was a very well-buried secret. I suppose if you searched hard enough, you could find it. Still, he'd have to know where to look."

"Or know the history."

"Yes! Maybe that's why he seems familiar to me," MJ said. "Could he be local?"

"I've never seen him before."

MJ looked thoughtful. "Maybe he used to live here."

Bailey felt her cross warm, and her insides tingle. She knew that her friend spoke the truth. She just didn't know how it fit with the whole picture yet, nor even what that entire picture looked like. But everything kept leading back to this strange developer who had sailed into their world.

"So, who is Martin Delahaye?"

MJ shrugged. "Well, one thing is for sure—he's the buyer, regardless of where he came from."

"There's something 'off' about him."

"We've gone over this already."

"No, MJ, I mean spooky off."

Her mentor nodded, acknowledging that she took Bailey's comment seriously, and said, "It's just a business deal, and as you already know, the only one in sight.

Heck, I half expected to be out of business in about six months or so before this came along."

Bailey squinted her eyes, searching for something.

"What?" MJ asked.

Bailey touched her cross. "I'm not sure. It's just… I can't get over how convenient these circumstances are for him."

"Martin's an opportunist, I'll give you that. And he's in the right place at the right time. But really, I think he will lose money in the end. The cleanup will take a long time; the ecosystem will take years to recover. I don't see how the values will go up anytime soon."

"Yet he keeps wanting more. First here, then it's the marshland, and now we find out the Tropical Palm is part of the deal too. Why would he pour money into an obviously bad investment?"

Margaret Jane threw up her hands. "I don't know, but it's time to take the money and run. Get out while we can. That's why you need to make Mobile work."

"Yeah, I guess so. I just keep hoping for some miracle solution. Maybe I'm just grieving." Bailey sat quietly, absorbed by this mystery, gently playing with her necklace.

MJ touched her protégé's shoulder. "Bailey, you gotta make Mobile work. You hear me?" Her tone was somber, one last counsel from her trusted mentor.

Bailey nodded but didn't say anything.

"Time to let go of this place. Mobile hasn't seen Bailey yet. Go over there and show them what you got."

Bailey managed a half-smile. "Thanks, I will," she said flatly.

MJ reached into her desk drawer, pulled out a set of keys, and tossed them to Bailey. "This is why you really stopped by."

Bailey caught the keys one-handed. "Well, I wanted to see you, too." She smiled big and hurried out the door and into her Jeep.

Chapter 41

Shrimp Po'boy

The next day Bailey drove over to Gulf Shores, finding the last parking space at Neptune Seafood. The line spilled out the door with folks waiting to buy an assortment of fresh catches. A man and woman worked behind the counter, assisting the customers like old friends. The man's silver hair and strong chin accented his striking features. He looked fit and confident, but not pretentious. *Must be Mark's dad. So that's what he'll look like when he's older.* Bailey delighted at the sight.

The woman's long blonde hair had been pulled into a ponytail revealing a smooth and friendly face. Her blue eyes had spotted Bailey out of the crowd. Wiping her hands, she came over.

"It's okay, he has that effect on all the women," she said, looking back toward the man behind the counter now helping another customer. "He is gorgeous, isn't he?"

"Uhmm... well... I don't... well."

She touched Bailey's arm. "I'm just messin' with ya. I assume, of course, you are here to see Mark, my son, and not his dad?" Her ambiguous expression revealed nothing.

Are you serious? "Yes! Yes, I'm here to see Mark," Bailey laughed.

"Good," she said, nodding in the direction Bailey had been staring. " 'Cause he's taken." She guided Bailey past the counter toward the back. "I'm Sara, Mark's mom, and," pointing with her thumb, "his better half."

"Nice to meet you." Bailey liked her spunky, playful manner. "I'm Bailey."

"We know. We've been expecting you. Mark's in back. Never seen him work so hard on a po'boy sandwich before." Then she called out to her husband. "Hey Nick, this is Bailey."

He looked in their direction and smiled. "Nice to meet you, Bailey. Welcome and pardon me if I don't shake your hand." He held up his plastic-gloved, blood-stained, fishy palms. "It's the lunch rush, so I'll catch up with you later."

Bailey waved. "No problem."

Sara extended her arm toward the doorway leading into the back rooms. "Go on inside, make yourself at home. Mark is in there somewhere. I've got to get back to the customers."

Bailey entered a sizeable storeroom. Canned food and spices lined the shelves, and a large walk-in refrigerator sat off to one corner. What looked like an ice chest ran the length of the back wall. Various types of fish filled this frozen sea. *Must be the fresh catches of the day.* Spotting an open doorway to her immediate right, Bailey ventured through and instantly found herself no longer in a pantry or anything that resembled a seafood store. Instead, she stood in their living room, clean and quiet. The pillows on the couch had been crunched just so, as if someone recently nestled there. Across the room painted in bright beachy pastel colors, Bailey could see the edges of a wooden kitchen table with matching white wooden chairs flooded by light from a large bay window. The sizzling sounds of something cooking crept around the corner, along with a delicious smell she knew all too well, fried shrimp. She heard the clanking of a pan.

"Mark?" Bailey called.

He poked his head around the corner, a red and white apron draped around his neck, and a frying pan in one hand. When he smiled, she melted.

"Bailey! You're just in time." Motioning with his head toward the kitchen table, he added, "Come on in and have a seat. I'm almost done."

"This is so cool. You'd never know there is a store out front."

"Yeah, it's pretty neat. They don't have far to walk to work."

She saw a picture on the wall of two boys, one of them a much younger Mark. The other she didn't know, but he looked familiar.

"Cute kid," Bailey said, and winked at Mark.

Mark snickered. "Oh yeah, that's me with my child-hood best friend, Thomas." Mark paused from his cooking and studied the picture. He looked sad and melancholy.

"Y'all still keep in touch?" Bailey asked.

Mark stirred the shrimp. "No, he died a few years ago; boating accident."

"Oh, I'm sorry."

"Yeah, me too." Almost robotically, he kept stirring as if lost in a memory. "He really died long before that."

Bailey didn't know what he meant, but now didn't seem the time to ask either.

Then Mark's excitement returned. "Okay, it's ready." He wiped his hands and pulled out a chair at the kitchen table. "Have a seat."

Fresh flowers welcomed her from a small center-piece vase. She grinned from ear to ear, just delighted by this inside picnic.

"I should probably warn you," she said. "I'm a bit of a connoisseur when it comes to the shrimp po'boy."

Mark smiled slightly. Steady and poised, he sat down two paper plates that could barely contain lunch. Lettuce, tomato, and fresh fried shrimp poured out the sides of the sandwich.

"Enjoy," Mark said confidently.

They both took a bite. The warm, lightly toasted bread melted deliciously into a perfect balance of soft and crispy. Usually, the bread dominated as the main event. Here, the bun played only a supporting role. Flavors exploded in Bailey's mouth. The shrimp had been lightly fried to perfection. The shredded lettuce crunched crisp and cold, the tomato sweet, finished with a sauce that could only be a family recipe, all perfectly accented by the toasty bun. The combination was... heavenly. No ordinary hoagie could match this creation.

Bailey closed her eyes. She moaned unexpectedly. "Mmmm." Then looked at Mark, her eyes wide with delight. "Ohh... this is fantastic!"

"Told ya, I make a mean po'boy."

"Mark, this is incredible! You could sell this all day long."

He bit into his sandwich. "Mmmm, that is good."

They ate. Then Bailey asked, "So what made you want to go to Mobile and leave all this?"

Mark gently wiped the corners of his mouth with a napkin. He glanced back at the picture of him and his childhood friend. "Partly because of what happened to Thomas. He used to live between here and Lost Key. His grandfather owned that old shack out back of the Tropical Palm."

"Really?" Bailey noticed this was the third time she'd heard of the old hermit and the run-down shack.

"Yeah, the guy was kind of a hermit. I met him a couple of times, but he liked to keep to himself. He had all kinds of old stuff in his house—pottery, and other trinkets. It looked like antiques. He even had this cool desk he claimed belonged to Captain Davenport."

Bailey didn't know who Captain Davenport was, and she didn't ask, because she didn't want to stop the story.

Mark continued. "He claimed there were all kinds of treasures hidden at the bottom of the bay from old sunken Spanish ships. Rumor has it the guy had been seen at night dragging sacks full of treasures he found back to his old shack. Oh, could he ever spin a tale about pirates in this area. Thomas idolized his grandfather. One night a storm came. His grandfather's small boat capsized, and he drowned. The loss just devastated Thomas. But that wasn't the worst of it. A couple of months later, his mom was walking home from the store and passed by the Cross Bones Bar at the wrong time."

"You mean the bar that is now my real estate office?"

"The very same. Anyway, some local yayhoos had gotten quite lit that night. They happened to be leaving just as she was passing by. They decided in their warped, intoxicated brains that it would be fun to scare an innocent lady. They started calling her names, whistling, offering crude invitations to party, that sort of crap. Then they wanted to look inside her grocery bag. She got scared and turned to run away. As she did, she tripped and hit her head on an old piece of cinder block leftover from the construction of the bar."

Bailey gasped and covered her mouth.

"She died of complications from that head injury a couple of weeks later. The boys seemed torn up with remorse. They kept apologizing over and over. But that didn't bring her back, nor did it console Thomas or his father. A local judge ruled it an accident and sentenced them to community service for public drunkenness. They never did any jail time."

"That's just terrible," Bailey said.

"Yeah. It got worse, too. Thomas' father drank heavily after that, finally got sick and died from too much alcohol. Those events changed my friend. Sometimes he would pretend to be different people. I figured he was just trying to cope. He'd lost all family connections here. He finally ended up in the foster care system. I tried to keep up with him, but he made it difficult. Last I heard, he was living on a boat which sank in the Caribbean. The accident killed him. But like I said earlier, the Thomas I knew died long before that incident."

As Bailey listened to this sad and tragic story, she wondered what Mark must have felt as he witnessed his friend's life fall apart and yet be powerless to stop it. She reached for his hand, touching it gently. Mark appreciated the gesture.

Then Bailey asked, "So, you never wanted to go into your family business?"

"Well, don't get me wrong. I like selling fish and all. But you know what I love is the community. I love the way my parents know everyone who comes in the store. You know what I mean, as much as they can. These patrons are more than customers. They're friends. Some have been coming in here since I was a kid." He looked out the window. His brow wrinkled slightly. "There's been so much change over the last years."

"That's why I want to sell homes in Mobile," Bailey said.

"And that's why I draw neighborhoods."

Bailey smiled slyly. "Ain't we a pair?"

Mark sat back, looked at Bailey, and returned the smile. "Ain't we, though?"

"You draw neighborhoods, and I sell 'em. I'd love to sell that one you showed me."

"That would be a dream."

"Well, it's not gonna be in Lost Key, that's for sure. If the oil hasn't already ruined it, Acheron Developers will, with their cardboard, no-imagination box designs," Bailey said sourly.

Mark sighed. "I understand, Bailey. I watched something similar happen here. Folks get scared, and then they sell out. Forget about creativity and potential. It all comes down to the highest bidder."

"Except in Lost Key. It's all going to the lowest bidder because that's what an oil spill does."

"I'm surprised y'all have any bidders at all. Who wants to deal with the cleanup?" Mark added.

Bailey looked away, rubbing the small cross that hung at the end of her necklace. She gently caressed it between her thumb and index finger.

"What?" he asked.

She looked directly at him with a steely, sober gaze. "That is curious, isn't it?"

Mark's eyes widened. "You can't be serious?" Bailey said nothing, but held his gaze. "Who would do such a thing?" he added.

"He would." She answered matter-of-factly.

"Even if he would do such a thing. How could he?"

Bailey looked away. "I don't know yet."

"What makes you so sure that what's-his-name… Martin, is somehow behind all this?"

Bailey looked at Mark again. *Should I tell him? Should I tell him that sometimes I just know things? Don't scare him away, Bailey.*

"Just a feeling," she said.

Mark just nodded respectfully.

You know there is more to this story, don't you?

Mark nodded again as if he had just heard Bailey's thought.

Finally, he said, "Well, I guess reality is waiting, huh. Which reminds me I have something for you." He got up and walked around the corner. Just a couple of minutes later, he returned with Bailey's cell phone.

"You got your car," she said.

"Yep, the police called yesterday, said it was all clear. Didn't they call you?"

"I've been at Keri's. Maybe they left a message at my place. I'll check. Everything okay with your car?"

"Yeah, everything was fine, nothing stolen, no damage."

"You going back to Mobile tomorrow?" Bailey asked.

"No, I'm going to take a few days. I need to gather myself. You?"

"I guess so." She shifted as if the chair had just become uncomfortable. "Probably. I don't know. I'll figure it out later."

Mark didn't press her further. He seemed in tune with Bailey, somehow knowing just when to give her space. In addition to Mark being a gulf coast boy, and having cool parents, and making the best po'boy sandwich anywhere, Bailey had room to be herself around him. She enjoyed this house behind the store, and she liked Mark. He seemed to genuinely care for her. Bailey felt comfortable here. Try as she might, she couldn't conjure any feelings of excitement about returning to Mobile, surprised how quickly the wind had gone out of that 'big dream.'

Chapter 42

Lost Days

The last rays of the sun waved goodnight as Bailey arrived at her beach house in Lost Key. She went inside and headed straight for the bedroom. As the afternoon had worn on, a sense of tiredness overwhelmed her. She even had trouble tracking the conversation with Mark and his parents toward the end of their visit. *I just got to rest my eyes for a second, and then I'll get ready for bed.* She lay down, and a sweet slumber enveloped her.

Bailey woke to a brightly lit room as the sun beamed into her bedroom window. *What time is it?* She spotted the clock on the bedside table. "Two o'clock!" *I can't believe I slept this late.* Strange, but she didn't feel rested. She rolled over on her back. Her body sank heavily into the mattress. *Just a few minutes more. Then I'll brush my teeth and change my clothes.* She dozed off again.

A knocking at the door woke Bailey. She looked at the clock, five p.m.

"Bailey!" A voice called from outside. It was Keri. "You in there?"

"Yeah, come on in," Bailey managed, feeling drained from the effort of responding.

"I can't. You locked the door."

"What? I never lock the door. It's just stuck." She plopped her head down onto the pillow again.

"No. It's not stuck, it's locked." Keri banged on the door some more. "Come on, let me in!"

"Alright already. I'm coming." Slowly, she sat up, made her way to the edge of the bed, and put her feet on the floor. She stretched her neck, tilting her head to one side, then the other. More knocking. "Okay, okay, I'm coming." She labored to the door and unlatched it. "Well, what do you know. I did lock it."

"Hey, what the hell is going on? You alright?" Keri blurted.

"Yeah, I'm alright, just tired." Bailey rubbed her eyes and yawned.

"Everyone thought you went back to Mobile. Ann called Margaret Jane 'cause she couldn't reach you. Margaret Jane called me 'cause she couldn't reach you. Your mom called everybody 'cause she couldn't reach you. Girl, you scared the crap out of us."

"Why would Ann call MJ? All she has to do is call me here, leave a message." The light on her answering machine blinked—ten messages were waiting. "Oh, maybe she did. Besides, I told her I was taking a couple of days."

Keri spoke more softly and touched Bailey's arm. "No, you didn't. You didn't call Ann. And you didn't call your mom either."

Perplexed by this news, Bailey said, "Really? I could have sworn I did."

The phone rang. Bailey plopped on the couch.

"Aren't you going to answer that?"

"Na, it's probably just a sales call. Let the machine get it."

Keri stared at her with a look of disbelief and concern. "I'll bet it's your mom," Keri answered the phone.

"Hello?… Yes, it's me, Keri… Yeah, she's here. She's okay… I'm right here with her… yeah… Okay, yeah, I'll stay with her a while."

Bailey shook her head and mouthed the words *I don't want to talk*.

"No, she can't talk right now… I'll be sure and tell her. Okay, thanks." She hung up. "Your mom wants you to call her later."

Bailey nodded and leaned back on the couch.

Pulling her arm, Keri said, "Come on, Bailey, let's get up."

"No," Bailey said, not helping.

Her friend persisted with another tug of her arm.

"I said no! I don't want to go anywhere. I just want to stay right here."

Keri let go.

"It's safe here." Bailey looked frightened.

"Okay," Keri conceded. "But you can't go incognito on everyone. Especially with bad dudes chasing you."

"Yeah, yeah, I get it. As I said, I thought I had called everyone." Bailey rubbed her face as if brushing away the sleepy cobwebs.

Keri looked at her friend. "You okay?"

"I will be. I will be, I just need to be here right now."

"All right, I understand," Keri said. Then she surveyed Bailey's cottage, and went to the fridge, opened it, and assessed the contents. "You don't have anything to eat."

"Don't worry about it. I'm not hungry anyway."

"I'm going to get you some food." She started for the door.

"I said I'm not hungry."

As Keri left, she said, "And you're going to eat it."

"Yes, mother," Bailey said, irritated at first, but finally letting a slight smile escape.

"She's coming by later." Keri's voice trailed off as the door closed behind her.

"Oh, great."

After a short while, Keri returned with a hot sandwich and some groceries. Bailey ate and felt better immediately. Keri left for work, but only after Bailey had assured her that she would be okay at least ten times. And only after Bailey promised that she would respond to all the messages on her answering machine.

Throughout the evening, she returned the calls, just as she had pledged. It felt good to have a task, and one she did not have to think up. She showered, straightened her house, and watched reruns of her favorite sitcoms on TV. She tried not to think, tried to just turn off her brain and take a break.

Later, Bailey's mom stopped by, along with her stepdad, Uncle Jed, and Aunt Lee. They brought some home-cooked food, enough for a few days. Bailey felt comforted and grateful for their visit. She was also glad when they left so that she could return to the snug, secure cocoon of her small beach house. She wondered how long her place would survive the rise of the condos along the Gulf. How long before what was happening to other areas happened here? *It's already happening.* The real question, she knew—could anyone stop it? Would anyone even want to? Yet, each time a thought popped into her mind about how to solve the impending demise of Lost Key, or a memory flashed of recent events, she would push them away, vowing to take a break from every worry, at least for today. Though now and then, she'd swear two vacant reptilian eyes were watching her.

I'll go to the town hall meeting tomorrow night, she thought. *At least I can voice my concerns.* She figured she would head back to Mobile after that. Nourished by the love of family and friends, food, and long stretches of mindless TV, Bailey fell asleep on the couch in her fortress of solitude.

She woke, again, to a banging. At first, she thought it was the paddle on the side of the boat, and she and Mark were still trapped. Two vacant gator eyes peered at her from the foot of the bed. She squealed briefly, and then the image was gone. The banging continued, and she realized it was coming from the front door.

Keri's voice came from outside. "Rise and shine, Sunshine. Time to get up. Bailey? Hey, you okay? Come on, let me in!" She pounded some more.

"All right already." Bailey unlocked the door and then flipped the latch back and forth. She couldn't remember fastening the deadbolt.

Keri pushed her way inside. "Still locking your door, huh."

"I guess so," Bailey said, still puzzling over the lock.

"Brought you some breakfast goodies. Your favorites and fresh coffee." Keri placed them on the coffee table in front of the couch, where Bailey had slept last night. "And today's copy of the *Mullet Wrapper*, in case you decided to come back to the real world."

Bailey smiled. "You're the best."

"Of course I am." Keri winked.

Bailey plopped back on the couch as Keri opened the bag and handed her a breakfast sandwich. The hot coffee felt good going down. Then she bit into the salty sandwich, a taste of perfection.

"Thank you," came the muted gratitude from a mouthful of breakfast biscuit.

"No problem." Keri slurped her coffee. "Well, you still look like you've been dragged out of a swamp," she said with a slight smile. "How are you feeling?"

Bailey shrugged. "A little more normal, some bad dreams."

Looking around, Keri asked, "Are you ready to come out of this place yet? Can't stay in here forever."

Bailey nodded, yes. "I thought I'd go to the town hall meeting tonight and at least cast my protest. Then, I'll head back toward Mobile."

Keri stopped eating and stared at her again.

"What?" Bailey muffled as she took another bite.

"The town hall meeting was last night."

"No, MJ said the meeting is Tuesday night. That's tonight."

Keri opened the folded newspaper. "That was last night."

"It's Wednesday?"

"Yep. Just one week till Mari Gras."

Bailey gaped at the newspaper as if she were in a time warp. The date read Wednesday, February 26, 1992. Somehow, she had lost a couple of days. More, the front-page headlines read 'Farewell to the Tropical Palm' with a picture of Max and Mary standing out front.

"Bailey?"

"But... I haven't been sleeping for two days. I remember Mom and them coming over just last night."

"Well, actually, your mom and Joe came Monday night and last night. Uncle Jed and Aunt Lee joined them last night. With all you've been through, no wonder your days are running together."

I can't believe I've lost track of time like that. Bailey's face looked both forlorn and frightened. She cast her friend a dire gaze. "Am I going crazy?"

Keri hugged her. "Don't read too much into this. You were chased and shot at. You can't expect everything to be normal the next day."

Bailey began to cry. She put her head in her hands. "My God, what's happening to me?"

Keri hugged her more tightly. "Maybe you're just overloaded. You know, like your mind and body have just got to shut down for a while."

Bailey sniffled and managed to say, "Yes, that makes sense." But she wasn't convincing. "I just couldn't take any more input." She rubbed her eyes, looked at the headlines again, then leaned back on the couch. She gazed vacantly at nothing as if she had no way to process this news, no energy even to figure out how she could have lost an entire day. Worse, she had missed the town hall meeting. She felt defeated.

"He's won," she said just above a whisper and in a tone of surrender.

"This is out of your control, Bailey."

"He took my town, and I didn't even speak up against it. I wasn't even there."

The two friends sat quietly with that harsh fact.

Then Keri said, "You did what you could, and that's enough."

Bailey nodded, but only slightly, and sighed deeply.

"What are you going to do now?" Keri asked.

"Well, I suppose I need to get back to Mobile," Bailey said flatly. "What else can I do?"

"Only when you're ready. I'm sure your boss will understand if you need a couple more days."

"I don't know. I need to get my Mobile career going." It felt sobering to say it out loud. She noticed the look of concern from Keri. "I'll take it slow. I promise. But I need to get back over there. I can't even remember if I have any appointments or not. Heck, Mandy has probably already stolen any potential customers anyway."

"Just take care of yourself," Keri pleaded.

"I will."

"Famous last words."

Chapter 43

Lady Worthington

Later that evening, Bailey packed a bag and began the journey back to Mobile. She couldn't make the drive this time without her yellow sheet-metal companion. *To heck with their rules, I'm taking it anyway.* With the top up, she felt surrounded by a bubble of coziness. Instead of heading straight for the interstate, Bailey prolonged the trip by taking the beach route to the next highway. As she drove past the Sea-n-Suds car wash, she spotted Cricket cleaning an old boat.

She pulled up next to him and rolled down the window. "Hey, Cricket, is that your boat?"

"Hey, Bailey. Yep sure is! Good thing the Mobile Bay isn't that deep. Coast Guard dragged her out. Police gave her back to me once they processed it."

It looked worse in the daylight than Bailey had imagined. Unpleasant memories of their harrowing escape rushed to her mind. She could almost hear the engine's hum, feel the spray of water, and the ping of the bullets hitting the boat. *It's incredible we didn't sink sooner,* she thought to herself.

"Maybe it's time for a new one, Cricket."

"What? No way. This baby's still got life in 'er."

"Suit yourself, but having seen this in the daytime, I'm not gonna be riding in it anytime soon." She hoped he understood that she was half teasing.

He did.

"Well, you didn't have any complaints last week."

"None at all. Honestly, I don't know what we would have done if you hadn't come along." She almost choked on the last words.

"Just glad we all got out safe. Hey, aren't you supposed to be in Mobile?"

"Headed there now."

"Kind of taking the long way, ain't ya?"

"Just taking in a little more beach time. See ya, Cricket."

"Take care."

About an hour and a half later, the skyline of Mobile rose high against the setting sun. As the Jeep crossed the long bridge, Bailey decided to exit through the Bankhead Tunnel. She wanted to see the old oaks again, feel the Mobile welcome. She emerged downtown, greeted by the same New Orleans style railings on the balconies. The same thick branches still hung low over Government Street, but Bailey didn't feel their welcoming embrace. This time, the trees didn't greet her like a warm reception committee. They just seemed indifferent. She felt indifferent.

A lighted square road sign blinked up ahead. Orange cones surrounded the signal so no one would accidentally run over it. Darkness settled in as dusk gave way to night. The crew had already left and the construction they had been working on, stopped. *Strange they would leave their sign on*, Bailey thought. Stranger still, the lights blinked the message, "Turn Here" with an arrow pointing left. Bailey stopped and surveyed the situation.

"Turn Here," the sign blinked. Yet, there seemed no reason to turn left. Cars were still traveling on the road ahead. So, this wasn't a detour.

"Turn Here," the sign blinked again with an arrow pointing left. A car horn beeped behind her. Startled, Bailey turned left onto Magnolia Lane. The street name sounded familiar. It also looked like she had been here before but couldn't quite recall when she had visited. Then she saw it just up ahead.

"The Worthington estate!"

The sign had steered her to the house that no one could sell, the house that Bailey had fallen in love with earlier. Only tonight, the amber glow of lights poured through the old windows. Someone was home!

She pulled over to the curb and parked. *Must be one of the agents showing it to prospective buyers. No, wait, that can't be. The lawyer is the only one with the key, and it's shown by appointment only.* Bailey saw no cars in the driveway. *Maybe I can get another look inside.*

She ascended the porch, and gingerly tapped on the entrance. A woman opened the door. She stood a little shorter than Bailey and appeared much older. Though Bailey guessed she was in her late 70s, maybe early 80s, her radiant, flawless skin made her seem ageless. Any wrinkles she had on her face only added to her elegance. The woman held Bailey with her penetrating blue eyes. Bailey couldn't look away. The lady dressed like someone from another time with a long flowing gown and lace front. Her clothing did not seem old-fashioned, but rather a higher standard.

The thought popped into Bailey's mind—*this is the way people ought to dress.*

"Good evening, my dear." She spoke with perfect diction. "What can I do for you?"

"I… I don't know." Bailey said, and she honestly didn't. She wasn't even sure why she was here, and she certainly had not expected to meet anyone.

The woman's face scrunched as if to convey that she would not countenance a lot of foolishness. Her eyes glanced down at Bailey's cross.

"May I see your necklace?" the lady asked.

"Oh, yes, certainly."

The woman gently took it in her hand and studied it. Her face relaxed and took on a look of surprise. "Where did you get this, my dear?"

"My mom gave it to me. She said it has been in our family for a long time."

The lady nodded and now seemed very excited to meet Bailey.

"I'm Lady Worthington. Please, won't you come in."

Bailey could not contain her astonishment. "Really? You're Lady Worthington herself?"

The woman chuckled. "Indeed, I am."

Almost giddy with excitement, Bailey followed Lady Worthington into the living room. The furniture had been uncovered and adorned the room with as much elegance as the hostess herself. Bailey marveled at the craftsmanship. Each piece antique, yet in such good condition, it seemed new. The couch and chairs invited her to sit, just as they had welcomed many before. This room had hosted dignitaries from days gone by. Memories had been made here. The soft lighting filled the space with a historic glow. Bailey wondered what kind of bulbs were in the fixtures. The atmosphere took her breath away, even more than her first visit.

Who could have staged all this? Bailey wondered. Someone had cleaned the house and added several pieces of furniture along with the light bulbs. A nicely framed old black-and-white photograph stood prominently on the end table. The picture had captured a man and woman each holding one hand of a young boy walking between them. Their smiles suggested that the boy might sometimes get mommy and daddy to swing him, too. *Wonder who they are? Where did the elegant lady come from?* Though her mind popped with questions, she kept silent, eager to behold the mystery unfolding before her eyes.

"Please, sit, my darling." The elegant hostess gestured gracefully toward the couch.

Bailey sat on the sofa in front of the coffee table, as Lady Worthington took a chair opposite her. Bailey noticed the grace of her every movement. The way she sat, the house, her dress—all embodied self-respect not seen anymore. None of this was to show off. Instead, it expressed a deep reverence for life itself.

Lady Worthington poured some tea with the same poise with which she did everything. She added a dollop of honey to each cup.

Carefully lifting the delicate china cup from its saucer, Bailey sipped the most exquisite tea she had ever tasted. The brew warmed her with a calm and soothing wave of relaxation.

"This tea is lovely," she said.

Lady Worthington nodded in appreciation. "You must have quite a few questions dancing in your mind."

For a moment, Bailey found herself speechless. *I must be dreaming. Or maybe I've finally lost it.* "Yes, ma'am, a few." She chuckled.

"That's good. First, you're not crazy. You haven't lost your marbles as they say. And... you're not dreaming either." The hostess let her words sink in.

Bailey felt the urge to ask a question but didn't. She continued trying to take in the experience, to stay present in the moment.

"This is a place after dreams," Lady Worthington said.

"I saw your home just like this. We all came to visit it, the real estate agents, I mean. While I was here, I had one of my daydreams. I saw this room with the furniture arranged just so, and there were people and laughter. I also saw you briefly looking out the window as we left."

"As I said, it wasn't a dream." Then she casually sipped her tea.

"I don't understand."

This time the elegant lady chuckled. "Understanding is overrated, my dear. But the most important thing is that you trust."

"Trust?"

The lady nodded. "Yes, trust your gift." She placed her drink on the table so smoothly that there was no clink, as if the cup and saucer were one piece. "Tell me, why did you come here this evening?"

Bailey thought for a moment. "I'm not sure. I didn't intend to. Maybe I was guided?"

"Are you asking a question?"

Bailey chuckled again. "Yeah, I guess that did sound like a question."

"What makes you say you were guided?" She focused intently, listening for Bailey's answer.

"Well, this may sound strange, but… I… um… saw a sign. I was driving up through the old tunnel. I had hoped to recapture some of the warm feelings of Mobile. I ran across a construction sign that said "Turn Here," flashing lights, and all. So, I did."

Lady Worthington nodded and said, "You followed the guidance even though you couldn't figure it out?"

"Mm-hmm," Bailey said.

"You don't think that is coincidence now, do you?"

Though Bailey couldn't explain why, she knew this meeting had not occurred by chance.

"No ma'am, I don't. I think… I think I was led here tonight to meet you."

"You were, my dear," Lady Worthington said calmly and with absolute conviction.

Almost instinctively, Bailey clasped her cross again. "You seemed to recognize this."

"That's because I used to wear it." She smiled slightly and picked up her teacup again.

Bailey's hand dropped to her lap, and her mouth fell open. *What?*

The Lady continued. "As did my mother before me, and hers before her, and on through the generations."

"Since my mom gave this to me, do you mean that we are related?"

"Oh yes, my dear, in the strongest way possible. We are related through the Spirit."

Bailey could hardly comprehend this revelation. She felt exhilaration mingled with the feeling that maybe she *had* gone crazy. But if this wasn't a hallucination, then she must be talking to a ghost.

The lady chuckled. "Forgive me, my dear, the world has not caught up yet. Some bonds are stronger than family, thicker than bloodlines. I'm speaking of the bond of your Spirit family. I know that all your life, you've felt like you haven't belonged, but you do. Our family spans many generations of time. Now it's your turn to bear the cross."

Bailey touched her cross again, which was warm and glowing. "I've heard that phrase take up your cross and follow."

"That is true. For you, dear, it has a slightly different meaning. For you are the bearer of *this* cross."

"What am I supposed to do?"

"Be yourself. It will guide you. Trust the love you feel inside. You are a vessel of divine healing."

"I keep hearing that—be myself."

"That is the journey of this life. To allow yourself to become the person you are."

"I'm not sure I understand."

"You will. Give it time. Understanding will come. But most important is that you trust."

"Trust who?" Bailey asked.

"Why yourself, of course." Then she set her cup on the table. "Well, it's getting late, my dear. I really must take my leave of you."

"Wait! Wait! This… is amazing. I could sit here all night. I need to know more. How do I…"

"You know everything you need to know. Trust what has been revealed."

"But what does that mean? I don't…"

Lady Worthington stood, and Bailey respectfully rose with her. She took Bailey's hands and looked deeply into her eyes. "The home you seek is already around you."

Bailey tried hard to comprehend, but she wasn't quite sure what Lady Worthington meant. She fervently wanted to sit with her all evening and ask every one of her million questions. For now, she had to trust that all the answers would come.

When they got to the door, Lady Worthington glanced back toward the living room and said, "Find the family that is supposed to live here. Then bring them to Mr. Stockton."

"Where do I look for the right family?"

She chuckled. "You've already found them."

"What? Who?"

"Tell Mr. Stockton they are 'worthy.' "

"But I don't know where to look."

"Trust yourself first, you'll know later. Good night, my dear."

With that, the Lady closed the door, and they parted ways. Bailey got into her Jeep just as sprinkles of rain began to fall. She started the engine and glanced back at the house for one last look. Now it sat dark, as she'd always seen it—as if no one had lived there in a hundred years.

I am losing it. I can hardly wait to see Ann tomorrow. She's not going to believe this!

Chapter 44

Right Person, Wrong Time

Ann listened intently as Bailey recounted the eventful meeting. Then she peered over her half-glasses at Bailey, her eyebrows drawing together. She looked pensive. Silently, she walked around her desk and sat in her usual chair opposite Bailey, who was sitting on the couch. Bailey shuffled, trying to get comfortable. Ann seemed to be in a quandary.

"You say you met Lady Worthington?"

"Yes. Last night. I had tea with her."

"At the house?" Ann asked again, raising one eyebrow.

"Yes, just as I said. She told me I've already found the right family for the house, though I don't know who that could be."

Ann removed her glasses and let them hang around her neck. She leaned back and let out a deep sigh.

She doesn't believe me. "I'm telling the truth. I promise," Bailey added.

"Bailey, I know you believe you are. But no one has lived in that estate for years. Then last night the lights are on? And you had tea with the owner?" Ann didn't say it, but her expression did… 'really?'

"Yes, that's right," Bailey confirmed, aware of how all this sounded.

"Look, Bailey, you've been through a lot. You still need more time to recover. I can't even imagine what it must feel like for someone to shoot at you." She leaned forward. "We're so glad you are okay. That is the most important thing right now."

Then Ann's expression changed from concern to something like disappointment.

"What are you trying to say?" Bailey asked.

Ann drew a deep breath. Bailey knew what was coming. *Oh, no!* Silence filled the room. Ann moved from her chair and sat next to Bailey.

"I've got to let you go."

Bailey blinked. She never imagined the meeting going this way. Yet, all the signs had been there. She'd just been ignoring them. She had no production and had become increasingly distracted by all the changes happening to Lost Key. Not to mention that she had made several missteps along the way. She was even unreachable for a few days. Ann didn't remind her of these things; she didn't have to. Bailey's inner critic relentlessly told her of every slip. Her body tensed from head to toe. Thomason Brothers had never really seen her talent because she had never demonstrated her best work. She had planned to come back and show them what she could do, just like MJ encouraged. Instead, she finally returned with a tall tale of having tea with ghosts in the unsellable home that has wrecked many agents better than her. *Of course, you have to let me go. How can you not?* Frustration gave way to tears. Now, she would never get a chance to prove herself.

Ann put her arm around her. "You've got enough on your plate right now without trying to start a new real estate career. Like I said, the most important thing is that you're okay." Ann squeezed her shoulder tenderly. "That was a terrible experience on Dauphin Island. They ever catch the men who attacked y'all?"

Bailey shook her head.

Ann gently turned her teary-eyed protégé toward her. "I still believe in you, Bailey. You're the right person for Thomason Brothers, but it's not the right time. You are just not yet ready for this. That's all. It's not fair to yourself to keep going. It's not fair to the company. Take care of yourself right now. Take care of your home. You can apply again next year. I'll still go to bat for you. Just give it time. Let all this turmoil clear away."

The words cooled the sting, but firing is firing. Bailey leaned her head onto Ann's shoulders and resigned herself to her situation. "I'm sorry," she muttered.

"You have nothing to be sorry about. Life happens." Ann consoled but did not apologize, nor did she need to. She had a responsibility to the company.

After a few minutes, Bailey slowly stood. Her body felt heavy; the wind was taken right out of her sail. As she left Ann's office, she turned to her broker one more time.

"Thank you for everything."

Ann only nodded. Bailey realized how odd it must sound to thank her boss for getting fired. But it seemed warranted in this case. Ann had covered for her as long as she could. Bailey just never found her stride. Besides, her boss was right. She needed time to heal from this trauma, before taking on all the demands of being a new agent in a new town.

"You don't have to clear out your desk today if you don't want to," Ann said gently. "I have to ask for your keys, but I'll meet you when no one's here if you'd prefer to collect your belongings later."

I can't believe this is happening. "Thank you, but I'd rather just get my stuff now."

"Okay," Ann said softly. Then she winked and said, "Something tells me we haven't seen the last of Bailey Evans."

Bailey handed the keys to Ann. Then, she hugged her once more before walking to her cubical to clear out her desk. For the most part, folks greeted her politely. Yet every glance or every awkward aversion of eye contact felt like hot pinpoints of light, each one burning "Look, there is the latest one that didn't make it." Although the recent events were beyond Bailey's control, she still felt humiliated. All the sensors, all the defense mechanisms that generally shielded her from her internal critic, no longer worked. *You failed. You're a failure.*

Remy came over. He hugged her. "I'll miss you, Bailey."

"You have been a great friend, Remy. Thanks."

Bailey walked toward the door, carrying a cardboard box of her things. The walk of shame for her. She heard condolences and good wishes from almost everyone.

Even Mandy came over and said, "Good luck, Bailey. I hope you find your niche."

Her salutation sounded sincere. Bailey looked at her. She didn't have the energy to deal with Mandy. She walked away.

She sat in her Jeep, her eyes leaking uncontrollably. She let the tears flow. *So, this is it? It all comes down to my*

Jeep and me? Bailey didn't quite know where to go. Her apartment in Mobile felt like a cold hotel in a foreign land. *No, I can't stay here. Can't sit in this parking lot either.*

Bailey cranked the engine and drove. She headed home on I-10, eyes fixed forward, as if under a hypnotic spell. No music blared on the radio. The hum of the tires grinding against the pavement the only sound. Her dream of selling high-end homes in Mobile had evaporated like a morning mist. Next year might as well be another lifetime. Alabama had turned out to be no 'sweet home' at all. An hour later, she passed a Welcome to Florida sign. She shook her head, trying to clear the mental cobwebs. All she wanted was to climb into her bed and bury herself under the covers, yet her heart sank at the thought of going to her beach house. Instead of a fortress of solitude, now it felt more like a black hole. If she went through that door, she might never return. Lost Key was disappearing. There was no future over the horizon, and she had no moves left.

Yet, there remained one place she always found life, like an oasis. Soon she turned down that old familiar dirt road and saw the welcoming sight of the dolphin mailbox.

Chapter 45

Fake

"I know, I know," Keri spoke into the phone. "She's been like this all weekend. Well… when you've lost your dream, that's a pretty big honkin' deal, and you know how our girl sleeps when she's stressed… at least she's here and not shut up in her house… I will… believe me, I will. I'm taking a few days off. I'll watch after her. … Okay, Irene, no worries. … Yeah, that will be fine to bring some food tonight, but I think it's better if she stays here. Yes, I will. … Okay, bye." She hung up and sighed.

"Mom?" Bailey said, her back turned outward as she lay on her side, covered almost entirely by a blanket. Only a part of her head stuck out the end. She had stayed buried in this position on Keri's couch for the past two days.

"She speaks," Keri said, looking at the talking lump of blankets. "Yes, of course your mom, who else calls ten times a day? Come on, Bailey, you got to snap out of this. You are starting to freak me out."

No answer. Keri pushed her with her foot. "Hey, you listening to me?" Bailey lay motionless. Keri pushed harder.

"Hey, watch it!" Bailey's head popped up long enough to warn her friend with a leave-me-alone kind of glare, and then promptly covered her head again.

Keri grabbed the blanket and yanked the covers off. "Enough! Now get your ass up!"

For the first time in almost three days, Bailey sprang to life. Her eyes blazed as if a wild beast had possessed her body.

Keri, startled by the sudden transformation, backed up as fast as she could.

Bailey-beast moved toward her. "I... said... leave... me... alone!"

As Keri backpedaled through the door, her left heel caught the edge of the door frame. She stumbled backward out onto the deck. The sight of her friend falling transformed Bailey from beast back into herself. More concerned than irritated, she pursued Keri out the door to keep her from falling off the deck and into the waterway. Keri's eyes darted wildly. Fright filled her face as she groped for something to steady herself. The realization dawned that she would not regain her balance.

"Keri!" Bailey yelled. In a last-ditch effort, Bailey reached for Keri. But her fingers grasped only air. Keri went tumbling off the deck and splashed into the channel. The attempt to save her friend stretched Bailey a bit too far. She could not stop her forward momentum. She also plunged over the side of the deck, and she splashed right next to Keri. They surfaced, heads bobbing like corks. They faced each other, treading water.

"You okay?" Bailey asked.

Keri nodded. "Yeah, you?"

"Yeah... I'm so sorry, my friend." Bailey spat some water.

Keri smiled. "No need to apologize. You've been through it. I was starting to worry you might never come out from under that sheet."

"I'm working on it."

They paddled toward the lower dock where the WaveRunner floated.

"Maybe I'll become a high diver," Bailey joked.

Keri chuckled. "You'll have to work on your form. I give that last dive a one… maybe.

"Aaahhhh!" Bailey screamed as she saw something moving near the bank. At first it looked like the bulbous eye of a gator.

"It's okay, it's Snaps!" Keri said as she paddled toward their sea turtle friend.

Bailey let out a big sigh of relief. "Snaps, you scared the crap out of me."

"What's he got in his mouth?" Keri asked.

As she reached for the object, Snaps dropped it and swam back into the reeds.

"What was it?" Bailey asked.

"It looked like a gold coin, but I'm not sure. It sank to the bottom."

"Is Snaps bringing you treasure now? You've got pirates on the brain."

"Well, I was going to share the bounty with you, but just forget it," Keri said teasingly.

As they climbed back onto the boat dock, the phone rang.

"I'll get that; it's probably your mom again. It seems like she calls about every twenty minutes."

Bailey reached for a nearby towel and began to dry herself off.

"Jade! Thank God you're okay!" Keri's voice echoed from the living room. "Where have you been? Everyone is looking… slow down, girl; I can hardly understand you… What? Seriously? But that's bizarre. Are you sure that's the same batch of oil I sent you?… Okay. But more importantly, are you safe?… Where are you?… I'm coming to… No, don't hang up… Okay, okay."

Keri hung up and turned to Bailey, who was already standing in the doorway.

"That was Jade from the Dauphin Island Marine Center."

"Is she okay? Is she safe?"

Yes, but she sounds terrified. She won't tell me where she is. Said she had to go but would call back soon. I'm worried, Bailey."

Bailey let out a sigh. "Whew. I'm so glad she's alright."

"She wanted me to know something else, too. It turns out the oil sample I sent her, you know the one we gathered from the beach, is not crude oil, at least not the kind of spill you'd find from a drilling platform."

"I don't understand. What does that mean?"

Keri shrugged. "I'm not sure. She didn't explain the details. She was talking so fast it was hard to keep up with what she was saying. Something's got her spooked badly." Then Keri looked confounded and tilted her head to one side. "That doesn't make any sense. If it's not crude oil, then what is it? And what's it doing in my Gulf?"

Neither spoke for a moment.

Bailey scrunched her forehead, processing this new information. "You mean the oil is fake?"

"Well, yeah, I guess that's what that means. It's not raw crude that they would send to a refinery."

Bailey stared off, pondering.

"What?" Keri asked.

The oil is fake! She'd found the missing piece of the puzzle, the critical clue of the mystery. It all fell into place now. Bailey put her hand on her forehead and walked a few steps into the living room. "Of course!" she said.

"What? What, of course?" Keri asked.

Bailey was pacing now. "Of course! It all makes sense! That's it!"

"What's it?" Keri pleaded.

Bailey looked at her friend and said, "The oil spill is fake!"

"Okay, let's assume you're right," Keri said. "But… how would you fake an oil spill? Who in the world would bother?"

"Acheron Developers , that's who."

"You're serious."

Bailey stepped closer. "You bet I am." She had a resolve in her voice, and her azure eyes gleamed with conviction for the first time in a week. "Listen, when my Jeep first ran through the oil that day on the way to the Tropical Palm, I thought it would strip the paint for sure. I even took it down to the Sea-n-Suds car wash thinking Cricket might know how to get that stuff off and preserve the original color. But it washed away with soap and water as if there'd never been any oil on it at all."

"Okay, well, that fits Jade's findings," Keri said, looking puzzled.

"There's more. Remember last week on the beach? You were working in an area where the oil had been collecting." Keri nodded. "Your crew was trying to rescue any wildlife that might have been affected. You were showing me what happens when the oil gets on the wings of a bird, for example, it can't fly anymore."

"Sure, sure, I remember. If it gets in the gills of the fish, it suffocates," Keri added.

"Remember when we were cleaning that bird, you commented that this seemed different than other oils you had encountered, less sludgy?" Again, Keri nodded, still waiting for how this connected. "Remember how relieved we felt when we removed the oil from the wildlife?"

"Yes, yes, and I was surprised how easily it washed off. Then I sent it to the Dauphin Island Marine Center for examination."

Bailey made her point. "Acheron Developers is trying to purchase large blocks of land in Lost Key. It would be the largest land development project in the area. They say it's good for business, good for our suffering economy and all that stuff. Martin is going to turn it into cheap tourist rentals and make a killing. And isn't it odd that most of the oil leaking ends up near and around Lost Key all the time? It hasn't spread out to Panama City, or Destin, and hasn't gone to Mobile Bay."

Keri stood. "Yes, I noticed that. And, it's unbelievable timing. Why would a developer still want to purchase contaminated marshland?"

"Exactly! Too convenient," Bailey said.

"Are you suggesting that someone is dumping oil into Lost Key on purpose?"

"Not someone… Martin! Or someone he has hired. On the ferry ride home, Cricket told us he saw men trolling back and forth as if they were fishing. He said they weren't nice and didn't even look like they knew how to fish. That's how he happened to be at Dauphin Island that night. He didn't want to run into them anymore. What if those two men Cricket saw weren't fishermen? What if they had been dumping oil or fake oil in the Lost Key Bay and the Intracoastal Waterway? Then, that would drive the price of real estate down, and Acheron Developers gets all the land way cheaper because nobody would want it anyway."

"Wow! That's a wicked plan," Keri said. "Real oil spills damage the ecosystem, sometimes for many years. Nobody wants to go swimming and get a tarball on their bathing suit. They would be ruining their own property."

"Not if the oil is fake. Then it's a lot easier to clean up, as we have already seen from my Jeep and the bird we rescued. So, once the real estate deal goes through, the cleanup is easy. Also, since the spill is localized, there will not be a lot of widespread press about it, so there's no PR problem."

"Plus, any evidence disappears, washed away with the tide," Keri said. "So, the ecosystem is not permanently harmed at all."

"Exactly!"

"Like I said, wicked plan." Then Keri asked, "So you think they burned Marine Center to destroy any potential evidence?"

"Yes, I do."

"That's incredible!"

"We've got to stop them," Bailey said.

"What? Stop them? How do we do that and not get killed in the process?"

Instead of answering, Bailey peered off into the distance again. It seemed that the thought of getting herself killed didn't even register, or if it did, it came in a distant second to her concern of Lost Key being developed by this phony pirate oilman. Just then, she felt the tiny cross she wore around her neck grow warm. The temperature changed enough, so she knew it wasn't just her body heat warming it. As she touched it, images flashed through her mind, grainy and gray, again like an old movie. She saw a young boy in tears; she saw Martin in handcuffs; a party at the Tropical Palm Café; a new development in Lost Key, but not the one Martin had proposed. This one looked like something out of a storybook—playful, and fun.

"Bailey?" Keri said, and gently touched her friend on the shoulder.

Bailey realized Keri had been calling her name more than once. The movies in her mind faded, the cross cooled, and she came back to the deck.

"What are you seeing?"

Bailey gathered her thoughts, then nodded. "I just got a lot swirling through my head, a lot to take in, you know."

"That's the understatement of the year," Keri said.

Bailey looked away again. More images played across the screen in her mind. She saw Cricket in his boat with another person as clear as any recent memory, but it hadn't happened yet. She felt compelled to make it happen.

"We need Cricket's help. We need him to go back to his fishing spot in Lost Key. Only this time, there's someone that's supposed to go with him." She squinted. "It needs to happen tomorrow night." Bailey looked at her friend. She could tell from her concerned stare and scrunched brow that Keri was unsettled and worried, but trying to stay calm. Bailey touched her shoulder. "It's okay."

Keri nodded. "Sure, okay."

But Bailey could tell she wasn't.

Still holding her cross and again with the same otherworldly gaze, she continued. "And I must find Mark. He's already seen the future."

"Um, I'm not sure what you're talking about," Keri said.

Bailey didn't explain. She continued peering into some invisible portal. She nodded a few times then turned back to Keri. "I must get to Lost Key Realty and stop this deal... and..." She stopped, as if hearing a message. She looked directly into Keri's eyes. "Go find Cricket. Tell him to get his boat ready and wait for my call."

"You want me to go with him? Am I the other one in the boat?"

"No. You go to work. You're supposed to be on your job when it happens."

"Huh? When what happens?" She grabbed Bailey by the arm. "Tell me what happens."

Bailey said, "We're gonna take him down."

"Who, Martin? Oh, Bailey, I don't know about that."

"Just find Cricket, tell him to get his boat ready, and wait for my call. There's not much time. Got it?"

Keri paused. "Okay, got it. What are you going to do?"

"I've got to find the Antoines." She walked toward her Jeep. "I've found their home." Then she stood upon the side rail and looked over the roof at Keri. "There's something else about Martin... I'm not sure yet, but I'll let you know when it's revealed to me." Bailey lowered herself inside, cranked the engine, and sped off.

"Yes, of course," Keri called after her sarcastically. "Go find the Antoines. Got to find the Antoines. Who are the Antoines? Don't worry about me. I'll be right here waiting. Waiting for you to tell me what the hell is going on!"

Chapter 46

Time's Up, Thomas

Bailey knew she had all the pieces of the puzzle now. She just wasn't quite sure how they all fit together. She took a deep breath, then slowly let it out. These mini visions were not new to Bailey. She'd been experiencing them since she was a little girl, and always treated them as childish, like an imaginary friend that she kept secret. Usually, her more logical adult self would brush the insight aside, analyzing the "real situation" and crafting a more sensible alternative. But now, really for the first time, she trusted her intuition. *Let it come to you, Bailey. Let it come.* Slowly she sensed the path ahead, not the whole way, but enough to follow. The next step was to find the Antoines, just as she had told Keri. She couldn't explain why and didn't need to. She just knew. But there was another step. First, she had to reach out to MJ again. She had to stop this deal, somehow. Beyond that was like looking into the fog. She trusted it would lift as she walked ahead.

Bailey drove her Jeep straight to her old real estate office and spotted MJ's car around back. *Great, she's here.* When she reached the rear door, she turned the knob with a firm, steady grip, and flung it open like it was the back door of her own house.

"MJ, you're not gonna believe this. The oil is..." The piercing dark eyes of Martin stopped her mid-stride.

"The oil is what, Miss Evans?" Martin challenged. He sat in one of the chairs on the other side of Margaret Jane's desk. A sharply dressed man in a three-piece gray suit was sitting in the other chair next to him—Martin's lawyer. Neither man stood to greet her.

Margaret Jane rose from her chair, grabbed Bailey by the arm, and pulled her toward the same door she had just entered. "Bailey, I'm in the middle of a meeting! It's inappropriate for you to interrupt like this. Now is not the time."

But Bailey didn't move. Instead, she stared into Martin's eyes. This time her head didn't hurt. This time her ears didn't ring, and the room didn't spin; the tremor in her hand, gone. A tide of strength rose within her. She stood taller, her legs strong underneath her, and her feet firmly rooted to the floor. She felt as unstoppable as the next wave surging from the Gulf. She pointed two fingers directly at her own eyes, then pointed one finger back at Martin.

"I see you," she said softly, almost whispering. No one said anything at first, then Martin huffed and smiled mockingly.

"Bailey!" Margaret Jane shouted.

Slowly, Bailey shifted her gaze from Martin and turned toward MJ. Her former boss's face flushed in anger.

"The oil spill is fake," Bailey said calmly and in a matter-of-fact voice. Still looking at MJ, she pointed at Martin. "He's behind it. He's trying to drive down the property prices."

Margaret Jane looked at her former protégé as she would a friend who had gone completely mad.

The man in the suit stood. "This is outrageous! Young lady, I'm the attorney for Mr. Delahaye. I ought to sue you and this company for defamation of character!"

"No! We ought to sue you!" Bailey fired back. "For fraud!"

Bailey stepped toward the man, and he moved back.

Martin remained seated but no longer smiled.

MJ moved closer to intervene. "Gentlemen, please excuse this outburst. Bailey doesn't work here anymore. She does not represent the views of this company." Motioning to the lawyer, she said, "Please have a seat. I'll be right back." Slowly, the man sat back down.

Somehow, Bailey could tell he was only posturing. He wasn't as strong-willed as he pretended.

Then MJ opened the door and said, "Bailey, can I have a word with you outside? Now!"

Bailey matched Martin's gaze with a fierce stare of her own. She started to comply with MJ's request but stopped just before stepping through the door.

Then she looked at Martin again and gasped.

"You're him! The boy in the picture." She stared as if finally seeing through the tinted windows of his eyes. She saw pain and intense anger. Except for the scar and longer, darker hair, he looked like an older version of Mark's best friend. "You're Thomas."

Her words landed with Martin. He no longer looked confident, and the smug smirk on his face turned to one of almost shock. He shuffled in his seat, averting his eyes as if looking for a hiding place. For the first time since Bailey had met him, Martin seemed vulnerable.

Then she turned and walked right up to Martin and leaned down, her face inches from his. "This is *my* home! *Your* time is up! Stay away from my family."

Martin said nothing but met her glare with equal intensity. His face flushed and jaw clenched. Playtime was over.

Bailey thought she might soon find out what an angry pirate could do. She glanced at the man in the suit. He broke eye contact, shaking his head. Bailey gave him the once over, like a gladiator assessing her opponent. She huffed dismissively. Bailey stood towering in front of the two men, newfound confidence rushing through her being.

MJ tried to interrupt, pulling at Bailey again. "You need to leave now!"

Bailey didn't leave. She stood her ground, focused on Martin.

Martin rose abruptly. "I've had enough of this craziness." He stomped out of the office, followed by his lawyer.

MJ started after them, but the suit turned and abruptly said, "We'll be in touch."

When they had gotten into their limo, MJ slammed the door of her office.

"Bailey, have you lost your mind?" She was almost in tears with anger.

"MJ, listen to me. You do not want to be in business with these people—"

"No! You listen to me! They are the *only* business, Bailey! This deal is going to save me, and this whole scrub-brush town. I'm not going to throw it away because you got a feeling."

"This is more than—"

"Stop it, Bailey! Just stop it."

Bailey stopped, taken aback by the fury of her former boss.

MJ paced a minute, sighed, then she gently touched Bailey's arm. "Look, I'm sorry about Mobile. Sorry that all this," she waved her arms, "is changing."

"At least tell everyone what Martin is up to," Bailey said.

MJ shook her head. "No! No, Bailey."

"You have to disclose this!"

"Disclose what? That a disgruntled former employee thinks there is a fake oil spill as part of a conspiracy to take over Lost Key? Bailey, I'm getting worried about you. Talk to someone, please. You've been through—"

"I'm not making it up, MJ!"

"I believe… I believe that you believe that, Bailey." MJ's countenance changed from anger to a look of grave concern. Again, she reached out to comfort her friend.

Bailey recoiled at her touch, not wanting consolation. She wanted to be heard. "MJ, you know me. This is for real. If you don't tell people, I will!"

Shaking her head again, MJ warned, "Bailey… don't."

"He can't just come into our house and do this… this… fraud!"

"This is not your house, Bailey. It's *my* business."

"But how can you—"

"Stay out of it!" the broker yelled. She paced, stomping back and forth. Then she sighed and looked at Bailey, her eyes softer now. "Bailey, I love you like a daughter. Please, I'm begging you, let this go."

Bailey drew a deep breath and let it out slowly. "MJ, please don't go through with this. They're crooks."

Margaret Jane frowned, then turned business mode. "They're buyers."

Bailey stepped closer. "He's not who he says he is. I saw it."

MJ groaned in frustration.

"I think his real name is Thomas. I saw a picture of him at Mark's house a few days ago. They were best friends as kids. Then his mom was killed by some locals right on this very spot when it used to be a bar."

MJ gasped, surprised by this new revelation. "You mean he's *that* boy?"

"Yes." Bailey nodded her head.

"That can't be right. Thomas died last year, I heard, in some kind of boating accident. Maybe that's why he looked familiar to me. He must remind me of that poor kid."

"MJ, he *is* that kid."

"So, he is not only dumping fake oil into the marsh, but now he's come back from the dead, too?" She shook her head. "Bailey, listen to yourself. Don't you hear what you're saying? You are not making any sense."

Bailey stared off into space again. "Back from the dead... I've heard that phrase before."

MJ touched Bailey's arm gently. "Go home; please get some help. Stop worrying about Lost Key." She looked at her watch. "Tomorrow at four p.m., this will all be over. I have to go, I have a lot of work to do, assuming I haven't lost them as clients."

Bailey knew that no amount of protesting would convince her friend to back out of this deal. Even if

MJ did believe her, and it looked like she wanted to, she would not act solely on Bailey's intuition or years of friendship. This transaction, for her, was a business deal, and more—her last chance. Tomorrow at four, the deal would be done. Bailey had just over twenty-four hours to solve the mystery of Martin, stop the closing, and find another buyer for the whole project. There was nothing more to say, and if she persisted, Bailey feared they might later regret it. Pressing her point might irreparably hurt their friendship. So, she just hugged MJ and left.

Chapter 47

Going Barefoot

$\mathcal{B}$ ailey stood statue-like next to her Jeep just outside the Lost Key office. Then she looked around as if disoriented. A wave of doubt crashed over her. *What am I doing?* She had no plan, nor any evidence of her claims about the oil or Martin, and no other buyer. Outside, away from the heat of the moment, she realized how crazy all this sounded.

Back from the dead? Really? But it sure felt good to stand up to that guy.

She climbed into the driver's seat. The blinds in the office were opened enough for Bailey to see MJ sitting at her desk, elbows propped up on the top, holding her head in her hands. She wanted to rush back inside and apologize for disrupting the meeting. Anything to make it okay. *No, give her some space right now.* Besides, this wasn't right. The thought of MJ losing the office left a heaviness in her heart, a sense of profound discouragement. But for Martin to be the buyer, well, that was just wrong. Try as she might, she could not let it go. She could not accept what she saw unfolding in Lost Key.

He's always one step ahead. Is there any place this guy can't reach? Almost superhuman. Her heart skipped a beat. *That's what he wants me to think. He's just a man, a crook, a pirate.*

355

Yet the feeling persisted that there was more going on with Martin, that he was not who he presented himself to be.

This is insane. You're imagining things. Go home, Bailey, you've lost it.

She looked again at MJ, still sitting at her desk, head down, resting on her folded arms. Shards of guilt and shame stabbed Bailey. Her stomach clenched. She felt an overwhelming urge to hurry back to her beach cottage and disappear for another few days. *Sounds like a good idea before you hurt anyone else.* She cranked her Jeep and started to drive away when the highway sign directly ahead flashed Mobile. She waited, about to dismiss this as overactive imagination, when the word Mobile shined again, as if someone had switched on a backlight then quickly shut it off. A renewed conviction surged. Go to Mobile and find the Antoines. There wasn't any logic to it. This decision was all gut-intuition, but it felt right. Bailey heard Remy's voice echo in her mind. "Go barefoot." She chuckled. *Okay, I'm going barefoot.*

As she drove, more of the path became clear. She pulled out her cell phone and dialed. Keri picked up on the other end.

"Keri, it's me… Yeah, I'm okay. Listen, I'm heading to Mobile… yes, that's right, to find the Antoines… I don't know why… I'll explain it all later. It will make more sense, then, I'm sure. Can you reach Jade?… Well, at least try… I need you to get a copy of that report… yes, the one that confirms the oil sample is fake. I need you to get your hands on that report and meet me at Lost Key Realty tomorrow afternoon no later than three forty-five p.m. Got it?… I'll explain everything. Oh, and

Keri, don't drive to meet Jade, take your WaveRunner...
Oh, that's great, you'll already be near there working.
I knew you were supposed to be working when it happens... everything will make sense tomorrow... One more thing. I think Martin is not who he says he is... What?... Oh that's right, Jacquotte Delahaye, back from the dead red, the pirate who faked her death. Oh my gosh, that supports my theory that he may be Thomas... a long tragic story, I'll fill you in later. Be very careful, my friend. Martin knows I'm on to him. I saw him at MJ's office just now... Since when can I hold my tongue... Listen, just get that report from Jade and meet me at the office tomorrow at quarter till four."

Bailey drove on toward Mobile. As she approached Interstate 10, the letters, along with the arrow on the highway sign lit up ever so briefly, again a flashing signal that only Bailey could see.

Ha! You've got to be kidding me.

She redialed her phone, more confident of her emerging plan, whatever that plan would be.

"Hey, Cricket... yeah, it's Bailey. Listen, I need you to go to the *Mullet Wrapper* and tell that cute reporter you like that you've got a huge story for her... Yes, you do... Yes, it is obvious—everyone knows you like her, even she does. Cricket, listen, get her to go with you in your boat, and take pictures of those fishermen you were telling us about... Yep, those are the ones. Go tonight. It has to be tonight... They'll be there... I got a feeling... Yes, she will go with you... I just know. Now trust me. This is very important. Take the photos to Sheriff Cotton. Then bring those pictures to Lost Key Realty tomorrow no later than three forty-five p.m. Can you do that?...

You're awesome!… Yes, okay, you do this, and I'll go fishing with you… Great! Remember tomorrow at quarter till four."

She dialed again. "Mark, it's me. Yes, I'm okay… Listen, I need you to do something for me." She wasn't sure how to bring up what she was about to say. "Mark, would you take that picture of you and Thomas to Sheriff Cotton in Lost Key? Tell him that I think this is the same man trying to swindle the town from its marshland."

Mark did not answer.

"I know I must sound crazy to you right now. But Mark, I just got this feeling that your childhood friend is still alive, and he's about to commit the biggest fraud deal this town has ever seen. I just need some proof that I'm right."

The deafening silence was all Bailey heard. Her heart quickened. She knew she might have just ruined something that could have been so good. But she had to ask. Too much was on the line with no time to explain everything. She just hoped he would take a leap of faith and trust her.

Mark finally said, "Okay, Bailey. I'll do it."

She sighed a heartfelt relief. "Thank you so much and beeeeee careful. I'm driving to Mobile… I will… yes, I'll be extra careful." She hung up.

The late afternoon sun would set by the time she reached Mobile. "*Okay, Margaret Jane, you need some proof, I'll get you some proof.*"

The plan, as she knew it, was in motion. Keri would pick up evidence of the fake oil spill. Bailey figured that since Jade had done Keri a favor, off-book, and off-hours, then perhaps she kept the results off-site. Maybe she had taken the test results home with her, so they weren't in the Dauphin Island Marine Center when it burned. Cricket would contact the local reporter from the *Mullet Wrapper*. It didn't have as broad an audience as the Pensacola News Journal, but it would be local press. Hopefully, they could get more evidence of illegal activities tonight as they photographed the men dumping the fake oil into the bay. Mark would also inform Sheriff Cotton that Martin might be an impostor. Maybe this would start a more in-depth background check into this mysterious privateer. She only wished she could find another developer, and none of the locals would even touch this kind of deal. She'd already asked around. She sighed. She felt calmer to have a plan, at least. She didn't know if it would work. If it didn't work, Lost Key really would be lost. Bailey flipped off her boat shoes and drove the rest of the way barefoot.

Chapter 48

Finding the Antoines

*O*kay, time to find my favorite family. Bailey tried calling them, but got no answer. So, she exited the interstate and headed toward their apartment. *This has to work. It just has to.* She turned into their complex and drove past the graffitied-over sign. The Antoines' car sat near the stairs of their building. *They're home.* The car parked next to theirs seemed familiar, but Bailey couldn't quite place it. She climbed the steps and knocked on the door. Ashly answered.

"Bailey!" she said, surprised, and glad to see her.

"Hey, Ashly. Good to see you."

Then in perfect unison, as if they had rehearsed it together, Ashly and another voice behind her said, "What are you doing here?"

The other voice belonged to Mandy. Bailey stood in the doorway, staring dumbfounded at her nemesis sitting in her former client's kitchen.

Ashly broke the awkward silence. "Mandy is picking up where you left off. We decided to try again to find a house," Ashly said, almost apologetically.

Mandy stood and addressed Bailey. "I'm sorry, Bailey. I didn't know you are still selling real estate. I mean, you were fired so abruptly. You found another agency?"

Bailey felt her blood boil, and her anger rise. Instead of losing her temper, she touched her cross and calmed down. *I don't have time for you right now.* She held the agent with a fierce, dismissive glare until Mandy finally looked away. Then Bailey turned her attention back to Ashly.

"I understand," Bailey said, her expression softening. "I'm sorry I left without saying bye. I always thought of y'all more as friends than clients anyway. And Mandy's right, I'm not officially working for Thomason Brothers or any other agency. I really don't know why I've come…" Bailey stopped talking, captivated by a picture on their wall. The old black-and-white photo showed a young couple walking their child, swinging their little boy between them. *This is the exact same photo in Lady Worthington's living room!* Her words echoed in Bailey's mind, 'You've already found them.' "

"Oh my gosh! You're the ones! You're the family!" Bailey said.

Ashly and Don exchanged a ' Do you know what she's talking about?' kind of look.

"I've come here today just for you," Bailey said, stepping closer. "Your home is waiting for you."

Andy almost shouted, "All right!"

Don walked next to his wife, gently putting his arm around her. "That's good news, and it's great to see you, Bailey." He hugged her.

Bailey knelt and hugged Andy. Then she stood and spoke directly to the Antoines. "We need to see it right now," she said. "Can you come?"

"I want y'all to find a home too," Mandy interjected. "But Bailey, since you don't work for any real estate company here, you can't show them anything."

"I'm not going to show them the house. Remy is," Bailey answered calmly. "He's arranging it right now."

Of course, Remy didn't know anything about this yet. But Bailey figured the universe was somehow orchestrating these events, so she reasoned that it wasn't quite a lie.

Ashly appeared as excited at Bailey's prospect as Mandy seemed annoyed.

Barely containing her anger, Mandy said, "Look, Mr. and Mrs. Antoine, I have a dozen listings right here, good houses in an affordable price range, ready to go."

They looked at one another and made several subtle facial gestures, again communicating in the secret language of a married couple.

Bailey repeated with emphasis, "Ashly, Don, I found your home."

Ashly asked, "Where is it?"

Bailey glanced at Mandy and then focused back on the couple. "It's downtown, a beautiful home."

Mandy's expression revealed that she knew which house Bailey had in mind.

Mandy laughed. "Bailey, you have lost it. They can't afford a home like that. They probably wouldn't even like the neighborhood, different class of people." She closed her mouth abruptly, seeming to regret the words that had just escaped. But a word spoken can't be retrieved.

"And just what class of people would that be?" Don said, irritated.

Mandy stammered. "Oh no, I didn't mean to suggest…"

"Your meaning was clear," Ashly said.

"I'm so sorry. I misspoke."

"Mandy, let's take a break," Don said emphatically. "We would like to visit our friend and see the house she has in mind. If it doesn't work out, we'll get back to you."

"But Mr. Antoine, these are good homes I've found. They are going to go fast. The market is hot right now."

"Thank you for the work you've done. We'll take our chances with the market. We'll let you know how this turns out."

"Well, I hate to bring this up, but you just signed a buyer's agreement with me. I'm your agent now."

Don picked up the agreement from the table and ripped it into pieces. "What agreement? "

Mandy fumed. Her face turned crimson, and her expression hardened. Bailey had never seen Mandy so unsettled, and she took some pleasure in this small victory. Mandy managed a goodbye, but it obviously took considerable restraint to remain professional. Then she hurried out the front door.

After she left, Ashly said to Bailey, "So you found us a home?"

Bailey smiled and bounced on her tiptoes. "Yes! And you are gonna love it!"

Then Bailey pointed to the picture on the wall. "Bring that with you and meet me there."

Again, the Antoines exchanged a ' Do you know what's going on?' kind of gaze, but they did as Bailey asked.

As soon as she got in her Jeep, Bailey frantically dialed Remy.

"Come on, pick up, pick up."

"Hello?" Remy answered.

"Oh, thank heaven. Hey, it's Bailey. I need a huge favor from you."

"Sure thing, what's up?"

"I need you to contact Mr. Stockton and open the Worthington house. I have a buyer."

"Oh no, what are you doing?"

"Listen, I mean it. I have a buyer. Since I don't work at any real estate company, I need you to do this for me. You can be the selling agent. I don't even care about the commission."

"Oh Bailey, I don't know."

"I have to do this, Remy, please, I'm not obsessing… I'm… going barefoot… Remy? Hello? Remy, you still there?"

"Okay, my friend, I'll set something up for next week."

"No, it has to be tonight, right now. We're already on the way."

"What! Bailey, that's impossible. It takes at least a week to get that set up."

"I know. I understand. Just try, would you?"

"Okay, I'll call him, but don't hold your breath."

"You're the best! Thank you so much!"

"Don't thank me yet," Remy said and hung up.

Chapter 49

A Home for the Antoines

A short while later, Bailey and the Antoines met Remy and Mr. Stockton at the old house in downtown Mobile, the lovely old home on Magnolia Lane, the home that nobody could sell. Bailey watched as the family got out of the car, their eyes wide as if eager but also uncertain. Ashly and Don exchanged glances. Bailey had seen that look before on other buyers—a mixture of excitement that this would be a dream come true, and apprehension because no way this would be affordable. Ashly and Don met each other in front of the car, held hands, and walked cautiously toward the house.

But Andrew bounded out of the car, laughing. "This is so cool!" He ran toward the front steps, and in two small leaps, landed up on the porch. Turning to his mom and dad, he asked, "Are we really going to live here?"

Don gave a quick, pleading look at Bailey as if to say, please don't be messing with us. Then he answered, "We'll see, son."

Once inside, they all exchanged greetings. Then Bailey watched and waited. With every passing moment, Ashly seemed to be falling more in love with the house. *They are the ones!* She recognized this reaction before among her clients. Connecting a family with their home had always been Bailey's natural gift. She had done her part and brought family and house together. Now, somehow, the real estate gods had to make it work out.

Remy whispered to Bailey. "I hope you know what you're doing." Then he introduced himself to the Antoines. "I'll be happy to show you around or answer any questions you like."

They thanked him and politely declined. The family wanted to wander and explore on their own. Bailey smiled confidently, as this was another good sign.

The Antoines meandered through the house, and now and then they heard Andrew exclaiming how cool it was, asking again if they were going to live there.

"Delightful family," Mr. Stockton said.

Remy began to fidget, shifting his weight from side to side. "Yes, they are, but eventually they'll want to know the price. What shall I tell them, Mr. Stockton?"

Mr. Stockton didn't answer at first. He looked at Bailey and said, "So, Miss Evans, what makes you think this is the right family for this house?"

Well, this is it. Now we'll know for sure. Mr. Stockton had said earlier that the owners were more concerned about finding the right family than they were price. But what answer should she give? They're nice people? Then she remembered something Lady Worthington had told her.

"They are worthy," she answered. Mr. Stockton stood straighter, and his eyes opened wide.

She could tell the words had hit home. Then she handed him the old photograph, the one from the Antoines' apartment.

"And they have Worthington approval," she added.

Mr. Stockton studied the picture for a moment. Then he smiled and extended his hand. "Miss Evans, we have a deal." He shook her hand, and then Remy's vigorously, seemingly very pleased.

Remy gasped, his face a bewildered look. "What just happened?"

"What just happened," Mr. Stockton said, "is that you have sold this house."

"I did? I mean, we did?"

"Indeed, you did. Now shall we call the family back in and discuss the price."

They didn't have to call, for just then the Antoines rounded the corner. They all moved to the living room and sat on the covered furniture.

Mr. Stockton beamed. "Mr. and Mrs. Antoine, how do you like the house?"

"We love it." Ashly put one hand over her heart. "It's breathtaking."

Don nodded and said, "Yes, it is stunning."

"All right!" Andrew exclaimed, pumping his fist in the air.

"This place is truly special." Ashly's eyes drank in the room. "I almost wish I hadn't seen it. Now, any other house will simply pale in comparison."

"Okay," Don said in a sterner tone. "What's the asking price?" He grabbed his wife's hand and sat up straighter, as if bracing for the bad news.

"Make me an offer," Mr. Stockton said.

"I'm sorry?" Don's face contorted in confusion and perhaps suspicion. He looked at Bailey with an expression of, so here comes the 'catch.'

"Make me an offer." Mr. Stockton repeated. "Those are the owner's instructions."

They heard a knock, then heard the front door squeak open.

"Hello? Anyone home?" Mandy called.

A family followed behind her, husband and wife with one young child, a girl. Their beautiful clothing indicated money. Without waiting for an invitation, Mandy escorted them into the living room.

"Mr. Stockton, I'd like you to meet Mr. and Mrs. Stevens. They're here with an offer."

Bailey practically jumped to her feet and said, "What!" her face red hot and the veins in her neck bulging.

Remy rose also. He put his arm on Bailey both to calm her down and encourage her to sit down.

"I got this, Bailey."

Reluctantly, Bailey sat.

"Mandy, this is highly inappropriate, and you know it."

Mandy glanced at Remy dismissively, then returned her attention to Mr. Stockton. "Mr. Stockton, I've been calling your office for a week now, trying to arrange a showing for this family. You haven't returned my calls."

Though Mandy's statement sounded more like an accusation, Mr. Stockton didn't respond, nor offer any apology.

"I just want you to know that another family, the Stevens, are very interested in this house." She motioned to the Antoines. "I know these are fine people; I'm just saying that the Stevens are ready to go. They have great credit, and they have approved financing for one million dollars." She placed extra emphasis on the one million dollars.

Don frowned and glared at Bailey.

Remy remained calm but said firmly, "I'm going to ask you to step outside, Mandy. When we are done, if Mr. Stockton wants to entertain your offer, he certainly can. But right now, you're interfering with our private conversation. This intrusion is completely unprofessional."

"I'm so sorry," Mandy said, feigning an apology. "I sometimes get overzealous when I just know I found the perfect family for this perfect house."

"Seriously? Oh, come on!" Bailey protested.

Remy looked hard at Bailey, and she shut up with a heavy sigh.

Mandy glanced at the Antoines, and then at the Stevens. In a polite southern voice, she said, "Y'all pardon me. I've created an awkward situation. We'll wait in the next room, and they can look at the house while y'all continue your discussion."

Bailey knew that Mandy had calculated this whole maneuver. She had achieved her purpose, to get an offer on the table before another was signed. Even the apology seemed rehearsed, all part of Mandy's strategy. Bailey looked at Mr. Stockton. He seemed unaffected by Mandy's dramatics. If anything, the estate manager looked irritated. He nodded politely. Mandy escorted the Stevens family on their tour.

Ashly took on the appearance of someone who just had her dream ripped right out from under her. "I don't know what I was thinking."

Don said, "We're sorry to have troubled you, Mr. Stockton. If that is the asking price or anywhere near it, that's way out of our league." He shot Bailey a disappointed, angry scowl.

They started to get up and leave when Mr. Stockton motioned for them to remain seated. "Before we were so rudely interrupted, I'd invited you to make me an offer, Mr. Antoine. I'd like to hear your answer."

Don answered, "What's the point, Mr. Stockton—to embarrass us? I can't make that kind of offer, not even close."

Mr. Stockton spoke calmly. "I'm not trying to embarrass you, Mr. Antoine. What kind of offer can you make?"

Don looked at his wife Ashly, and then back to Bailey.

Bailey said, "They've been pre-approved for a loan of up to one hundred seventy-five thousand."

Mr. Stockton looked at the couple. Don nodded agreement.

Mr. Stockton addressed Bailey and Remy. "I presume that's probably the high-end of their approval?"

Bailey didn't answer this time but looked to the couple instead.

"Yes, sir, it is, but we *can* manage that," Don assured. "Except, we don't have much money for a down payment."

Mr. Stockton rubbed his beard and said, "I'll make you the counteroffer of one hundred fifty thousand."

His words stunned everyone in the room. Never, never in Bailey's entire real estate career, had a seller ever countered *lower*!

"You mean you're countering at a lower price?" Don asked.

"That's correct, Mr. Antoine." He said it with all the seriousness and dignity of the man in charge of the estate. "Do we have a deal?"

Don looked at Bailey and Remy, checking to see if this was for real. Both Remy's and Bailey's eyes were bright with surprise and delight. They said nothing and quickly nodded their heads yes.

Don looked around the room as if convinced there was a hidden camera somewhere, and this was a cruel, elaborate joke. Then, he and Ashly shared their secret communication. Finally, he ventured his answer. "Okay, yes, Mr. Stockton, we have a deal."

Mr. Stockton extended his hand. "Congratulations, Mr. and Mrs. Antoine."

Don shook his hand tentatively, perhaps still waiting for the catch. Ashly screamed with delight, and Andrew did a double fist pump. Bailey and Remy clapped.

Mandy appeared from around the corner. "You've got to be kidding me! A hundred and fifty thousand dollars? What kind of scheme are you running here?"

Bailey stood, and this time Remy did not stop her. But Mr. Stevens did. Nudging Mandy aside, he walked over to the estate manager.

"Mr. Stockton, we love this house, and we're prepared to offer you a million dollars for it," he said.

Again, the room got silent. Mr. Stockton stood unhurriedly. "Mr. Stevens, thank you for your generous offer. This house has been sold to the Antoines."

"Seriously…"

"This is not a discussion, Mr. Stevens. The decision is final." He brought his attention to Mandy. "If you will kindly allow this family some privacy so they can celebrate their purchase."

Disgruntled, Mandy and her clients left, arguing with one another all the way to their cars.

Warm contentment coursed through Bailey as she watched the Antoines revel in the moment. Andrew continued to hoot and holler, running around from room to room. Ashly couldn't stop the tears any more than she could hold back the smile that accompanied them. Don just chuckled, shaking his head as he signed the documents Remy had already prepared. The real estate gods had delivered. Like sweet icing on a delicious cake, Bailey had bested Mandy in the process.

Then Bailey saw Lady Worthington. She appeared just past them on the other side of the group. The elegant lady gave a slow nod of approval as the long-awaited family had finally come home. She placed her hand over her heart, looked straight at Bailey, blew her a kiss, and faded like the mist. No one else saw her, and Bailey never saw her again. Except for telling Keri, she kept this vision as a treasured secret. A deep satisfaction welled within Bailey. She had sold the house that no one could sell, and somehow, it also felt like she had helped right an ancient wrong, helped heal an old family pain. Most importantly, she found the Antoines a home.

Chapter 50

Just One Piece Missing

Wanting to celebrate the moment, Remy convinced Bailey to meet him at the Seize the Day Café. Arriving first, she claimed an empty table on the porch. Late afternoon transformed into a beautiful evening, and at this time of day, the café wasn't crowded. Shortly, Remy brought her a French press, her favorite.

"You did it." Remy sat down and laughed. "You did it! You sold the house that nobody could sell. And right in front of Mandy! Ha! That was awesome!" He slapped the table in delight. The spoon and saucer clinked.

Bailey smiled, delighting in the experience.

"What's more amazing is that you didn't do this for money. You did this out of the kindness of your good ole heart, 'cause you love the Antoines." He lifted his mug, and they clinked glasses. "Beautiful, Bailey, simply beautiful. How did you know? How did you do that?"

Bailey shrugged. "I told you I could."

"No seriously, Bailey, how did you know they were the ones?"

Bailey looked at her friend for a moment. How could she explain the flashes of insight, the cross around her neck, the lighted signs, and the ghostly owners?

Finally, she said, "I just went barefoot." She winked.

Remy nodded, then laughed again with delight. "Well, here's to going barefoot." They clanked their mugs again.

Bailey looked back at Remy with a wry smile. "Would you like to hear what really happened?"

Remy set his mug down and brought his full focus on Bailey. "Absolutely," he said.

Bailey didn't open up to others easily, or to very many , but she felt safe with Remy. She thought he would honor this as a precious moment. Also, Remy had first told her to 'go barefoot.' He deserved an explanation.

"I meant what I said. I got a feeling, an insight, and I decided to trust it." Bailey then recounted the events that led her to the sale. She told about the bad guys, the oil being fake, her theory of why Dauphin Island Marine Center burned, Cricket's boat, all of it except for meeting Lady Worthington. Remy listened with rapt attention. He never questioned it and took every word seriously. When she finished, neither spoke. The silence sanctified the moment.

Then Remy said, "But how did you know the Antoines were the ones to buy the house?"

Bailey paused, staring at her friend, then answered, "Call it, intuition."

Remy didn't reply but accepted her incomplete answer. He raised his mug again. "Well, here's to trusting your gut." He sipped his coffee then said, "So, what's next? How do we stop these guys?"

"We?"

"You bet." He sat up straighter. "I'm in."

Bailey was touched that he wanted to be part of the solution. "Well, I've got to get some evidence back to MJ, and that'll hopefully stop the sale."

"When's the closing?"

"Tomorrow afternoon."

"Tomorrow afternoon! Tomorrow is Mardi Gras."

"Not over there. It's just Tuesday."

"How in the world can you get enough evidence by tomorrow afternoon?"

Bailey looked blankly, shaking her head. "It's gonna be tight, that's for sure. Jade's got some proof, a report, or something. That, by far, is the most important thing. If everything comes together, it should be enough. There's just one piece missing."

"You still need another developer to replace Acheron," Remy concluded.

"Yep."

Remy stared off into the dusk. Bailey sensed his wheels turning. "What?" she asked. "You got another buyer?"

"Ummm… no. I wish I did."

"Well, holler if you bump into any multi-millionaire developers on your way home. Hopefully, the property will be available after four p.m. tomorrow."

"Yeah, I'll be sure and keep my eyes open. You never know when you're going to run into a cash-rich developer just looking for a last-minute project," Remy joked. "But then you just did sell the house that couldn't be sold. So, I'd say anything's possible at this point." Remy touched her gently on the arm. "Be careful, my friend."

She put her hand on his. "I will. Thank you for being such an awesome friend."

"At least come back to Thomason Brothers with me and get the credit you deserve for this, along with a referral fee. Besides, Ann would love to see you."

"Thanks, but no thanks. Tell Ann 'hello.' I've got to get back. And I don't need a referral fee. Seeing the smiles on their faces and a closing for my friend is payment enough."

They finished their visit with a hug and promised to keep in touch.

Bailey climbed into her Jeep and called Keri.

"Hey, it's me. Any luck reaching Jade?… Well, keep trying… We've got till tomorrow to get that info on the spill. Hey, guess what? I sold the unsellable house! Yes! It's way cool. And I sold it to the Antoines… You know, the family with the cute little boy… Anyway, I'm gonna crash at my Mobile apartment tonight. I've got a few things to pick up there… Okay, talk tomorrow."

Bailey's plan was coming together. Now all she had to do was get whatever proof Jade had back to Lost Key Realty. Right now, she needed some rest and a good night's sleep. It had been a big, glorious day. Still, an uneasiness haunted her, casting a shadow on this bright moment. She couldn't help wondering, *Jade, where are you?*

Chapter 51

Finding Jade

ailey woke to the ringing of her cell phone.
"Yeah?"

"Hey, it's me," Keri yelled over the hum of her
WaveRunner and the wind howling into her phone.
"Listen, I just spoke with Jade. She said she's been getting some strange messages, really creeping her out. Bailey, you awake? You hearin' me?"

"Yeah, I'm here." Bailey sat up. "Where is she?"

"She's heading to the Bienville Mall. The one on
Airport Boulevard by the interstate."

"Yes, I know the one. Where do I meet her?"

"In the food court. She's got the information we
need. I'm working around the causeway today. I'm en
route, but you're closer. Can you go help her?"

The news jolted Bailey awake faster than her
favorite French press coffee. "Tell her to stay right
there. It's a public place, so she's probably safe. I'm
on my way."

Bienville Mall, a one-story sprawling structure, sat
on what used to be the outer edges of west Mobile until
the city continued to grow west. Bailey followed the mall
access road around to the Belk shopping center and
parked near the back in a space next to a planted tree

and another car. *This spot ought to give me some cover and a quick getaway if needed.*

She donned a baseball cap from the back seat along with some sunglasses. It wasn't much, but it was the best disguise she could come up with at the moment. The ball cap bore the Crab Island logo on the front, one of her favorite spots in Destin.

She started for the door and immediately noticed two men dressed in black hanging around the entrance. They didn't look like typical mall security, rather more like Secret Servicemen she'd seen on the news. *They must work for Acheron—Martin's minions.* One of them kept glancing at a photograph he held in his hand, comparing the picture to the faces of those who went inside. Bailey wondered whose face was in that photo, hers or Jade's? She adjusted her path to stay far out in the parking lot, making it more challenging for them to recognize her. She walked past the department store toward the food court entrance. That's when she saw a young redhead, with knee-high black boots, walking at a brisk pace toward the same entryway. *It's Jade!* Bailey raised her arm and started to call out but abruptly stopped as she noticed two men following her goth friend. *I doubt she could hear me anyway.* The men were dressed less conspicuously than the other two around the corner. Their shirts looked like something they might wear fishing or milling about the house. *Maybe they are just a couple of regular dudes.* Yet, they seemed intensely focused, eyes forward, and tracking Jade.

Without warning, a car screeched to a stop, it's horn blowing. It missed hitting Bailey by an inch.

"Hey! Watch where you're going!" the driver yelled.

"Sorry," Bailey replied, taking a step back as the car sped past.

She started toward the mall entrance again. Jade had just stepped inside, and the door was closing behind her. The two men walked faster. Their attention was still fixed straight ahead; they didn't even turn when the car honked. Any average person would have been naturally curious to see what the commotion was about. *They can't just be shoppers,* Bailey thought.

Seconds later, they hurriedly disappeared through the same door Jade had just gone through. Bailey quickened her pace.

Thankfully, it was busy for a Tuesday afternoon. Kids were out of school, and the parades had cranked up to full swing downtown for Mardi Gras. The food court brimmed with hungry patrons, forming a line at every vendor.

This is good. It will give Jade some cover.

Remembering Jade was vegetarian, she walked toward Farmer's Veggies but didn't see her friend. Across the way, Bailey saw the Japanese sushi vendor. *Maybe there,* she thought, since they did have meatless rolls on their menu. But as she approached, no Jade in sight. Bailey scanned the rest of the food court and found no other vegetarian options. She was about to give up the search when she spotted a red-haired girl wearing knee-high black boots standing in line at the Chick-fil-A. *There you are!* Thankfully, she didn't see the two men anywhere. *Maybe they're shoppers, after all, probably two dads on an errand. I guess I am paranoid.* Though relieved, it was still odd to see Jade in line to buy chicken when she had sworn off any kind of meat. *Stress eating, I bet.*

Bailey walked up behind the girl and tapped her on the shoulder. "Since when do you eat chick—" she had started to say, only to discover it was not Jade. "Oh, I'm sorry, I thought you were someone else."

The girl nodded and said, "No problem."

Panic rose within Bailey. *Where could they have gone? Have they taken her?* She hurried through the dining area out into the atrium. Many shoppers strolled past but still no Jade. Then she saw the two men sitting in some of the chairs and couches under the skylights. They were definitely not shopping but rather waiting. They didn't slouch the way she'd seen most men sit on a mall couch. Instead, they sat more upright, as if on ready. All doubt disappeared when one of them touched his ear and spoke into a tiny microphone. *They are after Jade!* A security guard lingered nearby, observing them with evident curiosity.

That means they don't have her, but they must know where she is, or else why sit there waiting? Jade, where did you go?

The lounge area was situated near the end of one branch of the wide indoor thoroughfare. Three stores occupied this corner of Bienville Mall, Belk on the left, Macy's at the end, and to the right... *of course!* Goth World. Jade must have discovered that she was being followed and ducked in there. They were waiting for her to come out.

Bailey ventured forward, hoping not to draw their attention. The two men frequently glanced toward the Goth store, like they were watching it. *Yep, Jade has to be in there.* Bailey pulled the brim of her cap down and continued into the atrium. She stopped at a kiosk selling necklaces, bought the first one she saw, and asked for a large bag. The attendant gave her a puzzled look but seemed happy for a sale. Bailey stayed close to the far wall, cap down, big bag in hand, looking inside the display windows pretending to shop until finally reaching the Goth store. She stepped inside and gave a glance back. The two strangers still sat, talking to one another. They hadn't noticed her. *Whew!* The dimly lit black lights inside the store created a stark contrast to the brightness of the mall atrium. Rows and carousels of shirts adorned the walls and filled the floor space, their brilliant multi-colored designs glowing under the purplish hue.

A young brunette girl approached. She looked like a younger version of Jade.

"May I help you find something?"

"No, thanks, I'm just browsing, waiting on a friend."

"Are you Bailey?"

Bailey startled. She had not expected to be recognized.

"Yes, I'm Bailey," she said, trying not to act surprised.

The attendant smiled broader, her teeth glowing white under the black light. "Your friend Jade asked me to keep an eye out for you," she said. "She's trying on outfits in our dressing room." She motioned to the back of the store.

That's brilliant. Good hiding place. "Thank you very much."

"You're very welcome. Let me know if there's anything else I can do for you." She smiled and returned to her duties.

Bailey pushed through the opening of a long, dark, plush curtain that hung from ceiling to floor, and entered the dressing rooms. There were three rooms on each side with long, black velvet curtains for doors. No one else was in there. Then she noticed a flicker of movement behind the last curtain on the left.

"Jade?" Bailey called.

"Bailey? Is that you?" a voice asked from behind the curtain. The slender, redheaded, freckle-faced young woman stuck her head out and peered apprehensively. She saw Bailey and sighed with relief.

"Yep, it's me," Bailey answered.

Jade reached for Bailey and, with trembling hands, pulled her into the dressing room. Jade struggled to compose herself, taking shallow, quick breaths. She kept glancing, wide-eyed, back at the dressing room entrance. Dark circles, not makeup, hung under her eyes.

"When is the last time you slept?" Bailey asked. "You okay?"

Jade almost started crying. "No, I'm not. Have you seen them? The men in black? They're everywhere." She glanced at the door again.

"Yeah, I saw them. I don't think those goons recognized me, though. Right now, we've gotta get out of here."

Jade's eyes darted again at the entrance. "Sounds good to me, but how?"

Bailey gently held her new friend by the shoulders. "Breathe." She took a deep breath. Jade mimicked her. "That's it; just take a few breaths." As they continued, Bailey felt a calm assurance from deep within. Then, in her mind, she saw Jade going up to the security guard, and then the two men at the back door leaving. She saw a chase, a WaveRunner, previews of things to come.

"Bailey? Hello?" Jade said. "So how do we get out of here?"

She refocused on her friend and stated, "I have a plan."

Jade's expression softened at the news.

"Did you bring the information about your research?" Bailey asked.

Jade reached in her purse and pulled out two, three-and-half-inch, square flat objects, one red, the other blue. Jade held up the red one. "It's all on here."

Bailey studied the object. It was the new floppy disk Jade had shown her back at the DMC.

"The oil sample that Keri sent me is not crude oil, not something you'd find from an oil spill. It's homemade, manufactured to look like crude oil. The proof is on this disk."

"I knew it! This is excellent news." Bailey said. "Jade, you may have just saved a town. So, what's on the other disk?"

"Oh, nothing, it's blank. I was going to make a copy but didn't have the new drives at home, and then, well, you know, the lab burned."

Bailey's eyes gleamed. "This gives me an idea. Okay, so here's how we're going to get out of here. I saw a security guard out in the mall entrance. I bet he's still there. He seemed to have his eye on those two creepy dudes following you. Now, we'll go to the entrance of this store. You'll hand me the disk with your results on it, slowly, so they can see you give it to me. Then, wait until someone's leaving the store and walk alongside them. Joining them will give you a second or two of cover."

"Bailey, I'm scared."

"I know." Bailey wondered if Jade was about to have a full-blown panic attack.

"Hear me out, Jade. Hurry right up to the guard. Tell him you need help and ask him if he could escort you to the other end of the mall. As you're walking, tell the guard those two men are following you. He'll call reinforcements and maybe even the police. That should scare them off."

"What about you?"

"Once the men see you give me the disk, I think they'll follow me anyway and leave you alone. Just to be safe, you stay with security."

"You *want* them to follow you?" Jade asked.

"I'm gonna slip past them. I parked my Jeep outside, ready to go. I'll get this information back to the local authorities and Lost Key Realty."

Jade nodded. Bailey couldn't tell how much Jade believed in the plan, but she trusted her enough to try it.

"You can do this, Jade. Once those guys realize you don't have the information, they will leave you alone. But you have to report this to the police! Then they'll leave you alone forever."

"I just don't think I can take any more of those threatening phone calls," Jade said.

"What calls?" Bailey asked.

"I've been getting these scary messages. Some man's voice says he's going to get me. Tells me what I was wearing that day." Jade's voice broke. "It really freaks me out, Bailey. Then he says my time's up."

Bailey jolted at Jade's words. "He said that? He said, 'Time's up?' "

"Yes, exactly that."

Bailey felt her anger rise, and she made no effort to suppress it. "The plan will work, Jade. Just get to security and tell them everything. We're gonna stop those calls."

Jade nodded sheepishly. "What about you? Will they leave you alone?"

"Yeah. I'll make sure of it." She paused, and her eyes grew distant, seeing something Jade could not. Then she said, "Hey, I've got another idea, slight change of plans. Come on, let's go."

Chapter 52

Escape

ailey and Jade walked to the entrance of the store and stopped. The security guard stood watchful nearby. The two strangers, still sitting on the couch, spotted them right away. Both stood and seemed surprised to see Bailey, too. *Good, that's what I was hoping.* Jade and Bailey faced each other. Then, Jade slowly handed Bailey a blue, square, plastic disk. Bailey tucked it under her sweater. They hugged goodbye, and Jade headed straight for the security guard, while Bailey headed in the opposite direction. Out of the corner of her eye, Bailey saw one man talk into a tiny microphone clipped onto the lapel of his shirt. *That's right; follow me. I've got what you want. Leave Jade alone.*

The mall officer watched intensely as the scene unfolded. Jade quickly walked right up to him. The guard towered over her, the top of Jade's head only reaching his chest level. His physique looked as dense as an oak tree. The men had started toward Jade, but when she reached the guard, they paused. The officer glanced back at the two, and they immediately turned and began talking to each other, obviously trying to act casual. Jade and the officer walked down the mall corridor away from them. As hoped, the men did not pursue. Instead, they headed toward Bailey. She saw one of them talking again into his lapel mic. *They must be alerting others to look for me. Good, at least Jade will be safe now with the officer.*

Bailey quickened her pace. The men matched it. When she reached the entrance to Belk's, she swiftly darted inside. She knew she only had a minute, maybe two, before they caught up with her. The exit to the parking lot was at the other end of the store, except the men from earlier still lingered just outside. One touched his ear and said something to the other one. Then they too entered the store, eyes searching, guarding the exit. Her adrenaline rushed as she realized that now four men were looking for her. Bailey turned left and squatted down, pretending to browse some shoes on a lower rack. Out of the corner of her eye, she saw her pursuers enter from the atrium. They walked a few feet farther into the store just past her line of sight. Crouching, Bailey scurried behind the two men and out into the mall. Staying low, she turned right, then darted into the next store, hoping they would keep looking for her in Belk's.

Whoops, this store did not have a back entrance. It was the next one. As Bailey turned to leave, she saw one of the pursuers had stepped back into the mall. She retreated. *Maybe he didn't see me.* She spotted a dressing room, grabbed a shirt on the way, and dashed inside. She cracked the door for a peak and saw one of the men at the entrance. Bailey held her breath as he scanned the room, spoke into his mic, and then left. He didn't seem in a hurry. *Whew!* Bailey exhaled. Still, time grew short. It wouldn't take long for them to realize she was not in Belk's. Cautiously she peeked out around the corner into the mall.

All clear, no bad guys. She hurried into the next store and made her way to the exit. She pretended to shop and waited. Bailey fell in with a group of three women leaving, arms full of shopping bags. When she got outside, she glanced behind her, checking to be sure no one followed. She hurried to her Jeep, more exposed now that the car beside it had gone. A yellow Jeep stands out; there aren't too many of those on the road anyway. Bailey hopped in and quickly started the engine. Just as she did, a black sedan screeched to a stop a few feet away. A man burst out of the car and headed toward her. She froze. No way! He was the same thug who had come after her and Mark on the beach, the same one who had shot at them from the bridge. He reached inside his jacket as he approached.

Bailey's stomach leaped into her throat as she muttered, "Oh no! Oh, no, no!"

Instinctively she slammed the gear shift into reverse and quickly pulled out of her space. She stopped, pushed it in first, and floored the gas pedal just as the man reached her door. Now holding a silver pistol in one hand, he grabbed the door handle with the other and yanked. The door opened, then immediately slammed shut as the Jeep hurled forward. Bailey heard a groan and loud cursing when the man fell and hit the pavement. Briefly, she watched as he became a shrinking image in her side-view mirror. She sped on through the parking lot, narrowly missing a shopper loading packages into her car.

"Hey, slow down!" the lady yelled as the yellow blur screeched past.

In her side mirror, she saw the man scramble to his feet, gun in hand, and run back to the sedan. He jumped in, slamming the door. Their tires squealed as they began to pursue. They had found her.

Mobile began to close in on her again. The city of wonder and sentimentality had transformed into a maze of death. She turned left into an old neighborhood. *There's no way I can go on the highway,* she thought, *they'll chase me down. The sedan is faster. And I'm not in a sports car this time."* She figured her best chance of escape would be back roads. She could still see them in her mirrors. The sedan kept pace, matching her turn for turn. She made a sharp right. The car behind her made the same right. Only this time, they drew a little closer. Bailey drove as fast as she could, but she knew it wouldn't be enough. Turning left, and then weaving right, she ran a stop sign and then a red light. Still, they followed. Bailey couldn't believe they were willing to risk exposure like this. The passenger, who had come after them on the beach, flung his arm out the window, holding a long-tipped gun. She heard the clang as he shot at her with the silenced pistol. *No! Not my Jeep!* For a split second, she thought of Cricket and the pain he must have felt as the bullets pelted his boat. *Seriously, Bailey? You can buy another Jeep! These men are trying to kill you!* She pulled the steering wheel hard left, then again quickly right. She couldn't tell exactly where she had traveled, but judging from the old oak trees, she believed her location to be somewhere downtown. Then she heard a loud pop. The car began to shake, and the steering became difficult to control. *They shot my tire!* It felt like her right rear tire. The flat tire forced her to drive at a reduced speed. Her hope of escape faded rapidly, the walls of the maze closing in.

Just then, she heard music coming from outside. She looked left and saw a Mardi Gras parade only a block away. Hundreds, maybe even thousands of spectators lined both sides of the street. Abruptly, she turned left and then eased off the right shoulder onto a grassy lawn. When the Jeep finally slid to a stop, she quickly turned off the ignition, jumped out, and ran toward the parade. She heard the car skid to a halt behind her. Two doors thudded closed. She knew who followed. Just as she reached the edge of the crowd, she glanced back to make sure. *Yep, those are the same two who chased us on Dauphin Island.* She wasn't as worried about the heavyset man. She could outrun him. But the other followed fast and determined, with a crazy, angry look in his eyes. She shuddered at the thought of what he might do if he caught her. What revenge would he take for that nasty blow to the head that she had given him back on the island?

Bailey ducked and dodged her way through the crowd. She fell in step with a float and waved to the spectators like she was part of the procession, zigzagging her way across the street also thick with people. Then she saw the crazy man emerge on her side, too; the other one nowhere in sight. *They must be working on both sides of the road.* Bailey twisted and turned, bumping shoulders and pushing a path through the jungle of people. Cat-like, she threaded her way down the street along with the parade. Every once in a while, she glanced back, still seeing the man in pursuit, his eyes locked on her. He navigated the thick crowd with surprising agility and speed. Then he spoke something into his sleeve. *Are there more of them?*

The chase had taken them to the heart of downtown now, near the end of the parade route. Perhaps it would've been easier to hide in one of the stores, maybe go to Dell's popcorn shop, or duck behind an alley. But one thought dominated the rest: run and keep running. However, now there seemed nowhere left to go, and no safe place to hide. An image of Keri flashed in her mind. *Yes! Keri is working the marsh in the Mobile Bay! If I can just get to her.* Bailey reached for her phone but found only an empty pocket. She remembered laying it in the passenger seat next to her. It must have bounced onto the floorboard with all the wild driving. The parade turned left up ahead, and then looked like it ended in a vast parking area. She thought of staying with the crowd. Yet, the sea of spectators hadn't provided protection, seeming instead like another obstacle working in her attacker's favor. No, she must stop this deal. She must find Keri. Then she saw him!

He had broken through the crowd of people, his eyes fixed on her like scopes on a target. He didn't even seem to be breathing heavily. Bailey raced toward the old tunnel and hit the little walkway. She coughed as the fumes from the car exhausts flooded her lungs and sickened her stomach. She glanced back and saw a flash from the end of his pistol. The tile above her head cracked and splintered as a bullet made an impact. She screamed and tried to run faster. The cross around her neck began to warm, bringing a strange comfort even as the agent of death loomed. A second whiz-crack shattered another piece of tile a few feet in front of her. *He's not trying to scare me. He means to kill me!* Finally, she emerged on the other side of the tunnel and breathed deep the fresher air. She sprinted down to the old causeway. Keri and a couple of other people had gathered about one hundred yards on the left. They were working just offshore in the marshy water in their boats, just like in her vision. Bailey kept her eye on her friend like a lighthouse in a storm. Keri spotted Bailey and immediately guided the small boat to the bank, jumped out, and started running toward her. A wave of relief and happiness swept through Bailey. Tears welled in her eyes.

"We've got to… get out of here," Bailey said, gasping for air between the words. Just then, Keri's eyes widened with a frightened look. Bailey didn't stop but glanced back and saw the attacker emerge from around the bend. He lifted his gun, pointing it toward them. They heard a whiz-thump. Dirt flew in front of them. They screamed and darted for the WaveRunner. Keri's coworker saw the attack, and this caught the man's attention. The attacker lowered his pistol and slowed, irritated by this interruption.

Just then, the black sedan pulled up behind him. "Get in!" yelled his partner. The gunman growled in frustration but climbed into the passenger's seat. The car sped toward them.

"We are not gonna make it!" Keri shouted. And they were not. Bailey surmised that the car would overtake them before they could escape. *This time I'm not gonna make it to the boat. We just need a few more seconds.* Bailey reached in her pocket and extracted the floppy disk she'd gotten from Jade. She held it up so the men could see the blue square object. Then she tossed it off to the side and kept running toward their escape. The car stopped, and the men got out to retrieve it. That provided the extra time they needed. Keri and Bailey jumped on her watercraft and accelerated toward the Mobile Bay.

Chapter 53

The Race for Lost Key

The craft rapidly bounced and skimmed across their brackish escape route. The motor whined a high-pitched hum, spraying an arch of water behind. Keri hollered over her shoulder. "Did you just toss Jade's report to the bad guys?"

Bailey leaned closer. "No! But they think I did. Jade had two floppy disks on her. That one's blank. She was going to make extra copies of her findings, but never got the chance. We staged it so that the bad guys saw her give that blank one to me. I was hoping they would think I had the information and leave Jade alone."

"You're livin' on the edge, Bailey! But I guess if you hadn't done all that, we wouldn't be talking right now."

"We've got to get to Lost Key Realty as fast as possible."

Keri yelled back over the engine and wind, "I'll take us up the Intracoastal Waterway. We can get pretty close to the bridge, but we'll have to run on foot from there."

Bailey understood this, but it helped to think it through out loud. Then, simultaneously, both said, "We need to call the office."

Keri handed Bailey her phone. "Here, you dial."

Bailey dialed. "Eddie! Eddie, listen to me very carefully. Stop MJ from signing those documents. I don't care if they're in a meeting; interrupt it… Eddie, just do it. Look, just put MJ on the line… Hello? Hello, Eddie, are you there?"

Bailey checked the cell signal, but the screen had gone dark. "Dammit! The battery's dead. Don't you charge your phone?"

Keri didn't answer. She didn't have to. Bailey wasn't mad at her but rather the whole situation. They raced toward the mouth of the bay, then took a left toward Lost Key. It would take a while to get there. Holding onto Keri, she put her head back and sighed.

"Don't give up yet! New plan!" Keri said, turning the craft sharply right, out toward the sea.

Bailey almost fell off but tightened her grip. "What are you doing?" Bailey protested.

"Trust me," Keri said.

Not far in the distance, Bailey could see a long, orange, cigar-shaped speedboat.

"Is that the same…" Bailey began.

"Yep, I think so," Keri answered and handed Bailey a small orange flag attached to a plastic pole. Typically, it was used to mark her spot in the water so other boats could see her when she was working.

"Wave this around."

Bailey stood up and started waving. The speedboat driver pulled out some binoculars and peered their way, then turned the boat toward them.

"They see us!" Keri said.

Suddenly, they hit a wave, as the water had gotten rougher when they transitioned from the bay to the

Gulf. Like a trampoline, the swell catapulted Bailey off the back and into the water. When she surfaced, she saw the man in the boat pointing toward her direction. Keri turned around, realizing Bailey had fallen off.

Quickly, she returned and pulled alongside to pick up her friend. "You okay?"

Bailey climbed back on board. She flipped her wet hair back and spat out some water through the side of her mouth.

"Sure, I'm okay. Bad guys are trying to kill me, a pirate is about to steal my town, and I'm soaking wet, stuck in the middle of the Gulf. Why wouldn't I be okay?"

The cigar boat pulled up next to them. One other man was on board, too. The driver's blond hair shimmered as if dyed by the sun. His bright blue eyes captivated them both. Bailey raised an eyebrow at his shirtless, tanned, toned beach-body.

"You gals alright?" he asked smoothly.

"We are now." Keri smiled.

Bailey rolled her eyes. "Every time we see y'all seems like I get soaked."

"I'm sure I don't know what you're talking about," he said, playing dumb.

"Yeah, right," Bailey retorted, wondering if he was only 'playing' at being dumb. Turning serious, she said, "We need a ride and fast."

She explained the situation as briefly as she could. Keri lowered an anchor on her WaveRunner to keep it in place till they returned. The men helped them aboard the craft—then, they raced toward Lost Key. Bailey couldn't believe their luck. They just might make it in time, after all.

Keri kept smiling at the driver. "Nice boat. Looks familiar."

He grinned. "We get around."

Chapter 54

Thomas

Thanks to the two good Samaritans and their orange speedboat, they arrived at Keri's houseboat at three thirty p.m. The journey took about a quarter of the time it would've taken them on the Wave-Runner. The boat pulled up alongside the dock, and the girls jumped out.

"Thanks so much," Bailey said, "you're a real lifesaver." She ran toward Keri's truck.

When Keri got on the dock, she looked back and winked. "You know where I live, come visit anytime." She smiled, and the dreamy guy winked. Then the boat sped off.

"Come on, Keri, we have to go!" Bailey yelled from behind her. Keri ran into the house, grabbed the keys, and sprinted for the old Chevy. They jumped in and took off for the real estate office, hoping it was not too late. They could've ridden the boat somewhere closer like the bridge, but they'd still have to run there on foot. So ultimately, Keri's truck was the fastest way.

As they ascended the bridge crossing the Intracoastal, they saw two men dressed in black standing along the railing. They were looking west toward Mobile. One of them had a pair of binoculars.

"There they are!" Bailey said, pointing at them. "Are those the same ones that have been chasing me?"

"It could be. Who else wears black in this heat? Besides, they could have gotten here much faster in a car. They're not locals; that's obvious. They're expecting us to come skimming across the water, not drive over the bridge."

Bailey began to panic. "What do we do? Should we turn around? Maybe we should turn around!"

"Calm down! Let's just drive right by." Keri reached over and grabbed Bailey's shoulder and nudged her forward. "Duck down. They're looking for two ladies, not one. And they are more familiar with your face than mine." Just as Bailey had gotten her head down, Keri said, "One of the dudes is looking right at me."

Instinctively, Bailey started to lift her head, but Keri pushed her back down. "Are you nuts! I said, stay down."

"Sorry, I couldn't help it," came the muffled apology.

Keri didn't say anything but drove steadily and calmly forward.

"He's taking a good long look that's for sure," Keri relayed. "He's leaning his head as though there was something familiar about me." She pretended not to notice his stare. Bailey could tell their speed remained constant as they casually drove right past.

She turned her head and saw Keri checking her rearview mirror. "He's looking through his binoculars again watching the channel. It worked!"

When they crested the bridge, and once the men were out of sight, Bailey sat up, and said, "Of course it did. I knew it would work all along."

"What? You did not. You practically peed your pants back there."

"I'm just sayin', it had to work. After all, those goons had never seen your truck and hadn't seen you up close. They were looking for two women on a WaveRunner. Not one gal in an old beat-up Chevy. You were right is all I'm sayin'."

"What was that? I don't think I heard you. I was what?"

"You were rrrr... rrrrr... right," Bailey said, feigning difficulty saying the word.

Keri playfully hit Bailey's arm. "I'm just messing with ya."

"Pay attention. We're here."

They pulled up to the red light at the intersection. The real estate office sat just across the way. A long black limousine had parked out front, and another large man dressed in a tacky Hawaiian shirt stood next to it, like a chauffeur guarding the front door.

"You gotta be freaking kidding me. Who are these guys, the island mafia?" Bailey said.

"Come on; we've come too far to turn back now," Keri said. "How do we get around this big Bahama dude?"

"Turn left, then park around back. MJ has a back-door entrance. We'll go in that way."

Minutes later, the old Chevy pickup crunched to a stop. Bailey and Keri jumped out and hurried for the door. They found it unlocked as Bailey knew it would be. MJ, Martin, and his lawyer, along with the local attorney, were sitting around the conference table. Instinctively, everyone looked up at their interruption. MJ put her pen down.

Then the local lawyer said, "That's it. Congratulations, everyone."

They were about to shake hands when Bailey yelled, "Stop! You can't do this!"

Martin ignored her. MJ stood up and spoke to Bailey in a compassionate tone. "Bailey, I had to…"

"The man is a crook, and this deal is null and void," Bailey interjected.

Martin's lawyer slowly stood. "What is the meaning of this?" he said coldly.

Bailey's cross began to warm. The man glanced down at it then back up to Bailey's eyes.

Bailey looked at MJ and said, "The oil spill is fake."

Martin stared at Bailey with a stone-cold gaze. Though he said nothing, his eyes sent a clear signal warning Bailey not to cross *this* line.

The lawyer protested. "Not that again. This young lady has lost her mind."

Margaret Jane sighed. "Oh, Bailey, we've been over this."

Bailey persisted. "He did it to drive the prices down so he could buy all our land for less than it's worth."

"That's preposterous! This accusation is a defamation of my client's character," Martin's minion yelled.

"That's a serious accusation," the local lawyer added.

"I have proof," Bailey said.

The room fell silent as all eyes fixed on her. *Well, I crossed the line now.*

Martin sat still and peered at Bailey.

You are wondering what proof I have, aren't you? So am I.

"Well, where is this proof, young lady?" the lawyer asked impatiently.

"It will be here soon," Bailey said.

Even Keri looked surprised. "You don't have it with you?" her friend whispered.

"I've heard enough," Martin said as he rose and gathered his papers. The men began to pack their briefcases to leave. "It was a pleasure doing business with you, Margaret Jane," he added.

MJ returned the gesture, but Bailey could tell that MJ took little pleasure in this deal, though she did seem relieved to get it all behind her.

Martin stepped toward Bailey and said, "I told you to leave my project alone." Then he whispered in her ear. "You'll wish you had."

As the pseudo pirate was about to leave, Bailey said. "No! You'll wish you'd never come here. This town is my home! Not your project."

She'd thrown down the gauntlet now, making a direct challenge to the marauder. What surprised her was how confident she felt. She stood ready to wrestle him if that's what it took to save her town.

Martin chuckled at her defiance and continued toward the front door.

Again, Bailey felt a strength course through her. She stood tall, powerful, no headache, no ringing of the ears, and her mind crystal clear. *Well, I did my part. I followed my instinct, trusted my intuition. Hello, universe? If anything is going to happen, now would be a good time.*

A faint siren echoed through the silence, growing louder each moment. Her necklace warmed and Bailey's mouth curved in a victor's smile.

"The sheriff is on his way," she said.

Martin's eyes darted frantically. Then he did something seemingly out of character. The man who'd been in control and unflappable, now bolted through the office and out the front door yelling instructions to his driver as he piled in the car.

"No, no, you're not disappearing this time." Bailey took off after him, yelling back at Keri. "Come on, hurry. He's getting away."

"I don't think this is a good idea," Keri said, as she followed Bailey. They scurried to Keri's truck and chased after Martin.

"Floor it!" Bailey yelled. "Don't let him out of your sight!"

They pursued, barely keeping the sedan in view.

"Look, they're turning up ahead!" Keri said. "That's the dead-end road leading to the Tropical Palm."

"Why would he go there?" Bailey asked. "That's not a good escape route."

When they arrived at the town's favorite diner, the parking lot had been almost half dug up since Bailey saw it last. The lot had several large holes carved out of it. The granite-man had parked the sedan sideways and stood next to it, arms folded, blocking their path. Martin splashed through the water-filled holes. Standing knee-deep in one, he started digging erratically with a small shovel.

"This is mine! This belongs to me," he yelled.

Bailey and Keri looked on, dumbstruck.

"What's he looking for?" Bailey asked.

"Maybe he's searching for buried—"

"Don't say it," Bailey interrupted.

"What else could it be?" Keri said.

Martin dug more frantically. "It has to be here," he yelled, his arms caked in muddy water up to his elbows.

They heard the faint sound of multiple sirens growing louder. Shortly, several police cars skidded to a halt around them. Flashing blue lights pulsated. The sheriff and two other deputies opened their doors, then stood behind them, guns drawn, aiming at the two men.

"This is Sheriff Cotton. Stop what you're doing and put your hands in the air!"

The big man did as they ordered and dropped to his knees.

Martin, however, kept digging. "Stay away from me, Sheriff! This is my property. Get off my land."

"Thomas Morales, you're under arrest," the sheriff shouted, staring directly at Martin.

"Who?" Martin feigned, despite the look of shock all over his face. "I'm afraid you've got the wrong man, Sheriff."

Bailey had never seen him this undone.

"I was right," Bailey said. "It is him!"

"Who?" Keri asked.

"Mark's childhood friend."

"But I thought that kid died," Keri said.

"Yeah, everyone did."

Then they both looked at each other and said simultaneously, "Back from the Dead Red."

Martin reached behind him with his right arm and drew out a pistol. He held it clearly visible but pointed to the ground. Bailey heard multiple clicks as the sheriff and his deputies cocked their weapons.

"Put the gun down, or we will shoot you," the sheriff said with an eerie tone of finality.

Bailey shoved open her door and ran toward the stand-off. Keri grabbed after her friend but to no avail.

"No! Don't shoot!" Bailey yelled. She ran right past the police and directly into the line of crossfire. Martin, seemingly caught off guard by this insane action, stood unmoving, staring at Bailey.

"Hold your fire!" the sheriff shouted. "Bailey, get out of there!"

Max had also run outside. "Bailey, get away from him!"

This is crazy! Bailey thought to herself as she tore past them. *What are you doing? Let the police handle this.* She knew this was dangerous, but her intuition prevailed over her cautious inner critic. She held her hand up toward Max, urging him to stay put.

Martin stared at her. Fury filled his eyes. "You cost me everything! I told you to stay away!"

Bailey's heart thumped hard in her chest. It was all she could do to keep from shaking.

You're gonna get yourself killed.

"It was awful what happened to your mom," she said calmly.

Martin's eyes softened ever so slightly. For a moment, he looked more wounded than angry. But a look of rage quickly returned.

Bailey took a slow step toward him. "What happened to you was wrong."

Again, the look of pain on his face.

"We have to make it right," Bailey said, and took another slow step closer.

"Can you bring them back?" he said coldly. "That will make it right."

Then his eyes went vacant. Bailey didn't think her heart could pump any faster. The tremor in her hand returned, worse than before.

Oh no, this is it. I've messed up. He's gonna shoot me, then they'll shoot him.

Just then, more cars arrived. Bailey kept her eyes fixed on Martin, but heard the thud of several doors closing, and then a familiar voice.

"Thomas! You're alive!" Mark said.

Martin's eyes brightened at the sound of his friend's voice. Bailey felt a tide of relief. *Oh, thank you, God. We might get through this after all.*

Mark ran past the police and stopped next to Bailey.

"I'm so glad you're here," Bailey said, barely able to contain her emotions.

Martin, or rather Thomas, stared at his friend, gun pointing to the ground, holding it more loosely now.

"Thomas died a long time ago," he said, as tears welled in his eyes.

"I've missed you, my friend," Mark said, his voice breaking.

"It's too late. I've got nothing left."

"You've got me. We'll find a way back."

Thomas yelled in frustration, then lowered his head and began to cry. He let go of the gun. Mark rushed to embrace his friend and held him tight. The deputies charged in and quickly placed the privateer in handcuffs.

The sheriff said, "You're under arrest for conspiracy to commit real estate fraud here in Lost Key, and conspiracy to commit murder."

The deputies escorted him to a patrol car.

Keri ran to Bailey and gave her a big bear hug, almost knocking them both into another hole. "Oh, I'm so glad you are okay!" Then she shoved Bailey with both hands. "You scared the crap out of me!" She quickly embraced her again. "Don't ever do that again."

"Friends forever," Bailey said.

Mary and Katie had sprinted outside too, joining Max and the celebration of this safe ending. Bailey saw MJ and Cricket approach.

The sheriff addressed several questioning stares. "Max called me as soon as the developer arrived. That's how we knew where to find you. Martin's real name is Thomas Morales. He grew up here till his mom was tragically killed one night just outside Lost Key Realty. Only then it was the Cross Bones Bar. He's wanted for real estate fraud in three states. The authorities believed he had died in a boating accident, till now."

Bailey walked over to Mark and put her arm around him.

Sheriff Cotton looked at MJ, and his expression softened. He took his hat off. "Good to see you again, Margaret Jane."

She blushed. "What in the world is going on?"

The sheriff explained. "Jade had not given Bailey the evidence but rather kept it, a clever trick." *More like a divine revelation.* "Bailey figured that the bad guys would think she had the information they wanted and chase her instead. It worked, too." He gazed at Bailey. "That was a very brave and dangerous thing you just did. Your actions probably saved his life." He scolded her with his eyes before continuing. "Jade stayed safe in the custody of the local police and kept the real disk. And," he said, motioning to Cricket, "there's also the pictures."

Mark put his arm around Bailey. "Glad you're okay."

Bailey leaned into his embrace.

The sheriff continued. "Cricket managed to get pictures of two men pretending to be night fishermen as they dumped fake oil right along the mouth of the Lost Key Cove." He held up a manila envelope. "This made it seem like that shutdown rig out there was leaking and would permanently contaminate the land, therefore driving the property values down. We picked up his two goons this morning, and they sang like birds. They confessed that they work for Mr. Morales. We are waiting on test results, but I'll bet ya a new boat, Cricket, that the stuff they dumped into the bay will match the same stuff in Jade's report."

"What about the guys who shot at us?" Bailey asked.

"We just arrested them at the bridge. Both carried unregistered concealed weapons. Ballistics is running a comparison with the data from Cricket's boat to see if one of them is the gun that fired at y'all that night. I'm confident we'll have a match." He extended his hand to Bailey. She returned the gesture. "I'd just like to shake the hand of the lady who saved this town."

The group applauded. Bailey said, "Well, it was a team effort."

"Whatever you say, ma'am."

"Sheriff Cotton?" Mark said. "What will happen to Thomas?"

"If all the evidence matches, then he'll be tried for the crimes he committed. He'll get jail time, but he also needs help. Sorry about your friend."

"Thank you," Mark said.

"Something still puzzles me," the sheriff said. "I did some checking into his background. He's ruined several towns in the name of 'development.' In each case, he assumed a different identity. It makes me think he's not really interested in building anything. So why go through the trouble of this real estate deal?"

"Maybe it's the Finders Keepers rule," MJ said. "The real estate contract allows him to claim whatever he finds."

"Then he really was looking for treasure," Keri said.

Bailey nudged her friend that now was not the time for pirate theories.

"You really think that backhoe is for soil testing?" Keri said, defiantly.

"Well, Thomas used to go treasure hunting with his grandfather right here on this land," Mark said somberly.

"So, the old hermit that used to live there was his grandfather?" Max asked.

"Yes," Mark answered. "After his grandfather died in that accident, Thomas spent a lot of time fishing and digging around this old point. He told me once that he felt closer to his grandfather when he's out there searching."

"That's so sad," MJ said.

"Yeah— also, Thomas and his grandfather made their own treasure chest. It's supposed to be buried somewhere around here. He could have been looking for that," Mark replied quietly.

The sheriff donned his hat and said, "That boy needs more healing than he'll get from prison. We'll do our best to provide proper treatment." Then he nodded to MJ. "Margaret Jane."

She returned the nod, trying to convey a professional gesture. "Sheriff."

Then he and his deputies left.

Bailey nudged MJ with her shoulder. "You and the sheriff?"

MJ shrugged and blushed. Then she hugged Bailey. "I'm so sorry I ever doubted you."

Bailey shook her head. "No apology necessary. I probably would've done the same in your position."

"Most importantly, I'm glad you're okay."

"Sorry you lost the deal, but you just couldn't sell to him."

"Actually, I'm glad this fell through. Besides, better broke than sell out to some swindler. You saved the marsh, Bailey, and the Tropical Palm."

"Yeah, but the town is broke, and I didn't save the company."

"Now that the oil spill is a hoax, I'm sure prices will shoot up. There'll be another buyer, a real one who cares about this place."

Just then, another car pulled up. Out climbed Remy and Ann from Thomason Brothers.

With complete surprise, Bailey said, "Remy?" while MJ simultaneously said, "Ann?"

"Hey, Bailey," Remy answered.

"Hello, MJ," Ann greeted.

"What in the world are y'all doing here?" MJ asked.

Bailey stared at Remy, speechless. He smiled like he was bursting with a surprise and winked at Bailey.

Ann said, "We have a proposal for you. I think you're going to love it."

Chapter 55

Storybook Plans

MJ crooked her head and half-smiled. "Okay then, let's hear it."

They gathered around a table inside the Tropical Palm.

Remy outlined the plan. "Thomason Brothers is very interested in developing a new community. We think Lost Key would be perfect. But rather than high-rise condos, we want to build homes, small cute bungalow-type houses. Most developments offer three or four cookie-cutter designs. Instead, we are trying something new. We have several basic components, but each home could be custom-built to suit the family. We imagine a community center in the middle, with shops, beach access, and something that looks like an old beach town. We want to create a village that tells a story of Lost Key long ago."

Bailey blinked, checking to see if she was in a dream. This plan sounded too good to be true. She couldn't wait to hear the rest.

MJ, glowing with excitement, asked, "Do you have any drawings, any plans?"

"We certainly do," Remy said. He motioned to Mark, who had pulled his sketchpad out of his satchel. He laid it on the table in front of them and opened it.

They all saw the same drawings that Bailey had fallen in love with back at the Seize the Day Café.

"This is one idea," Mark said. "Something I dreamed, a home I'd want to live in." Mark winked at Bailey.

"It looks like something out of a storybook," MJ said, chuckling.

Mark turned the pages, revealing more drawings and new renderings that Bailey had not seen before, each uniquely charming. The vision enchanted her beyond anything she had imagined. This new Lost Key would be a magical community.

"They're delightful!" MJ exclaimed.

Mark turned the page again, displaying another drawing from a broader perspective, a view of the whole project, including the community center with a pool, games, and shops. Perhaps best of all, it incorporated existing landmarks, old family-owned shops, and even…

"The Tropical Palm!" Bailey interjected. "When did you have time to draw these?"

"I sketched them a while back, when Thomason Brothers first had their eye on Lost Key as a potential development. I never thought I'd get to use them." Mark turned another page. "We're preserving the marshland as well."

Bailey grabbed his face with both hands and kissed him on the lips right there in the meeting. She quickly regained a semi professional composure. Mark stopped presenting and stood with a dazed look, smiling and staring at Bailey.

"This is beautiful!" MJ said. "Truly magnificent."

"You'll notice there's even a space for Lost Key Realty. Granted, it involves a bit of a make-over for the structure, but is still mostly intact," Remy said.

Ann added, "Maybe we can get the liquor smell out of here."

"Good luck with that," MJ scoffed. "We've cleaned, we've painted, disinfected, and even perfume-bombed the place. That smell comes with the building."

Ann nodded. "We'll figure something out."

Then Remy nudged Mark, who smiled even more fully, like a magician about to reveal his secret. He turned the page. "I have an idea about that too."

They all stared at a sketch of the real estate office, but it had a margarita bar built into the back that opened into the community. It was the cutest grass tiki-type tavern Bailey had ever seen. She laughed out loud. She couldn't help it and didn't want to. Then she blurted, "I love you." Her eyes widened as she realized what she just said. "Well… I'm… ummm… you know what I mean."

Mark continued to smile, and then he winked again.

"Just one thing remains," Ann said. "I know you're looking forward to retiring, MJ. So, we just need someone to oversee the project." She looked at Bailey. "We need a good broker we can depend on to manage the office. Someone we can trust. Someone who knows and loves Lost Key. Someone whose desire is to sell homes, not just property." She paused, still looking at Bailey. The whole room now looked at Bailey. "Anyone here fit that position description? You all know anyone who has those qualifications?"

Eyes wide, Bailey gasped and grabbed both sides of her face. "Me? You want me to manage the new office?"

A warm shiver ran from the top of her head to the tips of her toes.

"Yes, we want you, Bailey. More than that, our deal is contingent upon you accepting the position."

Bailey didn't have to think about it. She bounced several times on her tiptoes and said, "Yes! Yes! I can't believe this! It's like a dream."

Everyone applauded.

Ann said, "I have the papers right here." She slid them toward MJ. "We'll pay you a *fair* market price."

Margaret Jane didn't even read them. She grabbed her pen and signed it. "Deal."

Chapter 56

Bailey's Home

No one could remember the last time the Tropical Palm brimmed with such a crowd.

"I don't know when I've seen so many people in our diner," Mary said.

Locals and Mobile folks from Thomason Brothers packed the place. All had come to celebrate.

"SSHHH, everyone, SSSHHH, here she comes," Mary said.

The moment Bailey walked in, Max turned the lights up, and the whole place erupted with a giant "surprise!" Applause, cheers, and good wishes filled the café. The force of energy coming from the loving crowd caused Bailey to take a step back.

Keri rushed forward and hugged her friend and soulmate. "I'm so happy for you. Congratulations, girlfriend. You deserve it!"

Ann winked and said, "We all saw something special about you, Bailey. Way to go!"

Johnny clinked a fork on his glass, hushing the crowd. Bailey didn't recognize him at first because he wore a loud, tacky Hawaiian shirt. He was still wearing slacks and upscale casual shoes, but at least half-dressed for the beach. On the other hand, Robert also wore a loud, tawdry beach shirt, but he had completed his outfit with khaki shorts and flip-flops. He looked right at home in the beach scene. He smiled and nodded toward Bailey.

Johnny continued, "Ladies and gentlemen, thank you so much for including us in this surprise party. Thank you for welcoming us into your community. We are thrilled to have our new branch office here in Lost Key." He looked toward Bailey. "And, it's all due to this amazing lady standing here."

Cheers erupted again. Then Bailey spotted Mandy amongst the crowd. *Well, it is a company party after all,* she told herself. Much to her surprise, Mandy lifted her glass and nodded, respectfully. Bailey returned the gesture.

Johnny didn't hush the crowd this time. He let the wave of joyfulness diminish of its own inertia before continuing. "Without you, Bailey, we'd have never seen the possibility. Thank you. You are the only agent ever to sell the house that wouldn't sell. But more than that, thank you for helping us grow. Thank you for being the wonderful, amazing human being that you are. I've heard lots of rumors and stories of treasure out here, but I never believed a word, until now. Bailey, *you* are the treasure of Lost Key." He lifted his glass. "To Bailey!"

Unanimously everyone in the room echoed, "To Bailey!" Glasses clinked, jubilations erupted again.

Then Max yelled, "Margaritas on the house!"

Adulations exploded as if someone turned up the volume on the merriment. That ended the toasts and people milled about as Jimmy Buffett played over the jukebox. Bailey, overcome with joyful tears, had never felt so at home. She saw her family there too, beaming with pride for their little girl all grown up. Aunt Lee nodded as if to say, 'see, I told ya everything happens for a reason.'

Bailey walked over to her and said, "You're right, Aunt Lee," clutching her cross. "This thing really is a conduit."

Lee exchanged a glance with Irene. "Truth is, hon—I found it in my flea market."

"What?" Bailey was stunned but not angry. Aunt Lee and her mom had played a game with her.

"I found several of them, actually," Aunt Lee added. "A good while ago, an elegantly dressed elderly lady dropped them off at the Red Barn. She looked like she stepped right out of the past. Anyway, they were so beautiful; I saved them."

"We made up the rest of the story," Irene said and winked mischievously. "We thought it might give you an extra boost."

Bailey blinked and couldn't help but chuckle. *I bet I know who delivered those. Maybe one day I'll tell you two the actual rest of the story.* For now, she savored the feeling of her family looking after her.

Then Lee said, "But your gift *is* real. You know that now, don't you?"

"I'm starting to," Bailey said. Then she embraced them both.

Bailey spotted Keri, across the diner, standing close to the blond-haired dreamy-eyed speedboat Samaritan. She noticed a slight discoloration on Keri's finger as she cradled her margarita, no wedding band. Keri met her gaze, smiled, and raised her glass. Bailey returned the gesture and nodded her approval. *Good for you, my friend. It's time to move forward.*

Bailey looked out over the crowd of friends, family, and colleagues. She realized the home she'd been searching for had always been right in front of her. *She remembered Mary's words of wisdom—sometimes, you are home and don't know it.*

"Quite a group of people you have here, Bailey," Mark said.

"Yes." She smiled; she continued to gaze over the hodgepodge of friends and family. "These people, this place, this is my home." Now, when she looked, she saw all the parts of a perfect house. All the comfort she longed for, all the space to be herself. Everything a home should be.

The celebration lasted throughout the afternoon. When evening came, the party began to wane.

Bailey took Mark's hand. "Want to go for a ride?"

"You mean in your Jeep?"

"Of course. It's the only way to travel in Lost Key."

Mark paused almost reverently. Bailey knew he understood what the invitation meant.

"Definitely," he finally replied with a smile.

They walked through the half-dug-up parking lot of the Tropical Palm. Bailey chuckled. She'd caught Max stealing a few glimpses at the holes. *I'll bet he keeps digging for treasure rather than pave them over.*

They stopped a few feet from the Jeep, and she handed Mark the keys.

"How about you drive."

His eyes widened with that same astonishing who-are-you look he had given her back in the boat on Dauphin Island before accepting the keys.

"It would be my pleasure!"

"Just don't dump us over. And don't scratch it."

As they reached the Jeep, she added, "And don't get any dings on it."

"Can I go over five miles an hour?"

Bailey looked sharply for a moment, then her expression softened. "Sorry, let's ride."

"I understand. Let's go."

They climbed in, and he cranked the engine. She squirmed, trying to get used to sitting in the passenger seat. She turned on the radio.

"Take a left up there," she said. "The sun is setting. Let's drive down Old Gulf Beach Highway. It will be pretty by the water."

Mark beamed. "Sounds wonderful."

As they rounded the corner, the vast ocean expanded before them. The sun had just dipped below the horizon, casting a purple reddish glow in the few clouds that still hung in the sky. Here, by the beach, away from the artificial lights of civilization, the stars began to twinkle, dotting the universe teasingly with its mystery and beauty. Then suddenly, they had to stop!

At least a half dozen cars were in line, blocked by construction workers still repairing the road that got washed away.

"You've got to be kidding me!" Bailey said. She stood up and yelled. "Hey! It's time to go home already!"

Mark leaned his head out the driver's door peering along the stalled traffic. "I don't see any oncoming cars," he said. "The construction worker just hasn't signaled for us to start moving again. They seem to be having some trouble with one of the backhoes. I think it's stuck in the mud. That could take a while to clear."

He leaned back in the driver's seat. Bailey sat down. As if telepathically linked, they turned to each other. Neither said a word as both their smiles turned into giggles.

Then Mark said, "Hang on!"

He veered left and pressed the accelerator. They raced past the stopped cars. When they reached the construction spot, he edged the Jeep left, slightly into the water. A yellow blur flew past the worksite, spraying a large fan of water and soaking the men.

Just as they passed, they heard one of them yell, "Dang it, Bailey!"

Lights flashed and horns honked from the cars behind them. Bailey turned to see other vehicles following their example. She leaned over, cradling Mark's face in both her hands, and kissed him. The Jeep swerved, breaking their union. Bailey stood face-forward, her arms thrust high, the wind blowing in her face. She laughed with deep joy and pure delight. They drove on toward the sunset as the tune of "Sweet Home Alabama" spilled in their wake.

Epilogue

Keri stood ankle-deep in the marsh she loved. The fading sun painted the sky with deep reddish blues heading toward the black of night. She heard the splash of a fish flipping in the water to her left as she relished that moment between the day and the night. The chorus of night creatures would soon join the sounds of the wind and the waves as they prepared their song. The water rippled just off to the right, drawing her attention. Though in love with this swampy stretch, she remained ever alert. A ripple in the water could be an approaching snake, or worse, the wake of a gator. She squinted toward the disturbance, her eyes already adjusting to the dimming light. It didn't slither like a snake. She could make out a small head peeking just above the water. A grayish-green shell trailed behind. When a portion broke the surface, she could see the familiar heart-shaped discoloration on top.

"Snaps! It's you!" She splashed over toward the turtle. It turned left, then right, then stopped. "It's okay, Snaps. It's just me." The turtle cradled a shiny object in its mouth.

"What did you bring me today?" She squatted down to pick up the sea creature. Instinctively, it retreated into its shell, dropping the object into the water. She quickly grabbed it before it hit bottom.

"What have you found, Snaps?" She turned it over in her hand, studying it carefully. She held a gold-looking coin somewhat dulled from age and being underwater. She ran one finger around the uneven edges, tracing the roundish shape. It looked homemade or banged up. On one side, a cross had been embossed, surrounded by the words "Libertad." Carved on the flip side, she saw the face of a lady who looked to be wearing a crown, as if she were royalty, and a date which read 1785!

Keri gasped. "I knew it! Snaps, where did you get this?"

Acknowledgments

*I*t takes a village to write a book, and I could not have completed this one without the support and help of many friends, family, and colleagues. This story began as a fun exploration into writing. As much as books can be love letters, this is one for my wife, Sherri. She is the inspiration for Bailey and the whole story. Though the characters took on a life of their own and would argue their uniqueness and independence, several are inspirations from her life journey. Sherri, without you, this story wouldn't exist.

I would also like to thank:

Linden Gross, my writing Jedi master. So often, I just wanted to be "done." You were steadfast in your encouragement and showing me the real finish line and all that goes into a well-written book. You pushed me towards my best writing. Also, you connected me with the best resources. Keri Barnum, Lieve Maas, and your whole team are top-shelf. You truly provide a one-stop writing shop. I don't know that I'm a fully trained Jedi yet, but I've learned more of the ways of the force.

'Corie' Guzman-Thornton. Your creative journey inspires me to keep writing. Your beautiful painting made all the difference for the cover of this book.

My nephew Hunter Hutcheson. We are not only kin but kindred creative spirits. Our weekly calls are sustenance for my creative soul. Producing 'Excuse Me

Santa' with you is one of the epic experiences of my life. I look forward to more stories and films together!

Kristen Law Sagafi. What a happy coincidence to discover that we are both completing our first book. I still take delight in your reaction that reading "Going Barefoot" is as much fun as drinking fizzy cherry soda.

My "Chimps"—Alan Thames, Debbie Brincivalli, and Sally Watson. You are my tribe during my transition from the wonderland of executive presbyter to the magical world of writer/film producer. I'm grateful for your friendship and collegiality. Y'all keep me connected to my spiritual home.

Laurie Ferguson, my executive coach. You encouraged me to make room for creative Jeff to play and see this not as an ad hoc activity but essential work.

Glenn Small, for being the wise and steadfast 'Yoda,' guide. Hear my calling, I do! (*Yoda voice.*)

Ron Davidson, my spiritual brother and fellow traveler on this lifetrek. Keep on writing!

My friends and family who were excited about my new writing and filmmaking venture and were not surprised by this creative path.

Helen Attridge, our friend, and life coach, for helping me step through the portal and sit in the captain's chair of my own starship.

Mom and Dad, in so many ways, you made this whole dream possible. My love of stories began somewhere in the Storyville of my childhood.

Finally, thank you to Lost Key. Though I took author liberties with some of the geography and the institutions there, Lost Key is a real place that protects its seashores, loves its sea turtles, and is just brimming with that gulf coast vibe.

Author's Note

Thank you for reading my first novel. If you enjoyed it, your review would mean the world to me.

You can connect with me personally on my website, www.jeffhutcheson.com, and leave reviews at Amazon, Goodreads and Barnes & Noble.

Jeff

Made in the USA
Monee, IL
27 October 2021

80876888R10252